RANDOM
HOUSE

LARGE
PRINT

SPEAK OF THE DEVIL

SPEAK
OF THE
DEVIL

A NOVEL

RICHARD
HAWKE

R A N D O M   H O U S E
L A R G E P R I N T

Copyright © 2005 by Richard Hawke

All rights reserved.
Published in the United States of America by Random House Large Print in association with Random House, New York. Distributed by Random House, Inc., New York.

The Library of Congress has established a Cataloging-in-Publication record for this title.

ISBN-13: 978-0-7393-2582-7
ISBN-10: 0-7393-2582-5

www.randomlargeprint.com

FIRST LARGE PRINT EDITION

10 9 8 7 6 5 4 3 2 1

This Large Print edition published in accord with the standards of the N.A.V.H.

To Julia

How lucky are we?

SPEAK OF THE DEVIL

1

IF SHE HAD KNOWN SHE WOULD BE DEAD in another five minutes, maybe she wouldn't have swatted her son so hard. That's just my guess. His balloon had been drifting into my face, that was the problem. It wasn't bugging me, but it was bugging his mother. He was a towheaded kid with a round pink face. The balloon was larger than his head. I couldn't say one way or the other if the kid was having fun, but Mom clearly wasn't.

"Ezra, if I have to tell you one more time."

She seemed to be wound awfully tight for nine-thirty in the morning. But I've never been a parent, so I'm hardly the person to judge. Maybe the kid was an absolute handful and his actions drained his mother daily of her reservoir of patience. Maybe the reservoir wasn't terribly deep to begin with. Or maybe the two were running late that morning and Mom hadn't gotten her caffeine jangle for the day.

Maybe this, maybe that. Maybes all over the place. Cheaper than a dime donut, as my father used to growl.

It was a Thursday. Thanksgiving is always a Thursday, so that part is easy. Fall was playing out nice and slow. The trees in Central Park were more yellow and red than I'd seen them in years. A high, bright sun was sending down just about zero warmth through the bracingly crisp air. What they used to call apple-cider weather.

I was standing at the corner of Seventy-second and Central Park West. I wasn't supposed to be standing there. I was supposed to be making my way up five flights of stairs in a turn-of-the-century brownstone halfway down Seventy-first, swinging my bag of bagels and whistling a happy tune. I had fetched the bagels (three poppy, three sesame) from a place on Columbus that makes them on the premises, but instead of trotting directly back to Margo's like a good dog, I had drifted up the street, lured by the sound of crashing cymbals, and was standing on the corner dodging a white balloon and watching Mother Goose roll by. Big pointy hat. Oversize smile.

Mother Goose, that is. Not me. I was hatless. And I wasn't smiling. When I see a gun being drawn in a crowd and it's not attached to a cop or to someone I know and trust, generally speaking, I don't smile.

CENTRAL PARK WEST RUNS NORTH–SOUTH. The parade runs south. Been that way since the late twenties. Back then they used to release the big balloon figures at the end of the parade. There were only a few of them, so it wasn't as if the skies of Manhattan suddenly darkened with a flotilla of giant balloons. You couldn't do it today. You'd have scrambled F-16 fighter jets intercepting the balloons faster than you could blink.

I was standing on the west side of the street, directly in front of the Dakota, when I saw the gun being drawn. If you've seen the movie **Rosemary's Baby,** you've seen the Dakota, although they called it something different in the movie. In the book, too. Richard Nixon tried to get his suitcase in the door of the Dakota not long after he was bounced from the White House, but the residents there would have none of it. It's **that** kind of place. When I think of that story, it's actually Nixon's wife I imagine. Poor beleaguered Pat. I imagine her standing on the sidewalk with her skinny arms crossed over her skinny chest, one of her dull practical pumps tapping irritably against the pavement. **Well, Mr. I-am-not-a-crook . . . what next?**

The gun was a Beretta 92F. That's nine-millimeter. Eight and a half inches long, a fraction over two pounds. Magazine capacity of fifteen bullets. The Beretta is one of the most popular pistols these days with both police and military shooters. The guy holding this one was neither. And though it's a good-looking gun, I didn't suspect he was pulling it out simply so he could admire it in the morning sun.

I instinctively slapped at my left shoulder. My gun is a simple .38. Short-barreled snubbie. A simple workhorse. No fancy history. I use it in my line of work, which is private investigation. Margo calls it my associate, a little joke she picked up from her father, from when **he** was a private investigator and **he** used to call his gun his associate. This was before he took on a real associate. A junior partner. Which was me. Green, eager, fearless and, at the time, extremely pissed off.

Nothing came between my slap and my shoulder. My associate was back at Margo's, in its holster, up on the dresser. Safety on. Facing the wall.

The guy with the Beretta was up on the low stone wall that borders the park. It was a fluke that I had a clear view of him. There was a gap between the Mother Goose float and the marching band in front of it, a high-stepping troupe of teenagers from Berlin, Maryland, and I happened to be standing where I could see right through the gap. The man was about five-eight or so. He was wearing a green windbreaker, khaki pants, sunglasses and a baseball cap. I saw him unzip his windbreaker and pull the Beretta from his belt, then take a step backward and drop off the wall, out of sight.

The white balloon drifted into my face again. The mother slapped the boy on his small arm. Very hard.

"Ezra, for the **last** time."

I heard the boy begin to cry as I took off running.

As I hit the street, the shooter's head reappeared above the stone wall. He planted his elbows on the wall and took aim. His target was clear. The easiest of all. Mother Goose.

"Get down!"

I threw my bag of bagels at the float. It hit the float just below the platform where Mother Goose was standing. I yelled again.

"Get down! Gun!"

I got her attention. The pointed hat dipped my way, a look of irritation replacing her waving-at-the-crowd smile. I saw the spark from the Beretta across the street and heard the shot a half-instant behind. Mother Goose dropped to her knees . . . and all hell broke loose.

I was still running. A chunky policeman who had been stationed on the corner not twenty feet from the shooter reacted simultaneously to the gunshot and to the sight of a loony—me—racing from the curb into the parade route, yelling and shouting. He started for me. I cried out, "Gun! Gun! Gun!" and pointed toward the wall, but the cop wasn't hearing. He was going for his own gun. Behind him, the shooter rose calmly to his full height, swung the Beretta to the street level and fired again.

I swerved, crashing into a copper-skinned teenager holding a bass drum. More shots rang out as the drummer and I tumbled to the street. The shots continued. The drum head ripped as another of the marching band troupe—a tiny girl with a shiny alto sax—planted her foot on it. Blood was pumping onto the white bib of her uniform. Nothing had even registered yet on her face.

I got to my feet. People were scrambling

for cover, though here and there were pockets of onlookers who remained frozen, unable to process. The chunky policeman was on the ground, not moving. The Mother Goose float had halted, its Styrofoam wings still flapping mechanically. The shooter might as well have been standing at a carnival shooting gallery. He was pointing and shooting, pointing and shooting, pointing and shooting. To my left, a skinny guy in a Macy's T-shirt lifted off the ground with the force of the bullets slamming into his chest. **Pop! Pop! Pop!**

Hunched over, I scuttled across the pavement to the policeman. He was lying on his right side. I knelt down and shoved him onto his back. A piece of skull the size of a doorknob was gone from the right side of his head. Ignoring the gore, I unsnapped his holster and pulled out his service revolver, then ran to the near side of the float, putting it between me and the shooter. I ran along the float, flipping off the gun's safety, and came around the rear with the gun in both hands, aimed at the stone wall.

He was gone. A squirrel was perched on the wall almost exactly where the shooter had been. Tail high. Head high. Tense and alert. I suppressed a roaring urge to blow it to bits.

I took off running. Holding the pistol

down next to my leg, I crossed the street and started up the paved path that leads into the park. Some hundred or so feet in from the street, the path opens to a small plaza. There's a decorative stone circle embedded in the walkway. The word IMAGINE is inscribed in mosaic on the circle. The city did this after John Lennon was murdered in 1980 outside the Dakota, which was where he lived. **Him** they let in.

Compared to what had just transpired on the street, the plaza was eerily quiet. As usual, several kids were seated on the periphery of the IMAGINE circle, strumming guitars and softly singing "All You Need Is Love." A girl in an oversize army coat was arranging flowers on the pavement.

The paved path continues past the memorial into the park. Benches and bushes line the path for another thirty feet, until it comes to a small clearing.

That was where the shooter came from.

He dashed from the clearing onto the path and raced farther into the park, in the direction of the Bethesda Fountain. I chased. He turned to look back and saw me charging after him. His arms pumped even harder, and he reached the small bridge overlooking the fountain plaza. He veered left and started down the stone steps. As I approached the bridge, two police cars sped past on the roadway, their sirens shrieking out of synch. I reached the bridge and started down the steps.

Mistake.

The shooter was already standing at the bottom of the steps. In a wide stance. Facing me. Aiming the Beretta. Behind him, the wings of the angel in the fountain stretched majestically against the blue sky. I dropped as the gun barked, getting off three shots myself before I hit the steps. One of them took the shooter in the right shoulder, near the collarbone. The Beretta fell to the bricks as the shooter staggered backward.

I lunged, knowing the instant I did that it was the wrong thing to do. I was half running, half falling down the steps. Somewhere in the tumbling, I lost my grip on the policeman's service revolver. Below me, the shooter was hugging his bad arm with his good, taking Frankenstein steps toward his gun. He'd reach it years before I could.

A body went flying past me down the stone steps. It was a cop. Gun drawn and shouting. A second cop grabbed me from behind and stopped my tumbling descent. It was a good strong grip.

"Fucking move, you're fucking dead! Just freeze!"

I did. Below me, the other cop reached the

wounded shooter. With a nifty sweep of a foot, he brought the shooter to the ground. Ignoring the wounded shoulder, the cop jerked the guy's hands behind him and cuffed him. I was cuffed, too. I offered no resistance and no explanations. My cop was a tall, fierce-looking black man. His heartbeat was probably nearing two hundred blows a minute. Mine sure as hell was. Way too many engines running way too high. I relaxed into custody. There would be time to talk.

The shooter was dragged back up the steps and shoved into the back of a patrol car. My cop was joined by another one, his partner. Squatty guy shaped like a gumdrop. The gumdrop patted me down for weapons, then shoved me into the back of a second patrol car. I was separated from the front seat by a cage. The black guy got behind the wheel. Gumdrop took shotgun.

They did the next part without sirens, which surprised me. It also surprised me that they didn't take the eastern exit out of the park, or the exit to the south. Either would have taken us away from the parade mess. Instead, the two cars rolled west to Central Park West, where at least a dozen more police cars and several ambulances were already crisscrossing the street, lights whirling. The screaming had ceased. Now it was time for the crying. The crying and the wailing. People hugging people. People staggering in a daze. Faces registering disbelief, horror, shock. Gumdrop muttered, "Jesus goddamn Christ," as we inched our way forward.

The parade was in tatters. Band instruments were strewn all over the place. I spotted the Pink Panther far to the south, near Columbus Circle, hovering precariously above the street. The wind had kicked up, and the huge figure looked like it was being uppity, bucking and shifting against its ropes.

As we crossed Central Park West at a walker's pace, I spotted a second balloon. This one was much smaller. A white balloon. The towheaded kid was still clutching the string. As the stretcher bearing the boy's mother was being slid into the back of an ambulance, one of the EMS workers gathered the boy up into her arms, and the balloon drifted lightly against her face.

Ezra, for the last time . . .

The little boy released the string.

2

WE HIT BROADWAY AND WENT LEFT. I FIG-
ured I was being taken to the Midtown
North station on Fifty-fourth, a five-minute
drive, tops, with the cherry spinning and the
siren clearing the way. But the accessories remained undeployed, and as we drifted past
Fifty-third, I leaned forward in the seat.
"Boys. You missed the turn."

The driver said nothing. Gumdrop half
turned in his seat. "Shaddup."

The radio crackled, and a female voice
spit out a series of numbers and letters.
Gumdrop glanced curiously at his partner,
who nodded tersely. Gumdrop fished a
headset from the glove compartment and
put it on, glancing at me briefly as he leaned
forward to plug it into the radio, which sud-

denly went silent. I placed both the cops somewhere in their early thirties, which meant I was the senior man in the car. The driver looked up in his mirror and saw that I was still leaning forward.

"Sit back."

"Just so you know," I said, "I'm the good guy here."

"Sit. Back."

I sat back. We crossed to Ninth Avenue and passed a restaurant called Zen Palate. Margo loves that place. There are three of them in the city, the closest one to her being the one on Broadway in the mid-Seventies. She's dragged me there a couple times. I like half the stuff I've tried there with her. The other half tastes like cardboard.

Margo.

With all that had just happened, it was hard for me to imagine that Margo could still just be sitting up on her pillows, dressed in her oversize Rangers jersey, waiting for me to come back with the bagels. But maybe she was. Margo can balance on the precipice of a moment better than anyone I know.

The car hit a pothole, and my head slammed hard against the roof. I tallied no fewer than four ways I could have sued the city. A minute later, Gumdrop pulled off the headset. He turned to his partner. "We're supposed to get a bag."

The driver gave him a look. "A bag?"

"Yeah. That's what they said. We've got to cover his whole head."

The driver looked at me in his mirror. "You hear that?"

I nodded. "I heard. You're supposed to cover my whole head. Whatever the hell that means."

We hit another pothole. The driver swore softly, then glanced into the mirror again. "What's your name?"

"Malone," I said. "Fritz Malone."

The driver nodded. "You prefer paper or plastic?"

AFTER FETCHING THE BAG (PAPER) FROM A market on Forty-eighth, the cops drove to a spot under the West Side Highway, just north of the U.S.S. **Intrepid.** I could make out the tail wing of one of the jet fighters on the rear of the aircraft carrier. Before they put the bag over my head, the black guy blindfolded me. He was leaning in the back door, one knee on the seat. His part-ner stood behind him, looking around anxiously. Gumdrop looked pale. I'd have given him a cocky wink right before getting the blindfold, just to make him a little more nervous, but to tell God's honest truth, I wasn't feeling too happy myself.

Something was seriously wrong here. I had lifted a service revolver from a freshly murdered policeman, given chase to the shooter, and discharged three bullets from the police revolver, striking the shooter once in the shoulder. Taking me into custody was the right thing to do. But pulling the squad car over beneath the West Side Highway and putting a blindfold on me, that wasn't the right thing to do. The fat trails of sweat on Gumdrop's fleshy face told me that he knew it, too.

"What the hell is this?" I snapped as my world went black.

"Down on the floor."

The black guy took hold of my shoulders and guided me into position, semifetal, my ear against the hump. The cops got back into the front seat. The engine fired up. They spoke not a word.

This was all wrong.

Wherever it was I was being taken, the driver didn't take the direct route. Most of Manhattan is a grid. You go north–south, you go east–west. In the Village, it gets all screwy, as well as down in Chinatown and in the Wall Street area. But where we were, midtown, everything is straight streets and ninety-degree turns. From the floor of the car, I tried to track our course, but after several sets of turns that could only suggest redundancies and doubling back, I was lost. Which I assumed was the point.

I thought again about Margo. By now even Margo would have moved off the bed. She'd have heard all the sirens coming up from near the park, and she'd have flipped on her television. She'd be one of the many millions of New Yorkers who were now glued to their sets. What was I saying? Not just New Yorkers, people all across the country. The network jingle-meisters were probably scrambling right now to lay down little five-second tracks in just the right tone: solemn yet provocatively urgent. The graphics people would have worked even faster. Their work was probably already up on the screen, blending with the horrific images.

THANKSGIVING DAY MASSACRE
MAYHEM IN MANHATTAN
PARADE OF TERROR

Margo would be sitting at her kitchen table watching the breaking reports. I could picture her, bare feet pulled up onto the chair, the Rangers jersey pulled over her legs, covering her like a tent. Her stomach would be grumbling for want of bagels.

And she'd know. Margo knows me. The same way her mother knew her old man when he was still in the game. My being gone this long, she'd know that somehow I had gotten myself involved. But Margo also knows the odds. She'd know in her heart of hearts that in all likelihood, I was probably okay. As she likes to say, I seem to have been born under the watchful eye of the Saint of Reckless Dumb Luck.

Even so, she'd be having fingernails for breakfast.

WE STOPPED. TWENTY MINUTES OF DRIV-ing, by my estimate. Taking into account the little maneuvers to throw me off, we were still in Manhattan. I would have sussed out easily enough if we had traveled over a bridge or through a tunnel. My ear was close to the ground. Literally.

The two policemen got out of the car. Nothing happened for the next five minutes except that my calves cramped, first one, then the other. Finally, the men in blue returned and the rear door was opened. Unfolding me from the floor was not exactly a ballet, but we all did what we had to do. Outside the car, one of the cops adjusted the bag to sit straighter on my head.

"Thank you."

I was taken by both elbows and led forward. "Step up," one of the cops said. About twenty steps later, he said it again. I heard the click of a door being opened, and I was led inside. Even under the bag, I could practically taste the staleness of the air. I was somewhere cold.

We walked a few more feet and then stopped. I waited. After about twenty seconds, I said, "I hope you guys appreciate how docile I'm being."

Gumdrop told me to shut up. This seemed to be his specialty.

"Listen," I said. "I don't know what academy you two attended, but you've both got a lot to learn about bringing a person in. This is bullshit. Take this goddamn bag off my head."

Nothing. A moment later, I heard a small metallic squeaking sound. "Take three steps," the black guy instructed. My elbows were released. I took the three steps.

"Later," Gumdrop muttered, and I heard the squeaking again. Nothing. Then the ground shifted suddenly.

Elevator.

Going up.

I was pretty sure I was alone now.

3

SOMEONE WAS WAITING FOR ME WHEN THE
elevator door slid open. My arm was grabbed
tightly and I was yanked forward. I stumbled
a few steps and jerked free.

"Whoever you are, fuck you."

A gravelly voice muttered, "Just c'mon."

My arm was taken again and I let myself be
led forward. Tile floor, not wood. Something
in the slap of the shoes. My other senses were
already picking up the slack. We walked
about fifty paces before we stopped.

"Sit down."

I lowered myself carefully. The fingers of
my cuffed hands found the chair before the
rest of me did. Straight-backed metal chair.
I perched lightly on the edge. Between the
tumble down the steps at the Bethesda Foun-

tain and my being curled up on the floor of a police car, my muscles were beginning to show me their aches. Even so, I tensed my legs, ready to leap. The bag was lifted from my head. The gravelly voice sounded. "Oh shit."

The handcuffs were unlocked. I heard them being tossed onto a table as I kneaded the circulation back into my wrists, then I reached up and tugged off the blindfold.

I was in a room about the size of a small classroom. No windows, completely unadorned. The walls were painted infirmary green, circa several decades ago. A ridgeline of what looked like coffee stains ran about four feet off the floor along the wall facing me. Overhead, a bank of fluorescent lights buzzed, giving off cold, colorless light.

I was seated at the long end of a rectangular wooden table. The paper bag was on the table. So were the handcuffs.

Seated across from me was a large man in his late fifties. Huge chest. He was in a charcoal suit with a red tiepin. The tented handkerchief in his front pocket was a pale blue that somewhat matched his eyes, which were small, hard, clear and currently boring angrily into mine. His salty hair was cropped short and sat flat on his scalp, sort of a modified

Roman-emperor look. On the local news, you don't tend to notice the old acne scars. You see putty-colored skin, a twice-broken nose and an imposing ugliness that, in his job, seems to work in his favor. You also don't notice the labored breathing. The man in front of me looked like he had just finished a couple of laps around a horse corral.

"Hello, Commissioner," I said coolly. I massaged my right wrist again as I glanced about the dreary room. "I don't know. Perhaps maybe a nice landscape over there? Pick the place right up. What do you think?"

Police Commissioner Tommy Carroll came forward, resting his arms heavily on the table. "What the **fuck** are you doing here?"

I met his angry gaze with as placid a one as I could muster under the circumstances. "I don't even know where 'here' is."

"We're in the Municipal Building."

"Oh. Really? What floor?"

"Jesus fucking Christ."

I could practically see the gears spinning in his head. The eyes were like blue-tinted windows behind which the thoughts were tumbling at high speed. Carroll probed the inside of his cheek with his tongue, as if fiddling with a jawbreaker. He stared hard at me a few seconds. Then he checked his watch. "I need to be across the street in fifteen minutes. You can imagine the hell that's breaking loose."

"I've just been through a little hell breaking loose myself, Tommy. I gather you've heard."

"There were two guys with guns out there. That's the report I got. You were one of them?"

"Not my gun. I lifted it from a dead cop."

"McNally."

"We didn't have the chance to properly introduce ourselves." I indicated the bag on the table. "What gives, Tommy? Some bizarre new suspect-protection program? I know you've got budget crunches, but paper bags? What are we doing here? Why aren't we in a police station?"

"I can't talk right now." He looked at his watch once more. "Look. I need to hear your story. I need it short and sweet. We'll talk again later. And I mean soon. An hour. But I've got to be three fucking places at once right now, and one of them can't be here. For the record, you're not here, either. Now, what the fuck happened out there? Give it to me clean. And quick. I mean it."

Carroll glanced at his watch three more times in the two minutes it took me to tell my side of the story. As I spoke, his eyes moved to the wall behind me, as if maybe he was using it as a place to project my story.

"That's it," I said when I was finished. "How many casualties are we talking?"

His eyes snapped back to me. "First reports from the scene have seven confirmed dead. That could change, of course. It's nuts out there. We don't know what they're getting at the hospitals. Maybe we'll get lucky."

I sent an eyebrow up the pole. "You've got seven dead. One cop and at least a couple of kids. You might want to think about putting the word 'lucky' away for another day."

"Seven isn't seventeen."

"It's not zero, either."

He waved it off. "Were there any other people in the vicinity when you shot this guy? Did you notice?"

I shrugged. "Nobody else was by the fountain. I know that much. If there had been, I wouldn't have shot. Why? Are you looking for witnesses?"

"I'm just trying to picture the scene."

"I didn't see anybody."

"Look. I don't want you talking to anyone about this. Okay? Nobody. It's important. Not until you and I have had a chance to talk."

"This isn't a talk?"

"Not enough of one. I've got to get over to City Hall. The mayor is facing the cameras in about ten minutes. I'm sure he'll want me to say a few words."

Of course he would. My father had held Tommy Carroll's post for four years before his abrupt resignation nearly fifteen years ago. I know how it works. During the time my old man was top cop, it seemed that I used to see him more often on the tube than I did in real life. The other large reason for that was that he didn't live with my mother and me. He hadn't been married to my mother. He was married to another woman. The real wife. That's why I don't share his name. He and the wife lived uptown, in every sense of the word, just off Park Avenue, along with their two kids. So he didn't get down to see us all that much. It was less than a week after he stepped down from his post that he disappeared. Then no one saw him at all, not even the rich wife and the well-tended kids. It was soon after this that I met Margo's father. I hired him to nose about for the old man, and before the year was out, I had a PI license of my very own. It made it easier to join in the hunt. For all the good it did.

I was twenty-five then, a couple of years of John Jay already under my belt, followed by something of a flameout, then a couple of years behind a bar on Ludlow Street. Now I finally had a legal gun in my pocket. It wasn't exactly following in the old man's footsteps, but I'd say overall it has worked out fine. I'm my own boss. I fetch my own coffee. I answer my own phone. If I don't like a case, I don't take the case. Life could be worse . . . as that little flameout showed me.

And I'm one up on the old man's former colleague sitting across the table from me: I've had my nose broken only once.

Tommy Carroll leaned forward. "Look, I want you to sit tight—"

I cut him off. "I'm not going to sit in this hole waiting for you."

"I just told you, I've got to get the hell over to City Hall."

"I'll come with you."

"Not a good idea."

"Why not?"

"You know the Three Roses?"

"I know it."

"Go there. I'm sure they'll have the tube on. You can watch the show. Give me another ten minutes after Leavitt and I wrap things up, then come over to City Hall. You know Stacy, my assistant? I'll have her positioned out on the steps to look for you. She'll escort you in." He reached into his pocket and pulled out his wallet. He handed me a twenty. "Live it up."

"Thank you, kind sir," I said, pocketing the bill. "But may I say for the record that something is very fucked up here?"

He stood up. Tommy Carroll standing up is like an ocean liner rising up on its aft.

"You may say it," Carroll said. "But not for the record." He jabbed a thick finger against the tabletop. "There is no record."

COMMISSIONER CARROLL LET ME OUT through a basement door. It led out to the corner of Police Plaza, where on weekdays you've got a half-dozen or so food kiosks waiting to serve lunch to the hundreds of civil servants who've been up in the Munici-pal Building all morning, passing the city bureaucracy around from office to office and desk to desk. This being Thanksgiving, the plaza was deserted. Two police cars were parked at the curb on Centre Street. The two cops who had brought me in, plus the one who had collared the shooter, stood next to the cars. One of these patrol cars, I thought, should be parked in front of a hospital, not here.

"Avoid them," Carroll said. "Just circle around them and get to the bar. And I'm serious about this, Fritz, don't breathe a word to anyone until after we've talked. Promise me."

I nodded. A nod is not a promise. I was calling Margo the moment I got to the bar. And no big ugly police commissioner was going to stop me.

I traced a wide circle around the two police cars. Only Gumdrop looked over my way. I shot him with a finger pistol and trotted across the street.

The Three Roses is tucked into an alley-like street that sees all of a single wedge of sunshine for approximately ten to twenty minutes once a day, depending on the season. The bar is two doors in from the corner, between a pizza joint and a bail bondsman's office. I moved into the shadowed street, went flat against the wall of the pizza joint, and looked back over toward the cop cars. The police commissioner was talking with his men. Whatever he was saying, he was using his hands to emphasize his point, slapping the knuckles of one into the open palm of the other. I couldn't tell if he was angry or he was just being emphatic. My experience with Tommy Carroll is that there's not much difference. This went on for about a minute, then he checked his watch for maybe the hundredth time, turned and started back for the door he and I had used. One of the cops went with him. The one who had nabbed the shooter.

I went back down the shadowy street and into the bar. As Carroll had predicted, the television set was on. The handful of patrons were all gazing up at it. The expressions on their faces were pretty much identical. They were watching a replay of footage that had been taken several minutes after the Beretta had done its damage. The Mother Goose float was in the center of the screen. Several bodies were visible lying on the street and on the far sidewalk, being tended to by either EMS or regular folks from the crowd. People wandered in zigzags all over the street. An old-timer at the bar was shaking his bony head in dismay. "That's one fucked-up parade."

I asked the bartender for a glass of seltzer and took it to the rear of the place, where I wedged my shoulder into a corner so I could use the pay phone on the wall and still keep an eye on the television. Margo answered on the second ring.

"I misplaced the bagels," I said. "I'm sorry."

I heard a sound that I took to be a long breath being let out. Either that or my sweetie had suffered a puncture and was leaking.

"Where are you?"

"I'm in a bar."

"Ten-thirty in the morning," Margo said. "How colorful."

"Trust me. They're not letting too many colors into this place."

"I feel stupid asking, but you do know what happened up at the parade while you were out, right?"

"Don't feel stupid. Yes. I wandered up to take a peek."

"Before or after?"

"During."

There was another pause. "Are you okay?"

"I'm fine. A little scrape here, a little banged up there."

"You got caught up in the stampede?"

Up on the television, they were showing footage of the parade prior to all hell breaking loose. The Spider-Man float. The Pink Panther. A two-story dog poking its head out of a Christmas stocking.

"I got caught up chasing after the shooter," I said.

"Is that right? Hmmm. I'm not surprised."

"I'm not surprised you're not surprised."

"The television is saying that the guy who did it was caught. They say he was shot by the police."

"By the police? That's not what happened. I shot him, Margo. I chased him into the park. I winged him at the Bethesda Fountain." This was the conversation Tommy Carroll had warned me not to have. "But for the moment I think it would be best if you kept that piece of information between you, me and the pillow."

"What do you mean you shot him? Your gun's here. The cute little fellow's been keeping me company in your absence."

"I borrowed a gun from a policeman."

"Borrowed a . . . Why couldn't he just shoot him himself?"

"He was already dead."

There was another pause. The longest one yet. Finally she spoke. "Could you just do me one favor? Could you drag yourself away from your little bar and get back over here? We were having a very sweet morning until you went out for the damn bagels."

"I'd love to, but I can't, I'm sorry. Not yet. I've got a little sorting out to do on account of my sticking my nose where it didn't belong."

"You're going to sort it out in a bar?"

"It's a long story. To be honest, I don't know how it goes yet. I'm not even supposed to be talking to you."

"Me? What have **I** done?"

On the television, the picture cut to what appeared to be a scene from a Broadway musical. The stage held a mock-up of the broad side of an ocean liner, and a chorus of about twenty male singers in scrubbed white sailor suits, sailor caps and hundred-watt smiles were lined up at the rail, engaged in some sort of manic clog dancing. While their feet smacked out the vigorous patty-cake, their arms were swinging and jerking as they waved snappy red and blue semaphores in perfect unison. I have to admit, my musical-theater gene is profoundly underdeveloped, so maybe what looked like utter inanity to me was actually Tony-winning choreographic genius. Whatever it was, I couldn't figure out what it was doing on the television screen right in the middle of live news coverage of a bloody massacre.

A lifeboat appeared from above the earnest seamen, lowering on cables. A slender-waisted woman in a modified sailor suit designed to give her bare arms and legs maximum freedom and exposure was standing in the middle of the lifeboat singing her little lungs out.

Even from the rear of the bar, I could catch the tinny sounds of her voice. Her face was framed by a headful of blond ringlets that I was sure was a wig, topped by a sailor cap of her own, raked at the jauntiest of angles.

I recognized the face.

"What's on your screen right now?" I asked into the phone.

". . . They're showing a reporter standing in front of City Hall. Why?"

"Switch channels."

"Okay."

"You're looking for a girl singing in a lifeboat."

"A what?"

"It's a show. Broadway musical. You got it?"

"I got it." She laughed. "Gosh, Fritz, let's run right out and buy tickets! It looks great."

I asked, "Who is she?"

"The singer?"

"The singer-sailor. Who is she?" Margo writes for magazines. She knows who all these people are. The scene on the television had switched. I was looking at the same woman, without the blond ringlets, this time sitting on a cushy chair being interviewed by Katie Couric. The sailor woman was a redhead, which was how I had remembered her.

"That's Rebecca Gilpin," Margo said.

"And Rebecca Gilbert is?"

"**Gilpin.** Don't they have **People** magazine under your rock? Rebecca Gilpin of the TV show **Trial Date**?"

"**Trial Date.** Is that where a couple go out together first to see if they might want to actually go out together?"

"You're not as obtuse as I know you'd like to be. You've heard of **Trial Date.**"

She was right. I had. It was a popular TV show. Cops, robbers, lawyers, judges, juries, witnesses and suspects. I wasn't sure what its particular twist was, but it must have had one. It had been around for a while.

"Rebecca Gilpin is on the show?"

"She was. She left it."

"What did she play?"

"She was a prosecuting attorney. She was the character with no scruples. Lie, cheat, sleep with the enemy."

On-screen, Rebecca Gilpin and Katie Couric were enjoying a huge laugh together. Sisters. On top of the world.

"So now she's on Broadway?"

"Yep," Margo said. "Lies, cheats, sleeps with the enemy **and** she can dance and sing. Whatta gal, eh?"

I frowned. The old guy sitting under the television set launched into a world-class smoker's cough. "Rebecca Gilpin was Mother Goose in the parade today," I said.

"I know."

"The guy who killed all those people took a shot at her first."

"They're not certain about that," Margo said.

"I am. I was right there." The picture on the screen switched from the **Today** show footage. We were back to the scene of the parade, post-shooting. I asked, "Do you know if she was hit?"

The television showed two policemen. One was holding the pointy Mother Goose hat that Rebecca Gilpin had been wearing. The camera zoomed in as the cop holding the hat turned it in his hand to show something to his colleague. It was a pair of small holes. One going in, one going out. The second cop produced a large plastic bag. The hat went into the bag.

"Apparently, she's fine," Margo said. She added, "One bright spot for the mayor."

"The mayor? What do you mean?"

"You really do live under a rock. You don't know about the mayor and the Broadway star? Are you completely out of the zeitgeist?"

"Mayor Leavitt and Rebecca Gilpin are an item?"

Margo laughed. "An item."

"And everyone knows this?"

"Everyone but you, my sweets. Common knowledge."

The old guy beneath the television set hadn't stopped coughing. Ten more seconds of this and his ruined lungs would be on the floor.

"I'll call you," I said. And I hung up.

I DIDN'T WAIT FOR THE MAYOR'S AND Tommy Carroll's statements to come on the tube. I left the Three Roses and hoofed it up the street to City Hall Park. I noted that both of the police cars that had been parked across the street were gone. An uncommon quiet filled the downtown air between the bar and City Hall. Only my footsteps and my ricocheting thoughts. I was mulling over what Margo had just told me. Someone had taken a shot at the mayor's girlfriend. And following that, at his citizens.

And following that, at **me.**

The scene in front of City Hall was a regular Woodstock of media. Focus all those satellite dishes on a single spot out in the galaxy, and we probably could have initiated first contact.

The mayor was standing at the top of the stairs at City Hall. The bank of microphones in front of him looked like a muscular piece of modern sculpture. Dozens of cameras down on the sidewalk were aimed up at him. Just the way he likes it.

I voted for Martin Leavitt. It wasn't with the utmost enthusiasm that I had flipped the lever next to his name, but he was the devil I knew, and I'd been willing to give him a go. A rigorous district attorney in Brooklyn with an impressive collection of pelts on his belt, Leavitt brought strong law-and-order muscle to the post. Those are two of my issues; I'm biased that way. His prosecutorial zeal aside, Leavitt was also one of those pretty-faced politicians whom people seem to like these days. The younger Redford would have played him in the movie. At least, this was an observation Leavitt himself had been overheard uttering soon after his reelection. Allegedly, anyway. Page Six made some hay with the comment for a few days. The Sundance Mayor. Divorced after a brief marriage during the middle of his political climb to the top, Leavitt was frequently spotted in the company of high-profile women. Scorekeepers noted that the gentleman preferred blondes, though he was not beyond the stretch over to a redhead now and again. Leavitt's decision to have a dishy pop star sing the national anthem at his inaugural had been viewed by some as refreshing and by others as tawdry. I hadn't really cared either way myself, except when the singer mangled the high note.

Leavitt was closing in on two years into his term, and until recently, no one could have voiced any major regrets. The city had been in a sinkhole of debt when he took over the reins from his predecessor, and by putting a systematic squeeze on each and every department, Leavitt had prompted cries of mutiny throughout the five boroughs, but he had also managed to raise the levels of efficiency in the hitherto bloated and self-serving bureaucracies that had grown way too accustomed to living fat while their constituencies chewed on bones. In other words, he was putting the financial house in order.

Unfortunately, things had become a little unraveled in the arena that was Leavitt's strong suit. Law and order. A corruption scandal in his police department had flared up like a flash fire several months back, and with the impression that Leavitt's primary response to the scandal had been to circle the wagons around the upper brass while feeding some street grunts to the lions, the heat had begun finding its way to City Hall. Initially, the scandal had involved a group of cops in Brooklyn's Ninety-fifth Precinct who were being accused of, among other things, a years-long pattern of shakedowns of local drug dealers, falsifying evidence or even re-selling the evidence for their own gain, swapping drugs for sex with area prostitutes and generally trampling all over the neighborhoods they were sworn to protect. When the name of a noted Brooklyn prosecutor with whom then–Brooklyn D.A. Martin Leavitt had worked closely started appearing in newspaper accounts alongside the names of some of the accused cops, voices in some of the more mad-dog corners of the city had begun calling for Leavitt's head. Tommy Carroll's, too, for that matter. I hadn't seen that it would come to any of that. But then the apparent murder-suicide in early November of a pair of cops allegedly involved in the scandal had guaranteed exclamation points being slapped onto the story. The papers were calling it "The Bad Apple Scandal," "The Rotten Apple Scandal," etc. National press was beginning to pick up on it. A definite black eye for the Leavitt administration. Its first direct hit. And some nut opening fire on citizens

during the Thanksgiving Day parade was certainly not going to help matters. The darkened skies over City Hall had abruptly grown
just that much darker.

I was too far back to hear the mayor, so I
stepped over cables to a Channel 4 van. The
side door was open. A pair of engineers were
seated on canvas stools, smoking and watching the mayor on their monitor.

". . . shake the spirit of this great city. We
won't let it happen. That's not what we're
about. I want to repeat, there is nothing to
suggest that what happened this morning at
the Thanksgiving Day parade was a terrorist
attack. This was, it appears, a lone gunman.
The gunman has been apprehended, taken
into custody—"

Leavitt paused as a barrage of questions
from reporters took him out midsentence. I
could hear the cries both live behind me and
in the news van's speakers. Leavitt raised his
hands like a man at gunpoint and rode out
the cacophony.

"We don't have that information confirmed. As you can imagine, first reports on
something like this come flying in from all
sorts of sources. Including you folks in the
media. We do have him. That much I will
confirm. As to his condition? Was he shot? All

that? You're going to have to wait—" The mayor looked directly into the cameras. "**You** are going to have to wait as **I** am going to have to wait, so that we get one story and one story only. Perhaps Commissioner Carroll will be able to update us on all that, I don't know. He will speak in a moment. I—"

Again the mayor was interrupted. This time the tiniest trace of a smile came over his face as he listened to the yapping.

"Have I heard from Miss Gilpin directly? No, I have not. Do I know that she is safe and unharmed? Yes, I do."

Another barrage. Another smile. This one not quite as tiny.

"How do I know that? I'm the mayor. I know people in high places."

One of the engineers snorted. "Dude knows Rebecca Gilpin in low places, too."

I left the van and made my way back over to City Hall. Blue police barricades had been set up at the bottom of the steps. The reporters were calling out their questions to the mayor from behind the barricades. Commissioner Carroll stepped to the bank of microphones, which struck him near the abdomen. Behind him, whispering into Leavitt's ear, was Philip Byron, the deputy mayor. The mayor was nodding in almost exaggerated agreement to whatever it was Byron was saying to him. He looked like a circus horse.

I worked my way forward and spotted a **Times** reporter I knew well enough to hail. Henry Greene. He was leaning forward on the barricade, holding a handful of papers he had rolled into a cone.

"Greene!" I called out.

The reporter turned. He waved me over. "Well, if it's not my favorite German-Irish dick."

"You should be careful, using that kind of language."

He indicated the barricade. "How punk is this? Leavitt's got us in a mosh pit."

"You're all animals. I don't know why he waited so long."

"Animals. Right."

"So what are you hearing?" I asked. "Sound like straight dope so far?"

The reporter shrugged. "Fifty-fifty. They're holding back on some things. They always do."

I considered the report Margo had mentioned, that the parade shooter had been shot by the police. It's possible that this was simply a mistake resulting from the early chaos, but my better senses told me that wasn't the case. I should have been coming clean to the authorities that very minute in a well-lit room at a police precinct near Central Park, all the lousy coffee I could stomach, eager faces crowded around to hear my tale. Instead, I was scheduled to pop into City Hall for a hush-hush confab with the police commissioner as soon as he finished addressing the cameras. Greene was right. They were holding back. And I was one of the things they were holding.

Commissioner Carroll repeated the bare bones of what the mayor had said. He wanted to assure everybody that the crisis was already over. He offered his condolences to the families of the dead and wounded, got in a plug for the professionalism and efficiency of the New York City Police Department and suggested to people that they include an addendum to their normal Thanksgiving Day prayers. As he turned from the podium, Greene brought the cone of papers to his mouth and shouted out, "Commissioner! Why can't you give us an update on the gunman's condition? Can you tell us if he was acting alone? There've been reports of two gunmen. Can you comment? Is there anyone else out there we should know about?"

Carroll started to turn back to the microphones. As he did, he spotted me. He dark-

handed me the paper cup. I tried to hand her a smile, but she wasn't accepting gifts. "Door," Carroll said gruffly as she exited.

It closed with a delicate click.

The commissioner balled his hands together on the desk. "I'm supposed to be in Tortola."

I wasn't sure what I had expected him to say, but "I'm supposed to be in Tortola" would have been way down on the list.

"Nice place, Tortola," I said. "I went down there a couple of years ago. Very good snorkeling. I went nuts for the parrot fish."

Tommy Carroll picked up a remote and switched on the television. A grim-faced blond woman with helplessly blue eyes was holding a microphone to her chin. Kelly Cole. Ubiquitous Kelly. Channel 4.

"According to Mayor Leavitt, the gunman has been—"

Carroll muted the sound. He frowned. "What were you and Greene talking about just now?"

"Nothing."

"He's a wiseass. That question about McNally? A good cop is killed defending the people of this city, and this pipsqueak reporter thinks he can get smug on me."

"That's his job," I said.

"To smear the New York City Police Department?"

"Seems to me the cops over in the Ninety-fifth have been doing a fine job of that all on their own."

Carroll scowled. "I thought I told you to stay at the Three Roses until we were finished up here."

I pulled the twenty out of my pocket and placed it on the desk. "Sorry, Tommy. The place was making me feel like I needed to take a shower."

"We've got a real problem going on here, Fritz."

"As they say in the old country, 'No shit, Sherlock.' "

"The mayor and I are counting on you to cooperate."

"Cooperate with what?"

Carroll unballed his hands and leaned back in the chair. He gazed out the window over his left shoulder. It occurred to me that those picnic tables near the subway entrance were probably a decent fit for the commissioner. He looked out the window a few seconds, then let out a gravelly sigh and turned back to me. "The shooter has been identified as Roberto Diaz. Born in Puerto Rico. American citizen. Lived in Brooklyn. Divorced.

Last worked for a company called Delivery on Demand. It's a messenger service."

"I see."

"He left a month ago. Quit."

"Okay."

Carroll leveled me with a look. "You didn't shoot him."

"I didn't **what?**"

"You didn't shoot him, Fritz. Just start getting that notion into your head. You're not leaving this office until it's there."

I leaned back in my chair. I noted again the commissioner's labored breathing. Tommy Carroll had been a heavy smoker ever since I'd known him. He'd quit lately. I wondered if he'd quit too late. He dipped his large chin toward his chest, his eyes inviting me to speak.

"I shot him, Tommy. I hit him in the right shoulder."

He was wagging his head even before I'd finished talking. "You didn't shoot him, Fritz. Officer Leonard Cox shot him."

"Who is Officer Leonard Cox?"

"He's the cop who shot Roberto Diaz."

"Did he shoot him in the right shoulder?"

Carroll nodded.

"Did he shoot him out by the Bethesda Fountain?"

Another nod.

"While giving chase?"

"Of course. What else?"

"Well, I don't know what else, Tommy. Since we're obviously stringing fantasies together here, maybe this Officer Cox shot Diaz because Diaz was running around with a flowerpot on his head, and the new rule is no flowerpots on the head on national holidays. I don't know. What the hell is this all about?"

As Carroll was raising a hand in a gesture to quiet me down, the phone on his desk rang. He picked it up, still looking at me, and listened a few seconds. Then he said, "No. Not yet." He listened a few more seconds, then grunted and hung up. "That was the mayor."

"I hope he's not wearing a flowerpot on his head."

"You're talking to him in five minutes."

"Okay, Tommy, can we get everything out on the table? Why was I taken away from the scene and shoved onto the floor of a police cruiser with a bag over my head? Why was I taken to the Municipal Building? Was Diaz run through the same routine? Where is he now? And last but not least, why am I supposed to start pretending that I didn't shoot the guy in the shoulder, or anywhere else, for that matter? I'm seeing the mayor in five minutes? Fine. I'll give you two of those minutes to tell me exactly what the hell's going on, or I'm walking out of here." I indicated the television, where Kelly Cole was still yammering into her microphone out in front of City Hall. "Forget Greene. Kelly and I are old pals. You can tell the mayor to tune in to the Channel Four News for all the latest."

Carroll looked as if he would be quite happy to see my head come off my neck and crash to the floor in pieces. He cleared the telephone to the edge of the desk with his arm, as if making room to lunge forward and grab me by the collar.

"Leavitt knew about the shooting in advance."

The words came in loud and clear, but I had to run them through the filter several times just to be sure. "He knew Diaz was gong to shoot up the Thanksgiving parade?"

"Not exactly. He didn't know the specific details of what was going to happen. He didn't know the where or the who or the when."

"But he knew?"

"He'd been warned that something might happen."

"And he did nothing to stop it?"

"You're not listening. I just told you. He

didn't know what or where or when. Believe me, we were working on it. The parade was an obvious target. I tried to get him to cancel the damn thing, but in this town that's like asking someone to cancel Christmas. Leavitt wasn't about to do something like that. Especially now, with all this other crap coming down. People like a parade. It gets their mind off stuff. The whole point was not to go public."

"I'm not following you."

"Diaz contacted the mayor a couple of weeks ago. Of course he didn't give us his name. It was a note. He made . . . let's just say he made some demands. I can't go into details."

"Can I assume they were unreasonable demands?"

"Of course they were. You know how it is, we hear from nutcases all the time. It's almost always them just blowing off steam. Nothing comes of it. This guy, who could say? He wasn't specific about his threats. They never are. But we weren't sitting on our thumbs. We were working to worm him out, but obviously he acted before we could get to him."

"What were the demands?"

"I just told you, I can't go into details."

"Is that what I should tell Kelly Cole?"

"You're not telling Cole anything. Maybe I

haven't impressed on you the seriousness of this whole thing. We have seven known dead out there, including one of our own. We've got more who are injured. Some of them pretty badly. So we might lose a few more."

"Half an hour ago you were calling these numbers lucky."

"Fuck half an hour ago. Now is now. There's nothing lucky about any of this. It's a nightmare. But it's not half the nightmare it's going to be if word gets out that the mayor was warned in advance. You know how it works. It doesn't matter that no one knew where or when or any of the details at all. The only thing that matters is the mayor was told someone was ready to do some real fucking damage in this city, and that for all our efforts to stop the guy, the damage was done. We're not putting that word out. Simple as that."

"So you're manipulating the truth."

"Fuck the truth."

"Nice," I said.

"That's how it is."

"So what about Rebecca Gilpin?"

"What about her?"

"The shooter aimed at her first. I was right there. The first bullet was a head shot on Mother Goose."

"What of it?"

"What do you mean, 'what of it'? Apparently the whole world knows that Leavitt is fluffing the pillows with this woman. Come on, Tommy. Diaz was trying to kill the mayor's lady friend. Don't tell me he wasn't. He was making it personal."

Carroll grumbled, "I told him to pull her from the parade just in case. Easy enough to do. Put out the word that she's got a twenty-four-hour flu. He presented it to her. Let me tell you something, Fritz, this is a woman who doesn't listen. If you've got two seconds, I can tell you how much patience I've got for celebrities."

"Okay, so why are you trying to twist the truth about who shot Diaz?"

"Politics."

"Explain, please."

"You're a citizen. We're damn lucky you're a licensed snoop, even though the gun you used wasn't the one you're licensed to shoot. But at least you're not some trigger-happy Joe Everybody grabbing a gun and running around trying to be a hero. But even with you being a private dick, it's not a good picture. Vigilante justice is something we can do without."

I understood. "But a cop chasing the perp, winging him in the shoulder and taking him into custody, that's a good story. That's clean. That's 'Hero Cop Saves City from More Hell.' Am I reading the headlines correctly? A good apple? Is that what you're angling for? A little positive news for once?"

"It's close."

"Close. What am I missing?"

Before he could answer, the office door opened and in walked Martin Leavitt. Without a word, he strode to the television set, where he moved his hand over the controls like a wizard doing a little conjuring. He turned to the police commissioner. "Where's the sound?"

Carroll picked up the remote and pushed the mute button. Kelly Cole's voice was twice as loud as any of us were prepared for.

". . . this horrifically tragic day. A spokesman for St. Luke's confirmed just a few minutes ago that the still-unidentified gunman died of wounds inflicted during the shootout with police that had resulted in the gunman's being taken into custody. Apparently, the suspect was struck—"

I was out of my chair. "**Died?** I shot him in the fucking **shoulder!**"

"You didn't shoot him," Tommy Carroll said flatly. "We just went over that."

Mayor Leavitt slammed his hand against

the television's power button. The screen
went blank. His face was pale as chalk.
"We've got a problem."

Carroll rose from his chair. "No, we don't.
We're fine. Fritz here is on board. We've just
got to talk it all out a little more."

Leavitt turned to his police commissioner,
looking at him as if the man had just grown
avocados out of his ears.

"No." He pointed at the blank television.
"Not that. I just got a call. From him."

"From who?"

"**Him.** The goddamn nightmare. Who do
you think?"

Carroll looked confused. "The nightmare
just died at St. Luke's Hospital, Martin. You
heard the girl. Settle down. It's over."

"No. You're not listening. I just got a call.
From **him.** There's no question about it. It
was him." Leavitt was working to keep the
waver out of his voice. He was only somewhat
successful.

Tommy Carroll came out from behind his
desk. He stepped to within five inches of
the mayor. A huff and a puff and the mayor
would've gone down. Carroll's voice came out
with an eerie softness. "The shooter wasn't
our guy?"

Leavitt was shaking his head. "He must

have been put up to it by our guy. A trigger-man. A partner. Something like that. I don't know. The point is, our guy is still out there. He's not dead."

Carroll repeated dully, "He's not dead?"

"And he's not finished. Do you want to know what he said?" The mayor ran a hand through his hair. He took a few seconds to compose himself. God help me, for a moment I thought the man was going to cry. "He asked me if **now** I believed him. He said the nightmare has just begun. That's a quote. The nightmare. So you know this is the guy, Tommy. And by God, you can be sure this time I do believe him. I sure as fuck believe him. The bastard."

I watched as the police commissioner's face went from putty to crimson. I briefly thought he might put a fist right through the hand-some mayor's face. Then he spun in the direction of the television. The towering police commissioner was a hell of a lot quicker than I would have expected. Squeezing a growl through his clenched teeth, he swung his arm backward, clamped hold of the television and shoved it right off the metal stand. It crashed to the floor. The tube exploded with a loud **pop.** An instant later, the office door flew open and Carroll's assistant ran in. The commissioner took one heavy dinosaur step in her direction.

"Get the fuck out of here!"

Stacy fled. I went over to the door. The young woman was running down the hallway as if fleeing a fire. I closed the door. Carroll's cheeks were puffing with rage. Leavitt raised his hands as if appealing to a crowd for calm. Which, in a sense, he was.

"Okay. Hold on. Just stop. Slow down." He took a beat. "We've got a problem. We need to solve it."

The steadiness had returned to his voice. He stepped around Tommy Carroll and over to the desk, where he picked up the phone and hit a few buttons. "Philip. We're in Tommy's office. Get in here." He disconnected the line. Looking up at me, he shook the phone receiver in my direction.

"I'm not offering you a choice, Mr. Malone. Simple as this. You are cooperating."

5

MARGO SPARED ME THE TRUDGE UP FOUR flights. She met me at La Fortuna, right down the street from her apartment. It's a dark cozy place with old opera LPs and framed photos of opera singers all over its brick walls. Margo once ran into Pavarotti here. He was sitting alone in the garden out back with a cappuccino and a basket of biscotti, reading a paperback copy of **Lonesome Dove.** She managed to join him, using her own enthusiasm for the book as a wedge, and by the final biscotti, Pavarotti had agreed to let her interview him for part of a fluff piece she was putting together for **New York** magazine. The tenor wrote her a three-page appreciation letter after the piece appeared.

The owner of the cafe beamed like a brand

new mother as I stood at the pie counter trying to decide.

I put my finger on the glass. "The blue-
berry looks like the one today."

She pulled out the pie and slid a large slice
onto a plate, using her knife to scrape some of
the extra goop. She indicated Margo. "And
what will it be for the princess?"

Margo answered, "I'm not really hungry,
Mrs. Valella. I'll just steal a few bites from the
big guy."

"You want the cappuccino?"

"Two," I said. "The big guy doesn't share
everything."

Margo and I retreated to one of the small
tables next to the wall. Enrico Caruso looked
over my shoulder as I took my first bite of
pie. His mouth was wide open, as if he expected me to funnel a forkful his way. Margo
looked like rain on a sunny day.

"You could have been killed."

I nodded. " 'Could have' is the road to un-
necessary suffering. I wasn't."

"But you could've been."

"That's true for everyone," I said. "You
never know when the bus is going to flatten
you. It's why you want to seize the moment."
I tapped my fork against my plate. "How
about a piece of pie?"

She ignored me. "At the exact moment you were running around getting shot at less than a block away, I was probably sitting in bed painting my stupid toenails."

"It would have been stranger had it been the other way around."

"Oh, shut up. Think about the families, Fritz. Think about all the funerals they're going to be having over the next couple of days. And there I was painting my toenails. I feel horrible."

"Are we juxtaposing the tragic with the trivial?"

"I guess we are."

"And are we getting anything out of it? I mean besides anguish?" She screwed her mouth up into a pucker. With Margo, this is usually the equivalent of a pitcher going into his windup. I waited, but she simply remained that way, her eyes narrowing to slits. Finally, I asked, "Do you have something to say?"

She unpuckered. "Forget it."

"Look, the whole city is shaken up," I said. "Unfortunately, that's the point of these kinds of things."

"The point. I like that."

"See? You're edgy."

"How about we don't talk about it?"

"Okay." I picked up the fork and shoveled the piece of pie into my mouth. "They sure do good pie here, eh?"

She was crying. And I was an idiot. It was quiet crying. A pair of tears ran down her cheeks, followed by another pair. I felt something on my leg. It was the toe of Margo's shoe. She was locating my shin, and when she found it, she gave it a not insubstantial kick.

"I hate you," she said in a barely audible voice. She reached a hand across the table and I took it. Mrs. Valella arrived with our cappuccinos. She gave Margo the sort of sympathetic look only an Italian mother can give.

"He will keep you safe and warm, princess," she said to Margo, setting down the cappuccinos. She shot me a withering look.

Right?

When we got back to Margo's, I explained the situation to her as best I could. Before leaving City Hall, I had been sworn to secrecy, and had I thought that telling Margo might in any way put her in danger, I'd have remained mum. And she would have understood. But I needed to talk it out—so much of it made no sense to me—and next to her father, Margo is the best sounding board I know.

I swore her to secrecy. She crossed her fingers and said, "Sure." The tears were gone.

"I have a job," I told her by way of getting into it. We were in Margo's living room. One entire wall of the room was taken up with books. Floor-to-ceiling. A former boyfriend of Margo's built the shelves for her. He even installed one of those moving ladders that glides along a horizontal pole for reaching the high shelves. Good craftsman, but in the end, a lousy boyfriend. I was seated in a wicker chair across from the wall of books. Margo was in no one place for longer than twenty seconds. We were due at her parents' for Thanksgiving dinner, and she had promised her purple cabbage casserole. She flew in from the kitchen and landed a cutting board in my lap.

"Job is good," she said. "We like job." She ducked back into the kitchen.

"We'll see if job is good," I called in to her. "The mayor wants me to look after his girl-friend."

"Really? That's the job? So you get to meet Rebecca Gilpin."

"So do you. We've got comps to go see her

in her big Broadway show tonight. That is, if you want to go."

Margo poked her head out from the kitchen. "Tonight? You've got to be kidding. What the hell is she doing running around on a Broadway stage tonight? Someone just took a shot at her in the Thanksgiving Day parade. Is she a nut?"

"That's pretty close to how I put the question to the mayor," I said. "And he was pretty much in agreement with me. But it's what she wants to do."

Margo groaned. "The show must go on?"

"Right. It's some form of thespian testosterone. The mayor took a call from her while we were huddling in Tommy Carroll's office. Not to disparage our good mayor, but from what I observed, he's not the only one who wears the pants in that relationship. His plan was for all the theaters to go black tonight. Because of Thanksgiving, a lot of them had already decided not to do a show. But Rebecca Gilpin's is one of the ones scheduled to run tonight, and apparently, the woman wants to make a statement by, yes, going on with the show."

"What the hell is the statement?" Margo asked, bringing a large knife and a head of cabbage to me. "**I'm an insensitive idiot? I have can-do spirit?**"

"**Can do** what? Can do tap-dance across a crowded stage with a bunch of gay sailors? I'm with you. She should take the night off and think about all the people who weren't as lucky today as she was."

"From what you told me, it wasn't luck, bubba. You saved her life."

"I threw a bag of bagels at her."

"You said she ducked. The bullet would have gone right into her head."

"I still call that lucky. Anyway, the short version of all this is that Leavitt wants me to be her personal shadow."

Margo took the knife from me and gave the cabbage a few whacks. "Like that." She handed me back the knife. "But I don't understand. The killer was killed."

It was Philip Byron who had suggested that if I needed to explain to anyone why I was Rebecca Gilpin's bodyguard, I should say there was some concern about copycatters. Nutcases who find inspiration in high-profile tragedies and try to get in on the action.

"I'm supposed to tell you that they're afraid someone might try to do a copycat thing and take a shot at her," I said.

"But that's not it?"

"That's not it."

"This is the sworn-to-secrecy part?"

"It is." I told her about the mayor's having

received a phone call after the parade massacre from the person who had been taunting
him the past several weeks about an immi-
nent public tragedy.

"You mean the guy who did this is still out
there?"

"The guy who did it is dead. But the guy
who was behind it is still very much with us.
And he told Leavitt today that the nightmare
has just begun. That's a quote."

"What the hell is this all about, Fritz?"

"I don't know. Tommy Carroll said this
was all being handled on a need-to-know
basis and that I didn't need to know."

"And you agreed to that?"

"I didn't agree to anything. Well, no. That's
not true. I agreed to keep my mouth shut
about my shooting this Diaz character in the
shoulder. For the time being, anyway."

"Diaz. The dead Diaz."

"That's him."

"Whom you shot in the shoulder."

"Correct."

"But whom we're being told was killed by
a policeman."

"Correct again."

"And he died of a shoulder wound."

"He died of a bullet to the brain."

"Which you didn't inflict."

"Which I didn't inflict."

"**That** was the policeman?"

"Officer Leonard Cox. Our hero du jour."

"But that didn't happen at the Bethesda Fountain, right? You said that after you clipped the guy's wing, both of you were taken into custody."

"And driven in circles with bags over our heads."

"Jesus, Fritz. What was that about?"

"My opinion is that it was just a stalling tactic while Tommy Carroll and the mayor scrambled to come up with a plan."

"That would account for the blindfold and the dipsy-doodle driving. But what about the bag?"

"You have to remember, they didn't know who this other person was. The trigger-happy citizen who grabbed a cop's gun and went running after the shooter."

"You."

"Me. They didn't know who or what they had on their hands until they got me somewhere they could talk to me."

"And what's wrong with a station house?"

I shrugged. "Too many witnesses? That's my guess. That's why the bag in the first place. As best as I figure it, they wanted to make sure that if a photographer somehow happened to snap a picture of this trigger-happy person being led into the Municipal Building, it would be that much more difficult to identify him."

"Why would they need to hide the person's identity?"

"You're not going to like my answer."

"Try me."

"It's just supposition."

"Supposition me."

"In case the guy who walked into the Municipal Building under police custody never walked back out."

"Explain."

"Until they had a chance to talk to this live wire who's running around shooting off policemen's guns, they didn't know for certain that he wasn't part of the whole parade-massacre plot. Maybe he's not Mr. Brave Citizen after all. What do they know?"

"So?"

"So, Tommy Carroll made it pretty clear to me that the mayor's number one priority is to keep a lid on this whole thing. If word gets out that Leavitt had even an inkling about this in advance, and didn't do everything in his power to stop it . . ."

I paused. Margo finished the thought. "He's screwed."

"Big-time screwed. Forget Bad Apple. This would bounce him right out of there."

"So if you'd been a part of the conspiracy, you're saying you think they would have killed you?"

"It's only speculation," I said.

"Pretty wild speculation. I know you've run into some unsavory cops now and then, but this sounds more than a little far-fetched."

I said nothing. I just continued chopping. I could tell the moment it hit her. Her jaw dropped slightly and disbelief flooded her eyes.

"So . . . wait. Is **that** what happened to what's-his-name? Diaz? Oh my God. You said he wasn't killed out by the fountain. Where **was** he killed?"

"If you listen to the TV, he **was** killed out by the fountain. Resisting arrest. One shot to the shoulder, one shot to the skull."

"By the police."

"Officer Leonard Cox."

"So is that really who shot him in the head? In the Municipal Building?"

I plunged the knife into the remainder of the cabbage. "According to Tommy Carroll, that's one of those need-to-know things that I don't need to know."

Margo eyed me. "Fine. But are you going to settle for that?"

"What's your guess?"

She stepped over to me, took the cutting board from my lap and put herself there. She looked deeply into my eyes.

"No fucking way."

She took the words right out of my mouth.

6

WE TOOK THE 7 TRAIN OUT TO LONG Island City. Margo's parents lived on Starr Avenue, near the Silvercup Studios. The subway
was relatively empty. It was difficult to tell
whether the blank expressions on the few rid-
ers' faces were your standard-issue blank expressions or if the parade massacre was a
contributing factor.

The fatality count had bumped up to nine,
which seemed to be where it was going to
level off. This was a scale-down from ten,
when it was determined after speaking with
witnesses that one of the apparent victims
had actually suffered a fatal heart attack just
minutes before the bullets had started flying.

The oldest victim was a fifty-three-year-old
math teacher from Rumson, New Jersey. The

youngest was fourteen, the girl with the alto sax. Ezra Fisher's mother had fallen somewhere in the middle. Twenty-seven. From Fort Lee, just over the George Washington Bridge. Single. No other children besides Ezra. When I heard this, the first thing that came to mind was the boy's white balloon floating off by itself, higher and higher over the ruined parade.

We like to push bruises. I don't know why that is.

There were several eyewitnesses who claimed to have seen a second gunman. A man running along Central Park West with a gun. The police vigorously denied these reports.

MARGO'S FATHER WAS SITTING OUT FRONT when we arrived. The house where Margo grew up was built in the mid-fifties. It is a compact little place with a cement porch overlooking a small front yard that has flat rocks where you'd expect grass. The grass is out back, where there's also a picnic table, a birdbath and, in season, a modest vegetable garden. The house is two stories high, with an attic and a basement. It looks pretty much like all the others on the block except for its one novel feature, a long narrow ramp that runs at a shallow angle from the cement porch out over the flat rocks, ending right at the sidewalk. The ramp is wood—very solid—with two-inch-high strips running across it every two feet, sort of like the rungs of a ladder. The ramp allows Margo's father to wheel his chair from the porch to the sidewalk. The strips help him keep the trip from getting out of hand.

Charlie Burke waved his cigar at us from the porch. "Happy Hanukkah, you two lovebirds."

"Shalom to you, too, Charlie," I said as I stepped onto the porch. I carried a shopping bag with Margo's cabbage casserole.

Charlie stuck the cigar between his teeth and gave me his hard grip. "You're as ugly as ever," he said.

"You, too."

Margo landed her hands gently on her father's shoulders and went in for a soft kiss on his rough cheek. "Happy Thanksgiving, Daddy."

"Well, we've had better ones, haven't we?"

Margo straightened and her father studied her face. "That whole mess was close to your apartment, honey."

"I phoned Mom."

"I know you did. You're a good girl." He

looked up at me. "They say the guy worked for a messenger service."

"That's what I heard."

"That's sort of like working for the post office. What kind of nut does something like that?"

"The worst kind," I said.

"But they got him. Only good news of the day."

Margo took the shopping bag from me. "I'm going inside." She looked from her father to me and back to her father. "Save the world, men."

She disappeared into the house. I could hear the high falsetto of her mother's lavish greetings. I lowered myself lightly on the wrought-iron railing. Charlie was working up a blue haze with his cigar.

"It's not over, Charlie," I said.

He cocked an eyebrow at me. "Oh?"

"The guy they took down. Diaz. He was a stooge. Or a partner. Something. Whatever he was, he wasn't the person behind the shooting. He was behind the gun. But he was following orders."

"Keep going."

"Diaz was executed. At least that's how it's smelling to me. The police had him in custody with a shoulder wound. Nothing life-threatening."

"The TV says he took one to the head. DOA at St. Luke's."

"Maybe so. But he wasn't shot until after he was in custody. The police cruiser that took him to St. Luke's took a detour first, to the Municipal Building."

Charlie had a beanbag ashtray in his lap. He tapped the end of his cigar into it, snuffing it out. "You get a better news station than I do, Fritz. I missed all that."

"The version you got goes down easier."

Charlie frowned. "What's this about? Where'd you get all this?"

I gave him the story. He listened without interrupting. When I was finished, he stared down at his dead cigar.

"That need-to-know crap is crap," he said. "You just tell those bastards you need to know and that's that."

"I know it's crap, Charlie. But you've got to imagine the vibe at City Hall. It was so thick in there you **couldn't** cut it with a knife. Everybody was keeping their cards very close. Nobody was about to tell me any more than they figured they had to."

"Yeah, but you've got leverage. You've got a story they don't want you telling."

"I know that. And that's my key back in the door once things have cooled off a little. They leaned on me and I let them. For now."

Charlie was looking past me out toward the street. He used to do this back when we shared an office. As he put it, he did his best thinking out the window. I remained perched on the railing and waited. With little effort, I could transform the spiky gray-haired fellow in the wheelchair into the less grizzled version—the guy who used to be mistaken sometimes for Gene Hackman—leaning back in his worn red leather desk chair, looking out the window for invisible pieces of puzzles to fall magically together.

He snapped from his reverie. "A cop was killed out at the parade."

I nodded.

"Cops don't like cop killers."

I nodded again.

"So they took this Diaz character out. Pure and simple. No trial. This was the police commissioner putting the gag on you."

"Him and the mayor."

Charlie scoffed. "Screw the mayor. I don't give a damn about him. He's just a pretty face. It was Carroll, wasn't it? Let me guess. He pulled your father on you, didn't he? Of course he did. Commissioner Scott, blah blah blah. Loyalty to the old man's memory. He told you to be a team player, right? They're like a goddamn little mafia over there. You know how I feel about Thomas Carroll."

"I've gotten your drift over the years."

"So I'm right, aren't I? He put his big arm around you and walked you over to the thin blue line."

"I think you're taking it a little far, Charlie. But okay. I didn't go running out the door into the arms of the first reporter I saw. That's not my style, in any case. Especially when I don't have enough of the story myself. If you taught me anything, it was not to go off half-cocked."

He chuckled. "If I taught you anything."

"Carroll's ass is in a sling over this Bad Apple affair. He didn't come right out and say it, but it's no secret. Call me a sentimental old fool, but I cut him some slack."

"I'll just call you a fool."

"They're all ready with a copycat story if something else happens soon," I said. "Except we both know that will crumble pretty quickly. Leavitt's all freaked out that his girlfriend might be a target again. That's why Carroll sold my services to the mayor. You should have heard him, Charlie. I got a real silver-plated recommendation."

"I hope you're charging your premium rate."

"That's something else you taught me. Sliding scale."

"You slid this one up, I hope."

"I'll be able to cover the rent."

Charlie took hold of the wheels of his chair and gently rocked himself forward and backward. Aside from staring out the window, Charlie also used to be a pacer. You could make out the shiny trail he'd left on the wood floor of the office. Now he was reduced to this tiny ticktocking of his wheelchair. The movement was slight, but the coiled energy in his arms was heartbreaking to see. The man wanted out of that chair.

"They're wasting their nickel sticking you as a bodyguard," he said. "They should be cutting you loose to go find the son of a bitch who's behind all this."

The memory of a white balloon bumped gently against my cheek.

"I plan to keep my eyes open," I said.

"And your back covered?"

"And my head down."

Charlie laughed. "By God, I guess I did teach you a few things."

"Meanwhile, I've got to hook a line onto the mayor's celebrity girlfriend tonight. She's insisting on strutting around onstage, and Martin Leavitt doesn't seem to have the balls to shut the theater down."

"I heard him on television just before you got here," Charlie said. "That's his message to the city. 'The danger's over. Go about your business. Enjoy your turkey.' "

"Well, if someone really is still gunning for her, I guess I'll get to see it all over again."

Charlie looked out at the street. After a moment he said, "You might want to pick up another bag of bagels, Fritz. Worked pretty good the first time."

7

Times Square never takes a night off.
The electronic billboards and the zippers
and the commercials being projected onto
the sides of the glass buildings were all flashing and moving and blinking at their usual
epileptic-seizure-inducing speed. The funnel where Broadway and Seventh Avenue
merge was clogged with yellow taxis trying to get downtown, any random thirty
of which were unleashing their horns for
no apparent reason. I spotted one double-
decker tourist bus. There was a lone inhabi-
tant on the exposed upper level, wrapped in
an Eskimo-like parka, twisting this way and
that, a camcorder pressed to his face. As I
crossed Broadway, the steam pouring forth
from the Cup O' Noodles billboard looked
particularly inviting.

For all the dazzle and noise, the sidewalks were noticeably less packed than usual. A clown sat on the large sidewalk space in front of the Viacom Building, smoking a cigarette. His unicycle lay on the pavement next to him. His bucket was empty.

At the last minute Margo had opted out of joining me. The look of relief on her mother's face when Margo announced she'd be staying over with them for the night told me that it was the right decision.

"Now I can go spring that Swedish honey I've had stashed away," I'd told Margo. "Show her a swell time on the old town at last."

A look of alarm had leaped to Margo's mother's face. "He's kidding, isn't he?"

"He's kidding or he's dead," Margo answered. "The choice is completely his."

THE THEATER WAS NOT FILLED TO CAPACITY. The seat to my right, the one that would have been Margo's, remained unoccupied. To my left was a geriatric couple who looked to have been lifted intact from another era and deposited into G-12 and G-13. He was a frail man in a three-piece brown wool suit and red bow tie, with a fine shiny cane. She was in something vaguely deco and pale.

Her hair was like blue spun sugar. They leaned shoulder to shoulder to read the program together.

The show was the most ridiculous thing imaginable. In between numbers, there were a lot of slamming doors and fast entrances and exits, loud declarations intended to shove forward the so-called plot, a handful of huffy hands-on-hips speeches, would-be lovers misinterpreting mixed signals and one ham-it-up actor portraying a waiter who wrapped the audience around his finger from his very first entrance and made off with every scene he was in. The couple next to me loved him. Every time the waiter appeared onstage, the old man pointed his bony finger and announced loudly to his sweetheart, "There he is!"

With Rebecca Gilpin's first entrance, you'd have thought we were greeting the woman who had cured cancer. The audience leaped to their feet, applauding the skin right off their palms and calling out hoorays and bravos. A man seated in front of me—now standing in front of me—put his fingers to his mouth and sent out a series of whistles so piercing that I nervously eyeballed the old chandelier dangling from the theater's ceiling.

Everyone eventually settled down, and the actors, who had frozen into a tableau while riding out the spontaneous outpouring, swung back into action. Gilpin, making a comely dazzle out of her vintage frills, glided like a ballerina to center stage, where she delivered her first line in a voice that was somewhat huskier than I'd have expected.

"All I can say is, whoever called this a pleasure cruise doesn't know the gee-dee meaning of the word 'pleasure.' "

Right, I thought. This is definitely worth the risk of being shot at for the second time in one day. I checked my watch and settled in.

After the show, I headed backstage. As with most Broadway theaters, I had to go outside and enter a narrow walkway that led to the stage-door area. The union man at the door wasn't letting anybody in. He didn't even have a clipboard of names to consult.

"No chance, Mac. Not tonight. You gotta wait."

I showed him my PI license. He reached out and patted me on the accomplice. He shook his head. "You wait."

Good man. Exactly what I wanted to hear.

Some of the chorus members had already left the theater. I backed off to the far side of the alleyway to let them pass with as much flamboyance as they required. After about fifteen minutes, Rebecca Gilpin appeared. She was accompanied by the actor who'd played the waiter. I shoved myself off the wall and approached the stage door. The actress was giving the union man instructions.

"You're going to have to just wait, that's all. A car should be here any minute. Do you have any idea how many flowers I've got up there tonight?"

The union man scratched his freckled scalp. "Yeah, I do, in fact. Who do you think took them in?"

"Well, thank you. And now, if you'll just wait, it won't be more than a half hour, tops. They'll be going off to the hospitals for all those people who were shot this morning. Am I asking a **huge** favor?"

I stepped forward. "Miss Gilpin? I'm Fritz Malone. Mayor Leavitt told you about me."

She looked at me a moment with some confusion. Up close, her face was a series of sharp points. Nose, chin, even her eyebrows. Her ginger-red hair was pulled back in a severe ponytail. Her eyes were large, beautiful and unfriendly. She was wearing a silver fur coat that might have fed and housed a family of five for a year.

"You're the detective."

"We're going to need about twenty minutes," I said.

A finely etched eyebrow rose, but it wasn't Rebecca Gilpin's. It was the eyebrow of the actor who had played the waiter. I braced for the inevitable.

"Honey, if I were you, I'd take that deal," he said.

I ignored him: the cruelest punishment. I addressed the actress. "Is there a place you'd like to go? We have to talk. I need to explain how I operate." I conceded a sarcastic smile to the actor.

"Why don't we go to Barrymore's?" she said.

The actor piped up. "Or Joe Allen's."

"I'm sorry," I said. "But Miss Gilpin and I need to talk alone."

The actor quipped, "Detective? Let's see some ID." He snapped his fingers rapidly five or six times as he said it. He thought he was being cute. I sent a silent appeal to Rebecca.

"Okay, Stephen," she said. "I'm going with Mr. Malone. Thank you for the backrub, sweetie."

I watched a half-dozen zingers die on the vine. "Okay," he said. "I'll see you tomorrow."

I waited until he was several steps down the walkway. "I thought you were great tonight," I called out.

A hand rose. A frozen backward wave.

Rebecca Gilpin pointed her face at me. "Stephen is a laugh whore."

"Forget about Stephen. Let's go to Barrymore's."

The actress instructed the union man one more time. "Just please wait. I don't want to see those flowers when I come in tomorrow."

He and I traded a look. I didn't think that last request was going to be a problem.

I FELT LIKE I WAS LIFTING A SMALL BEAR from the woman's shoulders. I handed it to the woman in the coat-check closet, who smiled broadly at me. She was of Asian descent and wearing a red beret. She handed me a plastic stub. Number 101.

"I take it you're not a PETA person," I said to Rebecca Gilpin.

"Jack Nicholson gave me that coat. Who says no to Jack?"

"I hope when I'm balding and hiding the bags under my eyes behind tinted glasses that attractive women won't be able to say no to me."

"Give them a seventy-five-thousand-dollar coat and see what happens."

"So that's how he does it?"

"It doesn't hurt."

The hostess started to seat us at a table near the front of the restaurant, next to the window.

"We'd like a table in the back, please," I said.

"Follow me."

She planted us all the way in the back of the restaurant, next to the restrooms. Rebecca started for the chair against the wall. I stopped her. "That's mine."

She said nothing, but she made a major show of settling into the chair opposite me. Our waitress came over. I ordered a seltzer with lime. Rebecca asked for a glass of chardonnay.

"Let me guess," she said after the waitress had left. "You take the seat against the wall so you can keep an eye on the entire restaurant."

"Elementary," I answered.

"Everything I learned about law and order, I learned on my TV show."

I couldn't tell if she was trying to make a joke. And if you can't tell, it's not much of a joke.

"Fritz Malone," she said. "What is that?"

"That's me."

"I know it's you. I mean, it's a funny name."

"It's German-Irish. I'm a melting pot."

"You must drink a lot of beer. The Germans and the Irish."

"What's Gilpin?" I asked.

"English."

"And may I say, you speak it well."

"Oh, I see. He's charming, too."

I got down to it. "Mayor Leavitt is very concerned for your safety."

The actress had pulled out a compact and checked in the little mirror to see if she was still there. She seemed satisfied that she was. She clicked it closed. "The police killed that monster who murdered all those people."

Leavitt and Carroll had told me that Rebecca Gilpin was not being let in on the fact that Roberto Diaz had not been acting alone. She was under the impression that it was the concern over a copycatter that was the reason for my being hired.

"This town is full of kooks," I said.

She was studying me. "You're that man, aren't you? I just recognized you. You're the one who yelled up at me this morning just before the shooting started. You threw something at me."

"Bagels."

"Were you already protecting me? Did Marty hire you to keep an eye on me during the parade?"

I ignored the question. I had one of my own that needed answering. "Did Mayor Leavitt talk to you about canceling your appearance in the parade today?"

"Yes."

"Did he explain why?"

"He said his police commissioner had made the request. It's because Marty and I have been seeing each other. The commissioner just thought it would be a good idea if I kept a low profile. Hello? It's called **show** business?"

Our drinks arrived. The waitress fawned over Rebecca. She mentioned that she had tickets to see the show. My guess was that the waitress was an actress herself. Waitress? This part of town? Not exactly an Olympian deduction on my part.

Rebecca lifted her glass. "You didn't tell me what you thought of the show."

"I don't see a lot of musicals."

"So you didn't like it."

"They're not my flavor."

"You can say it, you know. I won't be offended."

"I didn't like it."

"None of it?"

"I enjoyed the intermission."

She paused with the glass near her lips. "That's cold."

She took the sip. She was dressed in a black sweater with a plunging neckline. Probably cashmere. It brought out the extraordinary alabaster of her skin.

"Do you have any reason to think that someone might want to hurt you?" I asked. "I don't mean because you're involved with the mayor. I mean because you're you. Have you gotten crank letters in the past? Any problems with fans? Stalkers, that kind of thing?"

"I was on a popular television show for five years. I played the bad girl. I got letters from people who loved me and people who hated me."

"The ones who hated you—any in particular who wrote you more than once?"

"I'm sure there were. You'd have to ask my publicist. I receive far more letters than I've got time to answer. Between the regular letters and the e-mail, we're talking in the thousands."

"That's a lot of fans."

"My character was extremely popular. Did you ever see the show?"

"I'm not big on television."

"I'm getting the idea that you're not big on entertainment in general."

"That would be the wrong idea."

She poked her tongue against the inside of her cheek. "What, then? I don't see you as the go-to-poetry-readings type."

"I pop up in all sorts of peculiar places," I said. "That's one of the great things about this town. More peculiar places than anywhere on earth." I took a sip of my seltzer. "Okay. Here's how it works. I'm going to be your shadow for at least the next couple of days. This means I'm in the lobby of your building when you leave in the morning, or whenever it is you leave. I'm there to wish you night-night. If you're going night-night someplace other than your apartment, then I'm there as well. Not to be personal, but I'm guessing this would be Gracie Mansion. In which case I'll pass you off to Martin Leavitt's people. When you travel, I'm in your taxi. No subways or buses, but I suspect that's not really a problem for you. If you go shopping, lucky me. I go, too. We don't have to **be** together. If you're having lunch with someone, I don't have to be at the table. But you're not out of my sight. And I'm going to give you a cell-phone number to call if you see or hear or taste anything suspicious or out of the ordinary. Anything. And I don't want you opening your mail. Don't even take it out of your mailbox. I'll do that. We might suspend delivery and keep it down at the post office. The same with packages. Especially packages. I'll have your doorman hold all deliveries. This guy Diaz worked for a messenger service. Nice way to deliver bad news, yes? And no takeout, obviously. If someone you know is coming to visit you, tell them to wait for you in the lobby. That's where I'll be. You'll phone me on my cell and let me know and I'll escort them up to you. I would prefer if you kept the number of people who know you're under my protection to an absolute minimum. What people like to call a need-to-know basis. Certainly don't tell the media. If I had my way, I'd have you stop doing your show for the time being, but I already know I'm not having my way. When you go places, don't pause in doorways. Get in, get out. If you want to take a car service, I arrange for it, you don't. During your show, I'll be all over that theater, backstage and out front. I'd prefer if you didn't go out for drinks after the show, but I'll let you arm-wrestle me on that one if you'd like." I gave her a smile. "Finally, don't accept candy from strangers and don't take any wooden nickels."

"Will you be by my side to help me brush my teeth?"

"No, ma'am. But keep the bathroom door closed and locked when you're doing it."

She gave me an appraising look. "That was quite a monologue. Have you ever thought about taking up acting?"

"I can't guarantee your safety, Miss Gilpin. But I can guarantee that anyone with an idea of wanting to harm you is going to have to work pretty hard to do it."

"Rebecca," she said.

The sound of the explosion came a half second behind the bright flash. It came in two stages, the second almost instantly atop the first. The first was like a large growl. A rumble. With the flash, I sprang to my feet and had already launched across the small table when the second sound arrived, and with it the bursting of wood and metal and glass.

Rebecca and I hit the floor together. I managed to slip my hand behind her head as we hit, giving it at least a little cushioning. Dishes and glass and wood and food and silverware rocketed over us. We were pelted, me more than her, as I had landed fairly square on top of her. A piece of the ceiling landed next to my head in a plume of plaster dust. I felt a sharp jolt to the small of my back, near my shoulder. At the same time, the roar was replaced by an anguished female scream from somewhere near the front of the restaurant. **"Oh my God! Oh my God! Oh my God!"**

The sound of a wailing car alarm was coming in from where the restaurant's front window had been. My eyes stung from the plaster dust, but I opened them anyway. Rebecca's face was inches away. There was a hook-shaped gash on her cheek and a nasty split in her lower lip. Her face was covered by a film of plaster dust.

Her eyes were not open.

A droplet of some sort plunked abruptly onto her cheek, followed by another, then another. The plaster dust absorbed the water where it hit and then began to streak in globby trails along her face. It was water from the sprinkler system. I twisted my head to see a pipe dangling from the ceiling. I also saw utter destruction up at the front of the restaurant. There was a big empty nothing where the coat-check closet had been.

I started to move, and pain shot through my left shoulder. I flinched. Water from the sprinkler was falling like mist from a fountain. Below me, Rebecca's eyes fluttered open. I should have been relieved. Not to say I wasn't on some level. But a mantra was already going through my head, which was beginning to feel like **it** had exploded.

Margo is safe. Margo is safe. Margo is safe . . .

8

I must have resembled a kid building a play fort. With my one arm that worked, I dragged two upended tables together in front of Rebecca Gilpin and created a little wall. Then I pulled my gun from my shoulder holster and, on my knees, rose up and peered over the wall.

Bang-bang.

Our waitress was on her hands and knees looking like someone trying to find a contact lens. Her blouse had been blown half off, and her exposed right arm was riddled with thick red dots. The restaurant had been only moderately full. Most of the patrons I spotted were moving, though some more slowly than others. There were groans and soft cries rising into the hazy air. I spotted a hand on the floor near where the waitress was crawling. When I realized that it was no longer attached to its arm, I bit clean through my lower lip. The sprinkler system had ceased. There were no fires. The floor was a thick milky puddle, with swirls of pinkish blood mixed in.

People were already coming in off the street to help or just to witness the chaos. I braced myself. This is what the more insidious bombers want, a fresh new crowd for explosion number two. Moths to the flame. I eyeballed each person who came high-stepping into the rubble. The other possibility would be that one of these people was picking his or her way through the mess to see if the target had been hit. I had no way to be certain, but I would have given better than even odds that the target was currently on the floor on her back, behind my little home-made fort.

The safety was off. My finger was on the trigger.

My heart was banging against its cage, trying to get out.

Rebecca let out a groan. "I can't move."

"Don't try."

She groaned again. I checked over the edge of my tables to be sure no one was marching toward us, then I turned and gave Rebecca a quick once-over. I didn't like what I found below her waist. Specifically, the left leg. A nasty chard of polished wood was lodged in her thigh, just above the knee, which itself looked like a bruised apple. Blood was pumping in small steady pulses from the thigh.

I set down my gun and scrambled around for a pair of cloth napkins. I knotted them together, then took hold of the two ends and spiraled the cloth into a narrow coil. I grabbed a small column of wood that looked like it might have come from a chair leg.

"Excuse me." Pulling Rebecca's torn skirt up to her waist, I held the piece of wood in place on the bottom of her thigh with the doubled napkins, then brought the two ends up around the thigh, crossed the ends of the napkins and bore down with all my strength, tying them off in a secure knot.

Rebecca asked, "What are you doing?"

"Hold on."

I located two more napkins, knotted them as I had the others, spiraled them and wrapped them around her thigh below the rig I'd just secured. I tied this one off even tighter than the first. Only then did I work the ugly sliver of wood from her leg.

"I think I'm going to be sick," she said.

The blood was still oozing from the

wound, but as I watched, the pulsing seemed to lessen. I picked up my gun and raised myself to look over the upturned tables.

A blue and red light was flashing on the faces of the people gathered outside the restaurant. The cavalry had arrived. I flipped the safety back on and holstered my gun. There was a small crowd of people standing near the remains of the coat-check closet. As I stood up, two of the people moved away, and I saw what they'd been staring at. It was the Asian coat-check woman. I recognized her red beret. It was still on her head, which was still on her shoulders, which were still part of her torso. But that was where she stopped.

My kicking the nearest upturned table proved enough—I discovered later—to run a hairline fracture on my little toe. I turned not a few heads from the grisly sight as I unceremoniously lost it.

"Goddammit!"

CAPTAIN REMY SANCHEZ OF MIDTOWN North's Homicide Division did some kicking of his own, but he had wisely picked a safer target: a harmless piece of plaster exploded into dust against the toe of his shoe.

"Copycat, my ass. What kind of a fool do you take me for, Malone?"

The fact is, I didn't take Remy Sanchez for anything remotely close to a fool. Sanchez was a thirty-odd-year veteran of the force who, through patience, solid work and, some would say, an uncanny ability to learn little tidbits about his superiors that those superiors would as soon no one know, had climbed steadily up the thin blue ladder from his days as a beat cop in Fort Apache in the Bronx to the point where he could now look out over a vast array of uniformed men and women and tell them what the hell they were supposed to do. He was a gentle-looking man. The eyes of a poet. Tight black curls showing inroads of gray. Married with children. I had met his wife on several occasions. She was quiet, nice. One got the feeling that if anyone ever harmed a hair on her head, calm and steady homicide captain Remy Sanchez would quietly see to it that it was the last hair on the last head that the person ever had the opportunity to harm.

He obviously wasn't buying the copycat story. I hadn't thought he would, but it was my job to stick with it.

"Okay, Malone. Look me in the eye and tell it to me again. Roberto Diaz takes a shot at Miss Gilpin as he's spraying bullets all over the Thanksgiving Day parade, and not fifteen hours later, some fry brain who has also gotten the bright idea to go after the mayor's special friend is up and running with a fripping **bomb** that he manages to place in the coatcheck room of a joint where Miss Gilpin is sipping merlot with a private eye?"

"Chardonnay," I said. Sanchez showed me the fire in his poet's eyes.

Crime-scene tape had been set up outside the damaged restaurant to keep the onlookers at a distance. Half a dozen ambulances were parked in front, along with two fire trucks and I couldn't say how many cop cars. The news media had also arrived in force, and minicam lights were floating and bobbing on the sidewalk as if a band of coal miners were outside the restaurant doing calisthenics. I spotted Kelly Cole, as well as some reporters from the **Times,** whose offices were just up the street.

"Malone!" Kelly started toward me, but Sanchez directed one of his cops to head her off.

"You're welcome," he said to me.

The injured were being taken out on stretchers. Remy Sanchez and I stood next to the EMS crew stabilizing Rebecca for her trip to the ambulance. She had gone into shock soon after I'd tied off the tourniquets. A little crying, a little laughing, a fixation with the flowers in her dressing room that she wanted delivered to area hospitals.

"I'm going with her," I said to Sanchez as the EMS crew kicked the collapsible gurney up to its rolling position.

"The mayor is on his way here," Sanchez said.

"Of course he is. And if I were you, I'd make sure that not a single one of your men or women make a peep to the media about her."

"I don't like this," Sanchez said. "I don't care if Diaz was killed, you can't tell me this isn't related. There's a connection, and I'm going to find out what it is."

"Hey, when you find out, let me know."

The EMS crew was clearing the way to take Rebecca out. I looked around and grabbed a damp tablecloth off the floor. I asked Sanchez, "You got a handkerchief?" He pulled one from his pocket. I stepped over to the gurney. "Miss Gilpin?"

Her head had been secured. Only her eyes could move. I was surprised to see how much venom they held.

"Rebecca. It's fucking **Rebecca.**"

"Rebecca, I'm sorry about this. But I think an incognito exit would be favorable." I unfolded the handkerchief and set it over her nose and mouth and eyes, then lowered the damp tablecloth on top of her.

"Looks like she's dead," Sanchez muttered.

The gurney started forward. I turned to Sanchez.

"Hold that thought."

MY LEFT SHOULDER WAS DISLOCATED. I'VE had this happen to me once before. That time it had resulted from a plunge off the top of a building. A man with a gun had encouraged me to take the leap. Four flights down into an industrial garbage bin, just like you see them do in the movies. I'd landed on eggshells and coffee grounds, but those aren't what separated my shoulder. It was the thing underneath the eggshells and coffee grounds. An accordion. A nice-looking one, too. Red mother-of-pearl. Shiny white keys. The thing gave out a discordant yelp when I hit it. I'm sure I did, too.

The EMS crew popped my shoulder back into its socket at Barrymore's. The doctor at St. Luke's–Roosevelt outfitted me with a sling and a handful of painkillers and moved on to the more seriously injured. Rebecca was in surgery, having her leg worked on. I'd been able to get Margo on the phone before she heard about the explosion on the news, a phone call that had featured yet another long silence from her end of the line. "You do know," she had said finally in a quiet voice, "a very nice, stable dentist did ask me to marry him once."

I was still waiting for Rebecca to emerge from surgery when Martin Leavitt arrived. He was flanked by his deputy mayor. Leavitt came on like a hurricane. "Where is she?"

He spotted me sitting on one of the molded plastic chairs in the waiting area and veered in my direction. "What the hell happened? What were you two doing in a public place? I thought you were supposed to protect her. Do you call that protecting? Goddammit, what **happened?**"

His face was the color of my chair. Philip Byron pulled up behind him and watched with a look of bland amusement. I couldn't tell if he was amused at my being dressed down or at his boss's outburst. Maybe both.

"I'm waiting," Leavitt fumed, planting his hands on his hips. All heads in the waiting area were turned in our direction.

I rose slowly from my chair. My God, I was aching. "What say we go somewhere private?"

Leavitt took a beat, then looked around at the gawkers and understood what I meant. He snapped, "Philip." Byron lost the amusement and quickly escorted the two of us through the swinging doors into the ER hallway. "We need a room," he said to the first person he saw. A fellow in green scrubs led us into a small, dimly lit room with a solid metal table in the middle and a hulking X-ray machine hanging from the ceiling. No chairs. As I leaned against the table, Leavitt opened his mouth to speak, but I beat him to it.

"She's going to be fine," I said. "So am I, thank you. There's a woman who was handling the coat check at Barrymore's who is not fine. I'd say she was in her mid-twenties. Attractive Asian girl. She's dead, Mr. Mayor. I'm guessing the bomb went off very near her waist, because she was blown apart. Add her to the tally from the parade this morning, and I think we can all agree that it's been a bad day." This last part I emphasized with a simple barking of the words "bad" and "day." The mayor blanched.

I continued, "If you want to try tagging me with the blame for Miss Gilpin's injuries and cutting me loose, go right ahead. I'll even give you my services gratis for the day. It's your call. I'm in or I'm out. Executive-decision time. I'm sure you're up to it."

"Look," the mayor began. "What I—"

I wasn't finished. "Whatever the hell this is all about, this shooting, this goddamn explosion . . . something is not being handled right."

Philip Byron spoke up. "You can't talk to the mayor like that."

I ignored him. An image of Margo having joined Rebecca Gilpin and me for drinks after the show flashed through my head. I held up a finger and placed it directly in front of the mayor's nose. Solid as a tree. No trembling.

"I've known Tommy Carroll a long time. He worked with my father. Any obedience you've gotten from me so far, and my putting up with this need-to-know bullshit, that's because of Tommy. But I just want you to know before you say another word that, Tommy or no Tommy, we're finished with all that. You can bounce me or not bounce me, I don't really care. But I am now officially curious. I want to know exactly what the hell is going on. Need-to-know basis? I damn well need to know, and I damn well intend to. This is my city, too, Mr. Mayor, and this is my body. And I am not sticking it between your girlfriend and the next who-knows-what until I get some answers and know some things. Call me nosy, but I either get those answers from you or from Tommy Carroll or from whoever else happens to know them, or I start kicking over trash cans and knocking down doors. That's what I'm trained to do. Ask Tommy, if you want to. I'm good at it."

My finger was no longer without a wobble, so I withdrew it. In any case, Leavitt no longer looked like he was ready to bite it off. Philip Byron did, though. He looked like he wanted to eviscerate me for speaking this way to his boss. As for the boss himself, he was considering me with a placid gaze.

"Tomorrow," Leavitt said. "Gracie Mansion. Can you make it for breakfast?"

9

STOCKY LITTLE APELIKE FIGURES WITH pointy devil's tails and forearms the size of car batteries were taking turns beating me about the head and shoulders with baseball bats. There were three of them, and each time one swung its bat down over its head, the force of the blow lifted the creature right off its feet. Big flat hairy feet, like you might expect from the Abominable Snowman. The beating was being conducted in a decidedly democratic fashion, each creature taking turns. Almost metronomic. **Bam-bam-bam.** I was doing what I could to protect myself, but my efforts were only diverting the blows onto my neck and arms. Eventually, a voice deep down in my cerebral cortex told me to wake the hell up. I opened my eyes and the apelike figures disappeared.

I took a good long time in the shower. Not wanting to be groggy, I'd skipped the pain-killers the night before, and now the pain in my shoulder was killing me. I dressed and went down to the corner market, bought the **Post** and some aspirin, which I washed down with a cup of burnt coffee. I probably could've managed without the sling, but I couldn't see a reason for being excessively macho.

Gina Lombardi was putting out her mother's sign as I came out of the market. She frowned at my sling. "What happened to you?"

I opened my palm to her and tapped it. "Can't you see? Right here? This line means my shoulder is going to get dislocated."

Gina laughed. "Sorry. I just don't see it."

"Right. Neither did your mother last time I let her pore over my palms. No warning whatsoever. What kind of racket is she running in there, anyway?"

"Did Mama tell you that you have a long lifeline?"

"Something like that. She also said I would never be a millionaire, but I wouldn't starve."

"So far, so true?"

"So far," I said.

Gina shrugged. "So she missed a shoulder. You think this is rocket science?" She set the metal sign on the sidewalk. She had a few ears of Indian corn with her, and she attached these to the sign with some brown twine. I told her I liked the harvest touch. She tapped the side of her head. "Mama. She is always thinking."

I walked up to Houston and flagged a cab. The **Post** was in high-octane mode over the Thanksgiving Day horrors. Lots of pictures. There was a photo of Officer Leonard Cox, the city's newest hero, as well as a blurry shot of Roberto Diaz. It turned out that McNally, the cop Diaz had gunned down, had been Leonard Cox's partner. The two had been working the parade together. Usually a fluff detail. Nothing new had come out yet on Diaz. Peppered throughout the accounts was speculation that the bombing at Barrymore's might well be related to what had happened earlier in the day at the Thanksgiving parade. Silence on that particular subject from the police commissioner's office was not going unnoted. Amazingly, Rebecca Gilpin's presence in Barrymore's at the time of the blast had been suppressed. She was mentioned only in relation to the parade shooting. Somebody in a place of power had clearly expended some capital to keep the actress's presence at the restaurant out of the news. According to police sources, speculation was centering on the bomb at Barrymore's having been in a bag that someone had left with coat check. The coat-check woman wouldn't be offering any description, and no other witnesses seemed to be surfacing.

The cab dropped me off at Eighty-eighth Street. I relinquished my pistol to a security guard outside the gate at Gracie Mansion and submitted to a mild pat-down. There were two police cruisers as well as an unmarked car parked in front of the mayor's residence. Looking around the side of the mansion, I saw a police boat anchored in the East River about two hundred yards offshore, rocking in the choppy morning current.

I was escorted inside by a guy who looked like he could hold down a weekend gig with the Giants. Young, thick, with a military cut and no visible sense of humor. I figured size-17 shoes, but I didn't ask. Silent Giant passed me off to a woman who introduced herself as Emily Watson. "Not the actress," she said. "Obviously." She was around forty-five, skinny as a rail, salt-and-pepper hair pulled into a loose bun, with a sad, brave smile. She reminded me of a school infirmary nurse.

"Mayor Leavitt will be down in just a minute. He wanted me to ask if you need anything."

I had a dozen ready responses to that question, but I pocketed them. "Orange juice," I said.

"Right this way."

She led me into the dining room. It was powder blue and as perfectly put together as a museum display, which in a way it was. They give tours of Gracie Mansion daily, except for Sundays. And except, I assumed, the day after a pair of major municipal tragedies. The mansion is a stately classical white-frame colonial house built in 1799 by Archibald Gracie. The estate and its eleven acres were appropriated by the city in 1896 to be included in the new Carl Shurz Park, and for many years the house had served as nothing more than the concession stand and restrooms for the park. In the early forties, Big Bad Bob Moses trained his visionary eye on the building and oversaw its transformation into the mayor's official residence. The first mayor to reside there, Fiorello La Guardia, moved there in 1942. Allegedly, he complained about the drafts.

I took a seat at the far end of a long table, near three place settings, and I felt very silly when Emily Watson emerged from the kitchen with my crystal glass of orange juice on a little white plate.

"Fresh-squeezed," she proclaimed. There

was a seed floating on top, in case I had any doubt.

When Mayor Leavitt appeared a few minutes later, he was shadowed by Tommy Carroll. Leavitt appeared pensive but considerably less haggard than his police commissioner. He was in tan slacks and a blue Brooks Brothers shirt, the sleeves rolled up to his elbows. Leavitt had "famous-person hair," as Margo liked to call it. In his case, thick and wavy and cut just so. He gave it a hand-combing as he approached the table, and it fell right back into place. There was a nodding of heads and a muttering of names, and the two took their seats on either side of me.

Leavitt spoke first. "How's your shoulder?"

"Popped out, popped in," I said. "I'll get over it."

"Rebecca wants me to thank you for what you did for her last night. I want to thank you, too."

What I did for her. I sashayed her in full view from the theater to the restaurant directly across the street so that our mad bomber could have a nice good look at her. I couldn't have been more boneheaded.

I asked, "How is she?"

"I just got off the phone with her. They're going to keep her in the hospital for a few days. She'll be confined to bed. Probably crutches after that. But her spirits are good."

"No more show."

He rolled his eyes. "The damn show. No, she's officially out of it. That's at least one headache off our plate."

As if cued by the word "plate," Emily Watson appeared from the kitchen carrying a large tray. She set it on the sideboard and presented each of us with a plate of scrambled eggs and bacon.

"I forgot to ask if you have any dietary restrictions, Mr. Malone."

"I don't. Pig and chicken are on my menu. Thank you."

The tray included a thermos of coffee and a pitcher of cream. Emily Watson set those on the table, clicked her heels and disappeared.

Martin Leavitt played host, pouring out a cup of coffee for me. I couldn't tell if he was putting on a charm offensive for my sake or if I was supposed to believe that this was his true nature.

"I've filled Commissioner Carroll in on the concerns you voiced to me at the hospital last night," he said. I nodded. Carroll was watching me closely. He waved away Leavitt's offer of coffee. Leavitt had brought a file folder with him. He opened it and pulled out the top sheet of paper. "It goes without saying that none of this leaves this room."

He placed a plain sheet of white paper next to my plate. A short letter was typed on it. No date. No address.

Mayor Leavitt,

You don't want to see your lambs slaughtered, do you? For a million dollars you can save your city from horrible pain. Take this seriously. I will hurt the city and the people you love. Trust me, it will be bloody. I hate you so much. You are filth and dirt. If you believe me, wear a red tie to the theater on Wednesday night. If you don't believe me, live with the results. Enjoy the show.

Your Nightmare

I looked up. "When did you receive this?"

"A little over two weeks ago. Tuesday the eighth."

"And 'the show.' I'm guessing that's Miss Gilpin's show?"

"It was opening that Thursday."

"Was it a known fact that you'd planned to attend the opening? Was it publicized?"

Leavitt shrugged. "It certainly wasn't being treated as a secret."

"Is this the original?"

He shook his head. "It's a copy."

I looked at Carroll. "Forensics?"

Leavitt answered for him. "Like we told you yesterday, we're keeping this contained."

"Maybe you are," I said. "But I think your Mr. Nightmare has some different ideas."

"So it would seem. We're proceeding with caution," the mayor said. "Which is where you come in."

"Oh? And where do I come in? I was under the impression after last night that I was already out."

Carroll spoke up. "We'll explain."

I looked at the letter again. "Okay, then, the hundred-dollar question. Or, I guess, the million-dollar question."

Leavitt nodded. "I wore a red tie."

I cocked an eyebrow at Carroll. The commissioner looked as if he might have entertained a few apelike creatures of his own overnight. His skin sagged and his eyes held none of their usual crisp alertness. "Of course we weighed it," he said. "You don't like to hand over a psychological victory just like that."

"But you also don't want to be stupid, right?"

"Exactly. Right off the bat, the prick got us into a lose-lose."

"Score one for Mr. Nightmare."

"He chose the right goddamn name," Leavitt muttered.

"So he could have been anywhere," I said. "He could have had a ticket and been seated near you. He could have been outside the theater when you arrived. Or up on the roof of a building with a pair of binoculars. Anywhere. For all you know, he might even be someone in the show. Or someone working for the theater."

"I do not like being jerked around by this creep," Leavitt said emphatically.

"And you're convinced that it wasn't Diaz who sent the note?"

Carroll answered, "We know there were at least two people involved, Diaz and whoever left the bomb at Barrymore's. It seems likely that's the same person who phoned the mayor to gloat yesterday after the parade shooting."

"Maybe the shooting was unrelated," I said. "Maybe the guy who wrote this letter saw a chance to piggyback on the parade shooting. Maybe the bomb in the coat-check room was all he was planning from the beginning."

Leavitt looked to Carroll. "We've considered that," the commissioner said. "But I've got a gut feeling on this one. We're feeding the 'two unrelated incidents' story to the media, but I'm sure as hell not buying it. I smell a real nut job here, Fritz. Make that a pair of them. We got one. We got Diaz."

"Correction," I said. "You had Diaz. You had a man who could have told you something about what was going on, except that someone blew his brains out. Before we go any further, I want to know what that's all about." I turned to the mayor. "I **need** to know."

"We're getting ahead of ourselves here," Leavitt said.

I picked up the creamer. "That's okay with me. We can get back to you and your red tie in a minute. I need to hear what happened to Diaz and why."

"He had a second gun," Tommy Carroll said.

The creamer froze in midair. "He had a second **what?**"

"A pistol. Strapped to his ankle. A Tomcat."

"The arresting officer missed a **weapon?** Tommy, don't ask me to believe that."

"Do you hear me bragging about it? You

don't get more fundamental than a basic pat-down. But what can I tell you? Cox retrieved Diaz's Beretta, then shoved him into his cruiser. He just wanted him out of there. He missed the other gun."

"Jesus Christ, Tommy, a six-year-old with a month of television under his belt knows you pat down a suspect."

"So maybe I should start enlisting god-damn six-year-olds. I just told you, I'm not happy about it."

"Let's hear about the head shot."

The mayor and the police commissioner shared another look. I couldn't read the look. Might have been nothing. Might have been something. Either way, I was ready. My bull-shit meter was primed and humming.

Carroll shifted in his chair. "After I cut you loose at the Municipal Building, Cox and I went back up to get Diaz."

I stopped him right there. "Tell me again why it is that your boys brought Diaz and me to the Municipal Building instead of a precinct house. From where I sit, that don't smell good."

"Control. We didn't know who or what we were dealing with yet. Or how many were in-volved. For all we knew, there were snipers stationed at all the precinct houses, waiting for us to bring their man in. It was a diversionary tactic that reverted the timing of things back into our control."

"But you had no reason at that point to think it was anything but a lone gunman."

"Wrong. You're forgetting, we already had **two** possible shooters in custody. Diaz wasn't the only one running around waving a pistol. We didn't know what we had. We took the precaution."

The "precaution" of avoiding taking dangerous suspects directly to a police station. The needles on my bullshit meter were dancing wildly.

Carroll continued, "When Cox and I got up to where Diaz had been secured, Diaz pulled his weapon."

"The Tomcat."

"Exactly."

"The Tomcat that Cox had failed to detect."

"Correct."

The needle continued to flick. "I assume he was still cuffed."

Carroll nodded. "He was cuffed."

"I saw him being cuffed at the fountain. At least Cox got that part right."

"Don't be an asshole, Fritz. Cox's partner had just been gunned down by this punk. You might want to cut the man a little slack."

"I saw Cox cuff Diaz behind his back," I said. "That must have been a hell of a thing, for Diaz to contort himself all over the place to get the gun out. How exactly did that work, Tommy? He somehow got the gun out with his arms cuffed behind his back, and then what? Was he turned away from you and Cox when you came in? Was he aiming over his shoulder?"

"He was cuffed to the table."

"Oh. The table. So you uncuffed him, then cuffed him again, this time to the table."

"Right."

"One hand?"

"Correct."

"Other hand free?"

"Correct."

"Free to pull out his pistol when you and Cox are coming in the door. My goodness, it's almost his lucky day."

"Lucky days don't end up at the morgue," Carroll said. The mayor grunted his agreement.

"Okay," I said. "So Diaz pulls his pistol. What then?"

"Cox drew and fired."

"And he hit Diaz right between the eyes."

"Not exactly. But close."

"Did Diaz get his shot off?"

Carroll shook his head once. "He did not."

"That's fast shooting on Cox's part," I observed.

"For which I am grateful."

I took a sip of my coffee. The eggs on all three plates were untouched and going cold. I looked over at the mayor. "How's all this sound to you?"

"Officer taking a man into custody and failing to detect that he has a weapon? Frankly, I'd like to have his badge. But we have special circumstances here."

I picked up the letter.

Enjoy the show.

Your Nightmare

Tommy Carroll leaned forward. His shadow eclipsed my plate. "You make instant decisions and then you live with them. You know how that is. Listen, Fritz, we want our citizens to feel that they're safe. That's our job. 'Hero cop kills massacre suspect in shootout in Central Park' versus the ugly and embarrassing truth. I like choice number one. Either way, the scum is dead. Cop-killer scum at that. It's a shortcut to justice, but in the end it's still justice."

"In the end it's a cover-up, Tommy. You

know your history. The cover-up's always the thing that ends up biting you more than the crime itself."

Mayor Leavitt chimed in. "We're trying to control history this time, Mr. Malone. That's why we're telling you all this."

"We need to catch the guy, Fritz," Carroll said. "He's still out there. We thought we had him yesterday. We thought Cox killed him. But Cox only killed part of the problem."

I quoted, " 'The nightmare has just begun.' "

"We're not releasing the information that Nightmare contacted us two weeks ago," the mayor said. "Categorically not. I hope I'm clear on that, Mr. Malone. It's crucial. This letter does not exist."

"We're calling him Nightmare?"

The police commissioner answered, "This is an operation. We need a name for it, and that's the name we're going with."

"It's an operation no one knows about," I observed.

"Exactly."

"You don't even know if it's one guy or a half-dozen."

"Doesn't really matter at this point," Carroll said. " 'Nightmare' covers however the hell many of him there are. Or them. I don't give a damn about that right now. Beginning in another hour, my next headache is the press. They're clamoring for a clarification from us about why we think the two incidents aren't related."

"I saw that Rebecca Gilpin's presence at Barrymore's was surgically removed from the news accounts. Good work on somebody's part, but how long is that going to last?"

"Not long enough, I'm sure," Leavitt said.

"Why not just say she was there? Try your luck with the copycat story."

"Because the story stinks," Carroll answered. "This was a fricking bomb. Not the most sophisticated bomb, but still not something a copycat freak is going to whip up in one afternoon. We put the blanket on Miss Gilpin's presence at Barrymore's partly to buy time. But also because at this point, if the word gets out, the chance of an actual copycatter increases. As of this moment, Miss Gilpin is essentially under house arrest. Nobody gets to her. As soon as she's stabilized, we're taking her out of the city to an undisclosed location. Nightmare has had two cracks at her. That much, at least, is over." Carroll gave me a rueful look. "Shortest job you've ever had."

"He doesn't mention her specifically in his letter," I said.

"Taking a shot at Rebecca was strictly to piss me off," Leavitt said. "I'm being messed with here, Mr. Malone. That's part of the M.O."

"And you're sure about that?"

"I am."

"What about the possibility that someone might have a specific beef with Rebecca? Or a fixation? You know the kinds of loonies who latch on to celebrities. So far, she's the common link here."

Carroll responded, "Fine. Of course. That's just it. It could be all of those things or none of them. Hell, I'd love to think that getting Miss Gilpin off the scene shuts down the problem. That'd be nice. But how stupid do I look? This Nightmare character is clearly a psychopath. We have no reason to think that he's gotten his ya-yas out and is just going to go away. He wants something. Besides the thrill he must be getting from blowing people away, he wants his goddamn million dollars."

"So if you're not planning on letting people in on the fact that this nutcase is trying to blackmail the city, what exactly are you planning to tell them?"

"First thing we're doing is we're sticking with the story that the two events are not related. We don't want people thinking we're suddenly under siege. Unfortunately, Miss

Gilpin is the key to that, and we don't know how her situation is going to play out. It's going to take a lot of spin once people discover that she was in that restaurant. But right now the plan is to isolate the two incidents. The parade? Diaz did it. Diaz is dead. **Loco cabeza.** Hero cop to the rescue. All is well. Case closed. On to the next incident. The bombing at Barrymore's? We just don't know at this time. God's truth. But we're going all out to find out who's responsible, and as soon as we know, we'll apprehend the responsible party or parties. That's the line. It's also the truth."

"It's nice when those two coincide, isn't it?" I picked up the letter and read it one more time. "Do your investigators know about this?"

Carroll fielded the question. "There's nothing in that letter that assists the investigation."

"I would think that its very existence assists the investigation."

"Our teams are sifting through the restaurant. They'll put the bomb back together. That might tell us something. They're interviewing everyone they can locate who was at or near the scene last night."

"Nobody's interviewed me," I said.

"We know what you know," Carroll said.

I indicated the letter. "And I know more than most."

Leavitt folded his cloth napkin precisely and set it on the table. "Commissioner Carroll says we can count on you, Mr. Malone. I knew your father. Not terribly well, but we had some dealings. And of course I knew his reputation. I had great respect for Harlan Scott."

"So did I," I said, maybe a little more tersely than I needed to.

"Tommy says you caught his best genes."

"Well, Tommy ain't the most poetical hen in the house. But I'll take the compliment."

Leavitt nodded. "I understand you were planning at one time to follow in his footsteps."

I glanced over at my father's successor, who was giving his fork a hard look. "I took a few steps in that direction," I said. "Some things happened and I made an adjustment. I decided the badge might be a little too heavy to carry around after all. I like being a little lighter on my feet."

Carroll set the fork down, made sure his eyes were nice and dead by the time they met mine. The mayor didn't seem to notice. He leaned forward and took the letter from me and gazed at it grimly. "We want you to help us stop this creep from doing any more damage, Mr. Malone."

I picked up my coffee mug. "I'd be happy to, Mr. Mayor. But genes or no genes, I don't know what you think I can do."

"We're going to pay him," Leavitt said.

"You're going to **pay** him? You're going to give this creep a million bucks?"

"That's what he wants in order to stop. I'm not going to have him ravaging my city. He's proved his point."

I looked from Leavitt to Carroll and back again. Good poker faces. "I'm guessing you gentlemen didn't bring me here to see if I had a spare million on me."

"You're going to deliver the money," Carroll said flatly. He reached out and placed a hand firmly on my wounded shoulder. "That's what you're going to do. And then you're going to never breathe a word about it."

NIGHTMARE HAD DELIVERED A SECOND letter. He'd left it in an envelope in a freezer bag, tucked beneath the handful of frozen turkeys that remained in the horizontal cooler at a Gristedes grocery store two blocks from the mayor's residence. A call had come in to the City Hall switchboard at around three-thirty in the morning. The caller was a male with a slight Hispanic accent who identified himself as "the mayor's worst nightmare." The operator described him as soft-spoken. The caller had said, "Tell the mayor that if he wants to stop the killings and is ready to talk turkey, he should go buy one at the Gristedes on York. No delay. If you don't deliver this message immediately, the blood will be on your hands."

The operator had contacted Philip Byron immediately at his home and played the message for him. Byron had phoned Tommy Carroll, and the two met in front of the Gristedes within the hour. Carroll was armed with a warrant to seize the store's security-camera tape for the past twenty-four hours. Not ten minutes after they arrived, they were joined by two members of the police department's bomb squad who'd brought a pair of sniffer dogs. Two clerks, the night manager and four customers were evacuated to a coffee shop two blocks away, where a patrolman was assigned to keep them from leaving until Carroll questioned them. Tommy Carroll and Philip Byron stood next to a barrel of pumpkins while the bomb squad and their dogs traveled up and down the aisles and through the rear storage area. The letter was located beneath the turkeys within five minutes, but Commissioner Carroll had instructed that it not be removed until the bomb sweep was completed.

The men from the bomb squad gave the store a clean bill of health just after five in the morning. Carroll put the plastic freezer bag containing the envelope and letter into a holiday gift bag that he'd appropriated from a display near the front of the store, then led Philip Byron up the block to the coffee shop to question the people they'd detained. Nobody reported seeing anyone poking about in the horizontal freezer section. Carroll took statements from the four customers as to what items each was shopping for in the Gristedes at that hour of the morning. He had them photographed by the patrolman, took their names and addresses and released them. Then he badgered the night manager and the two clerks for descriptions of the people who had come into the store after midnight, which was when their shifts had begun. One of the clerks, a lanky black guy with a silver earring, remembered "a couple of bitches that can kiss my ass" who came in around two o'clock and tried to walk off with two pints of Ben & Jerry's. "They was dustin', dude. High as a kite. You want to arrest somebody, those muthafuckas is prime."

The two "muthafuckas" aside, the only customer coming into the store between midnight and three-thirty who'd drawn any of the employees' attention was a nun who, according to the night manager, arrived at around three.

"It's just not something you see a lot," the night manager said. "She had all the nun stuff on. The big hat and everything?"

The clerk with the earring corroborated. "Total penguin, you know what I'm saying? Got the big old blinders on? And our lady's tall, too, Jack. Like six-one or something. That shit's all fucked up, man."

The nun hadn't purchased anything. According to the night manager, she'd come into the store, disappeared down one of the aisles and was back out the door in five minutes.

The smart-mouthed clerk chimed in again. "A religious fucking experience. Little lady penguin, man. What's that about?"

After questioning the employees a little longer, Carroll and Philip Byron accompanied them back to the store, where Carroll procured the security tapes. Byron had phoned the mayor to alert him to what was going on. Leavitt met Carroll and Byron at the front door of Gracie Mansion and took them directly to his office in the rear of the mansion, overlooking the East River, where they studied the security tape and the contents of the plastic freezer bag.

That was then. Approximately six o'clock in the morning.

I got my look at around eight.

10

"It's a man."

"What do you mean, it's a man?"

"I mean it's a man."

"That's a nun."

"It's not really a nun."

"You've got X-ray vision?"

"Just wait a second. You'll see."

The Gristedes had eight security cameras in the store, though only four of the eight were recording at any one time. The screen I was looking at was divided into four equal squares. Each camera's image appeared in one of the squares for about ten seconds before the next camera in the rotation clicked in. The nun had made her—or his—appearance in the upper-right-hand portion of the screen just after coming into the store. Each camera recorded an image every two seconds, so the nun's movement through the produce section was staccato, like that of a figure in an unsophisticated video game. The nun moved in five of these stagger steps right off the screen. A few seconds later, the next camera picked her up.

Him.

It.

Tommy Carroll and I were leaning in close to the screen. Carroll had his finger poised above the pause button on the video player. Martin Leavitt was off by the bay window, watching the sun burning its way through the white sky over the East River.

"We're estimating around six feet," Carroll said. "It's hard to tell with that headgear. You see the pillar with the bananas on it? Top of the nun's head comes up around that second batch from the top. I called a patrolman to go in and get me a measurement."

"Nun. Six feet. We can nail this thing in no time."

Tommy Carroll looked up from the screen. "Your old man had a sarcastic streak. I liked it a lot better in him."

The next camera picked up the figure. A bag of some sort hung from the nun's right shoulder.

"This whole nun thing is screwy," I said. "Have we got ourselves a Norman Bates here?"

"Who's Norman Bates?"

"You don't know your Alfred Hitchcock?"

Carroll was still looking horrible. "Who's Norman Bates?"

"**Psycho.** The Hitchcock movie. Killed his mother, then dressed up in her clothes whenever he got the burr up his tail to go kill someone."

"This guy's not dressing up like his mother. He's dressing up like a nun. Whose mother is a nun?"

I shrugged. "Mother Superior? Mother. Nun. All I'm saying is the getup must mean something."

"Right. Something weird." Carroll turned back to the screen. "Here. Look."

He tapped his finger against the square in the lower-left quadrant. The image jumped as a new camera clicked in. The horizontal freezer stretched from the bottom of the image to the top. With the lens the camera was using, the freezer looked absurdly long. The nun appeared. First the wimple, then, in the next image, the entire figure. Two images later, the nun was bending over the freezer. In the next image, something shiny was in the nun's hand. It was the plastic freezer bag containing the envelope.

"Wait," Carroll said again. Over by the window, Leavitt continued to gaze out at the river, almost as if he'd lost interest.

On-screen, the nun was stuffing the freezer bag beneath one of the turkeys. In the following image, the nun was standing upright again. So far we hadn't seen a single image of the face.

"That's what the habit is about," I said. "It obscures the face."

"Wait," Carroll said a third time. The nun pulled something from the shoulder bag and turned away from the camera. Deliberately, it seemed. Carroll pressed the pause button just as the nun turned back. The wimple was tilted up, and the nun was looking directly at the camera. The nun was wearing a pair of aviator sunglasses and a ridiculously large, droopy and obviously fake mustache.

The nun was giving the camera the finger.

IT WASN'T UNTIL SEVEN YEARS AFTER MY father had abruptly stepped down as police commissioner—and disappeared soon after—that the courts weighed in to officially pronounce him dead. It would have been nice to believe that what had really happened was that he simply dropped out of sight by his own choosing and moved on to a quiet incognito life somewhere in the Caribbean, grizzly gray beard, open-collared shirt, leathery tan, maybe the occasional dalliance with the occasional turista. I doubt his wife would appreciate that version of events as much as I do, but that's a beef I've always had about Phyllis Scott: no imagination. Coupled with a haughty self-regard that leaves precious little room for the consideration of others. Funny thing, since she's a psychiatrist, and not an inexpensive one. You'd think that a healthy degree of compassion and empathy would be one of the job requirements. Imagination, too. But I guess not. Her practice has never been more booming. It seems there are plenty of wealthy, uncentered New Yorkers willing to spill their hearts and guts out to a cold machine like Phyllis Scott to the tune of two hundred dollars an hour. I don't get it. I'd think an hour in a room with a frisky puppy would do as much for a person's mental health and would cost a lot less money. But what do I know?

Phyllis runs her practice out of the first floor of the town house she shared with my father on Sixty-sixth Street, right off Park

Avenue. Beside the scores of bitter, befuddled, destructive, frightened and generally unhappy people who have spent time within the building's walls (I'm speaking clinically here), the town house has also been terra cognita to Paul and Elizabeth Scott, my father and Phyllis's two children. My half siblings. Elizabeth I like. She never begrudged me and my mother our status as the marginal second family. The open secret. Her kindness to my mother, especially, has always won rave reviews from me. Paul is another story, and not one I'd pick up and read if I had a choice.

Paul Scott was coming down the steps of his mother's town house as I approached. I had hoofed it over from Gracie Mansion after viewing the Gristedes tape and going over so-called Nightmare's latest message. When Paul spotted me, he darkened like a rain cloud. He stopped on the bottom step. I'm sure the height advantage made him feel superior. I noticed a slight discoloration next to his right eye. "What are you doing here?" he asked.

"I'm thinking about buying the place and wanted to come by and kick the tires."

"Very funny."

Paul looked a lot like his mother, a fact I'll admit gave him not unpleasant features. Unfortunately, he tended to do unpleasant things with them. He was doing one of those things now. This particular one made him look like he was sniffing a foul odor.

"I'm here to see your mother." I said. "Is the doctor in?"

"Why do you want to see her?"

"I'm selling raffle tickets. Want one?"

He made his sniffing face again. "She's busy."

"I'm sure she is. She's expecting me. I'll bet she's been primping and prepping for this day for nearly a week. I know I have."

"You're a real stooge, Malone, you know that?"

It was a point of honor with Paul Scott that he had never in his life uttered my first name. At least not to my face. The closest he ever got was a phase in the beginning of his voice-cracking years when he tried to get some mileage out of referring to me as "Shitz." I gave him ten free passes before rewarding him with a bloody nose. Immediately thereafter, his mother the top-shelf shrink declared that I had "anger issues."

"Mommie dearest summoned me a few days ago," I said when he showed no sign of vacating the steps. "We have an appointment."

"Professionally?" He sounded horrified.

"Not today, but who knows? Maybe I can fit in a little couch time before I go. I'm sure my unresolved conflicts would sink the **Titanic.**"

"I've got to go," Paul said curtly. And he went. No hugs, no kisses. I can't say whether his stiffness as he moved down the sidewalk was because he knew I was watching him or if he was having troubles with the stick up his tail. I headed up the steps and pushed the buzzer. A few seconds later, the door clicked and I pushed it open.

The black and white tiles of Phyllis's enclosed entryway were set at a diagonal, which I would think the more loosely tethered of her patients might find disorienting, even a little bit threatening. On the left was the glass and metal door that her patients used to access her waiting area and office. A second buzzer was required to gain entrance. The door to the town house itself was a heavy oak slab that required a little muscle to push open. There was a second click, and I leaned into the door with my good shoulder.

As my eyes adjusted to the darkness of the foyer, Phyllis's voice came from the rear of the town house. "I'll be right with you! Have a seat!"

I stepped into the living room and did

what I could to make myself comfortable amid leather and metal furniture not too terrifically designed for that purpose. I sat facing a large piece of modern art on the wall that I might have titled **Ode to a Bowling Pin in the Snow.** It was new since I'd last visited. Also new was a pair of large chrome gooseneck standing lamps set on either side of the tall bay windows, their chrome hoods inclined toward each other over a black lacquered Asian table like a pair of alien heads in consultation. The room was spotless. I checked to see if I'd tracked in any dirt.

After another minute, Phyllis came in from the dining room. I rose. Even in her early sixties, she moved with a liquid grace. She was wearing bone-colored slacks and a ribbed maroon sweater. She was painfully slender, essentially hipless. The hair pulled back from her angular face was frosted the color of fresh straw. Her expression, as always, was a little bemused, a little aloof. A gold bracelet jangled on her arm as she reached for my hand. "You're prompt."

"You said noon. That one's easy. Both hands straight up."

Her hand felt like gelatin. I didn't dare give it a real squeeze. I sat back down as Phyllis lowered herself into a leather sling chair across from me. She made an L of her arms, settling her chin into her hand. I imagined an echo from hundreds of sessions across the hall: **So, tell me about your childhood.**

"You just missed Paul."

"I saw him," I said. "I ran into him out front. He embraced me like the bastard half brother I am."

She allowed the bemusement to flower. "You threaten him."

"Because I pack heat?"

"You know perfectly well why. Because you're rough and Paul is smooth. You are your father and he is not."

I do enjoy chewing the fat with shrinks. They cut right to the heart of the matter. I asked, "Does he know that he had all the advantages of life and I had approximately half of them?"

"He does. Which is what makes his unhappiness all the more profound. His leg up hasn't exempted him from pain."

"Ha ha," I said. "Fooled him."

"What happened to your arm, Fritz?"

A copy of the **Times** was on the glass coffee table to my left. The pair of pictures above the fold told the story. I didn't.

"I banged it," I said. "I'll live."

Phyllis sat back in her chair and crossed

her legs. "How's your mother, Fritz?" She added to the body language by crossing her arms. A foot jiggled impatiently.

"She's fine. She's out in California visiting a friend."

"And how is her drinking?"

I took the question in the chest. As intended, I'm sure. "That's direct."

Phyllis blinked like a Siamese cat. "You'd prefer not to say."

"It's a question of what I think she might prefer."

"I take it, then, that she's still wrestling with it. It's very sad."

"She's enjoying her visit with her friend," I said.

"There's no need to be defensive, Fritz."

I gave her a false smile. "You know how it is."

"Actually, I don't. Why don't you tell me?"

"Some other time. You can put me on the meter."

"That's not very funny."

"Then by all means don't laugh."

"I was only asking a question," she said coolly. "I wasn't intending to probe." Her gaze broke away from mine. It looked almost like she was purposely showing me her profile, then I realized she was looking down at the newspaper on the glass table. "This is so wretched." She leaned forward and picked up the paper, scanning the front page. "What has this world come to? I can only imagine the kinds of people capable of acts like these. It's horrible."

"Can you?" I asked. "I mean, a person who did something as depraved as either of those killings—could he actually walk around afterward, behaving just as normally as you and me?"

"Absolutely. Psychotics can blend right in. They don't wear sandwich boards declaring their homicidal rage."

"That would certainly be convenient for the authorities."

"And so many of the people you see who **do** look like they're ready to pull out a machete in a crowded subway, it's all bluff and bluster. They wouldn't actually do it in a million years. It's all verbal. Their anger is precisely the result of their inability to act. Their impotence. The world has them so tied down and hamstrung that their only tool is to yell or rant or simply start looking like something the cat dragged in. Their social-misfittedness is their attack. Other than that, they couldn't be less dangerous."

I pressed. "What if it were one of your patients who commited one of these attacks? Therapists have the inside track, so to speak. If the person was under psychiatric care, do you think his therapist would be able to suss it out?"

"There's no saying. Could be. And don't think that after events like what happened yesterday, therapists all around the city aren't running a mental inventory of their patients to see if any of them have shown the seeds of this kind of violence."

"Did you run an inventory?"

"There's no avoiding it."

"Did you come up with anything?"

"If I did, I wouldn't share it with you."

"I wouldn't expect you to. Not the particulars. No names. But I mean in the abstract. Are any of the people you're currently seeing capable of something like what happened?"

She gave me a level look and paused before responding. "Yes. I'd say one or two of them are."

"You practice a dangerous profession," I said.

"Harlan used to note that as well. He said the two of us probably had deep-seated death wishes."

"Sure was a cheerful guy, wasn't he? How about the both of you chose professions so that you could help other people? That has a nicer ring to it."

She glanced down at the paper again. "There's no doubt that the police are going to be flooded with calls from people claiming responsibility. Events like these speak to the imagination of unwell people. I could probably launch an entire new practice with the people who are going to come out of the woodwork on this." She tossed the paper back on the table and leveled me with her ice-blue eyes. New subject. "I want to thank you for coming over, Fritz."

"What is it you want? When you called the other day, you were pretty tight-lipped."

"It's Paul. I think he's mixed up in something he shouldn't be."

"Trouble?"

"I don't know. Perhaps. Linda thinks he is having an affair."

"I see."

"But she's not sure. His behavior has been somewhat furtive lately. And he is keeping an erratic schedule. Paul tends to shut down when Linda tries to draw him out."

"Has she put the question to him?"

"No. She's too nervous."

"Have you?"

"Yes."

"Let me guess. He denies it."

"He gets angry. And yes, he denies it. The problem is, Linda says Paul came home one night last week with a shiner. Maybe you saw." She tapped her right eye. "He tried to pass it off with a story about getting hit on the street by a bike messenger, but Linda is certain he was lying. Paul is not a good liar."

"As a mother, that should make you happy."

"As a mother, I'm concerned about my son. Linda says he hasn't slept an entire night through in well over a week. He's scared about something. But we can't bully him into telling us what he's up to. He's a grown man." She considered me for a moment. "I would like you to look into it, Fritz."

"You want me to bully him?"

"I think you know what I mean."

"If he won't tell you, he sure as hell won't tell me."

"I don't mean for you to ask him."

"You mean for me to snoop on him."

Phyllis's sweater had an oversize turtleneck. She poked a finger into the loose fabric and twisted it as she spoke. "That's what you do for a living, isn't it?"

"I don't snoop on my family for a living."

"Paul and you are family only in the most marginal sense of the word."

"There are a hundred other private investigators you could call in for this," I said. "I can give you some recommendations."

"But I don't know what it is they're going to uncover."

"If they're any good, it'll be the same thing I'd uncover."

She released the collar. "What I mean is, I don't know what they'll do with the information once they have it. I really don't want strangers rooting about in my son's personal life."

"So then you **do** want me because I'm family."

She recrossed her legs with military swiftness. "You enjoy being difficult?"

"I'm just trying to get us both on the same page. You want me to snoop on Paul to see why he's getting into fights and can't sleep. You want to be able to tell me to keep my mouth shut about it when I find out what he's up to. And the reason I'm supposed to keep my mouth shut is because Paul and I share the same father. But I'm not supposed to view this as snooping on my own flesh and blood."

"You could care less about Paul," she said flatly.

"It might not be an affair. It might be something else. I just need to warn you that investigations don't always go where the client thinks they'll go. If I were to uncover something unsavory or illegal, why would I be inclined to keep quiet about it?"

"Because I asked you to."

"I see."

"I would be your client. I would be the one paying you for your services."

"No family favors."

"I'm not family."

I gave my head a scratch. "The overall logic is a little shaky."

"I'll pay you in cash, if it's all the same to you."

"I still accept cash. Fits so snugly in my wallet."

"Good. Then we have a deal." She sealed her own conclusion with a sharp nod.

I asked, "Does Paul know that this is why I'm here?"

"I didn't say anything to him about your visit."

"You knew that I was coming today at noon. You didn't go out of your way to keep him from seeing that I was coming by to speak with you."

She turned her palms to the ceiling. "Let him wonder. That's not really important. What's important is that you find out what he's up to and I'm able to see to it that he stops doing it."

"He's a grown man," I reminded her.

She considered me a moment. "You do remind me of Harlan."

"What would he have done in a situation like this?"

"I think you know the answer to that."

I did. "The old-school method," I said. "He would have grabbed Paul by the ankles and dangled him from an upstairs window until he coughed up the goods."

"Precisely."

"But you're going to count on my tact and delicacy?"

"Your tact."

"And what about my delicacy?"

The high-priced psychiatrist gave a closed-lipped smile. "I don't give a rat's ass about your delicacy."

Nightmare was one ballsy piece of work. Maybe brilliant. Maybe naively stupid. Reckless, to be sure. Contemptuous of authority. An attention hound. Insecure. Angry. Vainglorious. Deluded. And he liked to dress up in nuns' clothing.

Phyllis was right: could be anyone.

There are several fairly standard ways of handling a money drop. Often the person making the demand will designate a somewhat remote area where he (it's usually a he) can get a decent sense of who's lurking nearby. In the case of kidnapping, the kidnapper is holding the plumb card. So long as the hostage is still being held, no one is going to swoop down on the kidnapper in the middle of the pickup.

But in this case, Nightmare's hostage wasn't a single frightened person who was going to be released on a random street corner once the money had been paid and the kidnapper had safely blended back into the woodwork. It was the entire city. Or if it **was** one person, it was New York City Mayor Martin Leavitt. Whichever way you wanted to look at it, Nightmare held all the cards. And like I said, the way he was playing them was ballsy, brilliant, stupid and reckless all at once.

He wanted the hand-off to be done at the Cloisters Museum in the middle of a crowded holiday weekend.

In the coat-check room.

See? Ballsy.

"WHAT AN IDIOT," MARGO SAID. "YOU grab him right there. Or you follow him and grab him later. He's putting himself right in your hands."

And I was putting a calamari right in my mouth. It was a tad overcooked—when I chewed, it chewed back. Calamari is tricky that way. It either melts in your mouth or it refuses to go down without a struggle. I had a pilsner glass of Carlsberg Elephant at hand to help subdue the calamari. Across the small table, Margo was confronting a spinach salad of Olympian proportions. She seemed uncertain where to start.

Margo and I were in the back room of Miss Elle's Homesick Bar and Grill on West Seventy-ninth Street. Except Miss Elle had recently sold the place to a mystery writer named Dorian, and now the sign out front said Dorian's. But it still looked like Miss Elle's, the food still tasted like Miss Elle's, and the hurly-burly crowd of regulars at the small bar in the front were Miss Elle's regulars. So what's in a name? It was still a duck.

Margo was reminding me of Tinker Bell today, and I couldn't for the life of me figure out why. Technically speaking, there's nothing remotely Tinker Bellish about her.

"Can't do it," I said to her. "His note made it clear that if anyone tries to grab him at the museum, or if he's picked up later, we'll be seeing another bloody mess."

"If you nab him, how can he do anything?"

"For starters, he could rig himself with explosives. We know he has the means. He could blow. But even if it's not that, we have to worry about another accomplice."

"You mean you can't pick him up because

he might have instructed someone that if you do, they should wreak havoc again somewhere else in the city. Preferably where there are big crowds."

Margo was wearing a sort of leafy green blouse. Maybe that's why I was thinking of Tinker Bell. But maybe not.

"Exactly. The guy has a built-in insurance policy."

"But that's ridiculous. If you follow that line of logic, then you're talking about a person with total immunity. He could walk around the city with a sandwich board announcing, 'I'm the crazed killer! But nobody touch me or else!' "

"That's funny," I said.

"What's so funny about it? It's horrible."

"No. That you said sandwich board. Phyllis mentioned a sandwich board earlier."

"A riot."

"Two mentions of sandwich boards in one afternoon? And they went out of common use before you or I were even born."

"Cosmic."

"Don't be sarcastic, Mo. You go from pretty to gorgon."

"That's nice. You're calling me a gorgon."

"Figure of speech."

"Not really."

"In a way."

"Then so is 'sandwich board.' "

I picked up my Elephant. "Are we entering into an argument?"

"If we are, it would be one our silliest."

"What say we skip it? You are so far from a gorgon that the very idea makes me choke up with laughter."

Margo buried her fork deep within her spinach. "You look pretty calm to me."

The drop-off was to take place the following day. Saturday. Two o'clock, when the museum would be gagged with people. The mayor was being forced to play the tie game again. This time he was supposed to wear a green one. The note that had been fetched from the horizontal cooler at the Gristedes said that if Mayor Leavitt was ready to agree to the conditions of the rendezvous at the museum, he was to make an appearance on the six o'clock local news wearing a green tie. He was further instructed to include the word "Wisconsin" in his appearance.

We got the check. Margo had managed to eat most of her spinach salad. She had formed what remained into a little pyramid in the center of her plate. "Why Wisconsin?" she asked as I was calculating the tip.

"Who knows? Maybe the guy is telling us

where he was born. All we've got to do is question every person in the five boroughs who was born in Wisconsin. Or maybe it's for no good reason at all. The tie should be enough. It could just be part of the guy's game. Jerking Leavitt around."

The waitress came over and I handed her the check and the cash.

Margo asked, "Did you leave a good tip?"

The waitress was still standing at the table. I looked up at her. "Maybe you could answer that for me."

The waitress blushed.

Margo blushed, too. "Oops."

"You need to have your timing adjusted, sweetie," I said.

The waitress was flipping through the bills. "This looks fine. Thanks."

She left. Margo reached across the table and finished the last small sip of my beer. "That just popped out. Sorry."

"You can trust me. I'm a big tipper."

"I know you are. Sorry. So anyway. Wisconsin. How's Leavitt going to make a sound bite around the word 'Wisconsin'?"

"I'm sure he's got his best and brightest working on it. He told me that he's going to award a commendation to Leonard Cox this afternoon at around four-thirty. He'll get media coverage for sure."

"Do you think this guy will actually do something if he doesn't hear 'Wisconsin'?"

"Probably not, that's the thing. He's just playing Leavitt's nerves like a harp."

Margo frowned. "Ugly imagery."

She skidded her chair back from the table and stood up. Beneath the leafy green blouse, she was wearing a simple black skirt. Beneath the skirt were Margo's pale legs, poked into a pair of calf-high brown leather boots. As I rose from the table she trained her eyes on me and she pressed her palms against her hips, running her hands down along them several times as I rose from the table.

Pretty imagery.

12

I BROUGHT MARGO WITH ME TO ST. LUKE'S to meet Rebecca Gilpin. The cop posted at the door to the actress's hospital room was none other than the black officer who'd bagged me—literally—the day before.

"Remember me?" I said to him. "I was the kid with the lollipop in your backseat."

He indicated my shoulder. "We didn't do that."

I ducked my head and gingerly removed the sling. I gave the shoulder a few cautious swivels. The muscles weren't exactly baby fresh, but the level of ache was acceptable. I was sick of the sling already. You look like an invalid, you begin to feel like an invalid. I balled it up and handed it to a male nurse who was passing by. "I found this on the floor."

Margo asked, "Isn't that a little premature?"

"I didn't want it to go stiff from non-use."

Margo looked at me blankly. Then her cheeks went red. "I just had a naughty thought."

"Save it."

This time I got the policeman's name. It was a lot easier without a bag on my head. The name was right there on the gold bar above his shirt pocket. Patrick Noon. An expression of cautious distrust appeared to be Officer Noon's mien.

"I'm here to see the lady," I told him.

"No one sees the lady."

"I'm not no one. I'm her former bodyguard."

"No one sees the lady."

"If you'd just pop your head in and tell her I'm here, I'll bet—"

He cut me off. "No one sees the lady."

I turned to Margo. "Is this station beginning to bore you?"

She blinked slowly. "No one sees the lady."

I was surrounded by pod people.

"Ask her," I said again to Noon. "Tell her Fritz Malone is here."

He shook his head. "I've got my orders."

"From Tommy Carroll?"

"It doesn't matter from who."

I turned to Margo. "I guess you don't get to meet the famous star of stage and screen."

"Officer Noon is only doing his job," Margo said.

I was just about to ask Noon if he would at least pass on a message from me to Miss Gilpin when the male nurse reappeared. He was carrying a plastic IV bag.

"Excuse me," he said, and the officer moved to the side. I took a step in the other direction as the nurse opened the door. I could see Rebecca Gilpin in the far corner of the room, propped up in bed. She spotted me and raised a hand in greeting just before the nurse slid the door closed. A few seconds later, the door reopened and the nurse popped his head out. "She wants to see you."

I turned to Noon. "Who'd have thunk?"

"Five minutes."

The actress was medicated to the teeth. The smile she tried to give me as I approached the bed nearly poured off her face. She was as pale as her hospital gown. Her right leg was wrapped like a mummy's and elevated slightly on several pillows. A bandage covered her left cheek.

"You are, thank you . . . it's . . . my thank you." Clouds drifted across her eyes.

"You're welcome," I said. "Listen, I brought a friend to meet you."

"This was wrong, Fritz," Margo said. "I shouldn't be here." She addressed Rebecca. "Miss Gilpin, I'm sorry for what happened. Best of luck for a speedy recovery." She turned to me. "I'll wait in the hall." She left the room.

The nurse was changing Rebecca's IV bag. "How's she doing?" I asked him.

"There's a lot of pain. The leg's a real mess."

Rebecca said, "The bastard who did me I can kill him with . . ." The rest of her sentence came in an unknown tongue. A pool of tears appeared in each of her eyes. I took hold of the hand nearest me. She closed icy fingers around mine. "I'm beautiful," she muttered.

"Yes, you are."

Out in the corridor, Margo was entertaining Officer Noon with her story about getting smashed on martinis with the queen of Denmark while she was interviewing her in a suite at the Plaza several years ago. Margo loves that story. Any one of a hundred cue words will get her rolling with it. Even Noon appeared to be softened up by it.

"You could charm the pants off a statue,

couldn't you?" I said to Margo as we waited for the elevator.

"I wouldn't want to."

The elevator arrived. It was the size of some New York apartments.

"Wait," I said. "I'll be right back."

I retraced my steps. Patrick Noon watched me with a wary eye as I approached. "I was just wondering," I said as I reached him. "Are they going to spell you for the ceremony this afternoon?"

"What ceremony?"

"Cox. The mayor is planning to fawn all over him for allegedly taking out Diaz in Central Park. I was just wondering if you were going to be there?"

"I don't know anything about that."

"Nice irony, isn't it? A cop forgets to do something as basic as pat down a suspect he's taking into custody, and the next day he's a hero."

Noon said nothing.

"I'm just curious. Were you and your partner even on the scene yesterday? I mean officially? Are you supposed to be going along as so-called witnesses to Cox's so-called shooting Diaz out there by the fountain?"

Noon's eyes left my face for a fraction of a second. His glance took in the empty corridor. "We weren't there."

"Officially."

He nodded. "That's right."

"What do you think about the story of Cox's shooting Diaz up in the Municipal Building?"

"What am I supposed to think about it?"

"If you're like me, you're thinking that Cox was speedy on the draw in direct proportion to Diaz being pathetically slow." Noon said nothing. "I put myself in Diaz's position, and I think of at least two things I would have done. The second one is I'm sitting in that room with my pistol out and already aimed at the door five seconds after Carroll leaves me alone. I'm ready to shoot the moment it opens."

Noon appeared to concede the point. He weighed it with a little ticktock of his head. "What's the first?"

"The first is I never get into that room in the first place. I've just shot up the Thanksgiving Day parade. I've killed innocent people. I've killed a cop. I'm in custody in a police cruiser with the cop's partner. I'm screwed six ways to Sunday. But I've got a Tomcat strapped to my ankle. I don't give a damn if I'm cuffed behind my back, I get to the damn gun. I twist around in the seat any possible way I can and I shoot like hell through the gate. I take my chances."

Noon considered the scenario. Or maybe he was considering what he was going to have for dinner later that night. The man was hard to read.

"Interesting," he said at last.

"I think so, too. Either of my two stories sounds more likely than Commissioner Carroll's account. For one thing, why uncuff him and then recuff him with a hand free?"

"You cuff him to a solid object," Noon said. "That's procedure. You don't want him able to move around the room."

"But you don't want him to be able to reach for a gun and try to shoot you."

"They didn't know about the gun."

"Right. Of course. Listen. Do you know this Cox guy?" I asked. "I mean, personally?"

"Cox and I are from different precincts."

"What's yours?" I asked.

"The Seventeenth."

"What about Cox and McNally? I heard a reporter asking if they were from the Ninety-fifth."

Noon hesitated before answering. "That's right."

"The Bad Apple precinct. What were they doing all the way in Manhattan?"

"Parade duty," Noon said. "Overtime. You get cops from all boroughs."

"So you're not familiar with Cox? You don't really know him?"

"Are you a lawyer or just a pest?"

"What did Carroll say to the three of you when you were hanging around the Municipal Building? Before he and Cox went inside."

"I think we're finished talking."

"He didn't by any chance say, 'Stick around, Cox has some unfinished business with the guy who gunned down his partner,' anything like that? 'Hang tight, we're bringing a dead guy out here in a few minutes'?"

"What's all this about?"

"I'm just trying to see how many lies the commissioner is getting you and your partner to sign off on. I'm trying to figure out how deep a hero Leonard Cox is."

"Figure it out somewhere else."

"What's your partner's name?"

"Levine. Why?"

"No reason. I just collect names. Hobby of mine."

He let his breath out in a large sigh. "I'm just doing my job, man. Why don't you let it go?"

"Were you and Levine still there when Cox and Carroll brought Diaz out?" A thought occurred to me the moment I said this. "No.

Carroll had to get over to City Hall and face the cameras. Cox must have gotten help. Was that you and Levine? Did you help load the body into Cox's cruiser so they could take it to St. Luke's and have it pronounced dead?"

"You're done here," Noon said.

"Did you?"

"I said go."

"No, you didn't."

"I'm saying it now."

He took a step toward me. I didn't think he would be so stupid as to actually take a swing at me, but I braced. Though with my sore shoulder, I wouldn't have been much for blocking the punch if he decided to take one. He looked strong.

He didn't take the swing. He took the step, expecting I would back away. When I didn't, we were left as close as two moony kids at a prom dance.

"Well," I said. "Nice chatting with you."

I stepped away from him and rejoined Margo at the elevator.

"What was that all about?" she asked. "I thought you two were about to kiss."

"I'm not his type."

"If you were his type, I guess you wouldn't be mine."

"That's very narrow of you," I said.

She shrugged. "I'm narrow."

The elevator arrived. Again. We got on. Down the hall, Patrick Noon was watching us as the door slid closed.

"He's scared," I said.

"He didn't look scared to me."

I pushed the lobby button. The elevator jolted and started down.

"I got a lot closer than you did."

13

Philip Byron called on my cell phone just before six o'clock. "We're on."

Margo was rubbing Mineral Ice on my shoulder. Turquoise gel. Goes on cold, settles in hot. Amazing stuff.

"We're on," I parroted back to Byron. "Good. So the mayor got the Wisconsin thing in?"

"I just checked with Channel Four. It's in their footage. Is your TV on?"

It was, though it was actually Margo's TV. We were at her place. The volume was turned down low. We were watching whales spawn.

"Channel Four," I said. "I'll watch it. So everything's been taken care of at the museum?"

"We're all set there."

"And the money?"

"Everything's in place. We want this thing to go off smoothly and simply. No bumps."

"I hope our Mr. Nightmare wants the same," I said.

"You know where to meet?"

"I've got it."

"The mayor appreciates your service on this," Byron said.

"No problem. It'll be handy having City Hall in my pocket."

There was a pause. "That's not funny, Mr. Malone."

"Really? I sort of thought it was."

He hung up.

Margo asked, "Did the mayor say 'Wisconsin'?"

"Apparently. If you can pull yourself away from your copulating whales, we can see. Channel Four."

We muted the volume. I didn't want to hear the new anchor's version of the previous day's events and where things allegedly stood. The truth surrounding the pair of assaults had already split into separate pieces, each of which was traveling down its own track. The version I was privy to was a lot spicier than the one being broadcast. Not to mention that it held more facts. But when footage of Rebecca

Gilpin dancing her little fanny off in the dinghy started running, I barked, "Sound."

"Yes, master."

The attempt to keep mum on Rebecca Gilpin's presence at Barrymore's the night before was already crumbling. The theater had announced that the actress had picked up a flu and would be out of the show over the weekend. Her understudy would be going on. But rumors were materializing that Rebecca had been at the restaurant when the coat-check closet exploded and that she was anywhere from mildly injured to critically injured to already dead. A tearful fan out in front of the theater was convinced that the rumors of the actress's death were the accurate ones. A know-nothing overreacting to a rumor that is false is not news. They let the woman blubber on for a good ten seconds.

A spokesman for the mayor had been sent to handle the Rebecca Gilpin matter. Was she dead? Had she been at Barrymore's after all? Wasn't there a connection between the two Thanksgiving Day incidents? The spokesman had used up his airtime essentially declaring that he didn't know a damn thing.

"Fumble," I said.

"Why didn't they just let the story out in the first place?" Margo said.

"Desperate attempt at containment. Pointless."

"It's blowing up in their faces."

"Fumble," I said again.

The next story concerned Roberto Diaz. It didn't contain much substance. Diaz had lived alone in the Fort Greene section of Brooklyn. He was divorced with a young daughter. No other details had been uncovered. His neighbors had nothing insightful to say about him, but they were allowed to say it anyway. None of them "had any idea" that he was planning such a horrific thing as the attack at the parade. He was described as "a quiet man" who "kept to himself."

"Shush," Margo said when she heard the beginnings of my growl.

"It's what they always say."

"Just let them say it."

Details on the termination of Diaz's employment at the messenger service were reported as unclear. A spokesman for the company had weighed in with a "no comment."

Margo scooted to the end of the couch and brought a foot up onto my lap. I pretended to ignore it, but it kept batting me in the ribs. I finally took hold of it.

The mayor came on next. He was standing

at a podium along with a very uncomfortable-
looking Leonard Cox. Tommy Carroll stood
behind them, half out of the picture. Leavitt
praised Officer Cox for his courage and his
dedication to duty and all the rest. He told
him that the city was grateful. It was a very
polished presentation. The mayor was wearing a bright green tie. It looked absurdly inappropriate.

Leavitt took hold of Cox's hand and
pumped his arm vigorously. "The people of
this city are proud of you. I'm sure the people
of your home state, Wisconsin, are proud of
you as well."

"Message delivered," I said.

Margo said, "I think it stinks that they
want you to hand off the money. I don't
like it."

"The people of Wisconsin will be proud
of me."

Her foot kicked lightly at my ribs. "I'm serious. I don't want you to do it."

"Someone has to do it," I said.

"But why you?"

"I'm qualified."

"I hate it," she said. "I wish you sold shoes
for a living."

I balanced her foot in my hand and studied it. I vetoed a few too-easy cracks, then

lowered the foot back onto my lap. "I'll be fine."

She glowered at me. "I want a big juicy steak for dinner."

"You've got it."

"Something really rich for dessert."

"Name it."

"I want you to come back home tomorrow in one piece."

"I always have."

"Right." She sniggered. "Sometimes."

14

THE CLOISTERS IS A BRANCH OF THE MET-
ropolitan Museum of Art. I can get to the
Met from Margo's by walking directly across
Central Park. Catch me in a jogging mood
and I can make it there in ten minutes. But
the Cloisters is located in Fort Tryon Park in
upper Manhattan, a mile beyond the George
Washington Bridge and some six miles from
Margo's place. I'm not **that** fond of jogging.

I took the A train to 190th Street, where a
cattle-style elevator brought me up to street
level. They call this part of Manhattan Washington Heights. The area is essentially a long
bulge running north–south along the Hudson, rivaling in height the bare-faced Pal-
isades cliffs across the river in the state that
isn't New York. The rents are more reasonable

here than farther south in the city, and the racial mix is decidedly melting-pottish. In recent years the yuppies and neo-yuppies have purchased places in Washington Heights. There may not be a Starbucks or a Banana Republic on every corner yet, but housing wise you get more bang for the buck, especially if you nab a place with a view of the river.

The sun was out. The sky was blue. There was an autumn nip in the air. I was getting by with a light sweater, a Yankees cap and a checked sport jacket. There's a used-clothing place on Columbus Avenue called Housing Works. Margo and I had gone there just before they closed Friday night and picked up the sport jacket for fifteen dollars. It was part of my disguise. I'd be able to write it off on my taxes.

I met Philip Byron at a stone gate on the south end of Fort Tryon Park. He looked pale and unhappy. Next to him on the ground sat a large green JanSport backpack. It was bulging like an overstuffed sausage.

"Is that a million dollars in there?" I asked.

"You have no idea how difficult it was to pull this together so fast."

"Come on. A politician. A million bucks. Sounds like a finger snap to me."

"You'd be wrong."

I grabbed hold of the canvas strap at the top of the bag and lifted. Good thing I had used my healthy arm. "I hope Nightmare isn't a weakling."

"I don't like this," Byron said. "I can think of a dozen better ways to arrange a hand-off. He's got something in mind."

"Of course he does. And he knows we know it. And he knows we don't know what it is. That's about as level a playing field as we're going to get here." I hoisted the bag onto my right shoulder. It would have been easier to carry it on my back, but I didn't trust the torquing of my bad shoulder. I asked, "Where's the cop?"

Byron frowned at me. "What do you mean?"

"I mean you're standing on a street corner with a million dollars in a backpack. Our resident psycho is out here somewhere. Probably somewhere close. I'm not calling you a coward, I'm just saying you don't strike me as stupid."

"He explicitly instructed no cops. No one touches him."

"I know what he instructed. But I also know how the police operate."

My eyes traveled down the wide road.

There was a fair amount of street traffic, most of it coming into the park. A hot-dog cart stood near the gate. The vendor stood leaning against the cart, smoking a cigarette. Byron shook his head slowly. Another elevatorload of people had just come up from underground, most of them drifting toward the Cloisters. About two hundred feet from the gate, a large black man was stretched out on a bench, sleeping.

"Don't tell me it's him. A child could pick that up."

Byron shook his head again. "It's the nanny."

I followed his eyes. Across the street from where the man was sleeping, an Asian-American woman was seated on a bench with a blue baby carriage in front of her. She was reading a paperback book.

I asked, "Is there a real baby in there?"

"Video camera. Wide-angle lens."

"You're breaking the rules."

"Not really. No one said anything about not taking pictures."

"Will she follow us?"

"At a distance. Outside only. We'll be picked up inside by someone else."

"I thought Leavitt was keeping this whole thing as quiet as possible."

"The undercovers don't know the details. Their instructions are to act for my safety, and once they've seen you, for yours."

And with my checked sport coat, I'd be hard to miss.

"Remember what you said on the phone last night," I said. "We want this to go smoothly and simply."

"That's the plan."

"So no surprise interferences, right?"

"That's right. We leave the bag, he picks it up, it's over."

We started walking. From the corner of my eye, I saw the "nanny" closing her book.

"You don't even need me," I said, adjusting the bag on my shoulder.

"Commissioner Carroll wanted you."

"In case things go wacky."

"They won't. At least not on our end."

We reached the stone gate. The hot-dog vendor tossed his cigarette to the street and called out in a light Irish brogue, "Hot dog, Mac?"

I answered back, "My name's not Mac."

Byron was a step ahead of me, so he didn't see the guy's wink. Nor mine back to him.

LET NO ONE SAY, AND
SAY IT WITH SHAME,

THAT ALL WAS BEAUTY
HERE, UNTIL YOU CAME

I read the sign out loud. It was planted in the ground at the base of the park's heather garden. "Where I come from, they just say 'No Littering.'"

Byron was putting on a pair of sunglasses. Along with his short hair and grim stiffness, they made him look like FBI. We walked without speaking along the dregs of the heather garden. I'd been there in the early summer, when the air was nearly choked with fragrances from all the flowers. Now it was fallow and scraggly. The Hudson was visible off to our left. A wide blue undulating ribbon.

Fort Tryon Park is laid out in a series of grass terraces broken up by large outcroppings of boulders left behind after the glaciers wormed slowly through several thousand years ago. A six-hundred-foot promenade weaves around the boulders, leading to the Cloisters. We approached from the south, the dramatic view. A pair of black crows were dive-bombing each other above the medieval building's terra-cotta roof.

"Have you ever wondered what it would be like to be a monk?" I asked Byron.

"Never thought about it."

"No sex. No pockets. No television. Eat like a bird. Out of the rack before the sun comes up. Never harm a hair on the head of a fly."

"What are you talking about?"

"Monks," I said. "Monks and nuns. Monasteries. Convents. The cloistered life. Turning away from the world's distractions and focusing instead on the subtle rhythms of the spirit. Or maybe it's the soul. I can never remember what the difference is."

The sun glinted off Byron's shades. "I'm not following you."

"Just thinking out loud," I said. "Whoever we're handing over this money to obviously has some seriously crossed wires. You don't normally associate nuns and monasteries with public massacres and blackmail. I think our Mr. Nightmare is what psychiatrists would call conflicted. What do you think? A very unhappy former choirboy, maybe?"

"We're not here to analyze him. We're here to pay him off."

"What makes the mayor think this guy's going to go away after this? It's possible, I guess. But a million dollars in today's world isn't what it used to be. He could burn right through it and come on back for more."

Byron took a moment before responding.

"We've discussed that. But we feel we have no choice. The mayor has to protect the citizens of this city."

We reached the entrance and made our way up an enclosed winding stone walkway to the admissions desk. "Mr. Small," Byron said to the woman at the desk. "He's expecting us."

She indicated an arched doorway past the gift-shop entrance. "Right through there."

I followed Byron through the arched doorway and up a short flight of stairs. The museum's offices were at the top of the stairs. A bespectacled man with thick gray hair was waiting for us. He took us into a small office. Byron introduced us. He was Gerald Small, director of the Cloisters. Mr. Small was wearing a gray wool suit and a red-striped tie. He looked like he was bravely toughing out a migraine.

"I'm not happy with this," he said immediately to Byron. His voice was nasal and grating. "I don't enjoy being left in the dark. I want to be on record with that."

"There is no record, Gerald," Byron replied coolly. "But I hear you. And the mayor appreciates your cooperation."

"Appreciation is one thing. You were a little more specific when you called me."

Byron offered a reassuring tone. "The

mayor keeps his promises, Gerald. Mayor
Leavitt is very enthusiastic about the museum's restoration initiative. You can depend
on seeing the fruits of that enthusiasm."

"Fruits of that enthusiasm," I repeated. "I
like that." My enthusiasm was blandly received by both men.

Gerald Small retrieved a burgundy jacket
from atop his desk and held it out to me. I removed my checked jacket and put on the
burgundy one. It was a little tight across the
shoulders but not so bad. From my pants
pocket, I pulled out a small folding mirror
and a neatly trimmed false mustache with
gummy webbed backing. I affixed the mustache to my upper lip, checking in the folding
mirror to see that it was on straight. From my
shirt pocket, I produced a pair of black-
framed glasses. I put them on, removed the
Yankees cap, gave my flattened hair a finger-
combing against the grain, then turned to
Philip Byron. "Presto change-o."

"Where's the bag that was left on Wednesday?" Byron asked Small. The museum director opened a small coat closet and pulled out
a black canvas backpack. It was a little larger
than the green JanSport. Byron took the
backpack and unzipped it.

Across the top of the note retrieved from

the Gristedes had been typed: NOW THAT I HAVE YOUR ATTENTION. The note instructed that a million dollars in hundred-dollar bills be bundled and delivered to the Cloisters by Saturday afternoon. The money was to be transferred into a bag that had gone unclaimed earlier in the week. The claim number on the bag was 16. The bag and the money were to be returned to the coat-check room by noon on Saturday and stowed in cubby number 16. The note included the instructions to the mayor about the green tie, the word "Wisconsin" and the warning that any deviations from the instructions or attempts to detain or pursue the person claiming the bag would result in "more public blood."

It was now nine-fifteen.

After the museum had closed on Friday night, a team of technicians had arrived and installed a new set of security cameras, one for each of the Cloisters' two entrances and one in a large wicker purse that had been strategically placed in one of the cubbies in the coat-check room. I had my doubts that the Cloisters' hastily installed cameras were going to capture anything other than another disguise. But I wasn't running that part of the game, so I kept quiet. In addition to the technicians who installed the cameras, an explosives expert had made the trip up to the Cloisters on Friday evening and inspected the unclaimed bag. It was clean.

We transferred the money to the black bag and made our way to the coat-check room, where Gerald Small explained the system to me. "You clip a number to the bag or the coat or whatever it is they're checking. The bags you put in order in the cubbies. The coats you hang in order on the rack. You give the customer the plastic tag with the corresponding number."

"I think I can handle that."

"It's very straightforward."

"Do I accept tips?"

"No tipping."

"Shucks."

Officer Kevin McNally was being buried with full police honors at noon, and the mayor and Byron were attending. The operation was now officially in my hands. Before leaving, Byron told me that the undercover cop inside the museum was wearing a Giants jersey. Number 08. This isn't how numbers appear on Giants jerseys, so the chances of a second person showing up at the Cloisters wearing Giants jersey number 08 were essentially zilch.

Comforting.

The museum opened at nine-thirty. I fielded about a dozen customers right off the bat, and then a lull set in. The steadier stream began around ten-thirty. A Saturday madrigal program was being conducted in one of the galleries at eleven.

From my vantage point, I had an uninterrupted view of the entrance nearest me and a partial view of the one across from the admissions desk. From that entrance, if a person wanted, he or she could go directly into the gift shop before paying admission. I looked around and found the newly installed security cameras, but I couldn't tell if they were calibrated to take in the gift-shop entrance.

I handled my duties admirably. Seems I was born with all the right skills. My anonymity threw me a little at first; 90 percent of the people handing over their coats or bags looked right through me if they looked at me at all. But I assisted in their indifference with equal doses of my own. I was there to blend in, not stand out. One person, a fat boy with black bangs, tried to draw me out as he handed over a heavy brown coat—"Hey! Do you like white meat or dark meat?"—but his mother, nearly his twin in a scary way, snapped at him to shut up.

Just before eleven o'clock, I was engaged a second time. A jean jacket was thrust at me, accompanied by something small wrapped in white paper.

"Here you go, Mac."

"What's this?" I muttered without moving my lips.

Jigs Dugan offered his shit-eating grin. "Hot dog. Thought you'd be hungry."

I let the hot dog fall into a wastebasket at my feet. I took the jean jacket and gave Jigs his number.

"Thanks." He pulled a dollar from his pocket. "Where's your tip cup, Mac?"

"We don't accept tips . . . **sir.**"

"I'd join a union if I were you, Mac."

"Go away," I muttered.

Jigs shoved his fists together and cracked his knuckles. The scar on his right cheek hooked as he sneered at me. "They got paintings of naked women here, Mac?"

"If you're lucky, you might find a cherub. And you can quit with the Mac already."

Jigs drew my attention to the pager on his belt. "You need me, bubba, you just whistle," he said in a low voice. A tall man was stepping up behind him, shrugging out of a long black Burberry coat.

"The madrigal program is starting in a few minutes, sir," I said stiffly and loudly to Jigs.

He put on a sage face. He was completely aware of the man waiting behind him. "Madrigals? Well, that's good. Can't get enough of those madrigals this time of year, right?" He turned and bumped purposefully into the tall man. "Oops. Sorry, there, Mac."

The man had nearly a foot on Jigs. He gave him a pissed-off look. Of course, he had no way of knowing that the first person Jigger Dugan ever killed had given him one of those looks. The third one, too, if I have my stories straight.

HIGH NOON ARRIVED. HIGH NOON PASSED. The cop with Giants jersey number 08 made several passes in view of the coat-check room. People drifted in from the direction of the gallery where the madrigal program had just ended. A few of them came directly for their coats and bags. Nobody handed me number 16.

Jigs passed by about twenty minutes later. He had latched on to a pair of young women. One of them looked soft and doughy, a little homely. Her friend was taller, skinnier and glaring at Jigs like a hawk. Jigs stole a quick glance my way and touched a finger to his upper lip. My fake mustache needed centering.

———

ONE O'CLOCK. MY LEGS WERE TIRED. What they needed in this stuffy little closet was a stool. Conditions in my workplace were getting to me. Normally the coat-check person would have been spelled for lunch, but this wasn't normally. There was a million dollars in cubby number 16.

I considered the cold hot dog in the wastebasket. I turned around and made a face at the wicker bag holding the video camera. I started wondering what sort of junk was in the other checked bags. A little chill ran through me as I recalled the scene the other night at Barrymore's.

JIGS'S TWO WOMEN CLAIMED THEIR COATS at around two-forty. The tall one was chewing out the doughy one for giving "that creepy Irish guy" her phone number. The doughy one countered that he "was sort of cute." As she handed me her claim number, she added to her friend, "I can look out for myself."

Maybe so. But I know Jigs Dugan, and he can look after himself, too. Jigs wandered by some ten minutes later, smiling like a wolf.

"I found that cherub you were talking about, Mac."

IT HAPPENED AT TEN MINUTES AFTER THREE. I had entered into a fugue state, and it took a moment for it to register that I was looking at a blue claim tag with the number 16 on it. My heart took a running leap against my ribs.

A woman in her mid-fifties stood in front of me. She had graying brown hair cut in a fashionless bowl, sharp cheekbones and large eyes the same color as the tag she had just pulled from a purse. She was dressed in a long beige jacket and a pair of brown slacks. Of all the day's customers, she was making the most direct eye contact. Her thin eyebrows arched quizzically.

"I'm sorry. This is going to sound a little peculiar. But . . . well, I think something has been left here for me."

My cell phone was sitting open in cubby number 12, right below the million-dollar cubby. Jigs's pager number was programmed into the speed dial. The plan had been that in retrieving the backpack from number 16, with my back blocking what I was doing, I would hit the speed dial and fire off a call to Jigs's pager. The moment he got the call, Jigs was to make a beeline for the entrance area, eyeball the person retrieving the bag, then step outside and perform his invisible shadow act. It was a gamble—the note from Gristedes had been clear as to what the consequences of a tail would be—but Jigs Dugan was a man worth betting on. Besides, the note hadn't been addressed to me.

I took the claim tag from the woman's hand.

"I'm a little confused," she said again.

I didn't want to stare. I turned away, being sure to give the wicker bag with the hidden camera a full frontal view of the woman. I started for my cell phone, then hesitated. Something was wrong here. I reached one hand up to grapple with the bag while I quickly hit the few buttons on my cell phone with the other. Then I grabbed hold of the bag with both hands. Cubby 16 was slightly higher than my head. My bad shoulder practically burst into flames as I pulled the bag down.

She can't possibly carry this.

The woman was still talking. ". . . so maybe I should talk to someone first. Take a look at—"

She was reaching into her purse. From the arched doorway, I saw Gerald Small moving fast, one arm raised as though he were hailing a taxi. Out of the corner of my eye, I also noted a dark blue jersey, number 08.

I landed the backpack directly on top of the woman's purse. The counter rattled.

"Oh!" She pulled her hand back.

Gerald Small was charging forward. "Listen! Listen! I just received—" He stopped. He saw the backpack sitting on the counter. "Oh my **God**!"

He lunged at the woman. Speedy little devil. The woman screamed. I whipped off the stupid glasses and grabbed at Small. The man was growling like a deranged terrier. He had the woman by the arm. She was clawing at his fingers. "Let me—"

I did the job for her, peeling the museum director's fingers off her arm.

"Freeze! Police!" The cop in the Giants jersey had his gun out and was holding it at arm's length, both hands wrapped firmly around the handle. **"Freeze!"**

It wasn't clear who he was barking at. The barrel of the gun was hopping stiffly between the terrified woman, the ballistic museum director and me. Behind the cop, people were scrambling for cover.

A second pistol appeared. An old snub-nose. Somehow, amid all the noise, the telltale **click** of its being cocked sounded very clearly. The sound seemed to echo off the stone walls. The pistol's barrel was three inches from the undercover cop's head. It didn't waver so much as a millimeter. Steady hand. Practiced hand.

"You'll lower it, or it's off to the angels with you," Jigs Dugan said calmly. "Count of three. That's one, two—"

The cop lowered it.

Jigs didn't. Not right away.

15

IF ONE MORE PERSON HAD TRIED TO squeeze into Gerald Small's tiny office, the floor would have buckled. It held three comfortably. Four in a pinch. Five was not going to float. I dispatched the undercover cop. He was the largest of the five, and from where I sat—on a corner of Gerald Small's desk—the most expendable. What he knew, I knew, and I knew more.

The cop still had a chip on his shoulder about being drawn on by wiry Jigs Dugan. Jigs was leaning against a file cabinet with his arms crossed, taunting the cop with his best Irish smirk. The cop swore under his breath as he lumbered out of the room.

"Okay. Now there's a little more oxygen for the rest of us," I declared.

The woman who had arrived with claim number 16 was seated in the office's only chair other than the one behind Gerald Small's desk, which was occupied by its owner. She sat erect, with her hands in her lap. Once all the artillery had been put away at the coat check, I'd cautioned her, "This is a police matter. I'm going to ask that you remain silent for the time being."

She repeated what had already become abundantly clear: "I'm confused by this whole matter."

Gerald Small was huffing and puffing like an old Stanley Steamer. **I demand to know this, I demand to know that. I will not put up with people waving guns all over my museum. This and this and that and that.** A wavering finger took aim at Jigs, along with a wavering voice. "Who is that man?"

I answered matter-of-factly, "He's a friend of mine. Francis Dugan."

Gerald Small sputtered, "He could have killed somebody."

I stole a glance at Jigs. "True. Or he could have saved somebody."

"Or both," Jigs threw in.

"I **demand** an explanation."

"Mr. Dugan is my responsibility," I said. "I asked him to come to the museum. Philip Byron knows nothing about him."

That was when Gerald Small delivered his provocative bombshell.

"Philip Byron is missing."

"Missing?" For no logical reason, I looked to the woman as if she might be able to offer some illumination. But unless she had mastered the Queen of All Poker Faces, she was as clueless as the chair she was sitting in. I turned back to Gerald Small. "Who says he's missing?"

"I got a phone call. I was coming down to tell you. Philip never showed up at that officer's funeral. His car was found on Fort Washington Avenue, not more than a quarter mile from here."

"Who called you?"

"The mayor himself."

The woman in the chair brought her fingers to her throat. "My goodness."

Small went on, "The mayor asked about the money. He wanted to know if it had been picked up."

The woman opened her mouth to speak, but I raised a silencing hand. I knew that this was exactly what Philip Byron would have wanted had he been here. Containment. Gerald Small knew as little as possible about why a million dollars had been delivered to his museum's coat-check room for pickup. **There is no record, Gerald.** Whatever the woman would have to say about why she had shown up with claim number 16 in her purse, I didn't want her blabbing it here.

The backpack was sitting next to me on the desk.

"Why don't you stow that somewhere?" I said to Small. "We'll be back for it." I slid off the desk.

Small stared at me as if I'd just spoken in a rare Senegalese dialect. "Where are you **going**?"

I turned to the woman. "May I have your name, please?"

"Mary Ryan."

"Mary Ryan and I are going to get some air."

Small was on the verge of full apoplexy. "I need to speak with my staff! I need to tell them what's happening!"

"Nothing is happening," I said. "The police were running an emergency drill. The museum was cooperating. The drill was a success. You may thank them for their professionalism."

"I **demand** to know what this is all about! Who is this woman? What is she planning to do with all this money?"

Jigs pushed away from the filing cabinet. "Do we need a muzzle on this hen?"

"But I don't—"

"Shut up."

I turned back to the woman. "Miss Ryan?"

She rose from her chair. "Or is it Mrs.?"

"It's Sister," she said.

I took a beat. "Sister?"

"That's right."

"You're a **nun**?"

She answered with a gentle tilt of the head. Next to the file cabinet, Jigs Dugan crossed himself with demon speed.

"Oh shit. JesusMaryMotherofGod . . ."

16

SISTER MARY RYAN ASKED IF SHE COULD pause for a private moment in the Fuentidueña Chapel just around the corner from the stairs. I was sure I'd be struck dead on the spot if I said no. The nun crossed herself at the chapel entrance, then stepped forward, bowing her head before taking a seat in one of the rigid wooden chairs.

"What do you think?" Jigs asked me.

I shrugged. "I suspect whatever she tells us will be the truth."

"I'm old-fashioned, Fritz. I like my nuns in costume, thank you. Your nuns start looking like everyday Joes, we'll have to be on our best behavior all the time, just to be safe."

According to a placard on the wall, the polygonal apse that made up the Fuentidueña

Chapel dated from the mid-twelfth century and had originally been part of the Church of Saint Martin in Segovia. Included in the chapel were twelfth-century friezes from San Baudelio de Belarga, also in Spain, as well as sculptures from Austria, Italy and the valley of the Meuse River, wherever that was. The room was narrow, the ceiling was high, the stone walls were cold to the touch.

Sister Mary Ryan spent several minutes in prayer. When she came out, the prayer seemed to have done her good. All the creases in her face had smoothed out. She looked as if a little lamp were illuminating her from the inside. I've seen a similar trick work with Jigs and a glass of Jameson's. The problem with Jigger's lamp is that it usually tips over and sets everything on fire.

"Thank you," Sister Mary Ryan said.

Across the Romanesque Hall from the chapel was one of the outdoor cloisters. In secular terms, a courtyard. A pair of paths intersected in the middle, at a stone fountain that was dry as a bone. Arched walkways bordered the courtyard. We settled on one of the low stone walls, in a final wedge of the fast-falling sun.

"I'm with the Convent of the Holy Order of the Sisters of Good Shepherd," the nun volunteered. "An envelope arrived at the convent this afternoon. That claim tag was in it."

I asked, "How was the envelope delivered?"

"That was the peculiar part. It was left in a basket at the front door."

"A basket?"

"A large basket. Like a bassinet, really."

"You mean like a baby basket?" Jigs asked. "Like if you were going to leave a baby on the front doorstep?"

"I suppose."

"Did someone ring the doorbell?" I asked.

"No, it wasn't like that. Sister Anne had come through the door not ten minutes before. She received a phone call from someone. A man. He told her that a package had been left at the front door. He called it a gift, actually, not a package. He said that with love, reverence and respect, he was making a gift to the convent."

"Those exact words?"

"He repeated them in the note."

"The note?"

"The note that was in the envelope along with the claim tag."

"Do you have the note with you?"

She opened her purse, pulled out a letter-size envelope and handed it to me. A GIFT was typed on the front in an all too familiar font.

"Did he say anything else to Sister Anne?"

"He said there was a gift. He said we shouldn't let anyone take it away from us. He was adamant on that point. It says the same thing in the note."

I unfolded the piece of paper.

Sisters—

In love, respect and reverence, a Gift awaits you. It is yours. This is my wish and decree. You need not allow anyone to talk you out of accepting it. Do not let them. It is yours. I want this for you. You are deserving. You are purity. You are endangered. I love you so much. Your Gift awaits you at the Cloisters. You will claim it with the enclosed claim check. Today. After three o'clock. Please be trusting. Please be swift. I am your lamb. From slaughter comes Grace. I am in tears with happiness over your Gift.

A Friend.

I read the note through twice and handed it to Jigs. I stared out at the dry fountain until he finished it.

"Fruit Loop," Jigs said.

Sister Mary turned to him. "Excuse me?"

"Your so-called friend, Sister." Jigs tapped a finger against his head. "He's got some of the pieces in the wrong place."

"What is this all about?" she asked.

I asked, "I can trust you to keep a secret?"

She smiled. "Vows of silence are our specialty."

"This is related to the business at the parade on Thursday."

"Those horrible shootings?"

"Yes. And the bomb at Barrymore's."

"My goodness."

"Mr. Dugan is right. Your 'friend' has his good and bad in a serious twist."

"How much money is this we're talking about?"

"A lot. There's a million dollars in that bag. I'd say that's a few new coats of paint for the old convent, wouldn't you?"

Her tone was hushed. "A million dollars."

"You understand that we have to hold on to that money," I said.

"May I?" She took the note from Jigs and read from it. " 'You need not allow anyone to talk you out of accepting it. Do not let them. It is yours.' " She looked over at me. "You are telling me not to accept this money for my convent."

"He's responsible for the killing of ten people, Sister. He made an orphan of a three-year-old boy. Others are still in the hospital. If you'll excuse my saying it, this money is dripping in blood."

She looked out toward the dry fountain. "Of course."

I checked my watch. It was nearly five. The museum was closing. The sun had dipped behind the slanted roof, and the temperature had dropped a good ten degrees. I reached for the note. The nun's hand was trembling.

"What is this all about?" she asked.

"We don't know, Sister."

"I must . . . We must pray for him. We must find forgiveness in our hearts."

She stood and walked over to the fountain. I couldn't quite tell, but it looked as if she dipped her hand into it, dry as it was.

Jigs looked over at me. He spoke in a low growl. "First we catch him and beat the living shit out of him. Then we'll worry about the forgiveness part."

———

BEFORE LEAVING THE CLOISTERS, SISTER Mary had requested that she be allowed a copy of the note. Gerald Small had photocopied it for her.

"We'll be in touch," I told her.

I phoned Margo on our way back to the city, but she didn't answer. I left her a short, silly message that apparently hit Jig's funny bone.

"You'd buy the moon for that girl, wouldn't you?"

I called Tommy Carroll on his cell phone, but he didn't answer either. I was dumped into voice mail. I left him a short message, too. Not as silly: "He didn't show. He sent a nun instead. She knows nothing. I've got the cash. Call me."

We stopped at Cannon's on Broadway at 108th. We brought the million dollars inside with us. Jigs was still disgusted with the yuppie makeover the place had undergone several years back. In our younger days, Jigs and I used to include Cannon's on our rounds. It always felt as if we were stepping into a cave. Now a new glass front let in so much light from the street that you couldn't find a dark corner if your life depended on it. Large-screen television sets hung all around the ceiling. Football, ice hockey, motocross, every sport in the book. The old tables had been replaced; no more knife scars and cigarette burns. The bar had been refinished. And with the city's recent no-smoking policies, you could actually see from one end of the room to the other. Time was at Cannon's, you'd pick up your darts and have to throw them into a fog.

Jimmy Reese still worked the bar. Except for the blue polo shirt with the Cannon's cloverleaf logo on it, Jimmy remained unrenovated. His tomato face was a psychedelic of burst blood vessels. Jimmy used to be a boxer. When I was a teenager, I saw him fight a handful of times. He had a peculiar sideways punch that became his signature. At a given moment in the round, he would abruptly shift so that he was standing next to and just a little behind his opponent. It was a sudden move, and when the opponent would start his turn to face Jimmy, the glove would come up. **Pop, pop.** Rabbit punches, but hard ones. Jimmy called them "nose poppers." He could do it from either side.

At Cannon's, especially late at night when he got talking, you'd see Jimmy go sideways behind the bar and feign a few of the punches. On the rare occasions when a real tussle broke out between patrons, he'd land them. They were still plenty hard. Jimmy Reese had stabbed his first wife during a domestic dustup. She lived—it was a superficial arm wound—but she set her two meaty brothers on him. Jimmy managed to KO one with his sideways punches, but the other one took a cast-iron pan to Jimmy's skull. When his hair started receding a few years ago, you could see the flat spot where the bone reset poorly.

Jimmy's second wife was named Shirley. That marriage lasted five years. Shirley referred to it as a "five-year food fight," which, frankly, is putting a soft spin on it. Though Jimmy never stuck a knife in **her** arm. Nice thing, right? Getting credit for not sticking a knife in your wife's arm? At the time of his marriage to Shirley, Jimmy had his hand, here and there, in what he referred to as "off-the-record business." **Something to keep the little lady in furs.** "Some furs," Shirley would say, modeling her thin cardigan. Shirley wasn't a prude about Jimmy's activities except when she wanted to be, which was usually during their yelling matches. Jimmy's marginal criminality was always Shirley's ace in the hole. To be more precise, it gave her the pretext for threatening to play her ace in the hole. "I've got connections!"

she'd shriek. "I could have you put away!" And it wasn't bluster. She did have connections. A certain police lieutenant rising swiftly through the ranks was only a phone call away. And Jimmy knew she'd make the call if she wanted to, because he'd already seen her do it. Not on his account, but on account of her teenage son, who wasn't always mixing in those days with the finest elements Hell's Kitchen had to offer. Jimmy had seen the police lieutenant answer one of those calls in particular. He'd seen him come down hard on the boy.

Shirley loved the cop. Jimmy knew that. Anyone who knew Shirley knew that. It was a fact-of-Shirley. She never pretended to hide it. Jimmy swallowed the lump for five years until one day he finally stuffed his duffel and moved out. I found him at Butch's Tavern that night, and he sang me a sad sloppy song about the toll it took on him to share Shirley's heart with a cop. He actually got a little blubbery at one point, which was embarrassing for both of us. I was only seventeen at the time. It was later in the evening, when Jimmy was back in the whiskey fire and getting sufficiently nasty about Shirley's cop, that it occured to me I didn't really want to be sitting right next to him at the bar. I was thinking about Jimmy's sideways punch. His nose popper. Luckily for me, his fist was mostly occupied in squeezing his dirty bar glass. But I'd seen the punch. I knew how quick it was. And already, at seventeen, I was shaping up to be my old man's spitting image. My old man the cop. The fast-rising one. There was no telling when Jimmy might finally look up from his fingers and see the enemy's face floating in the mirror behind the bar. Sitting right next to him. Perfectly positioned. **Pop, pop.**

"Trouble in twos," Jimmy crooned as he ran a cloth over the bar in front of Jigs and me. I nodded a greeting. Jigs did his John L. Sullivan imitation, his fists circling ludicrously. Jimmy smirked. "Look at the twig. Bare-bones champion."

Jigs brought a fist forward in slow motion and tapped it against Jimmy's chin. "Ha. Rang your bell."

"My bell, my ass." Jimmy tossed a pair of coasters on the bar. "What do you hear from your mother, Fritz? The two of you have a great big turkey on Thursday?"

"She's out in California," I said.

"California? What takes her to the Golden State? She breaking into the movies?"

"A friend of hers moved out there, swears

she died and went to heaven. Queenie thought she'd go out for a visit and get the lowdown on heaven."

"She's not thinking of moving out there?"

I shrugged. "Could be. But I wouldn't put money on it. Her roots are pretty firm in the local pavement."

"So what'll it be?"

We ordered a couple of beers, mine with a half-pound burger on the side. When Jimmy headed off to put in my order, Jigs pulled a cigarette from behind his ear.

"You can't smoke that in here," I reminded him. "They'll put you in Rikers."

He ran the cigarette under his nose like a Montecristo cigar. "They can't toss me out for fondling the damn thing."

The bar was half full. Half empty. A matter of perspective. Jigs eyed a pair of Columbia coeds who were at a table near the door, giggling. He tapped the end of his cigarette against his lips. "I'd trade this for that."

"That might land you in Rikers, too."

"Ah, they're old enough for Cannon's, they're fair game."

"I thought you set up a date with your friend from the Cloisters," I said.

"Right. Allison. Mustn't forget."

"Her friend thinks you're a creep."

Jigs's eyes sparkled. "She does, I know. I'd

give away a good tooth to pin that one. Anger like that can be a beautiful thing."

"You **are** a creep, Jigs."

He put the cigarette back behind his ear and gave another glance at the students. "Maybe I am," he said wistfully.

Our beers arrived.

"Your burger will be right out, Fritz," Jimmy said. "The cow put up a good fight." He took off again.

Jigs picked up his beer. "So what's that brilliant mind of yours telling you? Who do you suppose thought it would be fun to kill a bunch of people, then give a million dollars to a nun? Who comes up with an idea like that?"

I took Jigs's question into my beer. I didn't know what in the world I'd been thinking, expecting Nightmare to waltz into the Cloisters and pick up his loot. Even with his no-touch insurance policy in place, it would have been an absurd risk to take. Tommy Carroll was running around hanging video cameras and planting fake nannies on the street while I was flattening my feet all day in a fake mustache and glasses, and for all we knew, our creep could have been sitting snugly at home saying Hail Marys to dirty pictures the whole time. Red tie. Green tie.

Wisconsin. NOW THAT I HAVE YOUR ATTENTION. Okay. He got it. And it turns out he didn't even want the million bucks.

I watched as Jimmy mixed a martini for a guy in a baseball cap down at the other end of the bar. He chilled, he mixed, he shook, he poured. A martini at Cannon's. If God really were Irish, like they say, the joint would have been in cinders. Past the end of the bar, on the wall, was the pay phone. A chesty woman in a blue denim shirt was hollering in it above the bar noise.

"Shit," I said.

Jigs cocked his head. "Something good usually follows 'shit'."

"The money," I said. "The note made a specific point that the convent keep the money."

"If it were me calling the shots, I'd have gone halfsies with them."

"No. What I mean is, he wants the nuns to have the money, but they don't have the money."

Jigs rubbed his fingers absently along his scar. "We have the money."

"Maybe you haven't noticed. This guy expresses himself in bold statements."

"You mean he might not be happy if he finds out the sisters didn't get the money?"

"Right."

"And he might decide to express that un-happiness?"

"I need to talk to the nuns."

"You think he's going to check with them?"

"For all I know, he was spying on us when we left the Cloisters. If he was, he saw who was holding the bag and who wasn't."

Jigs toed the backpack. "That sister couldn't have lifted this bag if her life depended on it."

"Doesn't matter. The note made a point of it. So did his phone call. I could've carried the bag to her car for her. Or delivered it to the convent myself. Damn. We should have taken the money to her car and arranged a switch for later."

"Who knows, Fritz? Maybe he was planning to knock the nun over the head and steal the money. The guy's a loony bin. There's no telling where he's coming from."

I slid off the stool. "I'm going outside to call the convent. If this guy calls them to see if they got the money, I need them to say yes."

"You're going to ask a Daughter of Christ to lie?"

"It's for a good cause."

I went out to the sidewalk. There was nothing about the lights of upper Broadway worth writing a song about. I called Information on my cell phone and got a number for the Convent of the Holy Order of the Sisters of Good Shepherd. I dialed and asked to be put through to Sister Mary Ryan. While I waited, I kicked myself for not contacting Tommy Carroll from the Cloisters to have him place a tap on the convent's phone. The sister came on a minute later.

"Sister Mary? It's Fritz Malone."

"Mr. Malone. I was just going to call you."

"I need to ask if you—Why were you going to call me?"

"We just received a call," she said. "Sister Anne received it."

My heart sank. "From him?"

"He wanted to find out if we had received his gift."

"What did Sister Anne tell him?"

"She told him that we received his gift but under the circumstances, we could not possibly accept it. She asked if he would come to the convent and meet with her."

"She shouldn't say that. That is definitely not a good idea." A fire engine was tearing up Broadway, its siren blaring. I had to wait it out. When I could hear again, I said,

"I guess it doesn't matter. I assume he said no."

"No, no. That's just it, Mr. Malone. That's why I was about to call you. He said he would love to come by. We're expecting him any minute."

17

I CALLED TOMMY CARROLL'S CELL NUMBER as Jigs and I sped up the West Side Highway. Jigs's old Ford Fairlane swayed like a waterbed as he coasted from lane to lane.

Carroll picked up on the third ring. He answered snarling. "Where the hell have you been! Do you know what's going on? What the hell's this crap about a nun picking up the money?"

I gave him the short version. Jigs was leaning on his horn. A slow-moving car in front of us drifted to the other lane.

"Holy hell," Carroll muttered when I told him about Sister Anne's invitation to the killer. "What is she planning to do, serve him tea and hear his fucking confession?"

"We'll be there in eight minutes," I said.

Jigs looked over at me. "Six."

Carroll asked, "Who's we?"

"I've got Jigger Dugan with me."

"Jigger . . . That's just great, Fritz. How the hell did he enter the scene?"

"I brought him in. No offense, but I preferred having an independent contractor watch my back on this one. I didn't want to end up with another bag over my head."

"You've got Francis Dugan and a million dollars cash in the same car? You tell that punk he lays a fingernail on any of that—"

"You're breaking up," I said. I cranked the window partway down and stuck the phone into the wind for a few seconds. Jigs chuckled. I pulled the phone back in. "Do you want to weigh in with a plan, Tommy? We're almost in Riverdale."

"Philip Byron is missing."

"I heard. But that's not the point. What do you want me to do when I get to the convent?" This time the connection really did break up. "I missed that. Say it again."

"I said shoot to kill."

I took a beat. "You mean like with Diaz?"

Carroll exploded. "Now, **you** stick to the point, you prick! Leave Diaz out of this. If you confront this bastard and determine it's definitely him, you take him out!"

"Take him out? Not in? No citizen's arrest?"

"Out."

"If he's just sitting there talking to a nun, I'm sure as hell not going to waltz in there and shoot him. Are you nuts?"

Jigs glanced at me. "That's nuts." He swung into the right lane to take the next exit.

Carroll conceded. Not happily. "Okay, then, contain him. If he's already in the convent, let it stand. You and Dugan stake out the exits, then wait. I'm sending a blue-and-white up there. Give me the address. I'm coming up, too."

I gave him the address.

"Whatever the hell you do, do not let this guy slip away. If you've got a problem with it, you tell Dugan he's got my okay to take the bastard out. Dugan's got no problems with pulling a trigger. You tell the little mick he can dip his dirty paw into that bag of money if he gets this guy."

"I'm not telling him that, Tommy. We'll keep the creep from getting away, but that's it. And tell your boys not to come in roaring with the lights and sirens. We have no idea what kind of firepower he'll be bringing. I don't think you want a bunch of nuns being held hostage in their own convent. **That** is a nightmare."

"This ends tonight," Carroll grumbled. He hung up.

"What's the word from Super Cop?" Jigs asked as he pulled to the end of the ramp.

"He called you a punk."

"I've taken worse."

"He called me a prick."

"Man has a potty mouth, Fritz. Better keep him away from these lovely sisters."

THE CONVENT OF THE HOLY ORDER OF the Sisters of Good Shepherd was located midway down a residential block. It was between a pair of apartment buildings, set back from the street. There was a semicircular drive leading to the front door and a low metal fence delineating the property. As we crawled slowly past, I spotted playground equipment near the rear of the property. The ludicrous image of a nun on a slide popped into my head. I didn't share it with Jigs. Across from the convent was a block of low brick row houses. The street was dark except for an oyster light coming down from the moon. There wasn't a soul to be seen. It was as still as a photograph.

I told Jigs to swing around the block and

go down the parallel street behind the convent. I dialed the convent's number on my cell and asked for Sister Mary Ryan.

"Is he there?" I asked when she came on the line.

"Not yet."

"I'm circling the neighborhood. The police are on the way."

"Sister Anne has told me to let you know that she wants the opportunity to speak with this gentleman when he arrives. She is adamant about this, Mr. Malone."

This **gentleman.**

"This man is extremely dangerous, Sister. I don't think that's a good idea."

"Sister Anne suspected that's how you would feel. She insists. His overture was made to us. It is our duty to minister to the broken."

"With all due respect, it's my duty and the duty of the police to see that nobody else is harmed. It's possible that this guy has added kidnapping to his list of holiday activities, Sister. He's not well, you're right. But what he doesn't need is an opportunity to create more mayhem. You'd be acting on his behalf by letting us take him into custody."

"How do you plan on doing that, Mr. Malone?"

"I haven't actually gotten there yet," I admitted. "If the police arrive before he does, it's their game. What I'm saying is that this will all go down much easier and better if it happens outside your convent, not inside."

"Once he steps onto convent property, he is protected by the Church. We are a sanctuary."

I lowered the phone. "They want to give the creep sanctuary."

Jigs shook his head. "Nuns."

I returned to the phone. "Sister Mary? This guy is not dumb. He knows the police are in touch with you. If he told Sister Anne that he's coming over, then I can tell you it's one of three things. He's either lying; he's planning to turn himself in; or he's got something up his sleeve. If it's the first, none of this matters. He'll be a no-show. If it's the second, he might be combining it with the third. He might want to go out in a blaze of glory. Maybe he thinks that dying on holy turf will give him a handhold on the Pearly Gates. Who knows? Or maybe he has this same sanctuary idea in mind, in which case Sister Anne is playing right into his hand. What I'm saying is that the best thing for everyone is not to let him run the show anymore. We need to take over the controls."

"Just a moment."

She muffled the phone. I could hear her speaking with someone else. It sounded as if they were both underwater.

"Mr. Malone?" It was a different voice.

"Yes."

"Mr. Malone, this is Sister Anne Claire. I am the prioress of the Convent Good Shepherd. Naturally, we want to cooperate."

"I think that's the best attitude, Sister."

"Yes. However, you have your job and we have ours. This man has accepted an invitation from me. I gave it in good faith. I will not be party to a trap. I am a sister of Christ. We do not lie and we do not set traps. If this man arrives, I intend to meet with him. I intend to hear him out and to offer my perspective and guidance."

"Well, the fact is—"

She cut me off. "I have not trained for all these years so that I might turn away at a moment of testing. I have to assume that after he and I speak, I will be suggesting that he volunteer to turn himself over to the authorities. But I want a promise from you. This man will not be harmed, and he will not be detained when or if he shows up here. Not until after I have spoken with him. I ask you to give me your word."

Jigs had reached the end of the block. I signaled him to pull over. He snuffed the lights. There was a plastic Santa hanging off the top of the chimney of the house on the corner. The Santa was illuminated by a spotlight from the front yard. He looked like a cat burglar caught in the act.

I said into the phone, "This thing will be out of my hands when the police show up. Which should be any minute."

"Will you be in contact with them?"

"Possibly."

"Then you give me your word. You vouch for this man's safety and make whatever arrangements you need with the police."

"Sister Anne, I can give you my word until I'm blue in the face. But I have no control over the New York City Police Department."

"We have seen tragic things happen in this city between the police and people they were attempting to arrest."

"We have. But—"

"If I cannot get your word for my visitor's safety, Mr. Malone, I suppose I do have an alternative."

I didn't like the way she put that. "What's that?"

"I can alert the media right now. You tell me, would the illumination of the television media affect the proceedings?"

I held the phone to my chest. "She's thinking about calling in the cameras."

"Savvy sister."

I brought the phone back to my ear. "I have to remind you that you're going out of your way to protect a multiple killer."

"And who should need more protecting?" Before I could answer, I heard a faint sound in the background. The chimes of a doorbell. "I believe I have a visitor." There was an unmistakable smugness in the nun's voice. "I must go." She hung up.

I turned to Jigs. "Drive!"

Jigs's Fairlane lurched forward, screeching on the pavement and nearly hitting a parked car as it swung around the corner. I was thrown against the door as Jigs swung the large steering wheel again and we careened around the corner.

"Stop here!"

Jigs hit the brakes as I was shouldering open the door. I tumbled out and had to move my legs double-time to keep from falling. I crossed the lawn of the apartment building and headed for the fence that bordered the property. Beyond the fence, I could see a figure standing under the light at the convent's front door.

I reached the fence still unseen. I climbed

over it as quietly as I could and hit the ground in a crouch. The figure at the door still hadn't seen me. He was about a hundred feet away. I yanked out my gun and sprang out of the crouch. I thought about calling out. I thought about taking aim at his knees. I was running at full speed when the door opened and the figure stepped forward and disappeared inside. The door closed. He was gone. I slid to a halt on a pile of damp leaves. I surfed them a good six feet.

18

I MADE MY WAY ALONG THE SIDE OF THE building. The ground-floor windows were dark and, in any case, were set too high to be of any help. Near the back of the building was a smaller window that was giving off a flat, harsh light. I spotted a copper kettle hanging from a wooden rack. Rounding the corner, I froze. A shadowy figure was at the back door, dropping a bulging black plastic bag into a garbage can.

I hissed, "Sister!"

"Oh!"

A wedge of light shone through the partially open door. I hated to do it, but I stepped into the light so she could see my gun.

"Oh!"

"I'm with the police," I hissed. "I'm sorry to scare you. I need to get inside. Quietly."

The woman nodded. I stepped into the kitchen and she followed. She was in a blue and white habit. She was olive-skinned, with gentle Asian features, and looked hardly old enough to vote. Cheeks like a chipmunk's. Her eyes were wide, staring at my gun as she sidled up next to a wooden stool.

"I need to know where the prioress would greet visitors," I said.

Her voice was barley above a whisper. "In the Great Room."

"How do I get there?"

She pointed at a door. "You go through the dining room. The Great Room is just past it, on the left."

"I'm going to have to ask you to stay here," I said. "How many other people are in the building?"

"We have fourteen residents."

I indicated the wooden stool. "Sit."

She scurried onto the stool like her life depended on it.

I WAS HALFWAY THROUGH THE LONG DINing room when my cell phone went off. I yanked it from my pocket. I wanted to smack it silly. It was Tommy Carroll.

"Where the hell are you?" he snapped.

I answered in a whisper. "I'm inside the convent."

"What?"

"The convent. I'm inside."

"What's happening?"

"The prioress is with a visitor. I'm on my way to eavesdrop."

"He's **there**?"

"Somebody's here." The long rough wood table where the nuns ate looked like something from the Cloisters, which is to say, from around the twelfth century. A large candle was burning in an iron holder in the middle of the table. Its flame was casting fidgety shadows on the walls. I asked Carroll, "Where are you now?"

"I'm a block away from the convent."

"Are you alone?"

"There's a cruiser here with me. I've got a uniformed. We're coming in."

"No. Just hold on. Send the cruiser down to the far end of the block. You stay where you are. He's essentially trapped. You keep your cell phone clear, and I'll call you if he's coming out."

"What are you planning to do?"

"Just plug up the street, Tommy."

"Don't you fucking tell me what to do."

"If you want a full-scale assault on a nunnery, go right ahead. I should warn you, the prioress has already made noises about calling in the media."

"Where's Dugan?"

"He's out there. Ford Fairlane."

"Where's the money?"

"With Jigs."

"Jesus Christ."

"I'm hanging up. I'll call you back. Five minutes tops."

I set the phone to vibrate and made my way to the dining room door, my gun at the ready. I moved out of the dining room and into a hallway. At the end of the hallway was the front door. From the room to my left, I could hear talking. I edged forward. The voice doing all the talking was a female's. Sister Anne.

". . . to thank you for coming. If you'd sit tight while I give our friend a call . . ."

A shadow passed over the buttery light at the same instant that I spotted a telephone sitting on a small table only a few feet from where I was standing. A second later, a woman stepped into the hallway. She spotted me and let out a cry. "Who are you?"

I ran past her into the room. A man with stringy hair and a patchy beard was already rising to his feet.

"Don't move!"

But move he did. He darted to his left and out of the room. I turned and sprinted back into the hall with the idea of drawing on him there. But I hadn't factored in the woman. As I ran from the room, we collided. She went down with a high soprano yelp. At the end of the hallway, the man was yanking open the front door.

"Stop!"

I took aim, but he was already out the door. I jumped over the woman and ran for the door.

He was angling across the grass toward the street. I took off. A fast-moving car braked to a halt in front of the convent, and the driver's door flew open. The guy swerved and changed direction, running toward the rear of the convent. Tommy Carroll lumbered from the car. His gun was out. I saw a small flash; the shot sounded a half-second later. His bullet clanged off the metal fence.

Carroll grumbled, "Son of a **bitch.**"

Our prey dashed into the darkness behind the convent. I followed some fifty feet behind, but his fuel was fear, which is the swiftest. As I raced past the rear kitchen door, I spotted someone coming around the far corner of the building. It was Jigs. He angled into the darkness behind the convent. An instant later, I heard a **thud,** followed by what sounded like a rattling of chains. Then I heard Jigs's voice, the low, deadly version.

"You can move, brother. Or you can live. Those are your choices."

Then I heard the cocking of his pistol.

THE GUY WAS ON THE GROUND, ON HIS back. One of his legs was slung over a swing-set seat, the chain curled around his foot. Jigs was next to him, on one knee. The barrel of his gun was pressed right where the man's eyebrows met. Amazingly, Jigs was smoking a cigarette. He must have been running with the thing dangling from his lips. Jigs looked up at me, squinting through the smoke.

"What say, Fritz? Should he stay or should he go?"

In the faint moonlight, the man's complexion already looked like that of a corpse. His eyes were wide in pure panic. They were the only part of him that dared move. Before I could answer, Tommy Carroll ran up to us. He stopped short. He hadn't heard Jigs's question, but that didn't seem to make a difference. He glanced at me, raising an eyebrow.

"He's unarmed," I said.

Carroll was fighting to catch his breath. "That can be fixed."

"Like with Diaz?"

I didn't even see the fist. It might have been a Jimmy Reese special. **Pop!** My jaw took the jolt. A flash of light split my vision and I backpedaled several steps to keep my balance. I hit one of the swing-set poles and grabbed hold of it. The chains danced.

"Let him up," I said to Jigs.

Another figure had appeared from the front of the building. It was a policeman. I recognized him.

"What's up here?"

Carroll answered, "It's fine. Get back to your car. Just wait there."

Officer Leonard Cox retreated. Not before he and I had traded a look. Not a terribly chummy one. I ran a sleeve across my mouth. A little blood. "Cox, huh? It's nice to know we've got a bona fide hero so close."

"Shut up," Carroll snarled.

Jigs tossed his cigarette aside. He removed his pistol from the terrified guy's head and slipped it into his belt. He grabbed hold of the guy's collar. "Get your feet under you, mate." With a swift yank, he lifted him from the ground. He reached into the man's pants pocket and pulled out a wad of twenties.

Holding him as if he might fall over otherwise, Jigs ran a quick check over the rest
of him.

"He's clean."

Tommy Carroll stepped forward and
showed that he had more than one punch in
him. He landed this one right in the guy's abdomen. This time the guy really would have
fallen if Jigs hadn't been holding him.

I started, "Tommy—"

A light came on, casting the scene in harsh
yellow. We all froze.

"Mr. Malone?"

Standing at the rear door was the woman I
had tumbled into in the hallway. Next to her
stood Sister Mary Ryan. The young nun was
there, too, along with three other nuns, each
in blue and white habits. The woman I had
tumbled into was standing with her arms
crossed.

We were outnumbered.

HIS NAME WAS GARY HARVEY. HE HAD RE-
cently been fired from his job doing road
maintenance for the city. It's not easy to fire a
city worker, but apparently Harvey had managed to make it happen. To begin with, he
chewed drugs like they were candy; we found

a baggie on him with an impressive assortment. Harvey didn't even seem to know what the different pills and capsules were, nor did he seem to care. He looked at the baggie as if it were his cherished child.

Harvey was not our man. Twice in one day, our man had sent a messenger: first the nun, now this guy Harvey, who knew nothing. Harvey told us he'd been approached in a bar near Yankee Stadium by a man he could describe only as "quiet." Carroll asked him what he meant by that.

"Quiet," Harvey repeated. "Spoke in this real soft voice. Almost like a whisper. You could barely see his lips move."

I pressed. "But what did he **look** like? White? Black? Hispanic?"

"Puerto Rican, I guess," Harvey said. "It's dark in the bar, you know? I wasn't, like, staring at him."

Carroll looked up beseechingly at the ceiling. "Jesus Christ." Sister Anne made a face.

Harvey said that after a few drinks, the "quiet" man asked if he wanted to make a little money. He had a package he wanted delivered. He would pay Harvey two hundred dollars to deliver it to an address in Riverdale. Harvey told us that he had negotiated for taxi fare above and beyond the two hundred. He seemed proud of this fact. His instructions were to not simply leave the package at the door but to deliver it personally. He was told that he would be invited inside.

"He told me to ask for a glass of wine," Harvey said.

Indeed, a half-empty glass of red wine sat on the table next to the chair where Harvey had been sitting when I'd rousted him from the room.

Tommy Carroll drilled him with several dozen questions about the quiet man. Had Harvey ever seen him before? Was there anything distinctive about the clothes he was wearing? Harvey told us that the man wore a wool watch cap. Dark blue. Or black. Maybe dark green. He said he was wearing aviator sunglasses.

"What about his hair?" Carroll asked. "Did it stick out from the cap? Long? Short? Kinky? Give us something, goddammit."

Harvey couldn't remember if any of the guy's hair had poked out from under the watch cap or, if so, anything particular about it.

"Doesn't matter," I said. "It could have been a wig. Face it, Tommy, the guy was invisible."

Carroll agreed. He was also disgusted. He

glared at Harvey, who was glaring at the half-finished glass of red wine. "This scum knows nothing." Carroll called Leonard Cox inside. Cox and I exchanged another cool look. Carroll instructed Cox to take Harvey back to the bar where he had encountered the guy in the watch cap. "Ask around. Put the jitters in the owner. Lean on the bartender. You know the routine. See if there's anyone who can give us anything useful."

Harvey went off with Cox. Carroll turned to Sister Anne, who had been sitting in an upholstered chair at the far end of the room. "I'd like to see that package, Sister."

Sister Anne had already opened the shoe-box-sized package. It hadn't exploded. That was the good news. Inside the box was a smaller box. It was addressed simply: ML. Carroll looked at me and nodded. Martin Leavitt.

"We need to take this with us," Carroll announced. "We've got to get the crime lab on it."

Sister Anne narrowed her eyes, but she nodded. "I understand."

Carroll cleared his throat. "We're in the middle of an ongoing investigation here. I'm sorry I can't give you the details at this point, but I'm going to ask for your cooperation in keeping all this to yourselves for the time being."

Outside, he muttered, "I want to see what the hell this is."

"Do you want my guess? It's nothing that's going to make you happy," I said. "This guy is all about pulling our chain. This is all one big sick joke to him."

Jigs offered, "Maybe it's a hand buzzer."

We took the package to Carroll's car. He set it on the hood and opened it.

Jigs was wrong. It wasn't a hand buzzer.

I was right. It didn't make Tommy Carroll happy.

19

I FLIPPED OFF MY CELL PHONE AND SET IT down on the table next to my plate.

"Confirmed. The prints are Philip Byron's."

Margo's chin was in her hand. Her other hand was holding her fork. She was letting the tines drop onto her bacon like a slow-motion jackhammer. Her appetite was gone.

"Everyone already knew," she said.

"They did. Now it's official."

"Horrible." She let the fork drop again. "Incredibly horrible."

She was right.

It was an index finger and a pinky. Severed. Bound together by coarse brown twine into the shape of a cross. In case there was any mistake about the intended shape, the nail of the index finger had been scrawled on: a crude happy face in red ink. That's what had been in the package that Gary Harvey had delivered to the Convent of the Holy Order of the Sisters of Good Shepherd. Even Jigs Dugan had gotten a chill.

No note. No new demands. No new hoops to jump through. Everyone was waiting. It would come.

Something would come.

Philip Byron's disappearance—his abduction—was under wraps. He had not made his appearance at the McNally funeral the day before. The police commissioner had ordered officers in the Washington Heights precinct to be on the lookout for Byron's car. It had been found where he parked it to meet me at the entrance to Fort Tryon Park. Martin Leavitt immediately imagined the worst. Since he was now in possession of a crude bloody crucifix made of two of his deputy's fingers, those fears had plenty of currency.

He was waiting.

Margo's eyes were darker than usual. "Let's go to Mexico."

"Okay. Where in Mexico would you like to go?"

"Anywhere."

"Coastal? The interior? You want ruins?"

"All of it. Any of it. Let's just go."

"Okay."

"Let's leave tonight."

I picked up my coffee mug and took a sip. "I'm Superman. I'll be fine."

"Superman's a jerk. He's loaded with personal problems."

"Batman, then. There's a real head case."

"Don't change the subject."

"Is the subject still Mexico?"

Margo set her fork down on her plate and looked across the table at me. "The subject is, my skin is crawling. What kind of person does a thing like that?"

"One with personal problems," I said. "A head case."

"Batman?"

"You see? It's all the same subject."

"Mexico." She rapped her finger against the table. "I'm calling a travel agent while you clean up."

"I'm not in the mood to clean up."

"Don't you want to do anything to please me?"

"Of course I do."

"Like what?"

I got up from the table. "There's no need to go all the way to Mexico." I came around to her side of the table. I cupped her elbow in my hand, and she rose like a feather on a draft. We stood a moment, saying nothing.

"You're a head case," she whispered, and touched her nose to my chest.

Her arm around my waist, she leaned precariously sideways and switched off the coffee machine on our way out of the kitchen. No chance I was going to let her fall.

TOMMY CARROLL WANTED ME TO MEET with Remy Sanchez. I saw him in his office at Midtown North.

"You heard about the fingers?" Sanchez asked before I had even taken a seat. He was standing at the window, tweezering the slats of his venetian blinds, peering out the window. He looked weary.

"I saw them."

"No shit. You saw them, huh? I missed that detail." He released the blinds and looked over at me. "I seem to be missing a lot of details these days."

I shrugged.

Sanchez frowned. "Cat got your tongue?"

"No. I just don't know what to tell you. If there's a big picture, I'm not seeing it, either. Just these little pieces."

"The commissioner wants me to fill you in

on Roberto Diaz. He wants me to empty the bucket right into your lap. Why do you suppose that is?"

"Why don't you ask him?"

"I did. I thought it might be fun to get your answer and his answer and see how well they fit together."

"That's your idea of fun?"

"When pieces don't fit together, the truth is usually in the cracks between them."

"That's too long for a fortune cookie," I said. "Did you make that up yourself?"

Sanchez turned back to the window. He fingered the venetian blinds again, then dipped his head to peer though the slats. Something caught his attention. "Do you know what a white shadow is, Malone?"

"A white shadow. No. I don't."

He peered a few seconds more through the blinds, then released them. "A white shadow is when something is off. It's when something out there is not quite the way it's supposed to be. It's close, but it's off. It's not throwing down the right kind of shadow."

"I see."

"There's a white shadow all over the crap that's gone down these past couple of days. Something's not right, I'm just not sure if my giving a damn is worth it." He pulled back his squeaky desk chair and dropped into it. He ran a hand carefully along his hair. It was glistening, with deep comb grooves. "My wife tells me I need to do a better job of picking my battles. She says life's too short."

"What battle are we talking about here, Captain?"

"I'm not sure. I guess that's the problem."

"I wish I could help you. But I'm just going in the direction people point me."

"Somehow I don't believe that. But okay." He fiddled with his wedding ring. "I guess we've all got a job to do." He released the ring and clapped his hands together. "Let's spread Mr. Diaz out on the table, shall we?"

ROBERTO TOMAS DIAZ HAD BEEN BORN IN San Juan, Puerto Rico, and moved to New York City when he was nineteen. A few years later, he married a Gabriella Rodriguez, who worked at the time as a dispatcher for a car-service company called FastCar, located on Flatbush Avenue in the Fort Greene section of Brooklyn. Diaz took a job driving for Fast-Car, which he held for just under two years. During this time, Gabriella became pregnant and took a leave of absence. On his way to drop off a customer at La Guardia Airport one afternoon, Diaz rolled the car he was driving. No one was seriously injured, but the customer sued, alleging driver negligence. He claimed to have seen Diaz taking a drink from a liquor bottle. A half-empty bottle of peach brandy was found at the accident scene, but there had been no way to determine if it belonged to Diaz. At the trial, Diaz spit on the customer, for which the judge held him in contempt of court and commanded him to jail for twenty days. FastCar lost the suit and fired Diaz. A month later, the customer was jumped by two men as he was returning to his apartment around eleven o'clock at night. He was beaten severely with a pipe. Both assailants wore ski masks. Before running off, one of the two attackers lifted his mask and spit on the victim. Gabriella Diaz swore to investigating officers the following day that she and her husband had been home together going through a baby book, picking out potential names for the unborn child. Diaz himself had produced the book and pressed it on the officers, showing them the different names that were circled. His behavior had been judged by one of the officers as "extremely hyper."

The mugging went unsolved.

Diaz held several different part-time jobs

while his wife was pregnant. After the baby— a girl they named Rosa—was born, Gabriella went back to work at FastCar, leaving the baby with her mother during her shifts. Diaz came by the dispatcher's office from time to time, just to hang around. Gabriella's boss told him he was not welcome, and on one occasion a fight nearly broke out. When two of the company's vehicles were vandalized soon after—obscenities spray-painted all over them, tires slashed—Gabriella was let go. It wasn't a week later that the police answered a domestic-disturbance call and found Gabriella Diaz bleeding from a gash in her forehead and baby Rosa on the floor with her crib inverted, shrieking and crying. Stripped to the waist and sweating profusely, Roberto Diaz had told the responding officers that his wife had hit her head falling in the shower. The officers noted that Gabriella's hair was dry, as was the bathtub when they checked. They also noted that blood from the wound had spotted the blouse Gabriella was wearing, but was presumably not wearing when she took her alleged tumble in the shower. The police discovered an ironing board set up in the kitchen, but the iron was nowhere to be seen. When asked, Gabriella told the police that the iron was broken, so she had thrown it away. When? The day before, she said. The officers put her down as a bad liar. Bad and scared.

No charges were filed.

The divorce came through less than a year later. Gabriella had found a new job with a company that cleaned office buildings after hours. Her schedule allowed her to spend time with Rosa during the day and to be away from her husband for a large part of the evening. Diaz had a job at that point, spotty work with a moving company. At nights he went to the bars. His daughter stayed with her grandmother until Gabriella came by after work to pick her up and take her home.

One evening Gabriella was vacuuming the corridor of a law office near Borough Hall when her husband appeared with a woman on his arm. The two were clearly stoned. The woman was in a skimpy hot-pink dress and wore a tattoo of a rose on her upper arm. Diaz referred to the woman as his girlfriend and demanded that Gabriella show the woman where the bathroom was. Gabriella pointed her in the right direction, and the woman sashayed down the corridor. An argument broke out between Gabriella and Diaz. One of the lawyers who had been working late responded to the hubbub in time to see

Diaz swinging the hard plastic part of the vacuum-cleaner hose like a baseball bat, right into Gabriella's mouth. The lawyer intervened and was met with enough violent swings of the hose that he required medical attention.

The lawyer's services for Gabriella Diaz's divorce proceedings were conducted completely pro bono. Alimony, for what it was worth. No child visitation. A restraining order. Diaz emerged from his five-month prison term for assault a single man and, if possible, an angrier one.

"THAT TAKES US UP TO A YEAR AGO," SAID Remy Sanchez, squaring a small stack of papers on his desk and setting them to the side. "Since that time, he was quiet as a mouse. He got the apartment in Fort Greene and seems to have kept pretty much to himself. We netted one complaint from a female resident of his apartment building who said Diaz used to leer at her whenever he saw her, but that's about it. He got the job with Delivery on Demand and held it until about a month ago."

"What were the conditions of his leaving?"

"The company didn't want to say at first.

But apparently, Diaz had been opening the packages he was delivering."

"Nosy?"

Sanchez shook his head. "Paranoid. Remember how Son of Sam said his neighbor's dog was telling him to go out and kill pretty girls on lovers' lanes? Well, Diaz didn't have a dog, but according to one of his coworkers, he was convinced that the packages he was delivering contained coded messages meant specifically for him."

"So Diaz was receiving messages from packages he was delivering."

Sanchez shrugged. "That's how it is with some of them. A nut job in Minneapolis had cereal boxes telling him to kill prostitutes and cut off their feet—you remember that one? He had a whole refrigerator full of them. First thing he did when the police found the feet was ask the cops to wear gloves when they handled them! He didn't want the police getting their grubby hands all over them. He had cleaned them all with peroxide. Just like the cereal boxes told him to."

"So that would have been Diaz's defense? 'Aliens were writing me secret messages telling me to shoot up the Thanksgiving parade'?"

"Commissioner Carroll wants you to put it together," Sanchez said. He emphasized "you." He made no effort to hide how he felt about it. "On this end? Diaz shot up the parade. Diaz is dead. Case closed."

"And you're wondering why Carroll is putting a freelancer on the trail of a closed case."

"I'm wondering if I should wonder," Sanchez said.

"White shadow."

"I'm not an idiot, Malone. I know damn well the parade shooting is mixed up with the bomb at Barrymore's. And now we've got Philip Byron's fingers coming to us in a box. And we're keeping quiet about it. This is all real bullshit. Give me the force your old man ran any day." He balled his hands together and tapped his knuckles against his lips. "Yeah. There's a white shadow, hombre. No doubt about it. All I can tell you, Malone, is to be careful. You step into a white shadow, guess what?"

"Tell me."

"You disappear."

20

I met Elizabeth Scott for lunch at Ouest. She was sitting at a table in the back room, next to the window, working on a Bloody Mary. She looked fuzzy. Her hair. Her eyes. Even the set of her clothes. I told her so. She's my half sister, we can lay things out fairly straight.

"You look fuzzy."

"Very perceptive, Fritz. That's exactly how I'm feeling."

"Rough night?"

"I've had rougher."

I took a seat. "How are the Bloodies?"

"Soothing. Stingy."

The waitress appeared. Her blond ponytail danced as if it were on a spring. I pointed at Elizabeth's glass. "One of those."

The waitress took off. Elizabeth's eyes followed as she took another sip of her drink.

"She's cute," I said.

Elizabeth cocked an eyebrow. "You want to arm-wrestle for her?"

"Take her," I said. "I'm loyal to the court of Princess Margo."

"Of course you are. So what's the scrabble there, anyway? Are you ever going to make an honest woman of that girl?"

"Maybe yes, maybe no."

"She's not pushing for it?"

"Her mother married a private eye. She doesn't want to be her mother."

Elizabeth made a face. "Who does?"

"I don't think you really have to worry about that," I said.

"Oh? Why's that?"

"Where would you like me to start?"

She put a finger to her lips. "Let's see. Phyllis starves herself so she looks like Audrey Hepburn, while I like a nice bloody steak every once in a while?"

"Okay. That works."

"She took a perfectly nice Jewish nose and had it whittled down to an afterthought, while I happen to be rather fond of my own lovely battering ram?"

"You exaggerate."

My Bloody Mary arrived. Elizabeth reached across the table and tapped my glass. "May the wind always blow you down. Or whatever that is."

I took a sip. Soothing. Stingy. Just like the lady said.

The brunch menu included a salmon-and-goat-cheese omelet. I ordered it along with a side of toast. The food arrived in under five minutes. Elizabeth took two bites of her eggs Benedict and moved on to my toast.

"I can call the cute waitress back and order some more toast," I said.

"Fritz, do I look like a girl with any flirt left in her this morning?"

"It's afternoon," I reminded her.

"Oy."

"Just trying to be helpful."

The restaurant was full, but unlike a lot of places, it handled sound well. An acceptable level of murmuring and occasional laughter. High ceilings, that was a lot of it. Except for the window tables, most of the seating was large plush red banquettes. It was a relatively new restaurant in the relatively restaurant-starved Upper West Side. The room was warm; the window next to me was dappled with moisture up to the table line. It brought a thin chill to my leg.

While we ate, we shot the breeze. Elizabeth shoots it better than most, even when she's nursing a hangover. As I finished my omelet, she was doodling a face with her finger in the moisture on the window.

I asked, "Anyone I know?"

"My du jour du jour."

"Not bad."

"No," she said, smiling prettily. "Not at all."

"Okay," I said, draining my Bloody Mary. "Let's get to it. What the hell do we know about what's going on with Paul? His wife and his mother think it's an affair. Does his sister?"

"Honestly, Fritz, why do you bother?"

"Phyllis says someone beat him up."

"So his affair is with a married woman, and the hubby got wise. Don't you watch your soap operas?"

"I told your mother I'd snoop. She seems worried. Don't ask me why, but I've always trusted Phyllis's instincts. So what can you tell me? Is it a rocky marriage? Linda has been like a ghost to me the few times I've met her. I don't get a reading."

"Linda doesn't exactly set the world on fire. But then neither does Paul. Should be a perfect couple, right?"

"Are they?"

"I honestly don't know. Maybe they've been having some troubles. It seems like every marriage does. Paul wouldn't exactly confide that sort of thing to me even if it was happening."

"Any idea who he might confide it to?"

"Not Le Phyllis, that's for sure."

"So what do we have? Two kids. Nice apartment in Murray Hill. I assume there're no major money problems."

"God love a trust fund."

"What's Paul's latest job venture?"

"The vocation-phobic Paul? Let's see. This week I believe it's fund-raising. Unless I'm already behind."

"Fund-raising for what?"

"It's a company you hire to help you with your fund-raising. I guess they write grant proposals, help organize parties, shake down corporations for contributions. Paul's managed to get himself on the boards of a couple of nonprofits around the city. He likes that sort of thing. He's a prestige freak, as you know."

"As I know."

"He hits me up for contributions. He hits up our mother. He hits up her friends. I guess it makes him think he's a real pro at fund-raising. Who knows, maybe he is. Maybe he's finally found his calling. High-end handouts. Though it's not the sort of thing that would have made Daddy proud: It's not what he would have considered manly work. I guess Paul is doomed to never figure that one out."

"It's been fifteen years. There's no Daddy to be proud or not proud about anything."

She held up a hand. "Tell it to Paul. He's the one stuck under the shadow. After all, he's always saying there's that one chance in a million that Daddy's still out there somewhere."

I let this pass. This was Elizabeth's fantasy every bit as much as she was saying it was her brother's. Which isn't to say I haven't woken in a full sweat myself a number of times over the years, thinking I'd just heard the old man's voice. Or felt the presence of his shadow in my room. That's the stuff ghosts are made of.

I pulled out my notebook. "What's the name of this company Paul's with?"

"It's called Futures Now." I jotted it down. Elizabeth asked, "Do you think he's having an affair with someone at work?"

I shrugged. "High percentage. It's either work, friends or from something else he does on a regular basis. That's your standard affair pool. I don't see him as the random-bar-pickup type."

"No. Not our Paul."

I put away the notebook. "I'll nose around. I'd go right to the source and ask, but he'd just lie to me. The way Paul feels about me, I could ask him his shoe size and he'd lie. But if he's fooling around, I'll get the name. I'll give it to your mother. She'll know what to do with it."

Elizabeth picked up her glass. "Nasty business you're in, Brother Malone."

I thought about a pair of severed fingers bound up in twine and delivered to a nunnery.

Nasty. To the extreme.

GABRIELLA DIAZ WAS NO LONGER GABRIella Diaz. She was Gabriella Montero. Mr. and Mrs. Montero lived in a brownstone in the Kensington section of Brooklyn, off the south side of Prospect Park. Their apartment was on the first floor. No one answered the buzzer. The buzzer for the second floor said ALVAREZ. I tried it. After a few seconds, the intercom crackled. "**Hello? Who's it?**"

I pulled a piece of paper from my notebook and held it close to the intercom and crumpled it.

"**What? Who's that?**"

I crumpled the paper again and muttered "Mungamumma" into the intercom. The door clicked. I pushed it open.

The front hallway was dark and carried a stale minty smell. A large mirror above a covered radiator offered me a chance to look at myself, but I didn't take it.

Up the stairs, a creaky door opened. A voice called out, "Who's there!"

I started up the stairs. The squawky tune they played, I might have been stepping on a succession of cats. A woman with a Medusa of salt-and-pepper dreadlocks caught up in a green bandanna was standing in a doorway at the top of the stairs. The tin sounds of a television program leaked out from her apartment. She was in a flower-print muumuu with her arms crossed tightly on her chest. I stopped three steps from the top. Such was her power.

"What do you want?" The voice was dark, with an island lilt.

"You're Mrs. Alvarez," I said.

She scowled. "Don't tell me what I know. Tell me what I don't know. Who are you?"

"My name is Fritz Malone. I'm looking for Gabriella Montero."

Some sort of voodoo pulsed in her eyes. "Get out."

"But I'm—"

"Get out!" She pointed down the stairs. "She don't need any more of you, Gabby don't. You leave this girl alone. No more. She can't be happy? You stop now. You go!"

"Mrs. Alvarez, I need to—"

"I tell you to go! No comment." She said it a second time, wagging her finger. "Nooooo comment. She does not see the bad man for many many year. She is married again. You can leave her alone. You quote **me.** I say, no comment. All those beautiful souls that bad man killed. It is horrible. Get out."

"I—"

She bent sideways and groped with her other hand just inside the doorway. As she straightened, she was joined by a long double-barreled shotgun that she hitched snugly under her large arm. The twin barrels drifted up several inches until their aim was approximately at my nose. The barrels were as dark as night. Ugly black. A grimace tugged at the sides of the woman's mouth.

"If I am not speaking loud enough, my friend can speak louder, okay? I mean this. I got no patience with you monkeys." She shook the gun.

I had my hands out, showing her my palms. You do it without even thinking. I kept my voice steady. "Mrs. Alvarez. Listen. I'm not with the press. I'm not a reporter."

The black barrels traveled a small circle. "Who are you?"

"I'm here on police business," I said. Not completely a lie.

Her eyes narrowed. "You are police?"

"Yes." The lie.

Her dreadlocks shook. "No. The police have been here. Gabby has spoken to the police. You are a reporter. You are another hungry monkey. I know the tricks. The girl knows nothing. You make her cry."

"I'm not a reporter, Mrs. Alvarez," I said again. "Put the gun down. Please."

The barrels drifted up to my eyes. "Who are you? Prove you are police."

"I am reaching for my wallet," I said. Gingerly, I reached into my jacket and pulled out my wallet. I flipped it open to my private investigator's license. Five good seconds would tell a person that the license had nothing remotely to do with the New York City Police Department, but I didn't give the woman the full five. Her gaze locked on to the license as I climbed the final three stairs. I held the wallet high, and as her gaze followed it, I reached out with my other hand and grabbed hold of the shotgun barrel, twisting it and yanking it from her grip.

"What!"

I dropped my wallet, broke open the shotgun and unchambered a pair of yellow shells. I picked at the end of one and turned it upside down. Fine granules drifted out. "What's this?" I demanded.

The disarming had punctured the woman's chutzpah. From the television inside the apartment came a burst of laughter. "Is sand," she said dejectedly. "I will not kill you."

"Do you have a license for this firearm?"

"It is lost. But I have it."

I resnapped the stock and barrel and leaned the shotgun against the wall. I made a point of pocketing the shells. I picked up my wallet from the floor and put it back in my pocket. "All those beautiful souls, Mrs. Alvarez. It's my job to find out why Gabriella's ex-husband killed them. We want them to rest in peace now, don't we?"

"Yes." A six-year-old had more volume.

I gave her my best smile. "Okay. So, as you were saying. About Mrs. Montero."

THE LITTLE GIRL WAS SHRIEKING WITH DElight each time the swing sailed forward and up. There was no chance of her falling off; the swing seat was a black rubber diaper that came up well past her waist. The man standing behind the swing was slightly built, with black curly hair and a closely trimmed mustache. He was wearing a gray jacket, a tie loosened at the neck. He appeared to be enjoying himself as much as the little girl was. There was nothing in the child's face to suggest that she was in any way burdened with the knowledge that three days ago her father had gunned down more than a dozen people at the Thanksgiving Day parade, killing nine of them, or that he had then been killed himself by a bullet to the head on the eighteenth floor of the Municipal Building. Nothing. Nada. The little girl was wearing white shoes, pale blue socks and a navy blue coat. Her shrieks sounded like a miniature police siren.

I stood next to the slide and watched for a few minutes. Sitting on a bench ten feet away from the swing set was Gabriella Montero. She was a small woman. She was clutching a large bouquet of flowers, her forearms resting lightly on an extremely pregnant belly. As Mrs. Alvarez had described. She was pretty. Dark hair, dark eyes, olive skin, full cheeks. I'd been standing at the slide maybe half a minute when her gaze started bouncing between her daughter and me. Her eyes grew darker each time they wandered in my direction. Finally, she sent an invisible signal to her husband. He looked over at me, letting the little girl's next back swing go by without a push. As I came forward, Hector Montero began slowly shaking his head. He left the girl to her swinging and stepped over to meet me halfway. The delighted shrieking had stopped. I spoke first.

"Mr. Montero, my name is Fritz Malone. I'm not a reporter. I'm a private investigator working with the police on the Thanksgiving Day murders. I'm sorry, but I need to speak with your wife."

Hector Montero had sad eyes. "We've talked with the police. Please. Gabriella has nothing more she can say."

"I know the police have been by. I still need to talk with her."

"We are just from church. You can come back tomorrow."

"I need to speak with her today."

"But why? Roberto is dead. He will hurt no one now. Why can't you leave us alone? This is a bad three days. Rosa . . . she does not know yet about her father."

The rubber swing was slowing down. Another few passes and it would be at a full stop. The little girl was craning her neck to look in our direction. On the bench, Gabriella had lowered her head.

"Roberto Diaz wasn't working alone," I said. "He was working with a partner. The partner is still dangerous. I need to find out who he is."

Montero held my gaze. "We don't know who is the partner. Roberto was not in our life. Please."

I pressed. "Other people could die. This man is holding a hostage. He's extremely dangerous. I know this is painful for your wife, but you have to understand."

"She is pregnant."

I glanced over toward the bench. "I see that. Congratulations to you both."

Montero reached up and stroked his small mustache. He let out a sigh. "Show me something. Do you have a badge?" I pulled out my wallet and showed him my PI license. He gave it a long look. "I will talk to her. Wait here."

He stepped back to the swing and lifted the little girl into his arms. She threw her arms around his neck and looked over at me with a disapproving face. Montero carried her to the bench and set her down. Gabriella handed the child the flowers and shooed her away. Rosa went to a nearby picnic table and began laying the flowers out on the table, one by one. Hector Montero spoke with his wife.

She listened, then nodded. Montero kissed her on the cheek and signaled me to come over. As I approached the bench, he joined the little girl at the picnic table. Gabriella Montero was struggling to stand.

"Don't get up," I said.

She had not gotten far. She fell back heavily on the bench and looked up at me. Her eyes were as black as the twin shotgun barrels I'd faced just a half hour earlier.

"I am in hell," she said.

21

LUCKY THING FOR CHARLIE BURKE, HIS local was just two blocks from his house. In the days before an idiot's bullet put him in a wheelchair, the lucky part had to do with Charlie's having to negotiate only those two blocks safely after too many pints. Nowadays the paltry distance between home and bar meant that at least Charlie could get himself there and back on his own with no real problem, weather depending.

He was at the bar when I arrived. He was gassing about the Giants to some poor fool who didn't know better. If Charlie had his way, a goon squad would be sent out to abduct Bill Parcells from his current coaching job, his retirement, his deathbed, whatever, and forcibly return him to the Meadowlands and chain him to the hometown bench. A long chain, of course, so he could still range up and down the sidelines and bite the heads off the referees.

Charlie's victim was caught in the "but" cycle. "But . . . but . . . but . . ." I could have told him that you can't elbow your way into Charlie's Giants rant. The best thing to do is drink your drink, find something completely different you want to roll around in your mind, and nod now and then. Charlie is perfectly happy to go it alone. Prime him just right, and he'll pitch his Giants tirade to a two-year-old.

I rescued the victim. I came up behind Charlie's wheelchair and announced in a loud voice, "Bill Parcells is a mouse."

"What!" Charlie whipped his head around. When he saw who it was, he started to introduce me to the guy he'd been lecturing, but discovered that he hadn't gotten the fellow's name.

I told the stranger, "Get while the getting's good."

He probably walked away a Jets fan.

"May I say you're looking lovely tonight," I said to Charlie as I swung into the just vacated chair.

"You may not."

Jenny Gray was working behind the bar. Her crow-black hair was pulled back from her pale face in a thick, shiny ponytail. She was already looking my direction when I called out to her for a Harp. She gave a slow nod, then pulled me a pint and had it passed hand-to-hand over to me. This had been Charlie's method for fetching his drinks ever since the shooting. When I was with him, I sometimes adopted the method. Bad habit.

Charlie tapped his glass to mine. "To the pot we piss in."

Fifteen years and counting, and I'd yet to hear him repeat the same toast twice. I took a hungry pull on the Harp. Charlie's quizzical eye was on me as I set the glass down. "You've learned something."

Someone had just punched up a Rolling Stones song on the jukebox. I saw Charlie grimace.

"I spoke with Diaz's ex-wife today," I said. "She gave me a name."

Charlie deadpanned. "You've already got a name, son."

Under the table, my foot found the frame of his chair. I gave it a nudge. The chair rolled backward several inches.

"Right," Charlie said, adjusting his chair back to the table. "So, what did she tell you?"

"It wasn't something she was keen to talk about at first. You should have seen her, Charlie. The poor woman. She had a three-year-old with Diaz, and she hasn't told her yet that her daddy is dead. She's about to have another baby any day. New husband. They've been hounded by the press, as you can imagine. The woman was shaking like a leaf. She didn't come right out and say it, but in a way, she feels sort of responsible."

"Responsible for what? Her former husband's rampage?"

"They were married for four years. She was nineteen when they got married. He was abusive to her, and she put up with it for too long. She's extremely religious. She feels that somehow she should have saved him. Or been able to change him."

"He was a psycho. If she wants to feel responsible for something, she should feel responsible for not killing him while he slept. He'd be dead, she'd be in jail, and nine people would still be alive. Is that better?"

"She's worried for her daughter. She's sick with fear about the girl having her father's blood. 'Tainted blood' was how she put it."

"That's ridiculous."

"That's you and me sitting here with our beers saying it's ridiculous. But from where

Gabriella Montero is sitting, it isn't so ridiculous. She told me she saw the devil himself in her ex-husband's eyes. She said the devil comes to the world dressed up like everyday people. 'Thousands and thousands of devils in the world' was how she put it. Everywhere you look. And Roberto Diaz was one of them."

Charlie lifted his glass. "I'm not going to argue with her."

The Stones song ended, and the muscles in Charlie's face relaxed as Tony Bennett took over. I went on, summarizing the years that Diaz and Gabriella had spent together. I told him about the guy who'd sued FastCar, about Diaz spitting on him in court and then later, the mugger spitting on him after he'd been beaten with a pipe. I told Charlie about FastCar's vandalized fleet and about the police assessment that Diaz had hit his wife in the face with an iron. I could see a double frustration in Charlie's expression. Diaz was dead, but to Charlie, that was too easy a punishment. Charlie would have preferred spotting Diaz at the bar so he could have gone over and grabbed him by the shoulders, hurled him up against the wall and offered up some **real** punishment. That was the first frustration. The second was that even if Roberto Diaz had been loitering at the bar, Charlie was stuck in his damn wheelchair and couldn't really do much about it. His roughhouse days were well over.

"Wife beaters should be skinned alive," Charlie said in a low voice. "Your Gabriella is right. She was married to a devil."

My glass was empty. So was Charlie's. This time I got up to fetch the beers myself. Jenny Gray was chewing on her lip as she took the empty glasses from me. Her black T-shirt was a tight fit. Plunging V-neck. A "tip teaser" was how she had described it to me once. Her skin was pearl white.

Jenny gave me a steady look. She pulled the beers without so much as a glance at them. "How's Margo these days, Fritz?"

"She's good, Jenny."

"We don't see her much."

"She's a busy girl."

"She still writing about famous people?"

"Among other things."

"I guess she's hit the big time. Must be fun work."

"It's a hustle. Margo works hard."

"Plays hard, too, I'll bet." I didn't answer. Jenny set the two beers on the counter. She was still giving me her steady gaze. "How about you, Fritz? Are you working hard?"

"Keeping out of trouble," I said.

She set a glass on the bar and shot it full of seltzer. "Your work **is** trouble." She picked up the glass. "Cheers."

I drained an inch from my Harp, then set a twenty on the counter.

Jenny ignored the bill. "So, you two are good? You and Margo?"

I nodded. "We're good."

"Any news on the way?"

"News?"

"About the two of you?"

I shrugged. "No news."

She allowed a thin eyebrow to rise. "So you're not that kind of good."

I took up the beers. "We're good, Jenny."

She scraped the twenty off the bar. "Tell her I said hi. Tell her I wish her continued good luck in the city. Tell her she should interview that Tom Cruise while he's still cute."

"I'll tell her." I took the beers back to the table. Charlie was watching me closely. "It's nothing," I said, setting the mugs down.

"I don't trust that one farther than I can throw her."

"I said it's nothing."

"It wasn't nothing before."

"Before is before."

"My girl is a hundred of that one. Listen, if I ever—"

I cut him off. "Charlie. Just drop it. Come on already." I slid my mug over and tapped his. He hesitated, putting a long look on me, then he lifted his mug.

"May the cat catch its tail."

THE NAME. ANGEL. GABRIELLA HADN'T been able to provide a last name for me. Only the first. She had pronounced it **An-hell,** which was the kind of irony you could beat a person senseless with.

Angel was an acquaintance of Diaz's. Gabriella hadn't been certain when the two first hooked up. She told me she had a vague memory of Diaz mentioning someone named Angel early in their marriage, but the name didn't really start cropping up on a regular basis until a couple of years later. Charlie picked up on this detail when I related it.

"Prison," he said. "They appear, they disappear, they appear again. Prison." I agreed; that's what I had concluded.

Gabriella encountered this Angel character in the flesh on only two occasions. The last year of her marriage with Diaz, he was away from home half as often as he checked in. It was clear to Gabriella that her husband was involved with drugs, running with a bad crowd. More and more, she said, Diaz arrived home high on God knows what, laughing, sweating, speaking a mile a minute, trash-talking people Gabriella had never even met, trash-talking the police, the mayor, all white people, the Jews, the Arabs, the president. And there was always Angel. Angel this and Angel that. **Me and Angel. You should have seen Angel.** Finally, one night, Gabriella did see Angel. She was standing at a bus stop on her way to her office-cleaning job when a silver hatchback drove by across the street, vibrating the entire block with a **thumpa-thumpa** bass blast from a deck of inverted speakers filling the entire hatchback area. The tires squealed as the car ripped a half circle in the middle of the street, pulling to an abrupt stop in front of the bus stop. **Thumpa-thumpa-thumpa.** Diaz came out of the passenger side, and from the driver's side came a tall mocha-skinned man in a muscle shirt, a silver bandanna and a pair of orange-tinted sunglasses. Gabriella described him as at least six feet and "with muscles he was proud of." He had a pencil-thin mustache. Diaz had made an overt point of being what Gabriella called "all lovey-dovey, like he was showing off for his friend." Diaz introduced Angel to Gabriella. She said that Angel had barely acknowledged her. She couldn't see his eyes behind his sunglasses, and if he even spoke to her directly, it was in a voice pitched as low as the thumping coming from the back of the car. Gabriella commented twice to me about the man's muscles. What she had said was, "There was no soul. Only a body."

"Prison," Charlie said again. "We lock them up, they pump it up. Nice damn system."

The second time Gabriella encountered Angel, he was trying to rape her.

Gabriella had turned her head away from the picnic table where her daughter was playing with the flowers. She had kept her tiny convulsions under control even as the tears flooded her cheeks.

She had just returned from work, she told me. It was five in the morning. Rosa was still with her grandmother. The apartment was empty. No Roberto. No surprise. Gabriella had showered, put on her nightgown and then gotten into bed, first pulling down the shades against the rising sun. She had drifted swiftly to sleep. The next thing she remembered, the sheets had been pulled back and a man was on top of her. She remembered a vanilla scent and a strong pair of hands forcing her legs apart, a low mumbling voice intoning, "Don't fight, don't fight, don't fight." She opened her mouth to scream, and one of the hands flashed up from under her night-gown and clamped over her mouth. Gabriella was staring wide-eyed into a pair of pale green eyes, open to no more than a slit. "They looked like the eyes of a goat." She recognized the pencil-thin mustache. Angel was just entering her when her husband appeared in the doorway and started shouting. Angel attempted to continue, but Diaz threw himself onto the bed and the two men tumbled to the floor. Screaming, Gabriella had hurried off the other side of the bed and run into the bathroom, locking herself in, where she listened to the sounds of the fight. Eventually, the sounds stopped and she heard the front door slam. She waited an extra fifteen minutes, crying and shaking uncontrollably. When she finally emerged from the bathroom, Diaz was passed out on the bed, the pillow under his head draining blood from a small cut on his cheek. She told me that she had wanted to turn her husband's head into the pillow and suffocate him.

Charlie had barely touched his beer. He picked up his mug and looked at me.

"I know," I said. "I know."

I TOLD CHARLIE THE REST OF GABRIELLA'S story as I accompanied him back to his house.

Charlie didn't like being pushed; he motored his chair on his own. The temperature had dropped considerably and the air smelled like snow. Charlie was underdressed in a sweatshirt and a thin windbreaker. He generated some heat, though, muscling the wheels of his chair. The orange glow at the tip of his cigar led the way.

I told him about Diaz showing up at Gabriella's workplace accompanied by the woman with the rose tattoo on her arm, and the lawyer coming in to take Gabriella under his wing. Gabriella said she had insisted on using her husband's infidelity—not Diaz's violence—as the stated reason for the divorce. Apparently, the woman with the tattoo was more than just a one-night stand; Diaz had taken up with her. Charlie gave me a suggestion on how I might want to follow up on that information. At the house, he let me wheel him up the long ramp.

"You seeing my girl tonight?" he asked, sorting through his keys to find the one to the front door.

"I don't think so."

He looked up at me. "You wouldn't be going back to the bar?"

"Of course not. I'm beat. I'm going home."

"Just checking."

I drove back to the city over the Queens-boro Bridge. The way there are so many lights on in Manhattan's buildings all through the night, it looks like you're driving into a cluster of stars.

I gave Jigs Dugan a call when I got to my place. I told him I could use his services if he could use a little cash. Light lifting, I said. Easy money. He was okay with that, so I gave him the details.

An hour after lights-out, I still wasn't asleep. I got up and put a little milk and bourbon together and got back into bed. The face of **An-hell** floated near my ceiling. Slitted eyes, pencil-thin mustache, silver bandanna on his head. I summoned an image of the old man. My father. **Get this punk out of here. I need some shut-eye.**

I finally slept. I looked for Margo in my dreams. I had to skirt around that goddamn Jenny Gray and her pearl-white neckline, but at last I found Margo. Laugh me to sleep, sweetie. I'll owe you. I'll gladly owe you.

22

TOMMY CARROLL'S ASSISTANT HANDED ME my first cup of coffee of the day. She was dressed in a powder-blue suit and looked as stern as an unsexed schoolmarm.

"You don't take sugar." It was a statement, not a question, and it happened to be correct. I looked to see if I could find a hair out of place on her head. Not one. I considered asking if she had a boyfriend. I was thinking Jigs, just to muss her hair up a little.

"Commissioner Carroll will be right with you."

"Thank you, Stacy."

The door closed behind her. Thirty seconds later, it opened again. I stopped blowing on my coffee and greeted Tommy Carroll. "Morning, Commish."

He grunted and moved directly to his desk. "Where are we? What've you got?"

I told him, "Angel something-or-other. An associate of Roberto Diaz's. Likely ex-con. Diaz looked up to him. Extremely violent. The guy tried to rape Diaz's wife several years ago with Diaz in the next room. Don't ask me why, but I'm getting a 'fearless' vibe."

"How'd you get the name?"

"Diaz's ex-wife. She told me she'd spoken with the police. How come you didn't get the name?"

"The officers who questioned Mrs. Montero weren't looking for an accomplice."

"Right. Of course. That's still our little secret."

Carroll gave me a hard look. "I don't need your wisecracking. Not today. We've got a deputy mayor out there, either dead already or getting whittled down as we speak. And this asshole could pounce again any minute. The mayor wants this over."

"Then maybe the mayor should unleash the full power of the best police force in the world," I said. "How about we look for a soft-spoken six-foot Hispanic ex-con named Angel Something? Pale green eyes. Possible pencil-thin mustache. Drug chewer. Violent. Maybe drives a silver hatchback with music booming out of the rear. Muscles on muscles.

Ice-cold blood. Aviator sunglasses. Jesus Christ, Tommy, I'm painting you a picture."

"We'll look for him," Carroll said brusquely. "Meantime, you keep looking. Get a last name."

I asked, "No more word on Byron?"

Carroll muttered, "Fucking Byron." He shook his head. "No. Nothing. Two fingers tied up like a crucifix. Real cute."

"I'm sure Byron didn't think so. What's the word you're putting out? There's been nothing on the news."

"Illness in the family. Out in the heartland somewhere, a thousand miles from here. It'll buy us some time."

"It wasn't Wisconsin, was it?"

Carroll ignored the crack. "The mayor wants this guy."

"I heard that."

"I'm going to give you Cox," Carroll said.

I was about to take a sip of my coffee, but I stopped. "What do you mean, 'give' me?"

"To help find this Angel character. I've had Cox put on special duty."

"I don't want him," I said. "Why don't you give your hero cop a trip to Disney World? A cop who doesn't pat down a violent suspect, then ends up shooting him in the face in cold blood? I'll pass."

"It wasn't cold blood."

"Whatever. I wasn't there."

"You need help on this."

I took the sip. "Give me Noon."

"Noon? What do you mean, noon?"

"Patrick Noon. The guy who stuck me in a bag for you. If you want to loosen up a cop for me, give me Patrick Noon. Or is he still tied up guarding Rebecca Gilpin's hospital room? Is that how our tax dollars are spent?"

"We're trying to keep this thing contained."

"Meaning what? Cox knows too much and Patrick Noon doesn't?"

Carroll worked a knuckle until it cracked. "Let me talk to Remy Sanchez."

"Sanchez would love it if you'd talk to him. He's not happy about being kept in the dark. You're containing this thing right up the rear, Tommy. How about the mayor just comes clean and explains to the city that we've got a problem and we're working on it? It's amazing how the truth can simplify matters. He should be unbottling this thing."

"We're getting fingers in a fucking box," Carroll said. "Marty Leavitt doesn't think that's going to make him look real good right now."

"Well, Mr. Marty has to start backing away from the political mirror."

"This isn't going to make anyone look good," Carroll said. "It's getting out of hand. I want it shut down **now.**"

I opened my mouth to respond, but Carroll's intercom buzzed. The commissioner practically destroyed the machine crashing his hand down on it. "What!"

It was Stacy. "Mayor Leavitt's on line one, sir."

Go figure.

Carroll snarled into the intercom, "Tell him to sit on it for a minute. I'll be with him."

"Sir?"

"Tell him to hold on."

The intercom clicked off. Carroll looked across the desk at me. "It's Monday. Byron got grabbed on Saturday. It's not going to surprise me if we hear from Nightmare again today, one way or another. Go find him. You're a pain in the ass, but you're a good bloodhound. Just go find this Angel character. Sniff him out and give him to me. And forget the Patrick Noon business. You might be Harlan's kid, but you don't run my police force. I'm putting Cox on this. He's a good cop. Plus he's motivated."

"McNally?"

"Exactly."

"That kind of motivation isn't always so good," I said. "I mean it, Tommy. Don't saddle me with a man I don't trust. I'm not working with Cox. I'll go kick down some doors and let you know what I find behind them. What you do with it is your business. Consider this a gift from me to the city I love. But I can take the gift back anytime and go home. It wouldn't be the first time I walked away from a client."

"Your old man was a fucking mule, too."

I stood up. "Now, Tommy, don't start with the compliments."

23

I SLIPPED INTO THE COURTROOM AND TOOK a seat in the rear pew. There were twenty long pews in all, room for at least a hundred onlookers. Besides me, three people were present.

A woman had misstepped coming out the door of a sporting-goods store, where she had just purchased enough gear to tackle Everest on her own. Juggling all the bags had allegedly contributed to the misstep. She hadn't seen the yellow tape on the edge of the step, nor the sign that read, BEWARE OF STEP, and she'd twisted her ankle. From what I could piece together, she felt she should have been given a verbal warning by the shopclerk or been encouraged to take the bags outside in two trips. Or maybe chaperoned out of the damn store in a miniature hot-air balloon. The ankle had somehow led to a neck brace (Exhibit A) as well as severe interference with the woman's livelihood, which had something to do with the music-video industry. She was sitting at the plaintiff's table, legs crossed, wagging a foot incessantly. The foot was adorned with no less than a four-inch heel.

The lawyer arguing the case for the sporting-goods store was named Lance Jennings. He had promised me on the phone that we could talk at ten-thirty. I was giving him until eleven. The judge called a break at ten-fifty-two. I introduced myself to Jennings.

"She's wearing stiletto heels," I said.

"Oh, I know. The champagne's already cold on this one. I'm going to ask the judge to have her go up into the witness stand in those beautiful stupid shoes, then step back down. In front of the jury. I just know she's going to wobble."

We went to a coffee shop. "I don't drink coffee anymore," Jennings said, shooing my money away. "Acid reflux." He asked for a cup of hot water and produced his own tea bag from a small container in his briefcase. "Green tea. I'm becoming a damn Chinaman." I ordered a cup of the acid reflux.

I had told Jennings on the phone that I

wanted some information about the Roberto and Gabriella Diaz divorce. After dunking his tea bag in his cup, the lawyer produced a blue manila folder from his briefcase.

"Sweet women marry assholes. Don't ask me why. This Diaz was a real hard-on. Paranoid, a classic. Thought everyone was out to persecute him and rip him off. First thing out of his mouth in court was that his wife and I were ganging up on him and we were out to get him. I think he eventually included the judge in the conspiracy. Or maybe it was his own lawyer, I can't remember. He would just go off. A real trigger temper."

"I understand you were able to get a restraining order on him."

The lawyer poked at his tea bag with a spoon. "Piece of cake. History of violence, no inkling of remorse. Plus, I was the prime witness to the beating he gave his wife."

"With the vacuum-cleaner hose?"

"These were no love taps. It was hard plastic. The prick was really whipping her with it."

"He supposedly also beat Gabriella with an iron."

"She told me. This is a man who cannot be trusted with domestic appliances. When I intervened, he turned on me. I still have a buzzing in my ear from it. I'll take it to my grave. The bastard."

"So what did you think when you heard it was Diaz who shot up the parade the other day?"

Jennings answered immediately. "I felt good that I helped separate him from his wife and daughter. I felt maybe I saved their lives."

"So then it didn't surprise you?"

"The shooting? I was horrified, of course, like everyone else. But when I heard it was Diaz? That's what you're asking? What can I tell you, it made sense to me. This guy had rage, Mr. Malone. Serious rage. I feel horrible for the people he shot. I guess you can't put out a restraining order to keep someone away from everyone else in the world. I guess that's called prison."

"Or the grave."

"Right." He took a sip of his green tea. "The final restraining order."

I told the lawyer what I was looking for. Angel. I didn't tell him why, only that I needed to track down Diaz's former colleague. Jennings caught on immediately.

"You think this Angel guy was involved?"

"I don't know if he was. I can only tell you it's important that I locate him. I was hoping maybe you could help. But I'm guessing Diaz didn't call in a gangbanger like Angel as a character witness at his trial."

"That would be a good guess."

"What about the woman? The one Diaz brought to your office, with the rose tattoo. Gabriella told me she and Diaz were an item. She also said she's obliterated the woman's name from her mind. She doesn't want to remember it."

Jennings smirked. "You mean the hot tamale? I had her called as a witness in Diaz's assault on me. As I'm sure you can imagine, she was not too cooperative."

"Hostile witness?"

"That's one way of putting it." He rifled through the papers in his file folder. "Here we are. Donna Bia. Ah, that's right. The lovely Miss Bia. How could I have forgotten?"

I wrote the name down. "Have you got an address?" He did. It was in Brooklyn, not far over the bridge. I wrote that down as well. "Job?"

"The official term is 'no visible means of support.' Except take one look at this one, and the means of support is pretty damn visible. Miss Bia was a hustler from the word go. I'm not going to use the term 'arm candy,' but I could."

"Candies like that usually prefer their arms

to have some money," I said. "Diaz sounds a little short in that department."

Jennings shrugged. "Drugs are candy, too, and our Miss Bia had herself a big appetite. I'm pretty certain Diaz was into some low-level dealing. Aside from the candy itself, dealing lets you flash a decent-sized bankroll now and then."

"How good do you think this address is?"

"Who can say? She might have made it up on the stand."

I flipped my notebook closed. "At least Bia isn't a dime-a-dozen name. I'll find her."

Jennings smirked again. "When you find this one, your fripping eyes are going to pop out. She's a twenty-something wearing dresses built for a ten-year-old. Seriously, you'll think she paints it on. I guess a person is supposed to lead with their strengths. This hellcat's got 'em in spades."

"Oh boy," I said. "I can't wait."

Jennings sipped his tea. His gaze went deep into the liquid. "Hellcat," he murmured again.

I TOOK A CAB OVER THE BROOKLYN BRIDGE. Hell of a piece of work, that bridge, with its towering cathedral-window supports and the swooping rows of cables. There's a story that Annie Oakley and Diamond Jim Brady threw a big party on the roof of a bar down on Water Street in 1883, the night the Brooklyn Bridge was officially inaugurated. Legend has Miss Oakley shooting the hat off one of the attending officials as he came down from the bridge and was heading into the bar. The thing is, you read up on Annie Oakley, you get about a thousand shot-the-hat-off stories. Put me in her day, and I'd have simply removed my chapeau whenever I was in the woman's presence. The way a gentleman is supposed to, anyway.

The address Jennings had given me for Donna Bia was just off Atlantic Avenue, near the Brooklyn Academy of Music. They call it BAM. Margo's a big BAM fan. I've probably logged a dozen shows there with her. I saw one there once that featured a chunky man dancing in a wool skirt. That one didn't exactly top my entertainment list for the year, but generally speaking most of the offerings are quality goods.

I stood on a warped porch and tried to shoo a cat away from my leg as I waited for someone to respond to my knocking. The cat had a bald spot near its tail and a mustache like Hitler's. The house was pale green. Two stories, the second one sagging a bit. There was a red glider couch on the porch, losing a battle to rust.

Donna Bia didn't live here. Not anymore. A plumber named Ray lived here. He answered my knock in jeans and bare feet, pulling on a dirty white T-shirt. The vibe he put out was that I was interrupting something and he was eager to get back to it. I asked him about Donna Bia, and he told me that he and his wife had bought the house from a family named Bia nearly eight years before. I showed him my PI license and told him it was a matter of life and death that I locate the Bias. He didn't seem impressed, but he told me to hold on. He shut the door. The cat and I looked at each other for two minutes, then the door opened again and Ray handed me a piece of paper with an address on it. "The Bias called me a couple of years ago to replace an elbow joint."

A woman had drifted into sight in the dark hallway behind him. She was in a fuzzy bathrobe, smoking a cigarette. I thanked Ray and accidentally kicked the cat as I turned to leave.

"Don't sweat it," Ray said. "The cat's a menace."

The Bia family had moved to an apartment building on Eastern Parkway, only a few miles from their old home. Specifically, Mr. and Mrs. Bia had moved there once the last kid had moved out of the house. I learned this from Mrs. Bia, Donna's mother. She was a frowning square-shaped woman wearing a faded pale blue apron. Nothing about her suggested a hellcat had sprung from her loins. She said she had not laid eyes on her daughter in over three months. The name Roberto Diaz meant nothing to her. I told her that it was very important I speak with her daughter. She shrugged, then stepped into the kitchen, emerging a moment later holding a piece of paper. Today seemed to be piece-of-paper day. She handed it to me. "This is where she lives."

I looked at the piece of paper, which bore a phone number: 917 exchange. Cell phone.

Mrs. Bia went on, "I had to give Donna a hundred dollars to give me this number. I told her if her father or me die one day, maybe it would be nice if she got a phone call. This is my own daughter. I have no idea where she lives. I don't think maybe she lives anywhere. All the time Donna is growing up, she is beautiful, and people tell her she is beautiful, and they tell me what a good future she will have. But you have to make good decisions to have a good future. Donna is nothing but bad decisions. So now? As far as I'm concerned, she gets what she deserves. We gave her a pretty face and a nice home. What more can we do?"

I thanked her for her time and gave her my card. "If you hear from her."

She slipped the card into her apron pocket. "I am not holding my breath."

From the hallway, I tried the number. I was spilled into a voice mailbox. The recorded voice was yelling to be heard above a background din. **"This is Donna! Not here. Leave a message and I'll call you!"**

I was tempted to leave her a message to call her mother. But I restrained myself.

THE MOVING COMPANY WHERE DIAZ HAD worked off-and-on was called U-Move. It was located in a cinder-block building off Fourth Street. A light-skinned black man shaped like a cheeseburger heard me out. His name was Rodney. He sat at a gray metal desk in a small cement room with a buzzing fluorescent light hanging overhead. A half-naked woman in gold boots glowered angrily from the calendar on the wall behind Rodney's desk.

Rodney was working on a medium-sized

pizza and a bucket of Pepsi. He offered me a slice of the pizza and seemed relieved when I turned it down. Rodney's job seemed to be to answer the phone and put the caller immediately on hold. He did it as easy as breathing.

I didn't exactly ask, but he explained how U-Move operated.

"We hire out a crew chief and a driver, that's all. Crew of two. We figure out from talking to the customers how much stuff we're gonna be moving. If it's a big job, gonna take more than two, we pick up extra manpower. We call them cash crew." Rodney plugged the hole in his face with a large bite of pizza, chased by a hefty splash of Pepsi. He continued, chewing as he talked. "Crew chief and driver are on the payroll. The extra manpower gets theirs in cash. Off the books. Less paperwork."

This last statement was borne out by Rodney's office. The only paper I spotted, other than the napkins on his desk, were the calendar pages below the half-naked woman.

Rodney folded a slice of pizza in on itself, lengthwise. I feared he would inhale the whole thing at once, but he didn't. He chomped down on it.

I asked him about Roberto Diaz. Rodney remembered him.

"Sure, we used him sometimes. What a jerk, huh? Shooting up the parade like that? I had no idea the guy was like that. We've been sweating it they don't find out and put the company's name in the paper. That wouldn't be so cool with the customers."

"Did he work here on a regular basis?"

The fat man shook his head. "He was never on payroll. He was strictly cash crew."

"How does that work? The cash crew. You just keep a list of available names?"

"Not really. We've got some, but that's mostly up to the crew chief to hire out. They got friends or people they know. We tell them not to hire garbage, but a good crew chief isn't going to hire garbage anyway. He's the one who's got to work with the guy."

"You didn't consider Diaz garbage?"

Rodney licked his index finger. It looked like he was licking a small sausage. "Nah. I mean, I didn't really know the guy. Saw him a couple times. He came in here once and put his feet up on my desk. I guess I'm lucky he didn't pull a gun when I told him to take them off. But he seemed okay. Nobody called in any complaints about him. Past that, I don't care."

"Let me tell you who I'm actually looking for," I said. "I'm looking for a friend of Diaz's.

A guy named Angel. You wouldn't know any-thing about him?"

Rodney answered immediately. "Shit, yeah, I know who you're talking about."

My heart hiccupped. "Is that right? You know Angel?"

Rodney nodded. "Bastard robbed one of our customers, better believe I know him. Son of a bitch walked off with a box of jew-elry and a box of booze. The woman we were moving caught him red-handed. He was stashing them away in his car. All sorts of hell, believe me. This woman busted Angel, and he called her a cunt to her face. Sweet, huh? Her kid was right there. We had to do the whole damn move for free to keep from being taken to court."

I asked, "How long ago was this?"

Rodney chased some pizza dust off his face. "I don't know. Two years? It's been a while. Maybe longer. Three years."

"I'm guessing Angel was cash crew?"

"Totally. Guy like that?"

"You wouldn't have an address for him, would you?" I asked.

Rodney shook his head. "I told you. No paperwork."

"How about a last name?"

"Angel? Sure. Ramos. Angel Ramos. What's

up? Is he in some kind of trouble? He call someone else a cunt?"

"He stole something."

"Yeah? What'd he steal?"

"A person."

"Shit. How do you steal a person?"

"Usually with violence."

The phone rang. Rodney strangled a napkin between his hands and picked up the phone. "U-Move. Hold on." He said to me, "So you're trying to find Ramos?"

"That's right."

"Hold on." He jerked open a side drawer on his desk and pulled out a sheet of paper. Finally, some paperwork. "Eight oh seven President. That's in the Slope."

"What about it?"

"We're moving a family out of there today. Started at ten." He checked his watch. "They should still be loading."

"What's that got to do with Angel Ramos?"

Rodney was finished with his pizza. He pulled a pack of Rolos from his shirt pocket and began picking expertly at the foil. "Angel's brother is a crew chief. That's how we got Angel in the first place. He's running the job in Park Slope."

My heart did another one of those hiccups. "Angel's brother?"

"Yeah. Victor. He's a good dude. Nothing like his brother, except . . ." Rodney loosened the top Rolo from the pack and popped it into his mouth. "They're twins. Creepy as hell, man. They look completely alike."

24

VICTOR RAMOS HAD AN ANGRY RESTING face. Smooth. No creases, with eyes that were like a simmering python's. Pale, like Gabriella Montero had said. A pale swamp green. He was seated on the front steps of 807 President, staring into space, when I came up the walk. Despite the cool temperature, he was dressed in a muscle T-shirt. A glaze of perspiration covered his skin. He wore a pair of canvas work gloves and looked like he probably stood six-one or so. His chest was broad, his biceps the size of small pigs.

As it turned out, the angry resting face was simply genetics. When I gave him my name and told him that Rodney at U-Move had said I would find him here, he cracked an easy smile. "Rodney. You bribe him with food?"

"He seemed to have that area covered," I said. I pulled out one of my business cards and handed it to him. The smile dropped away.

"You're looking for Angel."

"How do you know that?"

"Because **I** haven't done anything wrong. What is it this time?"

"When was the last time you saw your brother?" I asked.

The reptilian eyes rested on me a moment. "Last time was right before the last time he went to jail. Next time could be never, as far as I'm concerned."

"When did he go to jail?"

"This last time? About a year ago. Before that, a couple of years."

"Your brother go to jail a lot?"

"My brother's a fuckup. Yeah, he's got the prison thing down. He goes in for a little vacation, he gets to hook up with a whole new set of losers, then they let him out too early. Some system, huh?"

"What kind of things does he go in for?"

Ramos ran a tongue over his front teeth. "Pimping's a big thing. Angel don't treat women good, I can tell you that. But they come in useful for him. He goes in for all sorts of stupid shit. He's been hit for robbery, car theft, aggravated assault. Kid stuff for Angel. They've never nailed him on anything really big."

"But he's done big?"

"What am I going to tell you? You're the investigator. I guess you're investigating."

The door to the brownstone opened, and two men appeared, carrying a couch wrapped in a quilted moving blanket. Ramos sprang to his feet.

"Excuse me." He placed a hand on my chest and moved me aside as if I were a leaf. The two movers came down the stairs and carried the couch up a metal ramp into the moving van. "I can't talk," Ramos said. "That was my break. It's over."

"I need to find Angel."

"Last time I saw him, I tried to take his head off. Son of a bitch was trying to recruit my son for his street crap. His own damn nephew. Boy wasn't even ten years old."

"What do you mean, 'street crap'?"

"What do you think I mean? Drugs. He tried to get Ricky to be one of his delivery boys. It's a good thing I don't have a daughter or he'd a been trying to draw her in, too. He strings those girls of his out on his dope, then pimps 'em out so they can pay up. Last I heard, he was running a whole racket. Angel's nasty, man. What can I say?" He smiled again. "We both got the good looks, but I got the brains. Or maybe I married brains. My wife comes from just over there, Boerum Hill. That's where we're raising our family. We've got another kid on the way. I never told my wife about Angel trying to hook Ricky into his scene. That's me and my boy's secret. We talked it out."

The two movers emerged from the truck. The shorter one said to Ramos, "Fucking chest of drawers up there's made of lead."

"Save it," Ramos replied.

"Like to fucking chop it into pieces, what I'd like to do."

The two went back into the building. Ramos turned to me. "I can't help you. I mean it. I swore off Angel a couple of years ago. Far as I'm concerned, he's a dead man. I got my family. I got this job, which he almost lost for me once."

"How about a name?" I said. "Someone he's tight with. Your brother must have a main man."

Ramos grinned. "Main man. Listen to you. Only main man Angel ever had took a cop's bullet in the head when we was all ten. Angel saw it happen. He was right there. Been mister bad boy ever since. No redemption, no return, you hear what I'm saying?"

I heard what he was saying. I heard it

clearly. Ramos picked up a weight lifter's belt from the steps and strapped it around his waist.

"What can you tell me about Angel and a convent up in Riverdale?" I asked. "The Holy Order of the Sisters of Good Shepherd."

"Convent? I don't know, man. You mean like nuns?"

"Exactly."

"Hey, if any of them are young and pretty, that's about all I can think. Angel's got no time for religion."

"You just used the word 'redemption.' "

"Yeah, well, that's me, not Angel. Our mother took us to church when we were kids. Tried to, anyway. Angel'd take a handful from the collection plate when it came around. That's about how religious he gets. That and his name. Our parents sure wasted a good name on that one. They thought 'Victor' and 'Angel' would get us both off in the right direction. Our mother died when Angel was doing one of his stretches. The old man refused to let them bring him out for the funeral. He won't even talk about him anymore."

"This friend of Angel's who was killed by a cop. What was his name?"

"Willy. Willy Padilla. They were tight,

man. Blood brothers. Willy was a good kid, too. One of those kids who could always crack you up. Always goofing. That little kid could've gotten away with anything. Angel and I had an older sister used to say that Willy Padilla was going to grow up and really make the girls cry." He shook his head. "It was a really fucked-up thing."

"You have a sister?"

"You want to talk to my sister?"

"You tell me. Does she keep in contact with Angel?"

"Only if he can talk to the dead. You want to see my sister, you can go over to Green-Wood Cemetery. She married a guy who killed her about five months later. It's a hell of a family."

"I'm sorry."

Ramos looked past me into the middle distance. "Yeah, well . . . Shit happens, I guess."

"What happened to your sister's husband?" I asked. "Did he pay for it?"

Ramos returned his gaze to me. The smile on his lips was barely discernible and not particularly pleasant. "Oh, he paid. **Mi hermano** collected that debt."

"Angel?"

"Angel can be very talented with a knife."

"I see."

Ramos laughed. "Yeah. **You** see. My ex-brother-in-law, man? After Angel's little talk with him, he's not seeing so good anymore."

He waited for my reaction. I had one, but I didn't show it to him. "One more thing," I said. "Do you have any idea where your brother might be hanging out these days? Where was he living before he went to jail?"

"That's easy. Fort Pete. That's still Angel's turf. Is that what you're asking? You want to find him, here's what you do. A block off Culver, that's Murray Avenue. Take it north as far as the Eubie Blake Apartments. It crosses Viceroy. Then south as far as the big brick building where they clean linens. You know, like for restaurants. You can't miss it. Big brick place, takes up about the whole block. That's on Lee Street. That's the strip. You run that strip, including about four blocks over to Hanover Boulevard. And check out a church there called Sweet Music Methodist. It's just a shell. No church left, just rats and drug dealers. You work those two strips, and you check out that church, and if you can do that and stay alive, you might find someone who knows where Angel's at. I hope you got some cash. No one in that strip is going to give him up for free. You know what they say—gotta pay to play."

I pulled out my notebook and jotted down the information. I also wrote down the name of Angel's childhood friend. "One more thing," I said.

Ramos chuckled. "I thought the last thing was one more thing."

"Did you ever know Angel to fool around with explosives?"

"You mean like bombs?"

"That's right."

"Shit, yeah. Angel was the king of Molotov cocktails when we were growing up. He'd go down to the waterfront over at Vinegar Hill and smash them against the rocks. They float. I mean, the flames'll float on the water. Angel loved that. He'd set off two at once and watch them float off down the river."

"What about something stronger?"

Ramos shrugged. "The dude's been in three different prisons. You can learn a lot in prison. Knowing Angel? Wouldn't surprise me."

I thanked him. He shook his head.

"If you run into Angel, man, you're not going to be thanking me for nothing."

I FOUND A COPY SHOP ON SEVENTH AVENUE. It was run by a bird-boned young man from the Kashmir region of India. I learned this only because there had been an explosion in Kashmir the day before, and the young man behind the counter was arguing about it with an older man when I came in. The older man was brandishing an Indian-language newspaper like a handful of thunderbolts.

I couldn't have followed the politics of the argument even if I had wanted to, which I didn't. I wanted five hundred business-sized cards made up while I waited, and I didn't want to wait until the two gentlemen had found common ground on the Kashmir issue. I had my own mad bomber to think about.

"Excuse me," I interjected in a falsely polite voice. "Customer?"

I waited in a Starbucks nearby while my cards were being printed. I thought of calling Margo but remembered that she was interviewing a pop star today for an article in **Entertainment Weekly.** Or **Us.** Or **People.** One of those. Mustn't interrupt the intellectual musings of the pop star. The Starbucks was filled with pretty young women and baby strollers. I felt lecherous simply for being a man. One of the women smiled at me a trifle too long. A pair in the corner were laughing themselves to tears over God knows what. One of the babies threw up. All to the earthy aroma of caffeine and the sweet strains of Vivaldi in strings. Simply lovely.

My cards were ready. The argument over the bombing in Kashmir had subsided. I paid for my purchase, then took the subway to Fort Petersen. The train briefly came out of the tunnel at one point and revealed a gray world, a large half-empty parking lot, a Home Depot, a massive junkyard mountain and a distant hook of the harbor along with countless tractor-trailer compartments stacked up twenty high. Then the train plunged back into the tunnel, and all I saw in the window was a smoky reflection of my own face, along with the hip-hopper passed out in the seat across the aisle.

I got off the train at Culver Boulevard, the major artery running through Fort Pete. Beauty shops, nail salons, chicken shacks, clothes stores, barbershops, fish-and-chips joints, corner bodegas. I oriented myself using a bus map I'd gotten from the subway attendant, found my north and south, found the two streets Victor Ramos had offered as the boundaries of his brother's main stomping ground. I went a block east to Murray Avenue and for the next forty minutes made a pest of myself going into business establishments and handing out the cards I'd had made up in Park

Slope. Here and there were pockets of men, some older, some younger, hanging out in chairs in front of the bars and barbershops and Laundromats. I stopped and told them that I was looking for Angel Ramos, and I handed each of them a card. At the corner of Viceroy and Columbia, a teenager was selling CDs that he had laid out on a blanket. He wasn't doing much business as far as I could see, so I made him a proposition. I gave him fifty bucks, doled out a hundred of the cards and assigned him a region. I knew he might just take my money and dump the cards, but if you doubt humanity at every turn, I figure you might as well pack it in.

I continued passing out the cards and asking after Angel Ramos. I didn't expect anyone to cough him up, but I wanted the word to saturate his territory. I wanted to draw a reaction from him. I wanted to flush him out. My cell phone number was on the cards, along with an intentionally cryptic message:

Angel—

I died, you didn't. So why you doing this shit?

Amigo Willy

Seemed to me like a reasonable ploy. Curiosity is like a drug. When I was twenty, I lost a pretty good friend to a policeman's bullet. If someone were to hand me a card with a phone number and a bullshit message from my friend, I'd call.

I found the church that Victor Ramos had mentioned. Its glassless white stucco facade made it look a little like the Alamo. A sign above the door read: SWEET MUSIC METHODIST CHURCH/REV. SALLY BODINE PRESIDING. The front of the church was covered with graffiti, primarily large rounded letters I couldn't make out. Someone had also drawn a skeleton seated atop a horizontal guitar. The skeleton was holding a paddle that it was dipping into some ripples next to the guitar. The front door of the church was boarded over, and the chipped cement steps were strewn with beer and booze bottles. As promised, a small rat was standing guard, sniffing at one of the bottles.

The attached building was also abandoned. A large sheet of tin covered the front door. I pushed on the tin and it moved easily. A stale cold air sifted from within. No doubt the way into the church was through this building. A hole in the wall somewhere, I figured. I considered going in but decided that if Angel Ramos was inside and I were to come climbing unannounced through a jagged brick hole in the wall, I wouldn't get the chance to climb back out.

My phone went off.

"Hello?"

A voice much louder than I was ready for chewed into me. "What the fuck do you think you're up to?"

"That depends who's asking," I said. "Who's this?"

"This is Leonard Cox. What the hell are you doing?"

"I'm just trying to save the planet, one person at a time."

"Where are you?"

"I'm standing in front of the Sweet Music Methodist Church. From what I can tell, the music died long ago."

"Don't move."

"Okay."

"And don't go inside that building."

"One step ahead of you on that."

He hung up and I put my cell phone back in my pocket. I passed a minute trying to clear my head of every thought that attempted to intrude. It's hard work. An unfortunate image of Angel Ramos bursting into the bedroom of Gabriella Montero (formerly

Diaz) managed to get through, and I was working to push it back out when a police cruiser rounded the corner and screeched to a halt in front of the abandoned church. The passenger-side door opened as if on its own. I stepped over to the curb. The city's most recent hero cop was behind the wheel.

"Get in."

I got into the car and closed the door. Cox hit the auto-lock. I turned to face him. "What brings you to the hood?"

Cox held up something in his hand: one of my cards. "Real cute," he said. "Who told you about Willy Padilla?"

The question surprised me. "Who told **you** about Willy Padilla?"

He ignored my question. "Ramos has contacted the mayor."

It didn't take a detective to note that Cox had also landed Angel's last name. "When?" I asked.

"I don't know. Sometime this morning."

"How did he contact him?"

"E-mail."

I glanced out the window. I didn't imagine the information superhighway had made a turn into Sweet Music Methodist Church. "What did he say?"

"He wants ten million dollars."

"For the convent or for himself this time?"

Cox put the car into gear and pulled away from the curb. The light at the corner was red. Cox flipped a switch, burped his siren and pulled through the intersection. "Who the hell knows? Crazy spic nigger. He also sent a picture. Deputy Mayor Byron."

I took a sharp breath. "Dead or alive?"

"Alive. With a fucking Uzi pointed at his head."

25

COX AND I AGREED THAT HE WOULD DRIVE
me out of Fort Petersen and over to Flatbush
Avenue, where I'd be able to catch a gypsy
cab back into Manhattan. The subway
would have been just as quick, if not quicker,
but I think better with actual space to stare
off into. In the subway, except for the occasional elevation, you're literally in the dark.

As we headed for Flatbush, Cox told me
that the instant Commissioner Carroll had
shared the name Angel with him, he knew
who we were dealing with.

"I had that moving company on my list
for Diaz. U-Move. Carroll told me you'd
flushed out the name Angel . . . **bang.** I
know Angel Ramos used to work at that
place, too."

"So you're already familiar with Angel Ramos?"

"Anybody working the Nine-five who didn't know Angel Ramos might as well flush his badge down the can."

"The good old Ninety-fifth Precinct."

"One goddamn crack about that Bad Apples crap, and you're walking."

Not much of a threat, but I took the meaning. "Was your partner involved in any of that?"

Cox whipped his head to face me. "What'd I just say?"

"You said no cracks. That wasn't a crack, it was a question."

"The whole thing is hype," Cox said. "They're just trying to sell papers. McNally was clean."

"What about those two cops? The murder-suicide. That doesn't sound like hype."

"You want to stick to the topic?"

"Fine. Tell me about Angel Ramos."

"He's a punk. Big strong punk, but a punk. There's a lot of gang action back there in the hood. I'm sure that's no surprise. That church you were standing in front of like a fucking target is one of the hangouts for Ramos and his crowd. The guy's got a whole racket going. He's got a string of girls he likes to dole out. Running any drugs you can think of."

"So you've been keeping an eye on him?"

"We've got an operation here to try and clean the shit off the street. That means creeps like Ramos. Except all we've ever gotten him on is robbery and banging heads. He's slippery. Now, with this whole stupid Bad Apple stink, our operation's pretty much shut down. The criminals are having a nice laugh while the cops investigate the cops. Great way to clean up crime, isn't it?"

"Have you ever dealt with Ramos personally?"

"Hell, yeah, I've been in the bastard's face plenty of times. He's cold. A punk like that's not going to live to see thirty."

"Did you ever see him with Roberto Diaz?"

The radio began to crackle. Cox reached over and turned it off. "I never saw Diaz until last Thursday. Son of a bitch, too. I'm standing there at the parade with my thumbs up my ass and suddenly this old blind guy with a dog falls down right in front of me. He was having a heart attack. What the hell's a blind guy doing at a parade in the first place? I was down there doing CPR when the shooting started. Me and the blind guy were just about trampled to death by people running from the shooter. I didn't even see my partner lying on the street. I finally got clear and everyone was screaming that two guys with guns went running into the park. First time I ever laid eyes on Diaz was when he was down by the fountain."

I was tempted to ask him about the last time he laid eyes on Diaz—alive, anyway— in the Municipal Building, but I figured he'd just threaten to make me walk the last block and a half. We reached Flatbush and he pulled over. As I shouldered open the door, Cox picked up my Amigo Willy card from the seat. "What are you hoping for with this stunt?"

"Old gumshoe trick," I said. "Trolling for information."

"You're wasting your time. No one's going to respond to that."

Au contraire, I thought as Cox pulled off down the street. You just did.

TOMMY CARROLL WASN'T IN HIS OFFICE. Stacy informed me that Carroll hadn't been feeling well and that he had gone home. Stacy looked pale and unhappy. I wondered if she knew the scuttlebutt concerning Philip

Byron, but I didn't ask. I did go ahead and ask her if she had a boyfriend.

She gave me a suspicious look. "Why?"

"If you do, I think you ought to go see him, that's all. You look as if you could stand some TLC."

She hesitated a moment before responding. "I can't." The words came out almost in a whisper.

"So then you do have one. Why can't you go see him?"

Whatever minor veil had seemingly lifted quickly descended. She looked at me with robotic eyes. Even her blazer seemed to harden. "I will note for the commissioner that you came to see him."

"No need. I'll catch him at his place."

"I told you, he's not feeling well."

I dared to touch her on the shoulder. "Honey, your boss is likely to be feeling a whole lot worse before this thing is over."

IT WAS RUSH HOUR. I TOOK THE SUBWAY TO Twenty-eighth Street and walked the few blocks to Murray Hill. A pair of policemen were standing over what we used to call a drunken bum on the sidewalk at Lexington and Thirtieth. The bum was asleep. His head was leaning on the brick wall below a travel-agency window, which showed a large poster of a carefree guy and a dishy woman running along a tropical beach. It looked as if the scene were sprouting directly from the poor drunk's head, as if he were dreaming it. Not such a bad dream. Kind of made me want to tell the cops to just leave him be.

As I approached Tommy Carroll's building, the unformed thought that had been nagging me since my conversation with Leonard Cox finally formed. McNally at the parade. A cop from the embattled Ninety-fifth Precinct, far from home base. Gunned down by a shooter who—more and more, it seemed—had been acting on instructions from a known troublemaker from the self-same precinct. I rolled the thought around and played with it while I waited to be buzzed into Carroll's building, then put it away for later.

Betsy Carroll answered the door. "Oh my God, it could be Harlan himself standing there. Come in, Fritz. It's been too long."

She insisted on taking my coat. My .38 was in one of the pockets. I had a twinge, then I remembered that this demure woman was licensed and well trained. I recalled one of my first visits to a shooting range—in the basement of a building on West Twenty-second Street—and my father pointing out to me the small woman in the big goggles.

"They told me downtown that Tommy's not feeling good," I said. "I hope it's okay, my coming over."

Betsy Carroll gave me a measured look. She was pastier than I recalled from the last time I'd seen her, which had probably been around a year or so ago. The skin around her sharp cheekbones and usually pointy chin was beginning to fall. I realized that the pasty look was partly because of the contrast with her shoe-black hair.

"Tommy hasn't told you, has he?" she said in a low voice.

"Told me what?"

"He hasn't told anyone at work. I just thought you . . . Maybe because you and he . . . Oh, Jesus, Fritz. Tommy has cancer. The big stupid bear smoked himself to lung cancer and now it's got him. It's not good. He hasn't told you, has he?"

"He hasn't said a word."

"Then don't you say a word. He'd kill me. We were supposed to go to Tortola this week and get a little sun. Just, you know, **relax.** I had to look that word up in the dictionary and show it to Tommy."

"Jesus, Betsy, I'm so sorry. I had no idea."

"He's scheduled to start radiation in a few weeks, but he's not sure he wants to. Now with all this damn . . . whatever it is going on, he's not going anywhere. I swear, Fritz, the man is going to allow no time between working and dying to—"

She clamped her eyes closed. Her fists, too. A few seconds later, tears emerged from under the eyelids. She drew a sharp intake of breath and opened her eyes. "He wants to die with his boots on. The rest of his life comes second. It always has. All of it." She wiped her tears with the backs of her hands and gave the approximation of a smile. "Men."

"I need to see him, Betsy."

"Of course you do. Somebody always does. Wait here."

She disappeared down the hallway. I looked at a framed print of Grand Central Terminal on the wall, the print with the sunlight streaming through the cathedral windows as if heaven itself had just pulled up outside. A minute later, Tommy Carroll appeared at the end of the hallway. He was in silhouette and he filled the space. I heard his labored breathing before he spoke. "Come in, Fritz. I'm in my office."

The dark form turned and walked off. I followed. Betsy was standing at the open door to her husband's home office as I emerged from the hallway. She gave me a plucky smile as I entered, then closed the door behind me.

Tommy Carroll had loosened his tie and rolled his sleeves partway up his freckled arms. He was settling into a chair in front of a laptop computer. I noticed a short tumbler next to the laptop. Something brown, with a melted chip of ice. He hit some keys on the laptop, stared at the screen a few seconds, then pivoted the laptop in my direction. "You want to see what it's come to?"

I didn't, really, but I knew I would. It was Philip Byron, of course. The picture was from the waist up. He was seated or standing in front of a red wall. His left eye was red and swollen, and he had what appeared to be several cuts above it and on his chin. He was holding up his left hand, which was covered with a gauze bandage. A trace of red had seeped through. His expression was somewhere between mortified and extremely grim. Or maybe despairing and angry. I didn't really know the man. As Cox had said, the barrel of an Uzi rifle was planted against Byron's temple. All that could be seen of the person holding the rifle was the arm. Out-stretched to show as much of the rifle as possible, wearing what appeared to be a puffy black winter coat. Five million New Yorkers wear puffy black winter coats. Not that it mattered. We knew who the arm belonged to. Or, if not who owned the arm, then who had taken the picture. I knew the face. Even on the good brother, it was a disturbing face.

"He wants ten million dollars or else he kills Byron. He also says he'll kill more people. We've got twenty-four hours." Carroll looked at his watch. "Just under. At five o'clock tomorrow, he tells us where he wants the money delivered."

"Five o'clock. That's better than high noon."

"A punk like this likes to hide in the dark. He'll want the money dropped somewhere at night."

"Is this going to happen?" I asked. "Is he going to get his ten million dollars?"

Carroll hit a button on the keyboard and the image of Byron vanished. He hit another key and a new image came up. It was the face of Victor Ramos, with the addition of a thin mustache, above a slate board bearing a series of numbers and letters. But it wasn't

Victor Ramos. It was his twin brother. Angel Ramos's mug shot.

Carroll placed his finger on the screen just below Ramos's chin. The liquid screen ballooned slightly.

"He's going to get his throat cut, that's what," Carroll said. "You or Cox, or me if I have to. We're going to find him, and we're going to take him out."

"We can't do it that way, Tommy. You know that. If that's your plan, I'm done here."

Carroll's face grew crimson in a matter of seconds. "You're not done until I say you're done. Goddammit, Malone, I'll take **you** out!" He punctuated this last sentiment by slamming his fist on the desk. The force made his tumbler fall to the carpet. He let it remain. Carroll's shoulders and head were trembling as if he were caught up in his own private earthquake. Which, of course, he was.

"Betsy told me," I said.

He glowered at me. "Told you what?"

I said it again, slowly. "She told me."

This time he got it. We remained in silence a few seconds, then Carroll reached down and picked up the tumbler and set it back on the desk. He rubbed the spilled liquid into the carpet with his shoe. "She shouldn't have done that."

"I squeezed it out of her," I lied. "I had a hunch."

Carroll seemed to like that. "The great detective and his hunch." He produced a bottle of Jameson's from a desk drawer and poured a few fingerfuls into his tumbler. He barked out, "Lisbeth!" When the door behind me opened, he said, "Get me another glass, would you? Fritz here wants to drink to my **health.** What do you think about that, honey?"

We said nothing while Betsy went off to fetch the glass. She came into the room and set it on Carroll's desk. He tried to make eye contact with her, but she refused. She left without a word. I took a seat while Carroll poured out a shot.

"I hope you like it neat," he said, sliding the glass across the desk.

I picked it up and tapped it against his. "To your health." I thought of Charlie Burke's toasts. He'd have been unimpressed.

Carroll growled, "Just don't tell me you're sorry. I don't want to hear that from anybody. I've got no damn room for pity. I hate pity."

We threw back our drinks like a couple of

cowboys. Carroll refilled his, then aimed for my glass. I waved him off. "I'm good."

"Unless you want to be trapped with a drunken, pissed-off old man, you'd better leave."

"You should take the trip to Tortola, Tommy. Get away with Betsy and sit on your can for a few days. If not for you, for her."

He set down his tumbler, running his thumb back and forth along the rim before looking up at me. "I've already got the **Post** calling for my head. Now we've got a psycho out there ready to blow the deputy mayor's brains out. And I'm supposed to go off and play in the sand?"

"So far you've done a pretty good job of keeping the city from even knowing there's a psycho out there. We know who he is now. We'll get him. If we do it right, we'll even get Byron out alive. Then you and the mayor can work up some sort of cutesy story about his fingers. A buzz-saw accident while he was out in the heartland helping his old pa bring in wood for the winter, whatever you want. It'll all be over soon. Then take the damn vacation. It's not going to kill you."

The words were out of my mouth before I could call them back. Carroll acknowledged them with a bemused look as he took another sip. "You see? If I tell people what's happening to me, it's going to be just like that. Everybody tripping over their tongues."

"As if that's ever bothered you."

"No, you're right. I got thicker skin than that." He picked up a framed photograph from his desk. I couldn't see what it was. His voice lowered. "They'll railroad me right out of there, Fritz. You know they will. They'll smell the blood. Leavitt, the papers, all of them. It'll be 'Thanks for the psycho, thanks for the Bad Apples, you really screwed up royal, here's your gold watch, now get the hell out of here and go die somewhere else.' "

"**That's** pity," I said.

"That's fact! Fucking Leavitt. He's the one that really burns me. Candy-assed little play-boy. That prick should have stayed in Brook-lyn busting criminals. But he's too big for that. He's got to be goddamn mayor. Screw-ing his celebrity girlfriends and whatever the hell else he can get his hands on. Do you think Leavitt's big goal was just to be mayor of New York City? No chance. This is a guy who doesn't know when to stop. He's that kind of politician. As far as Marty Leavitt's

Alameda Free Library

1550 Oak St.

Alameda, CA 94501

510-747-7777

Date: 5/15/2018

Time: 5:56:02 PM

Fines/Fees Owed: $0.00

Total Checked Out: 2

Checked Out

Title: The likeness
Barcode: 33341004966346
Due Date: 06/05/2010 23:59:59

Title: Speak of the devil : a novel
Barcode: 33341004634936
Due Date: 06/05/2018 23:59:59

concerned, he's just stopping off here to piss on a few fire hydrants on his way up. The man has plans. Do you think he's about to let this Bad Apple thing take him down? Not if he can pin the damn thing on me and give me the boot. And if word got out that I'm being eaten alive, it'd just give him one more way to hold me up as damaged goods." He glanced at the photograph again, then set it back down. "I'm staying put. And we're getting Angel Ramos. That's all there is to it. If this Nightmare business explodes now, it could bring me **and** Leavitt down. What I'm telling you is that I'm not going down. Or when I do, it's on my own terms. I've busted my ass all my life to get where I got. I don't go out a loser. It's just not going to happen."

He snatched up his drink. For just an instant, he looked like the healthiest man on earth.

BEFORE I LEFT, I HAD CARROLL PRINT ME out a copy of Angel Ramos's mug shot. Betsy Carroll showed me to the door.

"You're not much for keeping secrets, are you?" she said.

"I'm sorry."

"Don't be. Secrets can eat away at people,

too. It would do him good to talk about it with someone."

"He didn't want to talk about it, Betsy. He just wanted to yell."

She pulled open the door. "You've got to start somewhere."

I hadn't been to my office since Wednesday, so I walked the eleven blocks up and over to Forty-first Street. I stopped off at a cash machine on the way and withdrew a thousand dollars. As I passed the library, I saw that the lions out front were each wearing an enormous Christmas wreath.

There was a pile of mail under the slot, and the door plowed it as I pushed it open. It's a small reception area, four chairs, a low black table covered with outdated magazines, one of those Don Quixote prints by Picasso. I pulled a man's daughter from the paws of a serial rapist a number of years ago and he thanked me with a midtown office. Nothing fancy, but a convenient place to put my feet up and to meet with clients. There's a receptionist's desk but no receptionist. At least not on a regular basis. I hire one now and then for a day's work when I'm feeling charitable. New York City's temporary help comes in all sorts of varieties, and I consider it cheap entertainment. The rest of the time, when the desk is empty, I tell the waiting clients that my receptionist had to run out for an emergency. Margo and I took in a James Bond movie a few years back, and while Bond was playing cutesy with Miss Moneypenny for the jillionth time, Margo whispered in my ear, "If you had a Moneypenny, I'd kill you." Before the night was out, we'd somehow transformed the name "Moneypenny" to "Dashpebble" and christened my nonexistent receptionist.

The mail was mostly junk. Some of it was semi-junk, and I tossed those pieces onto Miss Dashpebble's desk. The rest I dumped in the trash can next to the desk. I hadn't emptied the trash can for a while. Maybe it was about time to get one of those entertaining temps in.

I went into my office, which overlooks Bryant Park, behind the library. When the weather's warm, the place is swarming with people. Junior executives from all over midtown come to the park at lunchtime and loosen their ties or pull their skirts up to the danger zone and soak in the rays. Not for nothing do I keep my binoculars handy.

But a cold November Monday nearing seven o'clock? At a glance, I counted fourteen hardy souls bundled like Cossacks.

The red light on my phone was blinking, so I checked my messages. One was from my mother in California. She can never remember my cell number. She sounded garrulous and a little angry. Pretty typical. She said she was going to hold the phone out so that I could hear "the mighty Pacific." This was followed by ten seconds of silence. She came back on and said she was having a wonderful time, that she loved me and I should stay out of trouble. She gave a cackling laugh and hung up.

There were a few calls about cases that I'd stuck on the back burner, then a familiar voice calling me "Fritzy boy." It was Jigs. I put the message on speakerphone and dropped into my chair.

"Most boring day of my life, I think. You should pay me double. I shadowed that half a brother of yours, like you asked. He was very polite on the subway in the morning. Gave up his seat to a one-armed lady. A real gentleman. But I don't think he was sleeping with her. Too old, too fat, too black. Didn't seem like Paulie's type. I think I snooped out what you need, though. A woman he works with. They took lunch together at a Mexican place near their office. I've got it written down what they ate. He paid. No hand-holding, no footsies, but they seemed to have a lot to talk about. Then, around three-thirty, a coffee break in City Hall Park. This time she was crying. Paulie was patting her on the back like he was trying to burp a pet pooch. And for the hat trick, drinks after work. That's where I am now. The Raccoon Lodge on Warren. They're in a booth. I'm looking at the tops of their cheating heads as we speak. She's got a name, too. It's Annette Hartman. Redhead. Not bad. I wouldn't kick her off the Ferris wheel. Husband's name is Robert, but you play your cards right, I bet he'll let you call him Bob. They live at eight seventeen West End Avenue, and I've got to say, Fritz, it shocks me that people actually pay you to find out this kind of thing. This is too easy. I don't know why you're not a millionaire by now. So look, if these lovebirds decide to go somewhere and flap their wings in private, I'm off the clock. I've got a call in to the homely and fair Allison from the Cloisters. Say a prayer for your favorite altar boy, Mac."

I'd scribbled down the information as Jigs was giving it to me. Next to "Annette Hartman," I wrote, "crying." Before I handed the name over to Phyllis, I'd want to check on it. Chasing after spouses has always felt to me like bottom-feeding. Charlie Burke calls it "bottom-line feeding." It was a good thing Phyllis wasn't asking for photographs. That kind of work depresses me.

I pushed my chair back and put my feet up on the windowsill. Rodin got it wrong when he chiseled **The Thinker.** His guy looks like he might have been mulling over a tough chess move, but for real honest-to-goodness thinking, you've got to bring your feet up level with your head. So long as you don't fall asleep, the cranium will start clicking.

Click.

I had to find Angel Ramos.

Click.

I had to find him before the next sundown.

Click.

The demand for ten million dollars told me one thing: Ramos was losing his cool. It was an irrational sum of money. Call it a hunch, but to me there seemed a desperate smell in it. Whatever had been the purpose of all the pussyfooting around with the "nun" giving us the finger at Gristedes, the original drop at the Cloisters, the million dollars being designated for the Convent of the Holy Order of the Sisters of Good Shepherd and all the rest if it, things had now gotten more blunt. We had two severed fingers in a box, and we had an Uzi jammed into the side of Philip Byron's head. These recent events squared more clearly with the Angel Ramos I'd been getting to know, the punk who'd steal money from the collection plate and recruit his ten-year-old nephew to run drugs. Call it another hunch, but I didn't get the feeling Angel Ramos was intending to pass along his latest ransom demand to nuns or monks or anybody else. This was a grab. This was it. This was the enchilada.

My ploy with the Amigo Willy cards had gone bust. I'd figured a few crank calls, at least. I tried Donna Bia's number again, still not sure what I'd say to her if she answered. She didn't. I hung up without leaving a message. I looked at my watch. I glanced out the window. Finally, I looked at my feet. "You boys ready?"

They offered no resistance. I picked up the phone and called the rental place I use, up on Fifty-second.

"Saddle up my pony," I said to the person on the other end. He wasn't with the program, so I had to translate. I hung up and fetched my blackjack from my desk drawer.

A gift from the old man. When he was a beat cop, he'd lifted it from a man who had been number two to take over one of the big Italian crime families. The mobster told him he called it Betty. Betty had cracked some pretty notorious skulls in her day. I lightly slapped the blackjack a few times against my palm. Even with taps, you can feel the bones beginning to worry.

I went into the closet and pulled out my scratched-up bomber jacket and checked through the pockets to be sure I had my black watch cap. All set.

On my way out the door, I told Miss Dashpebble to hold my calls.

26

SISTER MARY RYAN WAS SURPRISED TO SEE me. She was in her street clothes again, and I wondered if she ever donned the penguin suit.

She cracked, "I don't suppose you're here to give us our million dollars back."

"I would if I could, but I can't."

I had been told by the nun who answered the door to wait in the front hallway. Sister Mary showed me into the Great Room. I sat in the chair where Gary Harvey had sat while we were grilling him. From across the room, Jesus looked down at me wearily.

The sister offered me tea and I accepted. By a seemingly invisible signal, the young nun appeared, and Sister Mary put in the order for a pot of tea. I gave the nun a simple smile and she blushed.

"Natividad cannot stop talking about what took place here the other night," Sister Mary said after the nun had left the room. "With every telling, the details get more and more exciting. The guns get bigger and bigger. She is especially glowing about your Irish friend."

"Jigs. Yes. Women do glow."

Sister Mary made a delicate tent of her fingers. "Sister Anne and I have been talking. We would like to contact Mr. Harvey. In the confusion of the other evening, we feel we didn't tend terribly well to him. I believe very strongly in fate, Mr. Malone. I feel that fate led Mr. Harvey to Good Shepherd."

"A cold-blooded killer is what led Mr. Harvey to Good Shepherd."

"The Lord utilizes His agents."

"No offense, Sister, but the Lord has lost control of that particular agent."

Sister Natividad floated into the room with a tray and all the tea goodies. She set the tray down on the table in front of Sister Mary. She said, "You must let it sleep."

"**Steep,** Natividad."

The nun's blush was even richer than the last. She stole a glance at me as she left the room.

"How old is she?" I asked.

"Natividad is twenty."

"That seems young."

"It is." She smiled. "The older we get, the younger it becomes."

"I mean to be a nun. I guess I don't really know at what age a person can become a nun."

"Technically speaking, there are no restrictions. Of course, with a person who is not yet a legal adult, there has to be complete agreement from the parents or from the legal guardian. In Natividad's case, she became a nun in the Philippines when she was seventeen. Earlier this year, her family moved to America, and she wanted to remain near them."

"I was under the impression that when you signed on, you became part of God's family. So to speak."

"That's true. But it doesn't mean you forsake your secular family. We're still very much in the world, Mr. Malone. As you can see, many of us don't wear habits anymore. Not to deny tradition, by any means, but we're not relics, after all. At least we hope we're not. We're attempting to bridge the more traditional aspects of who and what we are with the fact of our being in the modern world. God is in my heart. He is not in my clothes."

She had just started to lift the teapot and had to set it down swiftly as she burst into laughter. "Oh, my. Well, I surely didn't mean it to sound **that** way!" She laughed again, then reached once more for the teapot. She shot me a look. "I think the tea has had time to sleep, don't you?"

THE NAME ANGEL RAMOS MEANT NOTHING to Sister Mary Ryan. I showed her the picture. She studied it thoughtfully. "He's a criminal," she said. "That's what these numbers mean. He's been arrested."

"That's right."

"What did he do?"

"As far as what they've nabbed him for? Robbery, assault, theft."

She looked up from the picture. "And what he hasn't been 'nabbed' for?"

"I believe he's the person behind the Thanksgiving Day shootings and the bombing. I also think he's kidnapped the deputy mayor. The package that Gary Harvey brought by. It contained . . . Someone cut off two of the deputy mayor's fingers. I think the man in that picture did it."

The nun paled. "Oh, my."

"There's an ultimatum: ten million dollars

in exchange for Mr. Byron's freedom. Everything's pointing to Angel Ramos."

Sister Mary glanced back at the photo. "He looks menacing."

"That's a good way of putting it."

"He must be in torment."

"Maybe so. But what's more important right now is that we stop him before he can put anyone else in torment."

She set the picture faceup on the table, next to the tea tray, then changed her mind and turned it over. "We'll do anything we can, Mr. Malone. But I don't honestly know what that is. Besides to pray, of course."

"We'll take that. But what we really need is to locate Ramos. The piece that isn't fitting in is why it is that Ramos went through the whole song and dance Saturday with having us drop the money at the Cloisters, then calling you in. At the end of it all, we still had the money. If it was all just to deliver the package and let us know that he had Philip Byron . . . it doesn't make any sense. The convent is nowhere near Ramos's territory. But there has to be some sort of connection. There has to be a link."

"I can't imagine what it could be," Sister Mary said.

"How many nuns are in residence here?" I asked.

"Normally? Fifteen."

"Why 'normally'? You don't have fifteen at the moment?"

"We had a loss recently." She had picked up her teacup, but she didn't take a sip. She looked past the cup, off into space. "You probably heard of it. Unfortunately, the papers played it up. More and more, that seems to be what they do."

"When was this?"

"Oh, just last month. Near the end of October."

"You don't mean the Sister Suicide?"

Sister Mary lowered her teacup into her palm. "You might understand, we're not exactly fond of that term. It's terribly dehumanizing."

We were referring to a story that the papers had made hay with for nearly a week, just before Halloween. A nun in full habit had been found by a morning jogger in a wooded section of Prospect Park. She had apparently slit both her wrists. A suicide note had been left next to the body. As Sister Mary said, the papers had jumped all over it. **Sister Suicide.** I recalled the photo that had accompanied the story. It was taken when the woman was in her early twenties, before she joined the sisterhood. She was pretty, and that helped give the story legs for a few extra days. Attractive young nuns slitting their wrists in a public place aren't your everyday news story. The coverage had been typically sensational and morbid. I had to admit, it had hooked me a little.

Sister Mary Ryan said, "Margaret was a terribly troubled young woman. Of course, guilt is a useless emotion, but we're only human. It's there. All of us at the convent feel it. We can't help but contemplate that we failed Margaret. Her difficulties were known to us. From the moment she arrived at Good Shepherd, it was a struggle for her. She had already suffered considerable tragedy."

"You don't have to talk about it if you don't want to," I said.

"No, no. It's fine. It helps, actually. It's been especially hard on Natividad. Being so young. Until Natividad arrived, Sister Margaret had been our youngest. She was only thirty-three when she died. Natividad latched on to her immediately. I'd say she looked at Margaret as an older sister. We encouraged the friendship. For both their sakes, actually. Margaret . . . She had a drinking problem."

My reaction must have showed.

"You're surprised by the idea of a nun having a drinking problem?"

"I guess I am."

"I always find it surprising that people are surprised. It's what I was just saying. We're human. We're not saints." She gave a coy smile. "At least not yet. We're not without our problems, Mr. Malone. We're mortal, and we suffer mortal failings. We do have a focus and a path and a calling and the assistance of our faith, and those are all wonderful securities. But we're flesh, and not without sin. And I'm not going to pretend that Sister Margaret always made life at Good Shepherd particularly easy. She didn't. She represented a formidable challenge. But in many ways, I think that might have been the gift she brought to us, at great cost to herself. Her difficulties challenged us to show the true depths of our compassion. Alcoholism is such a wretched disease. In the end, I suppose it took hold of Sister Margaret more forcefully than we did. Along with all her sadness and all her troubles."

She lowered her head. An image of my mother rose in my mind. Two images, really. In the one, she was flashing her seductively appealing smart-aleck smile and raising her glass in a ribald toast. Shirley Malone, life of the party. In the other . . . well, let's just say the party had gone on a bit too long. A gem without luster. I shook the images from my head and picked up the photograph of Angel Ramos. I waited until Sister Mary looked back up before I spoke. "I'm sorry, Sister."

"I guess I shouldn't let myself ramble so."

"Can I ask you to show this to the rest of the sisters? As soon as possible? If any of them have even an inkling that they've seen this man before, or have any information about him, I need to know immediately."

She leaned forward and took the photograph from me. She studied it a moment. "I know you're going to find this man, Mr. Malone. I have faith."

That made one of us.

I GOT MY FIRST RESPONSE TO MY AMIGO Willy cards as I headed down the West Side Highway. It was a male voice. No discernible accent.

"You put these cards out?"

"Yep," I said.

"You think you're funny. Well, **fuck you.**"

He hung up. I punched in *69, but the caller's number was blocked. Probably a pay phone. Since I already had the phone out, I punched in the code for Margo. She answered on the first ring. "Hello, sailor."

Caller ID. It still creeps me out.

"What's new, pussycat?" I said.

"I should be asking you. Where are you?"

"Streaking past Riverside Church, on a bearing heading south."

"Any exit plans? Like maybe Seventy-second Street?"

"Afraid I can't. Not right now."

I gave her a brief rundown on my day. I left out the part about Tommy Carroll's cancer. An irritating voice in my head said, Need-to-know basis. When I was finished, Margo asked, "Where does that leave you?"

"I'm going back out to Fort Pete."

"Now?"

"Yes."

"You want company?"

"No. You stay put."

"What do you think you can accomplish in Fort Petersen, besides getting yourself in trouble?"

It was a good question, and I didn't have a good answer. "If Angel Ramos is holding Philip Byron out there someplace, I want to at least be in the ballpark."

"I'm not hearing an action plan here."

"I'll bob, I'll weave."

"Oh, great."

In front of me, a red sports car bobbed and weaved. It also swerved into my lane, nearly clipping my bumper. I hit the brakes and leaned on my horn. The driver shot a hairy arm out the window to show me his finger, but I wasn't impressed. I squeezed on the gas, running my bumper right up to his, close enough to kiss it. Apparently, I also muttered my innermost thoughts.

"What'd you just call me?" Margo asked.

"Nothing. Sorry." The sports car swerved back to its original lane. I swerved right with it.

"My last boyfriend never talked to me like that," Margo said.

"Neither does this one. A guy just cut me off."

"**I'm** going to cut you off."

As if on cue, our connection began to break up. The sports car did a little fake to the left, then roared on ahead. Margo was burbling on the phone and I almost lost her, but we got clear as I passed the railroad yards.

"What were you saying?"

"I was saying please come over tonight. I don't care how late it is."

"Or early?"

"Either way. This is where my fantasies of you holding down a nice job as a shoe salesman start to kick in."

"I'll be fine."

"Don't make promises you can't keep."

"Listen," I said, "how was your pop star today, anyway?"

"Are you trying to change the subject?"

"I am."

"My pop star had an ego the size of the Plaza hotel."

"Is that where you interviewed him?"

"Yes."

"But if his ego was the **size** of the Plaza hotel, and you were interviewing him **in**—"

"Hey. I don't want the last thing I hear from you to be a stupid joke."

"It's not the last thing," I said.

"But it was going to be a stupid joke, right?"

"That's in the ear of the beholder."

"Tell me you love me, then hang up."

"I love you," I said.

There was a pause. "Really?"

I hung up.

FORT PETERSEN AT NIGHT LOOKED PRETTY much like Fort Petersen during the day, except darker, and most of the shops had been replaced by iron gates. A couple of teenagers darted in front of my car in the middle of the block. One of them turned in my direction and made a pistol with his fingers. I held my fire.

The Ninety-fifth precinct house was a block off Culver. I pulled into one of the slots reserved for the local crime fighters and went inside. The old guy at the front desk studied my PI license as if it were an unusually well-written piece of pornography. If he had moved it any closer to his nose, he might have accidentally licked it.

"Who's your duty officer?" I asked when he finally handed my wallet back to me.

"Captain Kersauson."

"I'd like to see him."

The old guy picked up his phone. "What should I tell him it's about?"

"You shouldn't tell him it's about anything. I'll do that."

He paused a moment, eyeing me, then dialed a number. "Captain? It's Ross. There's a gentleman out here wants to see you." He cupped the mouthpiece and gave me a wink. "You see how I called you a gentleman? Even though you're uppity?" He went back to the phone. "No, Captain, he didn't. He's a private investigator from Manhattan." He listened, then cupped the phone again. "The captain wants to know if you're Dick Tracy."

"I should have such a jaw."

Back to the phone. "No, Captain, he's not. But he looks harmless enough to me . . . Uh-huh. Okay." He hung up the phone. "Captain Kersauson will see you now. Through that door, take a left, then twenty feet, take a right."

"Sorry about the uppity."

He waved me on. I twisted the doorknob and walked right into the door. The old guy chuckled under his breath as he pushed the buzzer.

Kersauson was waiting at his office door. He had a large head decorated with a marine cut. He could have stood to drop about thirty pounds, but I didn't plan to veer our conversation into the realm of personal upkeep. He was in his shirtsleeves and wearing his shoulder holster and gun, as if he were ready for a siege. I handed him my card. He barely gave it a glance. "What can I do for you?"

"I'm looking for prostitutes."

"Is that so? What do you think this is, tourist information?"

"I'm working a job," I said.

This time he gave my card a harder look. "Hell of a job. You getting paid for this?"

"I'm trying to track down Angel Ramos."

The problem with a good poker face is that it sometimes gives away the very fact that you're trying not to give anything away. The captain gave me an absurdly neutral stare for a good five or six seconds before he said, "Who?"

"Angel Ramos. He runs an ice-cream shop over on Viceroy Street. Gives it away to the kids for free. Coaches Little League in the summers. Tutors math in his spare time. I believe he's also president of the Rotary Club. No. Wait. I'm sorry. **Angel Ramos?** He pimps, pushes drugs, runs guns, beats up people and steals things. My mistake. Ever heard of him?"

I was glad the old guy out front wasn't here to see me getting uppity all over again. His boss didn't look too happy to see it, either. "What's this about?"

"It's about I need to find Angel Ramos. I understand he dabbles heavily in the flesh trade, among his other hobbies. I thought I might start by asking the girls on the street. Some girls like to talk, if you handle them right."

"What do you want with Ramos?"

"That's confidential information, Captain."

He replanted his feet. "We don't have a prostitution problem in Fort Pete, Mr. Malone."

"There are hookers five blocks from the

White House, Captain. I'm not smearing your precinct, it's part of the landscape. I just want to know where the girls are." I took my card from him and jotted a phone number on the back of it. "Here."

"What's this?"

"It's Police Commissioner Carroll's home phone number. I'm on special assignment. Call him. He'll tell you whether to chat with me or throw me out on my can."

"Wait here."

I waited. Three minutes later, he came back.

I asked, "Did you reach him?"

"I got him."

"What did he say?"

"He said to tell you where the whores are."

"Okay, Captain. I'm all ears."

CAPTAIN KERSAUSON CERTAINLY KNEW HIS precinct. Not eight blocks south of the police station stood the large brick building that Victor Ramos had mentioned. Like he said, it took up the entire block. Its black silhouette made it look as if a piece of the sky had been carved away. A sign out front said: THE NIAGARA COMPANY. It was an industrial concern that took in and laundered towels and sheets and linen tablecloths, from hotels and restaurants in Brooklyn and Queens and from across the river in Manhattan. At the far end of the block was a half-acre parking area separated from the street by a metal fence that stood about twelve feet high. Several dozen vans with the Niagara logo were parked in the lot. According to Captain Kersauson, it was a little bit like a shell game, trying to guess which of the vans was serving as port of call at any one time for the local prostitutes and their customers. Technically speaking, the fenced-in parking area was locked up tight, as were the vans. There was even an unarmed guard posted on the north end of the lot, in a little shack about the size of a drive-through photo place. According to Kersauson, the local flesh peddlers paid the guard not to look south.

I drove slowly down Brockton Street, along the fenced-in parking area, and pulled over to the curb at the end of the block and turned off my headlights. Across the street were several abandoned buildings with boarded-up fronts, interspersed with darkened brownstones. Scanning the block for signs of life, I didn't even see the woman approaching the car from the passenger side. At the **tap-tap** of her fingernails against the window, I started for my gun. I found the window switch instead and lowered the passenger window partway. She was a young black woman. Her hair was long and paper-flat, glistening in the minimal ambient light.

"You looking for a date?"

"I might be," I said.

"Might be shit. You out of gas or you looking for a date? What's your name?"

"My name's Fritz."

"Right. My name's Brittany. It's cold out here, Fritz. Why don't you let me in?"

"Door's open."

She tugged on the handle and let herself in. She brought with her a slight scent of cinnamon. She was wearing a tight denim blouse and a short red skirt. Not exactly winter wear. She ran her hands up and down her skinny arms. "It's cold," she said, giving a dramatic shudder.

"You ought to be wearing a coat," I said.

She turned a sneer to me. I'm sure it was supposed to be a smile. "Coat don't show me off," she said. "You want to look?" Before I could say no, she tugged at her blouse the way Clark Kent tugs at his shirt when he's about to go save the world. She flashed her breasts, then as swiftly covered them up again. "That's your free sample. You want to go someplace warm and see some more?"

"Have you got any friends?" I asked.

She made a face. "You don't want me?"

"I didn't say that."

She gave me a queer look. "What? You want two girls?" Then she laughed, showing me a cracked tooth. "You got the stuff for **two** girls?"

"I've got the money," I said.

"We ain't talked money yet."

"How much for three?"

"Brittany" fell against the door as if she'd been shot. Her body shook with laughter. "**Three?** God damn, you're an **animal.** What you gonna do with three girls? Don't you go telling me you're Mr. Super Stud."

"I like an audience," I said.

"I get it. That's cool. We got a special kinky rate. Three hundred dollars."

"Fifty."

"**Fifty?**"

"One hundred."

"For three girls?"

"It's a cold night, Brittany. I don't exactly see the cars lining up."

"One-fifty."

"Okay."

"Show me the money."

I pulled a wad of cash from my pocket.

She seemed satisfied. "Okay. I'm getting out of the car. Drive around the corner.

Halfway down's a streetlight that's out. There's a Dumpster. Stop there."

She got out of the car and crossed into one of the boarded-up buildings. I followed her instructions. A part of me wanted to just step on the gas and keep going. I was making this up as I went along. My thinking was that I probably had only one crack at trying to get information; why not gather together as many potential informants as I could? I hadn't been waiting two minutes at the broken streetlight when the passenger door opened and a lithe black man slipped into the car, pulling the door shut behind him.

"Give me the money."

I asked, "Who are you?"

"I'm the man with the girls."

"I don't see any girls."

"I got 'em."

"You've got three of them?"

"You're a hungry motherfucker, aren't you?"

I asked, "Is Donna one of the girls?"

"What are you talking about, Donna?"

"Donna Bia. I was told Donna Bia is worth three of anyone else. You say you're the man, so I thought I'd ask."

"I ain't got no fucking Donna for you, punk. This ain't fucking pick-and-choose. You want these three or you want to get the hell gone? Two hundred dollars."

"Brittany said one-fifty."

"Well, fuck Brittany. It's called inflation. Two hundred." I gave him the money. He stuffed it into his pocket. "Flash your lights."

I did. A few seconds later, I could make out three figures crossing the street. One of them pulled back a piece of the fence and let the others inside, then followed. They moved to one of the vans, opened the back door and disappeared inside.

"Showtime," said the man next to me. "What you do is you don't leave a mark on them, you got that? You hurt my girls, I hurt you. That's the only rule. Otherwise, enjoy."

He left the car and slid into the shadows. I removed my shoulder holster and gun and stashed them under the seat. I figured I might have to withstand a caress or two to help set the mood, and nothing tanks a mood like a snub-nose .38.

I got out of the car and found the place where the fence was unattached. I curled the fence back and slipped into the lot. I reached the van and jerked down on the rear door handle, pulling the door open.

The women were arrayed on bags of linen, like a trio of farmer's daughters in a hayloft. They were still dressed, which I was glad to see, though there seemed to be a heated contest as to which could hike her skirt up the highest. By an amazing coincidence, all three had forgotten to put on their panties when they'd gotten dressed that morning. Brittany spoke first. "We got us a party. Girls, meet Fritz."

One was wearing a platinum wig. The other reminded me of Mama Cass Elliott. I climbed into the van and pulled the door closed. Only the slightest light came through the front window. I sensed movement, and hands began poking and prodding me. "Whoa, whoa. Hold on."

The hands withdrew. Brittany's voice sounded. "There a problem?"

"I want the lights," I said.

"Lights? Oh, right. The man wants an audience."

I crawled over several soft bags and at least one bony thigh and stretched into the front seat, slapping around on the panel until I found the light knob. I twisted it and the overhead came on. I turned back around and leaned against a pile of the duffel bags. Six dull eyes settled on me.

"Whatever split you get from your middleman, you've already earned it," I said to them. "I'm not really in a frisky mood tonight, girls, thank you all just the same." My announcement received no reaction. The one calling herself Brittany rubbed her index finger list-lessly along her front teeth as if brushing them. I went on, "I've got three hundred dol-lars in my pocket. I'd like some information. If any of you can help me out, it's a hundred dollars. And you don't have to share it with whatever-his-name-is."

"Lenny," Platinum Wig said.

Mama Cass snapped, "Shut up!"

"I'm trying to get ahold of either Donna Bia or Angel Ramos," I said. "If neither of these names means anything to any of you, we're through here."

Platinum Wig spoke up. "What you want with them?"

"That's between me and them, but I'll tell you this: if I don't find them first, the police will. And it would be better if I do."

"You a cop? Shit. He's a cop."

"I'm not a cop. I just need to find Angel or Donna. Money in the bank, girls. Who's going to help me?"

The three looked at me as if they had each been struck dumb. Then Mama Cass reached into a small purse and extracted a cell phone. It was already flipped open. She held it deli-cately between two fingers.

I asked, "What's that?"

Brittany answered, "That's Lenny."

The rear doors of the van flew open. Indeed, it was Lenny. He was holding a cell phone in one hand and something I couldn't make out in the other. He flipped the phone closed and tossed it into the van. With a similar move of the other hand, a switchblade knife appeared.

"Out."

The three women scrambled out of the van and took off running, or in Mama Cass's case, galloping. Lenny gestured with the knife. "You, too."

"I'm pretty comfortable where I am," I said.

"You're pretty fucked is what you are. Get out."

I came down slowly off the duffel bags. I slipped sideways, and when I did, my hand ran quickly into and back out of my pocket. Lenny missed the move. He gestured again with the knife. "You tried to fuck me over. You give me the rest of that money, or I'm going to fucking cut it out of you." He backed away slightly to give me just enough room to get out of the van. As I did, he brought the knife up and shook it in my face. "Let's have it."

So I gave it to him. I would have preferred a downward swing; you get the full fulcrum effect that way. But I had to swing upward. I landed the blackjack just under the pimp's wrist. The knife fell instantly. My arm continued its upward swing, to a point just past my head. Lenny started to make a noise, but the sound never made it past his lips. I brought my arm back down, snapping my wrist sharply. Betty bounced off the pimp's skull with the telltale **crack.** He lost his legs and dropped . . . like a sack of linen.

Love that Betty.

27

I ALMOST RAN HER OVER. SHE STEPPED IN front of the car as I rounded the corner, and I hit the brakes. It was Brittany. She moved swiftly to the passenger door and hopped into the car. Her eyes were wide. "You kill him?"

"I didn't kill him. I just put him to sleep."

"He wakes up, he's gonna kill **you.** You still got that money?"

"I've got it."

"Gimme it."

"Is this a stickup?"

"Drive. I show you where's Donna Bia, you give me the money. That was the deal. You shoulda just asked me in the first place. You got a fucked-up way of doing things."

"I thought I was improving my odds," I said.

I followed her directions and in five minutes was driving past a wobbly-looking building with a small group of men milling about outside. A sign painted on the blackened window read: FLEA CLUB.

"That's it. You find Donna in there."

"In the Flea Club?"

"That's right. Gimme the money."

I pulled over in the next block. "If she's not there, I'm out three hundred dollars," I said.

"She's there. Bitch practically lives in that place."

"What about Angel Ramos?"

"I don't know. But if you got Donna, you got Angel. And I'm telling you, you got Donna."

I had an idea. I pulled out my phone and the piece of paper Donna Bia's mother had given me. I punched in the number and handed over the phone. "If she answers, find out where she is."

Brittany put the phone to her ear. A few seconds later, she gave me a wink. "Donna? This is Keesha. Where you, girl? You at the Flea?" She listened, nodding a few times. "Uh-huh. No. Nothing. Lenny was just asking, that's all. Says someone was trying to get hold of you." She listened again, nodded again, said, "Shiiiiiiit," then hung up.

She handed me back the phone. "Pay up."

I STUCK MY .38 INTO MY BELT AND UN-tucked my shirt, pulled my watch cap from my coat pocket and put it on. Not much in the disguise department, but it was all I had to work with. I was going to stand out in the Flea Club no matter what. As I approached the building I reached into my pocket and gave Betty a little squeeze. The **thump-thump-thump** of dance music oozed from the building.

I took several unfriendly glances as I entered the club and made my way to the small bar. There was a pool table in the rear. A cone-shaped lamp hung over the pool table; otherwise, the place was dark as a coal mine. The music was coming from overhead. I stood a moment to let my eyes adjust to the darkness, and when they did, they saw a half-dozen faces looking in my direction, none of them terribly impressed with what they were seeing. I asked for a beer. When it came, I imagined squeezing the bottle the way Popeye does with his spinach can, the beer leaping into the air and going in a neat hook-move right down my throat.

Some might say I was jumpy.

I affected a moody pose, drinking the beer slowly but steadily, staring at the bottle as if the two of us were discussing a breakup. I noticed people coming in and crossing to a ruby-colored curtain that hung over a doorway just behind the pool table. I deduced that the dance club was upstairs. I also deduced that Donna Bia must be up there, too. I quickly concluded that I should get myself upstairs. Brilliance like this should be packaged and sold at premium prices.

I paid for my beer and went over to the curtain. The two guys playing pool watched me with interest but didn't interfere as I pulled back the curtain and started up the narrow stairs behind it. The **thump-thump-thump** grew louder.

The upstairs was packed. I'd say a hundred people were crammed into a room designed for half that number. The floor was elbow-to-elbow, with people either dancing or giving it their best shot. An obnoxious lighting system bathed the crowd in a rotation of colors, red then green then blue, followed by a ten-second white-light strobe, then back to the colors.

I checked my watch. Ten-thirty.

I thought of the image on Tommy Carroll's computer screen. Philip Byron with his bloody bandaged hand, the Uzi pressed against his head. There's a point in certain investigations—not all, but some of them—when you're struck with the notion that you've gotten everything wrong. Investigating is a guessing game, after all, a matter of how much you trust a particular assumption and then the one that leads from that and the one after that and so on. You follow a path, but you need to remain mindful that it's a path you helped create. Charlie used to warn me in the early days about what he called the intoxication factor: **You can get yourself drunk on a single idea. You can go blind. That's not good. A better idea might come lumbering along, as big as an elephant, and you won't even see it. You've got to stay focused, but you've got to stay flexible.**

My problem was time. This wasn't an investigation of leisure, where I could put my feet up in my office and gaze down at the human ants in Bryant Park and systematically gather together in my mind the various threads or puzzle pieces or whatever you want to call them and see how things were looking. These kinds of investigations are a luxury. The information percolates, and all the useless bits eventually burn off until you're left with exactly and only what you need. But this was the **other** kind of investigation. I had a mutilated man with an Uzi to his head and the **Jeopardy!** theme song plinking away in the background. The thought that came to me as I stood at the entrance to the dance floor was that maybe I had allowed myself to become intoxicated with the unquestioned notion that Angel Ramos was the man of the hour and that maybe I was now standing gumshoed at the most ridiculous of all places, chasing after a nasty, degenerate, pale-eyed wild goose while time was **tick-tick-tick**ing away. The thought was a hammer blow to the gut. Philip Byron couldn't afford for me to be wrong.

Then I spotted Donna Bia. She was dancing near the DJ's station, twenty feet from where I was standing. Lance Jennings had painted a surprisingly accurate portrait with just a few words. Hellcat. Hot tamale. Also, I spotted the tattoo of a rose on the woman's upper right arm.

If I were to say that Donna Bia was wearing a little yellow number, I'd be underreporting. Miss Bia had hips like a Vespa motor scooter, high round breasts that were jostling each other for attention, and taut, dark woo-woo legs, all packed into a breathtakingly tight and skimpy taxi-yellow dress. The hem of the thing ran so high the woman could not have sat down without causing a minor riot. Her cell phone was clipped to her dress, next to her right breast, and she was dancing with her eyes closed and a self-satisfied sex smile on her face. Her clenched fists pumped the air in time with the music as her ample hips gave just the barest hint of swing to the otherwise grandiose pelvic thrusts. Imaginary sex at its best. As I watched the hot tamale sizzling out there on the floor, I knew this much: Her mother would not be proud.

Margo drags me out onto the dance floor now and then, and my general act is to shuffle in place while Margo runs vivacious rings around me, sort of like I'm a maypole. Something told me that where Miss Bia was concerned, I should keep my dance moves under wraps. It was clear that I couldn't attempt to speak with her here and expect anything other than a game of **What? What?** I considered stepping forward and just muttering "Police," flashing my PI license in the strobe lights and dragging her off the dance floor and out of the club under the guise of an arrest. But the backfire potential was too high. Besides, Lady Bia might simply slap her trap shut and demand to see a lawyer.

So I played dirty. Or rather, dirtier. Hell, it

had worked so far. I reached into my pocket and pulled out my cell phone, along with a fistful of twenties. I hit the redial button and put the phone to my ear. A few seconds later, the woman in the yellow afterthought plucked her phone from her elastic hem. I saw her mouth move and heard the words shouted in my ear: "Is Donna!"

"I'm over here!" I shouted back. "I'm waving my arm!"

I waved my arm. Donna continued dancing—or at any rate, her hips kept stirring the air—and she looked around until she spotted me. She frowned and yelled into the phone, "Who're you? What do you want?"

I held up the fistful of twenties. "I want to give you a lot of money!" I shouted into the phone. "All this! It's for you!"

I didn't wait for her response. I turned my back on her, pocketing the cash and the phone, and retreated down the stairs, through the curtain and back outside to the street. The shops across from the club were all shuttered. One of them—a Laundromat—had a blue plastic pony out front, the kind you feed a quarter to give a kid a ride. I crossed the street and waited next to the pony, arms crossed, leaning against the Laundromat's metal gate. When Donna emerged from the club half a minute later, pulling a flimsy sweater around her shoulders, I gave a sharp whistle. "Over here!"

As she stepped across the street, slipping the strap of a pillbox purse over her shoulder, I pulled the watch cap off my head. The perfect gentleman. She came up onto the curb and I inclined my head to the right. "You want to ride the pony?"

She gave me the look I deserved. "What do you want? Where'd you get my number?"

"I thought maybe we could talk."

"Talk fast, mister. It's fucking cold out here."

"We could go someplace warm."

Her eyes narrowed. "What's this about? You trying to fuck with me? I got a boyfriend'll slice your eyes out, you try to fuck with me."

"What I'm trying to do is give you some money in exchange for a little of your time."

"I could slap you, talking to me that way," she said. She took a beat. "How much money you talking?"

"Five hundred dollars."

"Shit. What you think you're going to get for that money? I told you, I got a boyfriend."

I gave her a long, deliberate up-and-down. "Look, I can give my money to someone else.

You're a piece of work, but you're not the last woman on the planet. If you want to sneeze at five hundred bucks, that's up to you."

Something passed over the woman; I could see it in the relaxing of her facial muscles. She moved a step closer, fingering the collar of her sweater. Her nails were hooked like talons. "You like how I dance? That it? I dance good, don't I?"

"Yes. You dance good."

"Uh-huh." She stepped closer. "You want to give a girl some money to watch her dance? A little private dancing? How's that sound?"

"Sounds good."

"I know someplace warm."

"I've got a car. It's just down on the next block."

She lowered her voice. "You go in front of me. You get in, and you get comfortable. And you get the five hundred ready. I'll be right behind you."

She had me pegged for a sucker. I could see it in her expression. She tried flashing her eyes to give out the pretense that she was suddenly all excited about what was to come, but it didn't really work. I headed for the car, and she followed about twenty steps back. I caught some looks from the people outside the Flea Club, but no one said anything. I reached the car and got in and leaned over to open the passenger door. Donna got in. I thought her dress was going to snap in two. She set her tiny purse on her lap. The contrived smile on her face froze, then vanished altogether. I was holding my .38 loosely in my hand, aimed roughly at her waist.

"Shit. What's that for?"

With my other hand, I pulled some twenties from my pocket and handed them to her. Her talons gathered them in.

"Your boyfriend," I said. "The one who'd slice my eyes out. We're talking about Angel, aren't we?"

Her eyes hadn't left the gun. "You a pervert or a cop?"

"Neither, last time I checked." I gestured with the gun. "Angel. I need to know where he is."

"I don't know where the hell he is. Put that thing down. I thought you wanted to have some fun."

I tossed a few more twenties onto her lap. "That's the nice way of asking," I said, then I raised the gun barrel a few inches, to the woman's easiest target. "This is the not-nice way. I'm betting you're not only pretty but smart. So just tell me where I can find him. I'll give you the rest of the money, all five hundred, and you can go back to the Flea and buy drinks for everyone. But I need to know, Donna. Angel is in big trouble. Seriously big trouble. If I can talk to him, I can keep it from being even bigger. There's already a noose around his neck. I'm the one who can keep it from being pulled. But I've got to talk to him."

"I don't know what you talking about. Put that fucking thing away."

"I'm talking about Roberto. Your ex-boyfriend. We both know what he did last week and how he ended up. And we're talking about your current boyfriend. Do you want him to end up dead, too?"

"Angel hasn't done nothing. What you want with him?"

"When was the last time you saw Angel?"

"That's none of your business."

"Have you seen him since last Thursday? Since Thanksgiving?" I counted out five twenties and held them up in front of her face. "It doesn't come any easier than this, honey. Free cash. One word, Donna. Yes? No?"

"No. I ain't seen him." She snatched the money.

"Okay. I want an address, Donna. I want a location. I'm going to drive, and you're going to give me directions." I hit the button on the driver's door armrest, locking all the doors. Donna flinched slightly at the **thunk.** I loaded my voice with ice. "You take me to Angel, you'll see the rest of the money. You play games? I pull over somewhere dark, and you're not going to be happy."

She tilted her chin upward defiantly. "You won't shoot me."

I touched her leg with the barrel of the gun and nudged at the hem of her dress. "Let's put it this way: I won't kill you."

"I don't know where he is," she said again. A slight tremor had slipped into her voice. "Angel doesn't live anywhere. He just crashes places."

"You know the places he crashes. We'll go on a little tour, you and me."

I pulled the gun back and turned the ignition. A part of me hated having to be such a creep, but in this business, you don't let those parts have any say in the matter. I thought of Gabriella Montero and the total lack of concern shown for her by the woman in the seat next to me. That helped. As I put the car in reverse, Donna shifted in her seat, swinging her knees over in the direction of the steering wheel. Her legs were impossible to ignore, as she knew full well. She snapped open her purse.

"Hey. I got an idea." She looked up from her purse with dark meaningful eyes. "I can call Angel. See where he's at."

I swung my gun hand over the back of the seat in order to look out the rear window. "Good idea." I eased the car backward, turning the wheel. From the corner of my eye, I saw Donna pulling her cell phone from the purse. In the brief instant before she lunged at me, it struck me how remarkably slender the phone was.

Pfffffffffffff!

Pepper spray. I jerked my head as it hissed from the tiny canister. A lot of it went directly into my mouth and I immediately gagged, but enough also misted into my eyes. Within a second they felt like they were on fire. I dropped the pistol onto the back floor as I pawed at my face. Donna cursed at me in Spanish, throwing herself across my lap. I heard the **thunk** of the doors unlocking. Grabbing wildly, I managed to get ahold of Donna's hair.

"Fucker! Let go!"

My cheeks took a raking from her dangerous nails and I lost my grip on her hair. But I got my first burning gasp of air. I tried to see through the tears welling up in my eyes, but there was only a yellow blur moving off my lap. I swung at it. My hand hit something hard. Her purse. I grabbed at it. Donna tried to wrest it from my grip, then lowered her head and sank her teeth into the back of my hand. I jerked at the purse and heard its contents spill out. Donna slapped at my face, then the passenger door opened and I lunged, but my hand managed to grab only part of her leg. A second later, I took a sharp hit on the side of the head. I released the leg and the door slammed closed. From the swiftly receding sound—a slowly syncopated **click, click, click**—I gathered that Donna had hit me in the head with her stiletto heel and hadn't stopped to put the shoe back on.

I remained sprawled on the front seat, working to find just one complete breath. Tears from my burning eyes were running down my face. How **stupid.** How utterly stupid of me. I tried to open my eyes again, but the burning sensation overcame me. I touched the spot on my head where I'd been hit. It was wet with blood.

Then I heard voices approaching. Chief among them was Donna's.

"There! That green one."

I shoved myself into a sitting position and beat spastically with my hand until I found my armrest, managing to find the door lock just as the voices reached the car.

"That's it." Donna again. "Right there. He tried to rape me."

Someone pulled at the door. "Open the door, motherfucker, or I'll fucking smash it the fuck in!"

I rubbed at my eyes and squinted through the blazing tears. I couldn't tell how many of them Donna had summoned, but however many they were, they began rocking the car.

"Get the fuck out of the car, you pussy!"

The engine was still running. When Donna had blasted me with the pepper spray, the car had bumped harmlessly into the one parked behind me. My chest felt as if it had collapsed under a weight of bricks. I straightened in the seat and took hold of the wheel. I couldn't see past the front of the car.

"He's trying to get away!" Donna screamed. "Stop him!"

The rocking became more violent, and it was joined by a pounding. I wasn't sure where it was coming from. I found the transmission and shoved it into drive. The pounding grew louder, then there was a **pop,** and bits of glass flew against me. The passenger-side window had been smashed. I could make out an arm coming through.

I twisted the wheel as far to the left as it would go and stomped on the gas. My fender grazed the car in front of me, but not enough to stop me. I swung the car out onto the street. Several people were running alongside me, shouting. There was a loud **bump** and the car shuddered. I might have hit someone, but I wasn't about to stop and find out.

I leaned forward on the steering wheel just as headlights appeared directly in front of me, accompanied by a loud car horn, which was the only way I knew I had drifted to the wrong side of the street. I jerked the wheel, trying to find my lane. I glanced in the rearview mirror, seeing only a receding yellow blur floating amid several darker ones. Up ahead, I saw a red light approaching. Seeing no other lights, I went through the intersection, then rolled my window down, let off the gas somewhat and stuck my head out into the cold night air. It stung like hell, but it was the only way I could breathe.

Holding the steering wheel with one hand, rubbing my eyes with the back of the other hand, all the while hacking like a retired coal miner, I made my way at a crawling pace out of Fort Petersen. When I reached Flatbush, I pulled over and called Margo. I draped myself halfway out the car window and fought through the crappy connection.

"I need you to call me a cab," I said. The words were like razor blades running on the inside of my throat.

There was a pause. "Okay. You're a cab."

My upper body collapsed against the side of the car. Laughing hurt even more than speaking, but I had no control over it. I was still holding the cell phone, though not to my ear. I could hear the buzzing of Margo's voice.

"Fritz? Fritz?"

— 28 —

MARGO POKED HER TONGUE AGAINST THE inside of her cheek and said nothing as I pulled Betty from my pocket and set it on the dresser. She was sitting on the edge of the bed holding a mug of warm mulled cider and rum. I looked at her in the dresser mirror.

"The pimp," I said to her unasked question. "He had a knife, I had Betty." I set my .38 on the dresser, next to the blackjack.

"Mr. Arsenal," Margo said in her quiet voice.

I leaned closer to the mirror. Margo had dabbed iodine on the several scratches I'd suffered from Donna Bia's fingernails. I looked like an Indian in his war paint. My eyes were still red, but much of the stinging had subsided. I had a walnut-sized lump just above my left ear, where Donna's stiletto heel had done its damage. Hellcat, indeed. Lance Jennings hadn't been kidding. I recalled Donna swinging her dishy brown legs in my direction and giving me that dark smile, just seconds before hitting me full force with the spray.

"What are you going to do about the car?" Margo asked, blowing lightly into her cider.

"The easiest thing is to report it stolen. There'll be a lot less explaining to do to the rental company if I say somebody stole it. It's insured against the damage."

"What about wasting the police time?"

I turned from the dresser. "I can call Captain Kersauson. I'll tell him not to bother."

Margo took a sip of cider. "So how much money did you end up handing over to all these sexy women tonight?"

"They weren't all sexy."

"How much?"

"I took a thousand with me. I came back with just under half."

"How sexy was the sexiest one?"

I unbuttoned my shirt and pulled it off. Gingerly. The evening's festivities had kicked up the injury in my shoulder. I balled up the shirt and made a two-pointer on the chair in the corner. I stepped over to the bed and snapped my fingers. Margo handed me the mug. "Yes, Allah."

I took a sip. Nutmeg. Cinnamon. Cider. Rum. My raw throat welcomed the blend. So did my bloodstream. "The sexiest one? That would be the girl who slapped me around. More curves than the Daytona Speedway."

"Aren't you funny."

"You asked."

I reached into my pocket and pulled out a small silver tube. Margo made a quizzical face. "Is that what I think it is?" I twisted the bottom of the tube, and a soft ruby nub emerged from the top. Margo placed a finger on her chin. "I think something a little softer would suit you better."

I set the lipstick on the bedside table and pulled a similar shape from my pocket. This one was a transparent vial. It was three quarters filled with what the police like to call a powdery substance. I set the vial down next to the lipstick.

Margo asked, "Is that what I think it is?"

"It's my catch of the evening. While I was flailing away blindly—literally—after the lovely Miss Bia sprayed me, I managed to catch her purse and knock some stuff out."

Margo picked up the vial and held it up to her face. "Artificial sweetener?"

"I guess one could make the argument."

"What is it? Cocaine? Heroin?"

"One of the above. Or some such cousin."

"So your take for the evening was drugs and cosmetics. This cannot have met expectations."

I pulled one more thing from my pocket.

"That's not yours," Margo said.

"It's Donna Bia's."

"You got her cell phone?"

I weighed the weightless thing in my palm. "Yep."

"You're looking smug."

"I'm feeling smug."

"Okay, Mr. Smug. Why don't you put away your toys and come to bed?"

She hopped off the bed and disappeared into the bathroom. I pulled open the drawer on the bedside table and stashed the goodies. I finished off the cider and rum, kicked off the rest of my clothes and fell heavily onto the rack. The bathroom door opened, then closed, and the overhead light went out. My former boss's daughter crawled into bed next to me. I sniffed the air.

"What's that?" I asked. "Eau d'intrigue?"

"I'm not as curvy as a racetrack. I thought a little booster might be nice."

"You don't need no stinkin' booster." I turned to her. "Besides, you've got plenty of curves. Who says you don't?"

"I can tell I ain't no Donna Bia."

"And I can't tell you how happy that makes me."

Margo turned to me. Her fingers found the back of my neck and started playing little games there.

"Try," she whispered.

I WOKE SOMETIME IN THE MIDDLE OF THE night. Margo's head was tucked under my chin, one of her legs thrown across mine. Her breathing was barely audible, like a tiny teapot not quite coming to a boil. My right hand was resting against her bare back. I wasn't sure how long I'd been doing it, but I realized I was running my thumb gently back and forth against two of her vertebrae. Not waking, she muttered something in her sleep and nestled even closer.

I looked up at the ceiling. Margo's bedroom is a corner room. Two windows. South and west. One of the windows—the one at the fire escape—has a security gate. Ambient light from outside hits both windows and sends elongated patchworks of shadows onto the ceiling. It's never quite the same pattern twice; it's a little like clouds in that way. When a car travels down the street, a new shadow appears, sliding along the ceiling atop the others. Sometimes it looks to me like a guillotine blade whooshing down. Margo will occasionally stay awake simply to watch the shifting patterns. She claims it's one of her favorite features of the apartment.

As I lay looking up at the patterns, one of those car-induced shadows ran its diagonal course along the ceiling. It was followed immediately by a second one, this one moving faster. I heard a squeal of brakes, and the second shadow halted partway along the ceiling. I heard the **thump** of a car door closing. A few seconds later, Margo's front door buzzer went off.

"Shit."

Margo stirred as I peeled her off. "What is it?"

"Company."

I got out of bed and reached for my pants. Margo scooted up onto one elbow. A gash of pale light cut across her face.

"What time is it?" She leaned sideways and squinted at her clock. "It's three-thirty."

The buzzer sounded again. I pulled on

my shirt. Margo slipped out of bed and into her bathrobe in one liquid move.

"Don't get up," I said.

"It's my apartment." The sleep was gone from her voice, replaced with irritation. She went into the hallway and hit the intercom button. "Who is it?"

The crackly answer came back: "Malone." I joined her in the hall.

"It's you," Margo said humorlessly. "You're here and you're down there at the same time. Ain't you something?"

I pushed the button to buzz open the front door. I went back into the bedroom and got my .38 and tucked it into the waist of my pants.

"Why don't you wait in the bedroom," I said to Margo.

"Who do you think it is?"

I stepped to the door. The across-the-hall neighbor was a photographer. Several months back, he was backing out of his apartment carrying a tripod on his shoulder and somehow managed to land one of the hard rubber feet directly on the peephole in Margo's front door, making a spiderweb of the tiny lens. I looked through the peephole now, but all I could see was a triangular view of the carpet. I heard the sound of steps in the stairwell, and a moment later, the edge of a shoe nosed into view.

A loud knocking sounded.

"Don't open it," Margo hissed.

We both knew it was a hollow request.

29

A NUMBER OF YEARS AGO, I WAS WORKING A case for a woman who was being stalked by her former employer, an art appraiser at Sotheby's. The man's inappropriate attentions while the woman was in his employ had spurred her to look for another job; she landed a parallel position with a smaller auction house. Marlborough's, on Lexington Avenue. It was soon after the woman started the new job that she began noticing her former boss lurking outside Marlborough's, as well as showing up on her subway platform at both ends of the workday. He also phoned her frequently at work, offering up perfectly transparent work-related pretenses for the calls, and also at her home, although these calls—technically anonymous and conducted in an ill-disguised low breathy voice—were characterized primarily by utterings concerning underwear and puckered flesh. A friend of a friend of a friend referred the woman to me, and I had agreed to stalk the stalker, in order to corroborate the woman's tale of harassment so that she could take appropriate legal action and keep the unhinged art appraiser away from her. There was no indication—neither from a look into the man's past, which I undertook to investigate, nor in his actions—that the art appraiser posed an actual bodily threat to my client. He was a perv and a pest, and she wanted him officially designated as such so that action could be taken to get him out of her life.

And so I had thought little as far as danger was concerned one afternoon when answering a pounding on my inner office door. As Miss Dashpebble was "out," I answered the door to find the art appraiser standing there mopping his forehead with a pale blue silk handkerchief. Only when I saw what he was holding in his other hand did I reconsider the danger issue. It was a pistol, by **my** appraisal, a real one. He fired it point-blank. He claimed later that he was attempting to drop it when it went off. There might even have been some truth in this claim, for he certainly proved to have a lousy grip on the gun, which meant that his tugging on the trigger—intentionally or otherwise—tipped the gun's barrel forward and down so that the bullet that might otherwise have made its way into my spleen instead followed a trajectory directly into my left thigh, some five or six inches above my knee. The man let out a gasp—as did I—then cringed, almost as if he knew what my response was going to be. I grabbed hold of the door frame with my left hand, delaying my fall to the floor just long enough to bring my right arm around in a clean, hooking swing, landing a potent punch directly on my assailant's chin. At that point, the three of us—me, him and the gun—clattered to the floor. In the now-and-again replays of the scene, often occasioned by my pulling open a door to someone's insistent knocking, the nonexistent Dashpebble lets out a trilling scream, swiftly dials 911 and asks for help, then steps over from her desk and cracks the troubled art appraiser over the head with the telephone. In real life, I picked up the pistol (using the man's blue handkerchief, in order to keep his prints intact) and tossed it far back into my office, then dragged myself over to the receptionist's desk and called 911 myself. By the time the EMS crew arrived, I was propped up against the receptionist's desk and wearing a blue silk tourniquet around my leg, swearing softly against the pain. The art appraiser was still in the doorway to my office, curled up in a puddle of his own tears.

Which is all to say that it was not a completely steady hand that pulled open Margo's apartment door. Ever since that incident with the art appraiser, when I answer someone's knock, my gaze does not first seek out the face. It goes for the hands.

LEONARD COX'S HANDS WERE IN HIS POCKets. He wasn't in his police uniform. He was wearing jeans and a black leather jacket.

"Cop Cox," I said.

"Malone."

"May I say how lovely it is to see you? Especially at this hour."

"You gonna let me in?"

I stepped back from the doorway and he came in. The scent of stale tobacco joined him. I made the introductions. Margo remained cool, opting not to mask her irritation.

"You'll excuse me if I go **back** to bed?" she said, aiming her italics as much to me as to Cox. Or so I thought. But she retreated down the hallway with a goofy sliding action, something like a modified cross-country skiing step, and I knew she was only half as peeved with me as she was putting on.

I turned to Cox. "What's this about? How'd you know to find me here?"

"You weren't at your place. I checked there first."

"Which doesn't explain how you tracked me down here. What's going on?"

"Carroll said you might be here."

"Come on."

He followed me into the living room. He pulled up short when he got there. "Jesus." His eyes scanned the hundreds of spines.

"That grumpy chick in the bathrobe eats books for breakfast. There're twice as many as you see. They're double-shelved."

"That's a lot of fucking books."

"Right. Well, she's a colossus. But my guess is you aren't here to borrow the letters of Harold Nicolson. Why have you been asking Tommy Carroll how to find me? Has something happened?" I sat down in the wicker rocker and motioned Cox to have a seat. He took the claw-foot chair.

"We found your car."

"We?"

"Somebody phoned in an abandoned car with a smashed-in window on Flatbush. It was a rental. We ran it and came up with you. You rented it this evening from Dollar on Fifty-second."

"Correct."

"You were talking to the captain earlier tonight. You told him you were going to lean on some whores to try to find Ramos."

"Yeah, that's more or less how I put it."

"Is that how you got your face scraped up?"

"Maybe. Or maybe I had a motor-skill meltdown when I was shaving. I hope you didn't come over here at three-thirty in the morning just to show off your sleuthing abilities. I rented a car, I went looking for Ramos among people who might know where he is. For this you ask Tommy Carroll where my girlfriend lives?"

"You ran into trouble."

"Stop telling me what I just did!" My explosion even took me by surprise, but I kept going with it. "Jesus Christ, Cox, you've got about five seconds to tell me why you're here, or else guess what? You're **not** here. What the hell is so goddamn important that Tommy Carroll had the nerve to give **you** this goddamn address?"

Cox hesitated. His eyes hardened. I didn't

care one bit for the smirk he didn't bother to hide. "Why don't you keep it down, Malone? You're going to disturb the little lady."

I was across the room in two seconds. Cox rose, which made it easier for me to get two fistfuls of his jacket. He was ready for me, though, and he landed a pair of piston shots to my shoulders. I backpedaled, releasing the jacket.

"Assaulting an officer," Cox said coolly.

"Trespassing."

"You let me in."

The desire to leap at him welled up again, but I held my ground this time and waited for it to pass. There's no gain in two cavemen pounding stones against each other's heads. I was as irked with myself for losing my temper as I was with Cox for provoking it. He remained standing with his hands at the ready, like a gunslinger in the middle of Main Street. I could see in his expression that he'd be more than happy for me to keep the discourse purely physical. He was at least five years younger than me and two inches taller, and his reactions were probably a little sharper than mine at this particular moment. I was tired, for Christ's sake. Pimps and blackjacks and prostitutes and pepper spray will do that to you, I don't care what anyone says. Besides, the last thing I wanted was for Margo to come in and see me and Cox grappling on the floor in front of the fireplace like a couple of rejects from a D. H. Lawrence story.

"I'm listening," I said. "Either give me something to hear or leave."

"You ran into Donna Bia tonight."

"For God's sake, Cox, please don't start in with the play-by-play again. Yes. I did. How do you know that?"

"I know it, that's all. What did she tell you?"

I indicated my face. "She let her fingers do the talking."

"Are we getting any closer to Ramos?"

"Is that why you've come over here at three-thirty in the morning? To ask me that? No. We're not. She pretended she was going to take me to him. She pretended she was about to call him. That's when she sprayed me."

"Sprayed you?"

"Pepper spray. It was in her purse. I guess a girl's got to protect herself."

"I guess she must have used up all her protection on you."

"What do you mean?"

"Donna Bia's body was found in the back

of a laundry van at the Niagara Company lot just after midnight. Her throat had been sliced from one end to the other."

My knees weakened. "Who found her?"

"Anonymous tip."

"Good old anonymous tip. Is that where she was killed? In the van?"

"Hard to say yet. But it looks like it. There's something else."

"What's that?"

"In her mouth. The M.E. on the scene found something in her mouth."

"Besides teeth and tongue?"

"A finger. Sliced off at the base."

I sucked in a sharp breath. "Hers?"

"A man's."

"Philip Byron's."

He nodded "M.E. says it was a fresh cut. He figures the finger got chopped near the same time Donna Bia got the ugly smile. Same knife."

"Ugly smile. I haven't heard that one."

Cox ran a finger across his throat in a lazy arc. "She was one real piece of ass, you know?" he said. "Serious good stuff. Our goddamn Angel is really getting out of hand."

———

COX STAYED ANOTHER TWENTY MINUTES or so. I pressed him, and he told me that on getting word of Donna Bia's murder, he had gone directly to the Flea Club to "rattle some of those nigger spics" and see if he could get any information about Donna's activities and whereabouts in the hours prior to her throat being slashed from ear to ear. That's when he learned about me. Not by name, of course, but the most cursory description was all he needed, especially once my window-smashed rental car was located.

"So you knew that Donna hung out at the Flea Club," I said.

"Sure. It's one of those spots."

"Why didn't you go looking for her once Angel's name surfaced?"

"You mean like you did?"

"Okay. Yes."

"I planned to. But it's not like I could put on civvies and just go walking into the Flea like you did. This is my beat. They know me. If I approached Donna publicly, that's a lot of eyes that have seen her getting the shakedown from a cop. Do you think she's going to give up Angel when she knows word'll come right back to him?"

I thought about this. It made sense. "Why do you think Angel killed her?" I asked.

"The one thing she did **not** do was lead me to him. The way she behaved in that car, he should have given her a medal."

"Maybe Angel didn't believe her story."

"Or maybe it was the fact that she went far enough to get in my car in the first place."

Cox made a snorting sound. "Ramos? Not a chance. Donna might have been his main hump but she wasn't like his wife or anything. He could handle her going down on other men. She was part of his cash flow, for Christ's sake."

"So why give her the ugly smile?"

Cox shrugged. "Got me. I think at this point, Angel's probably keeping himself so high there's no telling why the hell he's doing any of this. The finger shit? That's ugly. This boy's over the edge. Who knows? Maybe Donna shows up, tells him a private dick was using her to get to him. He asks her some questions, and she doesn't answer the way he wants her to. Boom. Out comes the knife. Or maybe he just figures he got lucky this time, and next time someone's going to squeeze her better than you did. But let me tell you something. You shouldn't try to overthink someone like Ramos. Don't try putting logic to it. He's a homicidal dope-head. He's been pissing blood since he was a kid. Guy like that is just pure evil, end of story. He doesn't give a crap about killing people. Killing Donna like that? If anything, it probably got his rocks off. By now it's probably already 'Donna who?' "

He asked for something to drink, and I went into the kitchen and got him a glass of water. If he had something harder in mind, he didn't say so. He set the glass down, then said there was one more matter he wanted to run by me.

"Guy I talked to outside the Flea told me that Donna had bitched a blue streak to him that she lost some shit from her purse when the two of you had your little fight."

"You might call it little."

"The guy said she was real upset."

"Yeah, the things we think are important. She won't be needing them now."

"So she did lose some stuff in your car? Can I have a look?"

"Hold on."

I went down the hallway to the bedroom. The bedside light was on. Margo was sitting up in bed, reading a book of poetry by Deborah McAlister. Her face was pinched into a frown.

"Those poems are going to give you wrinkles," I said.

"They're good."

"But you're frowning."

"It's called focus. There are layers within layers."

"Isn't that always the way?"

I went to the opposite side of the bed and pulled Donna Bia's phone and lipstick and drug vial from the drawer of the bedside table.

Margo folded her book onto her finger. "Hero cop still here?"

"He's leaving soon."

"I don't like him."

"I don't like him, either," I said. "We'll keep him off our Christmas list."

"As if." She scooted up on her pillows. "What are you doing with those things?"

"Donna Bia was found murdered a couple of hours ago. Throat slashed."

"Nice."

"Cox was curious about the stuff that fell out of her purse. Someone told him that Donna'd been crabbing about it." I came back around the foot of the bed.

Margo set her book down on the sheets. "Wait."

"What?"

She said nothing for a moment. She was thinking. Sometimes when Margo's thinking, she looks like her father, that same out-of-focus stare.

"Maybe he just wants the drugs."

I held up the vial. "This?"

"I don't like him," she said again. "What's he doing here?"

"I told you. He came by to tell me about Donna. He knew that I'd been with her earlier tonight."

The frown had returned. "Ever hear of a phone? Or waiting until a decent hour?"

"That's just cops," I said. "They don't give a damn."

"This is the guy you think shot Roberto Diaz in cold blood, right?"

"That's the man."

"He should be in prison, not sitting in my living room. I don't think you should give him what he's asking for. I don't trust him."

"Margo, I'm sure a cop like Cox can get ahold of all the dope he wants, if that's what he's into. He's hardly going to come all the way over here at three-thirty in the morning just to lift a little vial of whatever this is. Besides, he didn't even know what fell out of Donna's purse. He was just told 'stuff.' "

"That's what he's telling you."

"That's what he was told by some guy."

"That's what he's telling you."

"How would some guy he's talking to know the specifics of what fell out of the purse?"

"Maybe it wasn't some guy. Maybe Cox actually talked to Donna."

I heard movement from the living room, and I stepped over to the door and pulled it closed. Margo sat up higher on the pillows.

"Daddy always says to doubt."

"I know he does. And it drives your mother crazy."

"If this were that tall policeman. The black one?"

"Patrick Noon."

"If this was him, I'd let the scales tip toward believing him. But this guy?" She raised both hands, palms flat, then let one rise higher while the other dropped all the way to the bed. She lowered her voice. "That's a murderer in there, Fritz. That's all I'm saying. Heepy-creepy."

I looked at the three items I was holding. Margo was right, of course. My line of business is about doubt, not about trust. I've had more than a few meaty discussions with super-shrink Phyllis Scott on **that** topic in my day. I ran back Cox's story in my head. Simple. Clean. Believable. Still, Margo was right. From someone like Patrick Noon, it would be easy to believe. But with Leonard Cox?

I handed one of the items to Margo. "Put this away, will you?" Then I leaned forward and gave her a peck on the top of the head.

"Down here, stupid," she said, and I gave her a peck on the lips. "That's better."

I indicated her book. "Find us a sexy poem. I'll go ditch the cop and be right back."

I returned to the living room. Cox was standing in front of the bookcases. His water glass was on the coffee table. I noticed he hadn't touched it. He turned sharply as I came into the room.

"Everything okay?"

"Fine," I said. He didn't look convinced. "Just wiping up a domestic puddle." I handed him Donna Bia's lipstick and her vial of powder.

"That's it?"

"That's all I found."

"Those two things?"

"Right."

"Well . . . okay." He sounded doubtful. He pocketed the two items. At the door, he started to say something, then changed his mind and left without a further word.

Margo had the sexy poem all ready when

I returned to the bedroom. It wasn't from the book she was reading. She made it up herself.

"You're a talented chick, aren't you?" I said, turning off the light.

A warm foot touched my knee. "So I'm told."

30

I SHOWERED AT MARGO'S IN THE MORN-ing—early, before she'd gotten up—but had nothing clean to put on, so I took the subway downtown and worked my way into fresh skins at my place. I brewed up some coffee. I would've as soon flipped open my skull and poured it directly onto my brain, but the hinges were too rusty.

There were two messages on my machine, both from Captain John Kersauson of the Ninety-fifth Precinct. Apparently I hadn't given him my card, which has my cell phone number, so he'd found me in the book. He said he had called my office number as well. The first message was a request that I come into the station at my earliest convenience to give a statement to the detective in charge of the Donna Bia murder concerning my activities the night before from the time I left the police station, specifically those activities concerning the deceased. The second message had come forty minutes later and told me to skip it "for now." He went on, "I spoke with the commissioner. He says you're busy. Must be nice having a fairy godfather like that."

I had already determined that my first stop of the morning would be to see the fairy godfather himself. I recalled last night's encounter with the brooding thundercloud that was Tommy Carroll. No one would ever accuse him of being a happy man; that was never the cut of his suit. But I knew he was a proud man, hardworking and accomplished well beyond the crowd he'd grown up with. Unlike Martin Leavitt, whose aspirations— I believed Carroll was right on this—were aimed for even bigger and glossier brass rings than what he had already achieved, Tommy Carroll's boyhood dreams had been realized when he became police commissioner for the city of New York. Carroll had reached his Everest. When my father had gotten **his** nod to head the NYC Police Department, Captain Tommy Carroll had cornered me at one of the congratulatory bashes thrown for the old man and told me that my father was now the most important man in New York City. "Day to day?" he had said. "On the streets? It's all about the cops. They grease the wheels in this city. All the other crap that's New York, it doesn't happen unless you've got the cops. It's your father now who's going to make this city run. No one else. The man in that office? He's the king."

After my father's disappearance—once it became clear that the disappearance was, in all likelihood, permanent—and after the two subsequent police commissioners had shown the chinks in their armor, Tommy Carroll ascended to the throne and proved himself completely up to the task. I suppose you could say he was a happy man at that point. Or maybe "satisfied" would be the better word. King Tommy. The most important man in New York City, at least by his own calculus.

But now there was disease—rot—that couldn't care less how important he was. As far as cancer is concerned, we're wood and it's termites. Cancer doesn't give a damn. It's equal-opportunity, it'll hollow out anyone and everyone if given half the chance. I thought of Tommy Carroll standing at his desk the night before, raging impotently. He was an idiot, of course. As long as I'd known him, he'd been a heavy smoker. So this particular time bomb was of his own making. It was the consequence of his own choice. I suppose that's partly why his feelings about the mayor were so venomous. Leavitt was outside of Carroll's control. If Martin Leavitt concluded that he needed to knock his police commissioner off the top of Everest in order to keep his own ass clean, that was what he'd do. Carroll had no control over the matter. No wonder he was furious. He was being destroyed from the inside and the outside and there wasn't a whole hell of a lot he could do about it.

My cell phone went off as I was coming out of my building. That was when I remembered that I'd left Donna Bia's phone back at Margo's. It was garbage day, and the green monster was at the curb, roaring as its uniformed handlers tossed black bags of gruel into its maw.

"Hold on!" I yelled into the phone. "I can't hear you!" I stepped quickly to the corner, where I took the call in front of Rossetti's bakery.

The caller was Sister Mary Ryan.

"I'm sorry to call you so early, but I have something here I think you should see," she said.

"What is it?"

"I don't know. I mean, I don't know exactly what it means."

"Does it have to do with Angel Ramos? Did one of the sisters recognize his picture?"

"Not exactly that. But I think it's important. No, it **is** important."

The garbage truck was lumbering my way, black smoke belching from its vertical exhausts, the tin lid flapping. The roar grew.

"I'll be there as soon as I can!" I yelled into the phone, probably louder than I needed to. But then, my heart seemed to be running faster than necessary, too. I flipped the phone closed as the truck shuddered to a halt.

IT WAS SISTER MARGARET'S SUICIDE NOTE.

God should not test His weakest lambs. I am in too much pain. I'm sorry. I am not purity. I'm filth. I'm dirt. I can't endanger my sisters any longer. I won't endanger them. If God won't slaughter this filthy lamb for the sake of purity then this will be my final gift. Maybe there can be some speck of grace from this. I've failed. I hurt. God will spit on me

for this. He will shed no tears. I lost Happiness and I'll never know Her. Who is She? She must hate me as much as I do. I forgive everyone who has hurt me and I ask forgiveness from everyone I hurt. I hurt so much. I have failed. I am so so so sick. Oh Lord, what a useless filthy waste. Forgive me.

I looked up from the paper. I was seated once again in the Great Room. Sister Mary Ryan stood in front of me, picking nervously at her lower lip.

"You see?" she said.

I picked up the second piece of paper, the copy of the note that the nuns had received on Saturday.

Sisters—

In love, respect and reverence, a Gift awaits you. It is yours. This is my wish and decree. You must not allow anyone to talk you out of accepting it. Do not let them. You are pure lambs. They are filthy. I want this for you. You are deserving. You are purity. You are

endangered. I love you so much. Your Gift awaits you at the Cloisters. You will claim it with the enclosed claim check. Today. After three o'clock. Please be trusting. Please be swift. I am your lamb. From slaughter comes Grace. I am in tears with happiness over your Gift.

A Friend.

"You see?" the nun said again. "There's no question in my mind. The lamb? The gift?" She stepped to my side. "You see? 'I can't endanger my sisters any longer.' And then in the other one. 'You are endangered.' This note we received is obviously related somehow to Sister Margaret. That's not coincidence."

I studied the two notes again. She was right. If this was coincidence, then my skin was green and feathery and so were my eighteen toes. I indicated Sister Margaret's suicide note. "Is this the original?"

She shook her head. "It's not. As far as I know, the police still have the original. It was Sister Natividad who requested at the time that we procure a copy. I told you how close she and Margaret were. Natividad wanted to have a copy of Margaret's final words. The note was read to us over the telephone, and we copied it down and then typed it up. Sister Anne has some ambivalence about Natividad's . . . I don't want to call it **obsession** . . . with her desire to keep Margaret's memory vivid. Natividad refers to 'Margaret's final words' quite often. That's why when she had a look this morning at the note we received on Saturday, she burst into tears. She brought out Sister Margaret's note and . . . well, as you can see."

"I can."

"What do you think it means, Mr. Malone?"

I lowered the two notes and gazed up at the crucified figure on the far wall. Then I stood and turned to Sister Mary.

"It means I want to talk to your youngest nun."

WHILE I WAITED FOR SISTER NATIVIDAD to be summoned, I phoned Tommy Carroll's office. The commissioner wasn't in. I was put through to his faithful assistant.

"Commissioner Carroll is with the mayor," Stacy said.

"How does he look today?" I asked.

"Excuse me?"

"How does the commissioner look today? He went home sick yesterday. I was just curious how he looked to you this morning."

"He. Looked. Fine." It took nearly six seconds for her to say the sentence.

"Choosing your words carefully there, Stacy?"

"Excuse me?"

"I. Think. You. Should. Relax."

She asked sharply, "Do you enjoy giving everyone a hard time or just me?" No problem spitting that sentence out.

"Only the lucky few," I said.

"I will tell the commissioner that you called," she said officiously.

"Atta girl."

I heard what might have been a large sigh. "What is it? Is it something particular that I've said? I don't understand you."

"You do your job well," I said.

"Thank you."

"I'm just looking for the entry point to the rest of you."

"Well, I wish you would stop. It's rude. I'll have Commissioner Carroll call you."

"Tell him to have the Cloisters note handy, as well as the other notes from Nightmare."

"Cloisters note. Nightmare. I'll tell him."

"Listen. Now that we've had this brief moment of air-clearing frankness, could you tell me now how he looked this morning? How does the old man seem to you?"

"I don't believe that is in the purview of my job."

" 'Purview'? Aw, Stace, do we have to go back there?"

"Make all the fun you want, Mr. Malone. Go right ahead. It's fucking kick-Stacy week anyway." She hung up.

Very interesting. Layer upon layer.

Sister Natividad was brought before me. That was how it felt. The young nun's head was bowed, and she moved almost as if her ankles were chained together. Sister Mary was slightly behind her, seeming to push her forward by the elbow.

"I would like to speak with the sister alone," I said. "If that's all right."

"Of course."

I addressed the young nun. "Is there, um, someplace less great we could talk? Where would you be more comfortable?"

She answered immediately. "The fountain." I cocked an eyebrow at Sister Mary.

"Natividad can show you," she said. "I'll be in the office if you need me."

She left the room. Sister Natividad led me

through the large dining room, then took a left before reaching the kitchen. We followed a clammy corridor down to a large oak door that led out onto a small garden arbor. A gravel pathway defined the square space, as did a framework of weathered trellises bearing the empty gray limbs of what I figured were grapevines. Precisely defined strips of turned earth indicated dormant flower beds. In the center of the square was a small fountain, not much more than a glorified birdbath in which a silver burble of water rolled over itself. A pair of finches perched on the rim of the fountain.

Beneath one of the trellises was a wooden bench. The nun moved directly to the bench and sat down, and I took a seat at the other end. It felt absurdly like a courting dance. The nun spoke first.

"Margaret had a rule. She was not allowed to be sad here."

"Here. You mean out here in the garden?"

She nodded. "Sometimes it was only for a minute. Sometimes she could be here for almost an hour. Not often, though."

"What happened to Sister Margaret?"

She looked over at me. "What do you mean?"

"Why was she so miserable? Why did she kill herself?"

The nun answered without hesitation. "God was angry with her."

"Did she tell you that?"

"Yes."

"And why was God angry with her?"

"Because she drank, and because she could not keep herself from drinking. Even here. In God's holy house, she could not keep her sins away. Sometimes she was found on the floor. Passed out. Sometimes when she was drinking, she would say horrible things."

"Did she seek help? Did she try to go it alone, or did she look for help? Counseling? A.A.?"

"Yes. Sometimes. The meetings. She went to them. There were times when she was better, but they didn't last."

"When she killed herself. I'm assuming she was drinking at that point."

The nun looked down at the ground. "She was in a lot of pain this time. This time was different. She had . . . She was difficult to talk to. She felt hopeless."

"Did you have any idea exactly how desperate she was? Had she ever mentioned suicide before?" The young nun raised her head and looked for a long time out at the small fountain. I watched as her dark eyes began to glisten. She said nothing. "Natividad?"

"I should have known." Her voice wasn't much louder than a whisper.

"Why should you have known?"

"I just should have. She did not have to die like that. I should have been a better friend. I should have saved her. I knew she was in pain."

"But you didn't know she was going to kill herself. Isn't that right?"

The whisper again. "I don't know. Maybe I did."

A thought occurred to me. "Sister Margaret was found out in Prospect Park. All the way out in Brooklyn. That's an awfully long way from here."

"That is where she used to live. Before she joined the order."

"Is that why she went all the way out there to kill herself?"

She looked over at me. Her face seemed preposterously small inside the white wimple. Her cheeks pressed against the hard fabric. "I cannot answer your questions."

"Cannot or will not?"

"Margaret was my only friend here. I'm very lonely without her."

"Natividad. Did Sister Margaret have addiction problems that went beyond alcohol? Did Margaret have a drug problem?"

"No."

"You say that with certainty." Or, I thought, too quickly.

"Because it's true."

"And you would have known? If she had a problem like that, you would have known?"

"Yes."

I pulled out the picture of Angel Ramos. I'd asked Sister Mary to get it for me. I set it down on the bench between us. "Did you ever see Sister Margaret with this man?"

"No."

"Did Sister Margaret ever say anything about someone named Angel? Or Ramos?"

"No."

"Except for when she went there the last time, did Sister Margaret go out to Brooklyn often? Did she visit with her family?"

"Her parents are both dead."

"Any other family?"

"She did not see them."

"So . . . trips to Brooklyn? That you were aware of? For any reason?"

"No."

"Sister Natividad, are you keeping something from me?" She didn't answer. I tapped a finger against the photograph on the bench. "This man is responsible for the deaths of many people. In fact, he murdered a woman just last night. In Brooklyn, as a matter of fact." The nun started but remained silent. "Somehow this man knew Margaret. His note to the convent and Margaret's suicide note have too much in common to be coincidence. I don't understand the connection or why he's making it, but it's there. This man is evil. He's a bad man. He's a drug dealer, among plenty of other things. Do you think it's possible that Margaret . . . that your friend was somehow involved with this man?"

"I don't know. I don't think so."

"You don't **think** so."

"I don't know."

"But if anyone here knows, it would be you. Isn't that right? You were her best friend here. You two talked. You shared your thoughts."

"She talked to people at her meetings, too. When she went. She said she felt good talking with strangers. She said sometimes it was easier than talking with God. Or with the other sisters."

"You're talking about A.A. meetings?"

She nodded.

"Do you know where she went to her meetings? Did she go to the same place or did she move around?" I knew that some alcoholics prefer going to different meetings. "Grazing" was how it was put to me once.

"There is one she liked in Columbia."

"Columbia. You mean Columbia University?"

"Yes. It's not only with regular people but also with students. Margaret liked that. She used to tease me that I should come with her and meet a nice college boy."

"I didn't know nuns had time for nice college boys."

"It was a joke. She was teasing me."

"Did she ever mention anyone in particular who she enjoyed seeing when she went to the meetings?"

"Yes, she did. There is a man named Bill. She said Bill was a nice person. She enjoyed talking with him."

"Bill. Any last name?"

"I think no one says their last name."

"What was Margaret's last name, by the way?" I asked.

"It was King. She was Margaret King."

"You miss her," I said.

She smiled. "I talk to her every day. Out here, where she was happy."

I looked around the tiny arbor. It was pleasant but not a lot of space. A fifteen-by-fifteen square within which to be happy. I stood up.

"Well, when you talk with her again . . ." I stopped. I had no closer. I looked down dumbly at the young nun. I heard a splashing sound, and the finches darted from the fountain and over the roof of the convent.

A small smile flickered on the nun's face. "Maybe she was listening to us the whole time already."

I looked at my watch. Closing on ten. If that's the case, I thought, I wish to hell she'd start speaking up.

31

THE COLUMBIA UNIVERSITY MEETING OF Alcoholics Anonymous was held in the basement of St. Paul's Chapel, a barrel-shaped brick building on the east side of the campus. It was a windowless, bunkerlike room with mud-colored walls, the only illumination coming from a dozen banged-metal wall sconces that gave off little pie slices of dirty light. I had been told by the helpful woman in the administration office that every Friday and Saturday night, the place served as a college coffeehouse.

I came down into the room via a spiral stone staircase. The tables had been shoved against the wall, and several dozen folding chairs were lined up in a pair of semicircles, the open ends of which faced a cheap pine podium. The smell of caffeine permeated the room. Hell, the **feel** of caffeine permeated the room.

There was no one there. I'd called the number Information gave me, and the person who'd answered let me know there was a meeting at ten. I'd hoped to catch the tail end of it. Or, barring that, a straggler or two. But no luck. I went over to the industrial-sized coffeemaker on the chipped card table and put my hand on it. Still a little warm. I ran an inch into a Styrofoam cup and sampled it. Quaker State could have been their supplier. I emptied the cup into a potted ficus tree, realizing too late that it was a plastic potted ficus tree.

I pounded back up the spiral stairs into the sun. I had half a mind to pop down the few blocks to Cannon's and have my mother's ex-husband slide me a short glass. The next meeting in the basement was scheduled for twelve-thirty, and I wasn't going to hang around for that.

Halfway across campus, I got an idea. I retraced my steps to the bunker. I scribbled out a note on the back of one of my cards and propped it on the coffeemaker, tucked into the red plastic handle.

BILL. PLEASE CALL. URGENT.

Back outside, my cell phone went off just as I reached Broadway. It wasn't Bill. How nuts would that have been? It was Tommy Carroll returning my call. I ducked back inside the university gates to keep down the traffic noise.

Carroll got straight to the point. "Stacy says you've got something about Nightmare's notes. What is it?"

"Do you have his notes with you?"

"No. Just tell me what you've got."

I told him what I had discovered—actually, what Sister Natividad had discovered—about the similarities in the notes from Nightmare and the one written by Sister Margaret King sometime before she slipped into the bushes in Prospect Park and opened up both her wrists. Carroll listened without comment as I told him about my talk with Sister Natividad. I told him I wasn't convinced that Sister Margaret might not have had a drug situation on top of her alcohol dependency. "It's the only real link with Ramos that I can imagine. Margaret King was from Brooklyn. It's a stretch, but maybe there's something there."

Carroll gave me a long silence to listen to after I finished. Then he said, "Drop it."

"Drop it? Are you kidding? Margaret King

is the link between Ramos and the convent. The bastard was signaling that in his note. That's why I wanted to take a look at the other—"

"So what? So some dead nun is the link."

"You don't find that interesting?"

"What I don't find it is helpful. We've got until five o'clock to collar this Ramos prick. What your nun has to do with any of this doesn't get us any closer to finding him. Stay on point."

Two women walked by laughing. Graduate students. Or maybe even professors. One of them looked astonishingly like Jenny Gray. The Jenny Gray of six years ago. She looked over at me and broke off the laughter. It only made the similarity all the stronger. I lost a few perfectly good heartbeats. I could also feel the blood rising to my cheeks. I switched ears on the phone and shifted the topic.

"By the way, thanks for telling Leonard Cox how to find me this morning," I said. I went ahead and quoted Margo. "Ever hear of a phone? Or waiting until a decent hour?"

"You were with that girl in Fort Pete. She ends up on the slab. I'm not going to sit on my ass until the sun comes up before I find out what the hell went on."

"I guess your pocket-cop gave you his report."

"Don't you fucking 'pocket-cop' me, Malone. I'm the commissioner. They're **all** in my pocket. Don't smart-ass me. Cox told me you had nothing. He did say she scratched your face up pretty good."

"Ruined my modeling career," I said. "So anything on her murder?"

"Forensics might come up with something. Miss Bia was definitely killed in the van. They've determined that already. The body wasn't moved. But they might get something off her to tell us where she'd been before she was killed."

"Expect fibers from the seat of my rental car."

"They've been informed about that. The point is, Ramos either took off Byron's finger on-site, which I doubt, or else brought it with him. Forensics says it was still fresh. That tells me he had Byron somewhere nearby. The cops picked up a pimp who runs girls in and out of those vans. He's being worked on. He says an undercover cop was out there last night and took some freebies from his girls, then took a piece out of his skull with a jack. I've got a feeling it wasn't any cop any of us know about."

"You always had good instincts, Tommy.

Except you can drop the freebies part. Didn't happen. Listen, I'm a little unclear about a few things. Cox. He wasn't on duty last night. At least he wasn't when he showed up at Margo's. He was in his civvies."

"What of it?"

"He told me he's saturated in the hood. He knows all the players. Ramos. Donna Bia."

"Of course. That's how it works. Everyone knows everyone. My cops better damn well know the scum in their own territory. So what?"

"Nothing, I guess. I'm just not clear on all the logistics. Who found my car? Cox or the cops?"

"Cox is a cop. Or are you forgetting?"

"I still don't see the point of his coming by Margo's."

"I explained that. You spent time with this Bia girl, and you didn't call in a report."

"I guess I'd never have made a very good cop after all," I said. "Probably a good thing I bailed."

"I've got to get going. What's your plan?"

"To be honest, I don't really have one. I was all hot for the suicide nun, but you just threw water on it."

"Drop the nun," he said again. "Focus on Ramos. Think with your feet."

"I don't suppose you've heard anything

more—or I guess the mayor hasn't—from Ramos?"

"We heard Philip Byron's third severed finger last night inside that whore's mouth. The mayor thinks that's a pretty loud message. So do I."

"This thing is going to collapse all around him, Tommy. You know that, don't you? It's going to collapse around both of you. It can't stay contained. Cox said one thing last night that I agree with: Angel has lost it. Cox figures he's popping and snorting and shooting anything he can lay his hands on; he's probably given up sleep. He's degenerating. Last week, in a funny way, he was a smooth cookie about all this. Now he's slicing open his girl-friend's throat and sticking severed fingers in her mouth? I wouldn't hold much truck with this five o'clock thing if I were you. That was yesterday's rant. This is a million dead brain cells later."

"The minute I hear from forensics, we're hitting the pavement. We've got the Bia murder now. There's nothing we need to contain about a dead whore. I can flood the area with blue. We're going to get this bastard by the end of the day if I have to fucking send tanks down the middle of Culver Boulevard."

"I'm glad to hear you've got a plan," I said.

"Look who's talking."

———

I PICKED UP A RENTAL CAR AT NATIONWIDE on Seventy-seventh Street, just east of Broadway. There was an accident on the approach to the Queensboro Bridge, so I took the Queens-Midtown Tunnel. I hate tunnels. By the time I'm halfway through them, I've forgotten how to breathe normally and I'm drenched in sweat. I don't know why it's not as severe in the subways, but it isn't. Phyllis Scott has a theory or two about the tunnel thing, all Freudian, of course. Margo's got her own theory. Even Jigs Dugan has weighed in on it. I'm so glad everybody gets to take a crack at it. Here's my theory: I don't like tunnels.

Charlie Burke was eating a sandwich in front of his television. He was watching a movie about a pair of drag queens driving across the Australian outback.

"Where's Charlie Burke?" I cried. "What have you done with him?"

"Shut up. Do you want a sandwich?"

"Do I have to fix it myself?"

"Yeah. I just told the help they could spend the day out on my yacht. Sorry."

"What've you got there?"

"Peanut butter."

"And?"

"And bread."

"Jesus, Charlie, it's hell-in-a-handbasket time around here."

I found some honey in the cabinet and showed him what a more complete sandwich looks like. I asked if he was hell-bent on seeing how things worked out for the Australian drag queens or whether he could spare a few minutes to maybe help me track down a cold-blooded killer and save untold numbers of lives.

"It's your call, Pops," I said. "I know how people's priorities change as they get older."

Charlie picked up the remote and killed the TV. He asked me to fetch him a beer from the refrigerator and to get one for myself if I wanted. I passed.

"Full alert, eh?"

"Something like that."

I took a seat on the couch and laid out for him everything I knew to that point concerning Angel Ramos. I gave him all the pieces. We slipped right into our old shorthand. He asked a few questions along the way, all of them good. I had him completely up to speed by the time he'd finished his beer.

"You're talking fast," he noted, setting aside the empty.

"Philip Byron's only got five fingers, two thumbs, and maybe five hours left."

"I'd be worrying bigger than Philip Byron if I were you."

"I am, trust me."

Charlie wheeled himself over to the window and stared out. Less than a minute later, he wheeled back around to face me. "The question. What's a cop from the embattled Ninety-fifth doing all the way in Manhattan working the parade and getting gunned down by a lowlife from the same Ninety-fifth?"

"Kevin McNally?"

"Uh-huh. You're figuring Diaz was working as partner with Angel Ramos, right? So Ramos has planted him out there at the parade with a Beretta in his belt. Officer McNally gets shot. That's a Fort Pete shoot-out on the streets of Manhattan. Coincidence?"

"You hate coincidence."

"I surely do."

"I had this same notion last night, right before I went to see Tommy Carroll," I said. "I haven't had the time to even think about it."

"So think about it."

"What are you saying, that McNally was actually the target of the Thanksgiving Day shooting?"

"He got hit. We know that much."

"What about Rebecca Gilpin? I definitely saw Diaz take aim at her."

"One thing at a time, hoss. Stick with the cop for now. Okay, so there's a mess going on out in the Ninety-fifth. It's the Bad Apples. Is this McNally a Bad Apple?"

"When the mayor and Carroll were holding their press conference after the shooting, a reporter I was standing next to asked Carroll the same question."

"What did Carroll answer?"

"As I recall, he didn't. He bitched at me later about how the press was pissing on a fallen cop."

Charlie wheeled over to the desk where he kept his computer and fired it up. Before he was grounded in a wheelchair, Charlie's patience with things like computers and other similar gadgets had been nil. The last of the Luddites. But losing his range the way he had put a new spin on everything. Now he was Mr. Keyboard.

"Play it out," Charlie said as he waited for his programs to come up. "Say McNally was the target. Or one of the targets. Anybody else of interest hit?"

"I don't know. I don't think so. I haven't really focused on the other people who were shot. There was a woman with a little boy. I was standing next to them when Diaz opened up."

"That's the problem when the cops close the books as quick as they did on this one. All the good investigating that could be done is just stopped."

"Once they had Diaz in a body bag, they called it a day."

"They knew it wasn't a damn day."

"McNally's partner was there, too," I said. "Cox. He was also working the parade. That's two men from Fort Pete, plus Diaz."

"The hero cop. He sure didn't get hit. He chased the perp."

"I chased the perp."

"He chased the both of you."

Charlie's screen sizzled as a mountain scene appeared. He hit a few keys, waited, then hit a few more. "Where was Cox when his partner was hit? Do we know?"

"In fact, we do. Cox was helping a blind man who had suffered a heart attack. He was down on the pavement doing CPR."

"Okay. So if Diaz was trying to take out both cops, maybe he couldn't get Cox because Cox had dropped out of sight."

"If," I said.

"Everything is if."

Right. Doubt everything.

Charlie muttered, "Bad Apple," as he hit the keys again. Comfortable as he was getting with computers, he was still a two-finger man on the keys. He punched them hard, as if squashing an armored bug each time.

"It's a little screwy, don't you think?" I said. "If you want to kill your local neighborhood cop—or cops—why would you do something so elaborate, not to mention so public, an entire borough away? For that matter, how would Diaz and Ramos know that Cox and McNally were going to be working the parade? Or exactly where they'd be? See? It begins to fall apart."

Charlie was only half listening. He had brought up something on his screen. "Pull up a chair, Fritz. Let's get educated."

For the next half hour, we read through every account and reference to the Bad Apple scandal that Charlie could come up with online. I was familiar with the general thrust of the accusations. A number of cops in the Ninety-fifth had allegedly been turning the neighborhoods they were supposed to be protecting into little fiefdoms. It was alleged that illegal raids would be held on the homes of suspected drug dealers, sometimes preceded by false calls to 911 as a means of "justifying" the raids, and that money was stolen as well as drugs, which the cops would later either sell back to the original owners or tag as their own and return to the dealer with the stipulation that the cops be cut in on the profit when the drugs were sold on the street. One editorial cartoon showed several cops standing with their hands stuffed with cash, looking up at the clouds and whistling at the sky while, all around them, dealers and users feverishly went about their business. The accusations also reported some cops tipping off dealers to impending legit raids. Payback was in money, drugs, sex or any combination of the three. Blackmail sex was said to be a common occurrence. A cop with a baggie of dope, according to the reports, could demand sex on the spot by threatening to plant the evidence and proceeding directly to the arrest. One woman was reported in **The Village Voice** as having a regularly scheduled rendezvous with two officers from the Ninety-fifth for just this sort of shakedown. "They call it a 'baggie blow,' you know what I mean? They come right in my apartment and tell my son to go on outside. Then they hold up that fucking baggie and shake it like it's a little bell or some shit."

The most extensive report, a piece in the

Times, broke down the alleged police abuse into two categories: bullying and partnering. The first category was less scandalous. In many ways, this one was business as usual. Shakedowns, threats, minor blackmail, sex on demand. It was the alleged abuses in the second category that were threatening to make the Bad Apple story a significant one. Partnering abuses. Collusion. Mutual back-scratching. Working things out to the benefit of both sides. Blurring even the idea that there **were** sides. That sort of abuse on the side of the police was the worst imaginable. "Criminals with Uniforms" was how one of the headings put it.

Caught up in the allegations was Brooklyn district attorney David Sack, who was reportedly aware of the validity of some of the accusations but had been willing—unnamed sources said—to turn a blind eye, especially in the cases of falsified raids and falsified evidence, so long as he could count on a healthy conviction rate. When Charlie read this, he commented, "It looks good on the résumé." It was Sack's relationship with Martin Leavitt that had begun to turn up the heat on City Hall in recent weeks. The two had worked together closely when Leavitt was a prosecutor in Brooklyn. Leavitt was referred to in several accounts as having been David Sack's mentor.

"Mentor," Charlie said. "Isn't that someone who teaches his tricks to someone else?"

The final related accounts concerned the murder-suicide of the two policemen at the end of October. No specific motive for either act was expressly spelled out, though there were implications that it was a case of one bad cop killing another, then taking his own life. There were also rumors that the cop who was murdered was a stoolie who had been informing on his fellow officers, a bad cop working to save his tail. The two dead cops were named Jay Pearson and Thomas Cash. However, it was a second pair of names that caught my eye. Charlie's as well. These were the names of the first officers on the scene. The alleged murder-suicide had taken place in a junkyard some hundred yards from a Home Depot parking lot on the edge of Fort Petersen. Someone had phoned 911, reporting shots fired in the area. The closest officers to the scene arrived within minutes of the 911 call. They attempted to revive both of the men, but according to an EMS spokesman, Pearson and Cash had already "expired" by the time their colleagues arrived.

Commended for their efforts in attempt-

ing to save the men were Officers Kevin Mc-
Nally and Leonard Cox.

"How's that song go?" Charlie asked,
swiveling his chair away from the computer.
"They're just too good to be true?"

"What are you thinking?" I asked.

"A couple of things. You asked before how
it was possible for Diaz and Ramos to know
that two cops from the hood were going to be
working the parade and where they'd be
working it?"

"Right."

"What if they didn't know? What if one of
these wonderful cops told them?"

"Which cop?"

"I'm liking the one who didn't end up taking a bullet."

"You mean Cox set up his partner? But
why?"

"Could be one of a hundred reasons. I told
you, it's just a thought."

"Any other thoughts rattling around in
there?"

"Sure. Try this one. Cox and McNally first
on the scene at this junkyard? I buy that. But
how about Cox and McNally first on the
scene before there **is** a scene? And then they
proceed to make one."

"Make one what?"

"A scene. They shoot both the other cops, Pearson and Cash, then set it up to look like a murder-suicide. They leave the scene, phone in a fake 911, turn around and go right back."

"That's quite a set of thoughts," I said. "Do they come with any motives?"

Charlie rubbed at the back of his neck. "Motives for taking out the cops at the junkyard? Could be anything. You saw what we just read. You've got a damn orgy of corruption going on out there. Rotten cops tripping over each other. Hell, it could have been a crooked cop turf war for all we know. Or maybe Pearson and Cash were both Boy Scouts and the other two decided to take them out."

"And Cox setting up McNally at the parade?"

"Bad guys always turn on each other. Don't you know your Shakespeare? Look, I'm just gassing here, Fritz. Maybe Cox did the cop shooting at the junkyard and he was getting nervous about his partner knowing it. There are a thousand things it could be. We're not gonna answer it all sitting here on our asses."

Charlie wheeled himself to the refrigerator and got another beer. He cracked it open and took a long pull. He slipped the can into the cup holder on his chair and wheeled back over to the computer and shut it down. He took a second sip of beer, then gazed thought-fully at the zip-top ring as he plucked at it lightly with his finger, making a small **twang.** His chest expanded and he let out a largely silent sigh, still twanging on the zip-top ring.

"Some days I just want to burn this god-damn chair."

32

I WAS SIXTY FEET UNDERWATER WHEN I remembered that I was able to get in touch with Angel Ramos. Or at least I had a shot. A tractor-trailer was stopped in front of me. A yellow sign posted low on the rear door read: HOW AM I DRIVING?

"You're not," I muttered. "You're stopped."

The line of cars in the lane next to me was stopped as well. But at least they could see up ahead, even if all they could see was nothing more than lines of gleaming brake lights. All I had was the truck. J. B. HUNT was printed in mustard and black letters across the rear door. The letters blurred. It was sweat, rolling down from my forehead into my eyes. I took a breath, let it out. And again. Took in, let it out. I wanted to focus on Angel Ramos but didn't dare; I had to make sure I continued breathing. The traffic didn't move, but the tunnel seemed to. I cracked open a window. The exhaust fumes didn't help much. Not at all, in fact. Someone was honking his horn. It was me.

The tunnel moved again. The traffic began moving with it. Slowly. I switched lanes abruptly, taking the heat of angry horns. Three minutes later—or was it three hours?—the light appeared at the end of the tunnel and grew steadily larger. That's my mouth, I thought. When I get there, I can breathe.

I CAME OUT OF THE TUNNEL ONTO THIRTY-fourth Street. Traffic was a tangled mess. Horns were honking from all directions. I rolled down the windows and the volume tripled.

I called Margo.

"Where are you?" she asked. "It sounds horrible."

"I'm stuck in traffic. Listen, I want you to do me a favor. What are your plans for the afternoon?"

"Well, I was planning to sit here and eat bonbons all day, but I've got to get down to **New York** magazine and pitch a story idea. Why?"

"I want you to get Donna Bia's phone out of there. I'd come get it, but right now I'm heading the opposite direction. I want you to take it out to your father's."

"Okay. But why?"

"Go fetch it," I said.

She replied, "Woof," then set down her phone. A scooter came buzzing along in between me and the car next to me. Its engine sounded like a loud bee. Margo came back on the line. "Got it."

"Take a look at her phone numbers. Check out A and R."

"You're looking for Angel Ramos?"

"I should have done this last night," I said. "I blame you. You and your damn sexy poems."

"I didn't hear no complaining."

"I'm thinking this is what Cox was after last night," I said. "The phone."

"Yep. It's here. Just says 'Angel.' Do you want me to call him up?"

"No. Just give me the number."

She did. As I was writing it down, Margo said, "Whoa. Hang on."

"What?"

"Here's another one, Paco. You might find this one even more interesting."

"What have you got?"

"It's what Donna Bia's got. Or what she had. L. Cox."

"L. Cox?"

"On her phone."

"**Leonard Cox?** She's got Leonard goddamn Cox programmed into her phone?"

"That's what I'm looking at," Margo said. " 'L. Cox.' You be the judge."

The traffic mess unglued for about ten seconds, then jammed right back up again. I was too slow moving into the space. A car that looked like a running shoe squeezed in front of me.

"I'll be damned."

Margo asked, "What does it mean?"

"At the very least, it confirms what I've already suspected. Leonard Cox is one bad apple."

"We both knew that already."

"Yes. But now we're beginning to see just how bad."

I considered the thoughts Charlie had been throwing out. In particular the one about Cox having set up his partner to be shot by Diaz at the Thanksgiving parade. Cox's number being listed in Donna Bia's phone wasn't definitive proof that this was what had happened, not by a long shot. But Donna Bia was Angel Ramos's woman. Or his property. I recalled Cox practically drooling on Margo's rug when he was talking about Donna, and how he had seemed to know awfully well how things stood with Angel and Donna. I had the feeling Leonard Cox figured in there somewhere. He had practically lamented the pointless loss of a perfectly good sex object when Donna Bia had turned up with her throat slashed. If Donna Bia had Cox programmed into her phone, chances were strong that Angel Ramos knew how to get ahold of the neighborhood cop. Cox was on the wrong side. This wasn't just one of the bullying abuses the papers had talked about. This was the other one, the partnering abuse. Leonard Cox was in cahoots with Angel Ramos. Maybe it was uneasy cahoots, but as I saw it, that didn't really make any difference. The more I thought about it, sitting there stuck in traffic, the more convinced I was becoming that Leonard Cox had set up his partner to be killed by Roberto Diaz. This left almost everything else a complete muddle, but as far as puzzle pieces go, it was a nice shiny one.

"Are you still there?" It was Margo.

"I'm still here. And I might be here until Doomsday, from the look of things."

"Sad."

"Look. I definitely want you to get that phone out to Charlie. You never know, Cox might be planning to come back around for another look. There might be other good stuff on the late Miss Bia's phone. Get it out to Queens."

"Do you really think it was the phone he was after?" Margo asked. "How would he have known you had it?"

"I think you got it right, what you said last night. I think what happened after Donna had her fun with me was that she got ahold of Cox somehow, obviously not on her phone, and told him what had happened. Or she told Angel and he told Cox. However it happened, Cox knew she'd lost her phone in my car. The last thing he wants is for me to start scrolling through her numbers. It's definitely why he came over."

"Okay. I'll take off right now. After I swing by the magazine, I'll head over to Dad's. What are you going to do?"

I looked at the clog of cars and trucks all around me. The sense of permanence, of taking root, was growing palpable.

"I'm going to age gracefully," I said. "Right here on Thirty-fourth Street. Maybe you'll come by someday and visit me."

"Maybe."

"Get moving," I said.

We hung up. I surveyed the scene again. You, too. For Christ's sake, get moving. I checked the time. It was approaching two.

A minute later, it was a minute later.

33

Doubt everything.

I drove to Midtown North and asked to see Remy Sanchez. I was told that he had left five minutes earlier to go downtown for a meeting with the police commissioner. I returned to my car and got onto the West Side Highway, which was a safer road to run red lights on than the more congested so-called surface streets. I parked a block from One Police Plaza and jogged across the bricks to the glass doors leading into the building. I took a seat on a metal bench out front. Unless Sanchez had driven down with his cherry light spinning, I was pretty certain I'd beaten him.

I had. After a few minutes of waiting, I spotted Sanchez coming across the plaza. I rose from the bench as he approached.

"Captain Sanchez."

He stopped. "What are you doing?"

"I need to talk with you."

"You want to— Suddenly, I'm Mr. Popular." He indicated the glass doors. "**El jefe** wants to see me."

"I need to talk to you about the problems in the Ninety-fifth. It's important."

"That's not my precinct."

"I know. I also know that inside dope the rest of us never hear has a way of making its way from precinct house to precinct house. The old invisible stream."

"What if it does? Why should I talk to you about it?"

"I think there's a link between the problems at the Ninety-fifth and the crap that went down on Thanksgiving. I'm not exactly sure what it is."

"That still doesn't explain why I should talk to you."

"You know the latest on Philip Byron?" I asked. "Another one of his fingers ended up in the mouth of a murdered woman last night?"

He nodded tersely. "I got that."

"The guy who's holding Byron, he's a punk out of the Nine-five. I think he's got a substantial tie-in with some of the cops up there.

They might even be helping him stay hidden, I don't know."

"Does Carroll know all this?"

"Some of it," I said. "Truth is, I don't really know how much he knows."

"Look, I've got to get in there. Carroll said he's got to be somewhere at three. I don't know what all this is about. Why don't you just talk to Carroll?"

"I want street-level information," I said.

Sanchez smiled, but without much humor. "Muchas gracias for the demotion."

"You know what I mean. Carroll's half cop, half politician. That's the job. You're a captain, but you still hear the beer talk."

"Maybe I do."

"Let me give you a quote: 'When pieces don't fit together, the truth is usually in the cracks between them.' You remember saying that to me? You were talking about a white shadow. You said a white shadow was all over this thing. You were right. And right now I don't need the kind of light Tommy Carroll is going to shine on it. All I can ask you to do is trust me." I reached into my pocket and pulled out one of my cards. "There's my cell number. You said Carroll's got to be somewhere at three, so you're only going to be in there for half an hour. I'll stick around. Call me when you get out of your meeting. I just need to bounce a few things off you."

Sanchez looked at the card, then pocketed it. "I'll call you. It might be to tell you to stuff it, but I'll call you."

"Good. And listen, don't tell Carroll we talked."

He had pulled the glass door open. He paused. "Look at me, Malone," he said. "What do you think? Was I born yesterday?"

The sky had darkened while we spoke. Low gray clouds were settling in over the city. I had time to kill. I realized that Paul Scott's office was nearby. There was nothing I could think to do about Angel Ramos until after I'd talked with Sanchez, so I decided I might as well rattle a chain for my other client. I called Information and got the address of Futures Now. They were located on the west side of City Hall Park, near the Woolworth Building. I hoofed it over and took the elevator to the eighth floor.

"I'm looking for Paul Scott," I said to the woman at the front desk. The words FU-TURES NOW hung on the wall behind her in silver block letters. The woman was wearing a headset. They're plenty popular now, but they still make me think of air-traffic controllers.

She directed me to take a seat as she punched a button on her console.

"Paul? There's someone to see you." She looked up at me. "May I have your name, please?"

Almost without thinking, I replied, "Nicholas Finn." That's the name I keep at the ready for those times when my job requires an identity dodge. I've got a folder full of falsified Nicholas Finn documents back at my office. The name had been an easy one to choose. The real-life Nicholas Finn had died not ten feet from me back when I was still attending John Jay. It wasn't an easy death to forget. Let's say, impossible. Years later, when Charlie Burke suggested I put together an alias to have at the ready, Nick Finn had slid into my skin so quickly I'd felt an actual chill. Why I gave it to the receptionist, I can't say. She repeated it into the phone, then said to me, "He'll be right out, Mr. Finn."

A minute later, Paul appeared. He saw me and automatically scanned the reception area.

"Mr. Scott?" I said, standing up.

He fixed on me. "What the hell is this about?"

"I was in the neighborhood. I thought maybe you had time for a coffee."

"What's this about?" he said again.

I asked, "Is there a place we can talk?"

Paul said nothing. The receptionist was watching with increased interest. Paul glanced at her, then at me. "Come on."

I followed him through a door to a large room that was divided up into clusters of cubicles. The walls were celery green and the cubicles a pale blue. People were sitting at their desks tapping away on keyboards and talking softly on phones. In the center of the room was a copy machine. A woman with red hair stood in front of it. The lid was lifted and the lightning-blue light from the copier was playing over her face. She looked up as Paul and I paused at the door. Paul led me along a row of cubicles, past a room with a swinging door and into an office about the size of a roach motel. He ushered me in, glancing out at the sea of cubicles before closing the door. I looked around for a place to sit. The only chair was behind the small desk. Good breeding told me not to grab it. Paul didn't take it, either. He remained at the door, loading his weapons.

"What are you doing here, Malone?"

I flipped a conceptual coin. It came down on the side of not pussyfooting.

"Your wife and your mother suspect that you're having an affair," I said. "I was asked to look into it. It's a dirty job, et cetera, et cetera. I begged off, but Phyllis said she'd rather keep it in the family, so to speak. Better me than some other Joe Gumshoe. I've been preoccupied lately, but since I was in the area, I thought I should try to earn my nickel."

Paul's skin had turned the color of putty. "My mother is **paying** you to spy on me? I can't believe this. Does Lizzy know about this?"

The question was pure Paul. The nervous sibling. Paul Scott could be in a room all by himself, and he'd decide the shadows were ganging up on him. He hated that Elizabeth and I got along 100 percent better than she and he did. He hated this nearly as much as he had hated my relationship with our old man. I threw him a bone.

"I don't know."

"Bullshit. If Linda knows, Lizzy knows. That's great. I really love family secrets."

He showed no signs of moving from where he stood. Helen Keller herself could have read the body language. Made me think of a novelty doormat: NOT WELCOME.

I checked my watch. This had to go quick. I sat down on the edge of the small desk. "Her name is Annette Hartman. Her husband's name is Bob. Or Robert. I guess it depends on how friendly you are with him. My guess is that you're not. Friendly with him, I mean. Our friend Bob is left-handed. I mention that only to show off my sleuthing skills. You had a boo-boo around your right eye the other day, and your mother says Linda thinks you got clocked by your girlfriend's husband." I held my fingers to my temples and narrowed my eyes, as if I were receiving a transmission. "You eat lunch together, sometimes Mexican. Sometimes you go to the Raccoon Lodge after work, and if I'm not mistaken, Mrs. Hartman is at this very minute making photocopies of something that is too large to fit on the glass."

I dropped the telepathic act. "Look. Paul. Your wife is distressed, your mother is concerned, and for what it's worth, your half brother thinks you should keep away from other people's wives. If you and Linda have a problem with your marriage, or if you've got a problem with your life, find a long-term fix, not a short-term one."

As if on cue, a light knocking sounded on the door. Paul opened it. The redhead was standing there, a look of concern on her face. She handed Paul a folder.

"Here's the file you asked for," she said. She spoke stiffly, as if reading from a script.

Paul looked momentarily confused. "It's okay," he said. "This is my half brother."

"Your . . ." Her face relaxed. "Oh. Okay. I just . . . okay." She took the folder back from and looked past him. "Sorry." She moved off. Paul closed the door. I hadn't expected a smug expression to be on his face, but that's what was there.

"That was Annette," he said.

I tapped my finger against my head. "I figured."

"She's a friend of mine."

"We're all adults here."

"No. I mean, she's a **friend** of mine. We're friends. That's all we are."

"I've said my piece."

"For your information, Annette's husband is the one having an affair. He's an A-number-one prick. She deserves someone a lot better than him."

"But that someone's not you?"

"I told you, we're just friends. Work buddies."

"And your black eye?"

"Yeah. That was her husband. Annette's been worried sick that her husband was seeing someone. She wasn't positive, but she suspected. She confided in me and I told her I'd look into it."

"Look into it?"

He blushed. He knew he had blushed, and he wished he hadn't. Which only made him blush all the more.

"Yeah," he said defensively. "So what? She asked me."

"What does Annette do here?" I asked.

"Here? She's in marketing."

"What's your job?"

"Mainly development. Why?"

"Nothing. I've never worked in an office. I guess I don't know the part where the marketing person asks the development guy to spy on her husband for her. I don't know, Paul. Professionally speaking, you're taking a potential client away from the likes of me. That's more my game, you know."

It was a cheap shot, and I regretted it the moment I said it. Paul Scott's Daddy issues—and I knew he had them—were probably not finding a whole lot of resolution in this closet-sized office on the edges of Cubicle Land. The last thing he needed was me tweaking him for playing detective.

"Why don't you just get out of here?" Paul said testily. "Some of us have work to do."

Some of us have work to do. Honestly, it made me want to cry.

I pushed off the desk and he stepped aside.

"That way." He pointed, as if I'd forgotten which way we'd come. I heard his door close behind me. As I passed the room with the swinging door, it swung open and I nearly collided with the one and only Annette Hartman.

"Oh!"

She was still holding the file folder. A piece of paper slipped from it. I bent down and picked it up. It was a blank sheet, except for the handwritten words "Is everything okay?" I straightened and handed the paper to her. She blushed, too. Must be the effect I had.

"My name's Fritz Malone," I said in a low voice. "If you and Paul are fooling around, be smart. Stop. If not, I apologize."

She sputtered. "W-what?"

"As for your husband, I get pictures, I get names and places, I testify in court if you need that. I can put the fear of God in him. Or I can put it in the other woman. There are plenty of approaches. I can also suggest counseling, though there's one particular counselor I'd strike off my list in this case. Point is, it's a lot more messy when you use amateur help. The lines can get muddy. If you'd like I'm in the book. You should keep Paul out of it, even if he volunteers."

I had no hat, so I had nothing to tip. I winced a smile and moved on.

The receptionist was taking a personal call as I waited for the elevator. Either that or she was just too overcome with the giggles to help herself.

I was partway across City Hall Park when Sanchez called me. He said he could spare a few minutes, and we agreed to meet in the park. The wind had picked up, and the sky was definitely threatening to let loose. I veered off to a nearby Starbucks and got two overpriced cups. I returned to the park and eavesdropped on a pair of old men arguing about the election of '48, the Truman upset over New York governor Dewey. The Dewey man was blaming the whole thing on Dewey's mustache.

"I bet you can't name the last president who won with facial hair," the Dewey man challenged.

"Teddy Roosevelt!"

"Wrong. It was that other guy."

"Who?"

"You know. I can't remember the name. But you know. That other guy."

"It was Roosevelt."

"No. It wasn't him. Jesus Christ. What the hell is his name?"

It was Taft. But I minded my own business.

Remy Sanchez showed up and we walked down to the south end of the park, away from City Hall.

"How was Mr. Carroll?" I asked.

"That man needs to take a vacation."

"You're not the first person to say so."

"He wants me to pull every black and Hispanic undercover I've got and send them out to Brooklyn."

"To the Ninety-fifth?"

"It's like a convention of narcotics officers. He says this guy Ramos is a cop killer. I asked him what cop, and he said that's not important. He said, 'He's a cop killer and I want your men to know it.' It's red meat. I asked him if he wanted dogs up there. I meant it as a joke, but he thought about it for a minute."

I told him what I needed. Information about the alleged murder-suicide of Officers Pearson and Cash. Specifically, I wanted to know the watercooler talk about McNally and Cox and how they fit into the picture. I knew I hadn't raised a tame topic. Sanchez's eyes told me as much.

"What are you looking for?" he asked.

"I'm not sure. I think I'm looking for motive for Leonard Cox to want to take out his partner. I'm wondering if there's something in the whole Pearson-Cash thing that might be a key. Even in the papers, the story has a stink to it."

"McNally went down in the parade," Sanchez said. "Diaz shot him."

"I know that. And Cox was conveniently on the ground already."

"Meaning what?"

"Too many theories. Maybe it means nothing. But all the principals at the parade were from a precinct far, far away. The same one." I set my coffee down on a bench. "And I'll be blunt about it. Leonard Cox is as crooked as a corkscrew. My money says he shot Roberto Diaz in cold blood. You know that the 'hero cop in Central Park' story is a load of crap, don't you?"

"I hear people talking."

"Diaz was shot right over there. In the Municipal Building. That's where I was taken, too. Carroll floated a half-baked story that they were simply protecting the cop killer from the cops until things cooled down. The truth is, the mayor's been dancing with a blackmailer. He called a bluff, and Diaz shot up the parade. Carroll and Leavitt wanted to make sure Diaz didn't start singing about how Leavitt had blown it big-time. I figured when

Diaz got wasted in the Municipal Building, it was a combination cop-killer-revenge and shutting-up-the-blackmailer, all with one easy bullet. Remy, the guy was handcuffed to a goddamn table. Supposedly, he pulled an ankle piece that Cox missed on arrest, and before he could shoot, Cox blew him away. But now . . . " I trailed off.

"Now what?"

"Now I don't know what to think. I don't even know which lie to doubt."

"You're thinking Cox set up his partner, then swung by the Municipal Building to silence Diaz."

I threw up my hands. "I'm just one little man. What the hell do I know?"

Sanchez took a sip of his coffee. As he did, his eyes moved around. When he spoke, his volume had dropped by half. "I'm not telling you any of this, okay? That's straight?"

"I'm not even here," I said.

"Pearson and Cash. Bad apples. Word was that Cash had flipped. Or maybe just Pearson stank and Cash was straight all along. You hear both versions. I.A. was working him to hook some of the others. Don't quote me on this—don't quote me on **any** of this—but supposedly, Cash was wearing a wire when he was killed."

"A wire. Was he trying to hook Pearson?"

"I don't know. Could be."

"Cash was the one who was shot, right? Then it was Pearson who ate his gun?"

"Right."

"So maybe Pearson found out his partner was wearing the wire, and he took him out."

"A version of that is the one going around," Sanchez said. "It's nice and clean."

"You don't buy it."

"You tell me. If Pearson is crooked and he catches his partner trying to trap him and he kills him, is that the kind of guy who turns right around and discovers remorse? I don't think so."

My heart sailed over a speed bump. "So then someone killed Pearson and made it look like a suicide."

"Or killed both of them and then set things up to look like that."

That was one of Charlie's theories. It sounded just as plausible coming out of Sanchez's mouth. Maybe even a little more so.

Sanchez watched me as I processed what he was telling me. A thought occurred to me. Sanchez knew the thought already. He'd been waiting for me to have it.

"The wire," he said.

"What happened to it? If Cash was wearing a wire, it should have recorded the whole thing."

"That's right. It should have."

"But?"

"It's missing."

"The wire is missing?"

Sanchez finished off his coffee. "No one wants the papers to get ahold of that information. Not one word about Cash wearing a wire. If I see it tomorrow . . . Well, you don't want me to see it tomorrow."

"You won't. Not from me. Jesus, Remy. So whoever killed Cash and Pearson took the wire."

"That's how it looks."

I looked over at the Woolworth Building. My gaze drifted south, to the less descript building where Paul Scott worked. I wondered if I had done the right thing in there. My gut told me that Paul had told me the truth, that he wasn't sleeping with Annette Hartman. He was being her hero. Harlan Scott's son to the rescue. I knew plenty about that myself. My gut also told me that damsels and their heroes—even paltry ones—have a way of mixing it up at some point if they're not careful. Neither Paul nor Annette Hartman struck me as being the careful type. You could see it in their lonely eyes. Put another way, they both seemed susceptible to the easy mistakes. So maybe I had done the right thing. At least now they were both on notice. They both knew that the world was watching. So, okay. A good little day's work after all.

I looked over at Sanchez.

"Captain, it was nice not having this conversation with you."

34

IT WAS 3:25 WHEN I GOT BACK TO MY CAR. I had a parking ticket tucked under the wiper. A hundred dollars. This city doesn't tiptoe around when it comes to passive revenue streams. I got into the car and did an illegal U-turn and took a left onto Pearl Street. At Canal Street I waited at a red light, catty-corner from the entrance to the Manhattan Bridge. The elaborate bridge entrance has always reminded me of the Brandenburg Gate. I'm sure that if I ever got over to my forefather's homeland and saw the real thing, I'd stop making the comparison. But I have no such plans, so I think the illusion's secure.

It was 3:42 as I headed up Bowery. I approached Delancey, and a huge green ball bounded in front of the car followed closely by a little Chinese boy with his arms outstretched. I had to slam on the brakes to avoid hitting him. A woman—his mother, I assume—jumped from the curb and grabbed the boy by his collar and nearly jerked him off his feet. Her screeching slashed the air like razors. She jerked the boy in my direction and shook him violently. His moon face showed nothing. I couldn't tell if she was trying to make him apologize to me, or if I was getting read part of the riot act myself. The ball had continued untouched across the street and come to rest next to a newspaper box. My phone rang. The woman continued to rattle the boy as I answered the phone.

The caller was Bill from the Columbia University A.A. meeting. The minute I mentioned the name Margaret King, he groaned. "Jesus Christ."

"I was wondering if I could talk to you about her," I said.

There was a long silence.

"Well . . . okay. I guess."

The rain had started. Big fat drops splattered on my windshield. Loose newspapers in the street leaped to life in the gusty wind. I turned off Bowery. Hit the FDR Drive, headed north.

No traffic problems.
3:51.

I EXPECTED A MAN, BUT BILL WAS A BOY. A
student. He told me he was nineteen, a soph-
omore at Columbia, studying political science. He envisioned a future for himself that
included the United Nations. He told me
that he had gone on a tour of the United Nations Building when he was nine years old,
and the memory of the place had never left
his system. He was lanky, five-eleven, with a
not unpleasant strong-boned face, slightly
soulful, slightly sad brown eyes and a loose
awning of blond hair. We met at a place
called the Underground, directly across from
Cannon's. It used to be a bookstore, it used to
sell crystals, it used to sell used CDs, it used
to house the offices of a community weekly.
Typical New York City pedigree. Now it was
a coffeehouse, comedy club and college hang-
out. Students were draped here and there on
various pieces of ratty furniture as if placed
just so by a meticulous set designer. Bill and I
sat across from each other at a small table.
Someone had carved CHE SUCKS on my side
of the table. Radical Republicanism.

Bill was upset with Margaret King, even a

full month and a half after her suicide. She had deceived him. She had deceived everyone at the Columbia meeting. She hadn't told anyone that she was a nun. Bill found out only when the TV and the newspapers brought out their "Sister Suicide" stories. He described for me the shock, disbelief and anger he had to balance with his grief, and he said he wasn't yet sure which was going to come out on top. He was more direct than I would have expected from a nineteen-year-old. I suspected the experience of standing up in front of a group of people in a church basement and reliving your soul's lowest moments can do that. I didn't ask, but I learned anyway that Bill had been going to A.A. meetings since his junior year in high school. In his admirably frank manner, he told me that discovering his problem and beginning his cure at such an early age had made him feel older than he actually was.

"I don't really socialize much with my peers. I can't stand most of the stuff they talk about. I can't relate to it. I mean, I hope they're having fun. I guess they are."

He was a swimmer. He said he spent hours and hours in the pool doing laps. He had a bit of a crooked smile.

"I'm a little obsessive." He laughed. "If a

person can be a 'little' obsessive." He was drinking a cup of herbal tea. He stared into it a moment, then looked back up at me. There was a visible ache deep behind his eyes.

"I was teaching Margaret how to swim. She said she'd always wanted to learn."

I TRIED GETTING AHOLD OF TOMMY CAR-roll on my way out to Brooklyn, but he wasn't in. Neither was Stacy. The skies had opened up, the rain slapping sideways in a gusty wind. Despite the first wave of the evening rush, I made decent time. As I crossed the Brooklyn Bridge, the clock on the Watch-tower Building read 4:53. If Angel Ramos was sticking to his pledge, dangerous ground was shifting somewhere out there. My having not heard anything from Carroll told me that either nothing was happening, or if it was, I was out of the loop.

Fair's fair. He didn't know what I knew, either.

Margaret King had been raped and se-verely beaten when she was seventeen. The attack had taken place in Prospect Park. Bill couldn't be sure, but he suspected that the attack took place in the same part of the park where Margaret ended her life six-teen years later. As would happen after her suicide, the seventeen-year-old Margaret had been spotted by a morning jogger. The attack had taken place in the winter—February—and Margaret's prone body had been frosted with a thin layer of snow. The jogger had called 911, and Margaret was taken to New York Methodist Hospital, where her injuries were treated. She wasn't lucid at first, and when she finally did come around and begin to grasp what was taking place, she denied that she had been raped. Vehemently. When asked if she was saying that the sex had been consensual, she attempted to deny that she had been involved in sex of any sort. In this case, the doctors knew best, or at least better. A sexual-assault counselor was brought to Margaret, and the woman promptly had one of her eyes very nearly gouged out by the frightened seventeen-year-old girl.

I drove down the ramp at the end of the bridge and turned onto Atlantic, then at Court Street, I took a right. Five o'clock. I turned on the radio, then changed my mind and turned it off. I preferred the silence. I needed it. To think.

MARGARET KING WAS COMPLETELY UNRELI-able. At first she claimed that she had not been attacked at all. Not just not raped, but not even attacked. Later she changed her story. She said that she had been hit by a car and that the car hadn't stopped and that she'd staggered into the park and passed out there. Later, she said it was a van. Then a city bus. At one point, she even said that she had fallen out a window and crashed through a skylight.

"Margaret had a lying problem," Bill had told me during our talk at the Underground. "She said she was always lying, always making things up, always exaggerating. She said she couldn't help herself, she lived half in the real world and half in a bunch of fantasies. Heck, maybe not even always half and half. Falling through the skylight? She said she actually laughed later, when her nurse friend told her the details of the story. Margaret didn't even remember telling it. She said she remembered the little details, the made-up details, but she thought they had come from a dream. She was . . . she was a real troubled person. I guess from the very beginning."

Bill had taken a long look at the ceiling before going on. "Who knows? She's dead now. **That's** real. But maybe she lied all along. I mean, she did. She lied when she never mentioned anything about being a goddamn nun."

Bill's voice had remained calm and cool

and steady, even as he described how he had gradually found himself being drawn closer and closer to Margaret King. She was fourteen years older than he. He said she was pretty. He said she could be silly, girlish, even a little flirtatious. He said he worked to keep his feelings subdued and to keep his fantasies from getting out of hand. He knew that he was essentially a loner and that he was responding—or trying to keep himself from responding—to the simple attractions of an older woman with whom he shared a destructive drive. He considered himself an intelligent person, and he figured he had things in hand.

He didn't.

Margaret's story, as told to me by Bill, was that she had eventually conceded the obvious to the authorities and was willing to state that, yes, she'd been accosted while walking alongside a wooded area of Prospect Park, then dragged amid the trees, where she'd been beaten and raped and left in a tangle of bushes. She was humiliated by the experience. She also gave so many conflicting descriptions of her attacker that the police ultimately had nothing to go on. An investigation was launched, but nothing ever came of it. Margaret's attacker went untouched.

Bill's story was that he was keeping Margaret King afloat in the Columbia pool one afternoon in late September when a jolt went through him. Margaret was on her back, her arms outstretched. Bill was supporting her, with one arm in the small of her back and one hand lightly prodding the back of her knees to keep them afloat. Except for the two of them, the pool was empty. Bill said he was walking her slowly around in little circles while she—eyes closed—chattered away at him, mainly about her early childhood. Like Bill, Margaret had been an only child. The stories had a certain embellished ring to them, and Bill suspected that once again, Margaret was making them up. Her stories in the basement of St. Paul's sometimes touched on her early life, and those too often sounded exaggerated and fantasized. The versions she was telling in monologue while being supported in the swimming pool had the same unreliable tone. Bill told me that he honestly didn't remember what had prompted him, but Margaret had just concluded a whopper about a family vacation to Greece, where she and a little Greek boy named Spiro had hitched rides on the fins of dolphins in the Mediterranean, when the next thing he knew, he was bent over Margaret and kissing her strongly on the mouth. She responded. He slid his hand up from her back to support her head and keep it from bobbing beneath the water, and she curled her body and let it float into his. The kiss went on for what felt like ages. Bill had continued stepping along the bottom of the pool, and eventually the two bumped up against the side of the pool. They finally came up for air. Several minutes later, the two were wrapped together on the floor of the steam room of the men's locker room, lying atop a mountain of towels that Bill had grabbed from the laundry bin outside the showers. They made love in a short, violent burst, then remained on the towels, clinging to each other for several minutes afterward while the hot mist spewed from the steam room's floor jets, several feet away. Bill said that Margaret had cried and cried and cried.

It was, let there be no doubt, a hell of a story.

35

RUTH KING'S LEGS LOOKED LIKE BOWLING pins. The short woman filled the doorway as if she were blocking the way of something inside that wanted to get out. For reasons probably buried in some fairy tale I was told in my diaper days, I imagined scores of highly animated mice fleeing the house, swirling past the woman's boxy black shoes like little Pamplona bulls. The woman had a wide face and eyes set far apart, as if she had been stretched at the ears. Her hair was a fine nest of mousy brown going gray. Her dress was also brown and a little shiny. I fully expected a large hairy wart to sprout on the side of her nose.

"You're Margaret King's aunt?" I said.

Her lips were fat and cracked. "Yes."

"I'm sorry to bother you, Mrs. King, but

it's very important that I talk with you. A friend of Margaret's told me how to locate you. My name is Fritz Malone. I'm a private investigator working with the police on a case that . . . Well, it's a matter of life or death."

"What do you want with me?"

"There's a man out there who I need to locate as fast as possible. I have reason to believe that your niece was acquainted with him in some fashion and—"

"My niece is dead." She had a strong, clear voice, like a car horn.

"I know that," I said. "I'm sorry."

"What did Margaret have to do with this man? Who is he? I can't help you."

"The man is a murderer, Mrs. King."

And then a creature did appear next to her shoes, a hairless dog not much bigger than a rat. Its eyes were like jellied marbles, and its toenails clicked as it shifted nervously from foot to foot to foot, like maybe it had to pee.

"I can't help you," the woman repeated. The dog let out a yelp. My shoe would have fit over it perfectly.

"I'm sorry," I said again. "This will take just a few minutes, but I can't accept no."

"Did you say you're with the police?"

"I'm working with the police." I pulled out my wallet and showed her my card. It didn't make her swoon. The dog yapped again and resumed his I've-got-to-pee dance. Another day and I might have shown my ID to the pooch, too. "Five minutes, Mrs. King. You can set your egg timer."

A sharp sound erupted from her. I saw a flash of teeth. It must have been a laugh. She skidded the dog away from the doorway with her foot and stepped back. "Come in."

The television set in the living room was on. Some TV movie. A pair of beautiful people having a lip-quivering competition while the camera closed in on their faces. Ruth King waddled to the set and was about to turn it off.

I blurted, "Wait. Could you keep it on?"

"What?"

"Could you just turn down the volume?"

She honked. "You watch this?"

If Angel was back in form, they'd be cutting away from the movie to report the carnage. Ruth King turned down the volume, then set her knuckles on her hips. I braced for the spell. "Do you want some water or something?" she asked.

"No, thanks."

I reached into my pocket and pulled out the copy of Margaret's suicide note that Sister Natividad had copied. And I froze. The woman noticed.

"What's wrong?"

"Um. Nothing. I . . . I'll take you up on that offer after all. The water."

She stepped into the kitchen, trailed by her hairless rat. I could feel the blood rushing into my face. My breath even went short, as if I were suddenly back in a tunnel.

Angel Ramos was not our man. Rather, he was maybe one of our men, the way Roberto Diaz had been one of them. But he wasn't the only man. He was not the thinking man. If he was involved at all, he was muscle. He was a man who could pull a trigger or leave off a bomb or swing a knife, but this thing that had kicked up last Thursday was not his scheme. I knew it. The nagging feeling that had been with me on some level since the moment I'd entertained a doubt at the Flea Club . . . it was the **right** feeling after all. **Doubt everything.** I'd known it the second I pulled Margaret's suicide note out of my pocket.

Angel Ramos. In Fort Petersen. A punk, a hood, a lowlife since he was old enough to light his first cigarette.

Sister Margaret King. A nun way the hell up in Riverdale.

Trying to fit those two together had been like trying to force magnets at their similar poles. Why in the world would Angel Ramos jerk Leavitt and Carroll around for a million dollars only to hand it all over to an order of nuns that he had no apparent connection to? It had never made sense, and it was never going to make sense, because that's not what had happened.

The person who left the note instructing the Sisters of Good Shepherd to go collect their "gift" at the Cloisters had made one thing clear to anyone who was paying close attention. And Sister Natividad had paid close attention. The fact that she hadn't drawn the obvious conclusion was not her fault. That was my fault. I'm the one with the license to snoop. Such things are my business, not the business of some young Filipino nun with a ready blush.

The one thing made clear by the person who left the Cloisters note—and my bet was that it was evident in Nightmare's earlier notes as well—was that the person who had written that note had also had access to Margaret King's suicide note. That wasn't Angel Ramos, unless he'd happened across Margaret's body in the park before the jogger did and decided on a whim to copy down the contents. And I wasn't buying that scenario.

The note had been found by the police in

Margaret's coat pocket. Doubtless it had cir-
culated among a few of the blue, though
probably not all that many. Once the M.E.
had confirmed the obvious, that Margaret
King's injuries were self-inflicted and that this
was in fact a case of suicide, the thin file was
complete. No further investigation.

The dead nun's note would have been
passed on to her family. Her next of kin.

Ruth King returned with a glass of water,
trailed by the dog. I put the note back in my
pocket as casually as I could. It felt like I was
stuffing in a thirty-pound goose. I accepted
the glass of water and drained it. "I'm sorry to
ask this, but is your husband still alive?"

"Albert? He died ten years ago."

"I see. Do you have any other family? Any
children?"

"You mean James?"

"James."

"That's my son."

"Does James live in the area?"

"He lives in Manhattan."

"What can you tell me about him? I mean,
if you were to say what kind of person he is."

"I don't understand."

I was grasping, I knew, but I couldn't shake
the feeling that there was something in my
fist. "Let me ask you this. James and Mar-

garet, they were cousins, right? What kind of relationship would you say they had?"

She darkened. "He hated her. He blamed her for Albert's death."

"For your husband's death?"

"That's what he says."

"How did your husband die, if you don't mind my asking?"

"He grew weak. His heart gave out." She gave another honk. Not with humor this time. "It's a long story."

"Could you sum it up quickly for me?"

"Sure I can. We took Margaret in after her parents were killed. Then she—"

"Wait. I'm sorry, Margaret's parents were **killed**? When was that?"

"I told you, it's a long story. I thought you said you were in a hurry."

"I can hear this."

She shifted on her feet. "Albert's brother and his wife, June, were killed in their sleep by an intruder. Years ago. It was a dopehead trying to get some money. They caught him. He's in jail and that's where I hope he rots. Margaret was in her bedroom when it happened. She was sixteen. She heard it happening, the whole thing, and she hid under her bed. That's the only reason she lived. When he was finished butchering Ronnie and June, the man went into her room, too. But he didn't see her hiding. Girl peed herself lying there on the floor. Can you imagine? After this, she moved in with us. Then she had . . . You know about her attack?"

"I know about that. They never caught the man."

"For three months the damn girl pretended it didn't happen, or when she'd finally admit it, she made up all these different stories about what really happened. Then one day, out of the blue, she says it was Albert that did it."

"Your husband?"

"That's right. All those nutty stories of hers and **that's** the one she decided to stick with."

"Did . . . do you think—"

I'd never seen someone turn so red so fast. "He never **touched** that girl! Never! End of story. Albert was a kind person. He never even swatted bugs. That was my job."

"Why did she say it?"

"Lord, don't ask me. That girl had more problems than a math book. She said it and she refused to take it back and that was that. I begged her. I wanted to hit her, but I didn't. Of course it devastated Albert. It devastated all of us. There was a trial, the newspapers, the whole thing. I think back on that time and I want to throw up. In the end, it didn't stick, 'cause there was nothing to stick. He was innocent. Whoever it was who really did it to her got off scot-free. Margaret had already started her drinking problem. She had moved out of here already. **We** couldn't keep her. The Catholic Charities were helping her out. I saw what she was doing with that drinking, and I thought . . . God forgive me for this, but I thought, Good. Drink. Go ahead. If it doesn't kill you, maybe it'll kill the baby."

"What baby?"

"What baby? Margaret's baby. What baby do you think?"

"I'm sorry, Mrs. King. You're losing me."

"The baby. Margaret's baby. That girl was raped. It got her pregnant. All the nutty stuff she was doing and saying, she didn't tell anyone until it was too late. She'd refuse to have an abortion, in any case. She'd gotten all holy at that point."

"Did she have the child?"

"Oh yeah. She had it. Baby girl. She held her for all of ten seconds, then . . ." Ruth snapped her pudgy fingers. "Off to adoption. Never saw her again."

She leaned down and scooped the dog off the floor, then straightened and held it to her chest. It kicked, but she ignored it. I took ten long seconds of silence. My brain was going muddy. I wasn't even certain why it was I'd come out here in the first place.

"Mrs. King . . . there was a suicide note. Did the police return that note to you?"

"Yes, they did."

"Could I see it?"

She was already shaking her head even before I'd completed the question.

"Afraid you can't. James took it."

36

THERE WERE THREE OF THEM. ONE WAS IN the metal bucket, suspended from a small crane affixed in the bed of the green Parks Department truck. He had a chain saw and was running it like a knife through butter, hacking off the small limbs of one of the large oaks in Carl Schurz Park. The other two, on the ground, were taking up the fallen limbs and tossing them into the growling machine that was hooked to the back of the truck. The limbs came out of the chute on the other end, reduced to chips. A call to the Arsenal in Central Park asking after James King had led me to the eastern edge of Manhattan. I was lucky. The storm had passed, but not before cracking off part of a large limb on one of the trees in Carl Schurz Park. James King was pulling a little O.T. to help take down the rest of the limb.

The bulge of land where Gracie Mansion was situated was visible several hundred yards to the south. As I approached, the man suspended from the crane called out something to his colleagues on the ground. They both took several steps backward. One of them almost bumped into me. He placed a gloved hand on my chest. "Hold up, buddy."

I saw that a rope had been tied around one of the larger limbs, the loose end of it run through a Y in the tree and coiled around a large spike that had been driven into the trunk about five feet up from the ground. As I watched, the man in the tree worked his chain saw through the large limb. When he was halfway through it, it buckled downward but was held in place partway by the rope. The man continued with the saw. He broke through, and the limb dropped several feet, then jerked to a halt as the rope brought it up short. Instead of falling to the ground, the limb remained in midair, rocking back and forth. And ten dollars to the person who doesn't think of someone being hanged from a tree until dead.

I took a few steps closer to the truck. The guy who had stopped me asked, "You want something?"

"I'm looking for James King."

"You're looking at him."

"You're him?"

"No. Him." He jerked his gloved thumb toward the man with the chain saw. The man in the trees was wearing a white safety helmet and a pair of protective goggles. The goggles made him look like a bug. The man on the ground called up to him, "Hey, Jimmy! Someone here to see you, man."

James King pulled a lever in his bucket, and immediately the crane began to lower him. He gazed down at me as he descended, or so it seemed; it was difficult to tell because of the goggles. He held the chain saw up near his chest, as if at arms. The blade caught the sunlight on the way down. The bucket was swinging closer to me than I'd expected, and my temptation was to step back. I resisted it. For one thing, the wood chipper was only a few feet behind me. It was still running, still humming, still ready for whatever might be tossed into it. But more than that, an image flashed through my mind. It was of the boy at the parade. The boy with the balloon. It was the image of him standing by as his mother was being placed in the back of an ambulance. The shadow of the bucket swung over my head. But I didn't budge. This just wasn't the time to give, not even an inch.

The bucket stopped less than a foot from the ground. James King stepped out of it. He was still holding the chain saw at arms. Above him, directly over his head, the large severed limb continued to sway and rock, side to side.

37

IT WASN'T HIM.

He was an angry man, possibly a violent man. When he pulled off his helmet and goggles, I saw a man in his late twenties already losing his thinning hair. He had enough of his mother's face to warrant some sympathies. The thought even dashed swiftly through my brain that he had the eyes of his mother's dog. His skin was ruddy, recently and harshly burned by the sun. He wore a thick Fu Manchu–style mustache, in need of a trim. There was practically more hair on his lip than remained on his head. He lit up a cigarette while we talked, and the smoke seemed to leach right into his skin.

He sat on the retaining wall overlooking the river. He'd set the chain saw down gently next to him, as if he might snatch it back up without warning.

"I still hate her. I guess I'll rot in hell, but I can't help it. She destroyed my family. Here're my parents, taking her in, and what does she do? She puts a spike right in my father's heart. Then what? She turns around and becomes a **nun**? She was a little teenage slut, and then she becomes a nun? That's great, huh? I guess she's 'saved.'" He made the sarcastic quotation marks in the air. "How about saving my damn father? Ever think of that? Do you know what happens to a person's reputation when he gets accused of something like that? He got cleared, but so what? The stain is there, man. You can't get it out. Everywhere he went after that, you could just see it. He was the guy who maybe raped his own niece. He lost friends. He lost his job. His life was over, it was just a matter of waiting around until he died. Meanwhile, little bitch Maggie is off with her nuns. Well, I guess she finally got her ending, too. My crazy mother went to the funeral. Not me, man. No way in hell. As far as I'm concerned, they couldn't dig her grave deep enough. All the way to hell's what I'd like. Jesus. Don't get me started."

It was a little late to avoid. He finished his

cigarette and lit another one. The move was seamless.

"You know, when we were kids, I liked her. She was my only cousin, and we used to play together. Maggie kind of dropped me once she became a teenager. I guess that's normal, I don't know. She was getting into boys. Shit. Like I'm suddenly a frog or something? Aw, man, Uncle Ronnie and Aunt June. That nigger breaks in and kills them in their frigging beds. This is me rotting in hell again, man, but I wish he'd dragged Maggie out from under her bed and killed her, too. Why not? She's dead now anyway. But at least my old man would've been spared all that crap."

He threw his cigarette away in disgust. I half expected him to grab up the chain saw and start to work on the retaining wall. Instead, he stared off into space.

I looked past him to the river. Halfway across, a barge was being nudged upriver by a towboat. I don't know where they came up with the name "tugboat." I've been staring all my life out at the water that runs around this island, and not once have I ever seen one of those boats tugging anything. They **push.** They settle up against the rear of something fifty times their size, and they start pushing. I know it's a metaphor for something, but in all these years, I've never quite placed it.

James King was not Nightmare. He was **describing** nightmares, but that was as far as it went. He told me that he had taken Margaret's suicide note because he wanted to plunge a knife into it, to rip it into a hundred shreds, to spit on it and burn it. Phyllis Scott would no doubt posit that King had some "unresolved issues." Sadly, ravaging his cousin's final words probably hadn't given the man anything near the "closure" he sought. I was looking at an open wound sitting on the retaining wall. Open and oozing and aching.

But I wasn't looking at Nightmare. James King wasn't holding Philip Byron. He wasn't playing puppet master to Angel Ramos. When I'd checked in with the Parks Department administrative office at the Arsenal, I'd been told at first that James King was out of town, on vacation in Florida. A second look at the records had shown that—no—his vacation had ended just the day before. Monday. He'd remained in Florida an extra day to avoid traveling on the Sunday after Thanksgiving. Today was King's first day back at work. King confirmed that for me. So did his sunburned face.

But even more than all that was the simple fact that he made no effort whatsoever to disguise a character that seemed all too capable of going to a very dark place and considering very dark deeds. Charlie Burke says to doubt everything. Fine. But James King gave me nothing to doubt. He pleaded guilty to ongoing rage and to an impotent act of revenge on his cousin's suicide note. More than the fact that he had been more than a thousand miles away during the past week of carnage, those were his alibis.

I thanked him for his time. He placed his hands behind him on the wall and leaned back. For a moment I thought he was going to swing his legs over his head and follow his cousin to the grave. He looked miserable.

He looked off to his left. "Funny," he said.

"What's funny?"

"Nothing, really. I was just thinking about Maggie. She was a drunk, you know."

"I know about that."

"Yeah. A drunk and a nun and now dead. Some life. Back when she was a teenager, after my aunt and uncle were killed and everything? Before she got attacked and accused my father of being the one who did it, we kind of got to be friends again. For a little while. She really needed someone to talk to. For a while, it was me." He stroked his mustache as his thoughts turned a little more gently to the past. "She had a huge crush on the guy who prosecuted her parents' killer. Huge crush. She was all of sixteen and seventeen, and she kept telling me how she was in love and she bet he was in love with her, too, and how one day they'd get married and everything would be great. She'd be the queen in her castle. You know how girls can get."

"Sure," I said. From just outside the park, I heard several sirens. Police. Ambulance. I couldn't say which. From the corner of my eye, I saw two men in suits take off running in the direction of York Avenue.

King picked up the chain saw and cradled it in his lap. A second set of sirens kicked up. These seemed to be coming from the direction of Gracie Mansion. King hoisted the chain saw up onto his shoulder as if he were Paul Bunyan. A smirk of sorts—it was hard to tell—appeared beneath the mustache.

"If Maggie's dreams had come true, none of that other stuff would've happened. Maybe my father'd still be alive." This time he let out a small laugh. "And Maggie'd have been a big deal. Queen of the whole city."

"What do you mean?"

Something was definitely going on. A cop on a bicycle was pedaling our way as fast as he could.

"The prosecutor," King said. "Maggie's dreamboat. That was Martin Leavitt. He was a big hotshot in Brooklyn at the time. Mr. Law and Order. If she really could've landed him, she'd be fat and happy now. It would've all been different, just like she said. Up at that mansion. Might not be a castle, but I'll bet Maggie'd have been all right with that."

"Leavitt?"

The bicycle cop flew by, his legs pumping like twin pistons. His face was a mask of grimness.

King slid off the wall. "Hey, man, where's the fire?"

Still more sirens sounded. I wheeled around. The feeling came over me again, the one like I was in a tunnel. I was standing stock-still, but it felt like everything around me was rushing past at breakneck speed. It was enough of a feeling that I must have staggered. King grabbed hold of my arm.

"Hey, man, are you okay?"

38

PIER 17 JUTS OUT INTO THE EAST RIVER just a few blocks north of Wall Street. Until the early eighties, it was just one more on the growing list of Manhattan's abandoned piers, home to seagulls, drunks, junkies and a few gay men looking for another few gay men. The only feature of note was the nearby Fulton Fish Market, which operated out of mainly open-air stalls located along the water running north from the pier, primarily in the shadow of the elevated FDR Drive.

That all changed when an urban development group called the Rouse Company struck a deal with the city to develop the pier, along with a portion of the real estate adjacent to it, for commercial purposes. They called it the South Street Seaport. The original vision of the Rouse Company was an urban mall stretching all the way north along the river to the Brooklyn Bridge, a quarter mile away from the pier. This plan, however, would have required more cooperation from the people who controlled the Fulton Fish Market (a loose consortium of Chinese and Italian mafia, along with, of course, the fishmongers themselves) than those people were willing to provide. So the plans got scaled back somewhat. The Rouse Company recobbled the foot of Fulton Street and renovated the existing buildings, most of which dated back to the seventeen hundreds and the area's heyday as the city's thriving boatbuilding district, but which, like the piers, had become increasingly ghostlike over the years as New York's maritime identity diminished. Vintage streetlamps were installed, and a general "Ye Olde" flavor was mandated for the signage of the merchants who were subsequently lured to the area.

Meanwhile, out on Pier 17 itself, a three-story glass and metal structure was erected. A pavilion. A faux-weathered brass roof was bolted into place, and there it was: a large, light-filled shopping mall on Manhattan's East River. The Gap, Sharper Image, Banana Republic . . . only a shut-in or an isolated

Montanan doesn't know the general run of stores that populate these kinds of places.

There's general agreement that the success of the South Street Seaport mall has been somewhat less than what either the Rouse Company or the merchants who pay their exorbitant rents to do business there had hoped it would be. I can recall stopping at the place with Margo one Christmas Eve and our being two of seven shoppers in the entire mall; a hired chorus of around twenty had stood at the garland-wrapped railing overlooking the main floor and serenaded us with holiday tunes.

Probably the most consistently thriving businesses in the pier's mall are the ones on the top floor, the one with the most glass and the best views: the Brooklyn Bridge to the north, the Brooklyn waterfront and promenade directly across the river, and to the south, Governors Island and the top half of the torch arm of the Statue of Liberty.

This is the Pier 17 food court. And this is where Angel Ramos screwed up while attempting to plant a homemade bomb behind one of the large potted plants that dot the terra-cotta floor.

THE CROWD OF ONLOOKERS WAS SOME-what larger than what you generally get for these sorts of things. This was because, in addition to the naturally curious, several hundred shoppers and salesclerks had safely fled the pavilion as word spread of a madman somewhere in the building with a bomb. Even as I arrived, scattered pockets of people were fleeing across the wooden deck between the pier and the street with their arms over their heads. The police had already set up sawhorses and barrier tape. Several officers dashed forward to escort the panicked people the final few feet. One of the people fleeing the pavilion was old St. Nick himself. The big guy was dragging along a stumbling elf by the arm.

Behind the barrier was the row of police. Dozens of them and more coming. The patrol cars parked at every imaginable angle. And behind the police cars, funneled into the narrow Ye Olde cobbled area of Fulton Street, stood the crowd of onlookers.

I'd gotten a fragmented piece of the story from one of the cops mobilizing just outside Carl Schurz Park. "Some nut is holding a group of people hostage at Pier 17," he'd said. "They say he's got a bomb."

I parked my car at the base of the Brooklyn Bridge and jogged along South Street, in front of the fish market stalls. The gawkers were sparse here, and I was able to get right up to the barrier. I heard mutterings from some of the cops that the mayor was allegedly on his way. Not too many seemed thrilled by the prospect.

"We got our fucking hands full here."

"He thinks we got time for a fucking photo op?"

As Remy Sanchez moved from behind one of the stanchions holding up the FDR Drive, I called out to him: "Sanchez!"

He looked around, then spotted me. A policeman near me was trying to keep me from the barricade, but Sanchez called to him, "Let him in!" and I ducked under the tape. Sanchez was barking into his walkie-talkie. "No! Do you understand the word 'no'? Just wait, is what I said." He lowered the walkie-talkie. "Cox is in there."

"**Cox?** Where?"

He waved his walkie-talkie toward the pier. "In there somewhere. Son of a bitch. Rule number one in these situations is you stand down. Any cop knows that. Rule number one is **not** running like a madman across an open space and going inside. That doesn't make heroes, that makes dead men."

I looked over at the pier. The public space was a good hundred yards from the pavilion building. "So what happened?" I asked.

"A man was spotted acting suspiciously by a worker at one of the food joints up there. We think the worker confronted the guy. This is what we're hearing from some of the people who managed to get away. The worker was shot. He's still in there. Somehow the shooter managed to corral a bunch of people, and he's holding them on the top floor. We don't know exactly how many. He let one person go. A messenger. She says he's got a bomb. She says the guy's out of his mind. He wants money. He wants a helicopter. He wants a boat. He wants to talk to the mayor. Son of a bitch doesn't know what he wants. We're trying to establish communication."

"What he wants is ten million dollars," I said.

Sanchez made a long face. "Well, so do I. And how do you know this?"

"Long story."

"I take it this is our nut job from last week," Sanchez said.

"That's the short version."

"So he'll kill those people if it comes to it. We can't count on this being a bluff."

"I wouldn't count on it."

"Holy mother."

Sanchez's walkie-talkie crackled, and he barked into it. I caught the word "sharpshooters." I scanned the phalanx of police officers. I was surprised Tommy Carroll hadn't arrived on the scene yet. One Police Plaza was under a mile away. A police van was making its way slowly down the cobbled street, parting the sea of onlookers. Sanchez clicked off his walkie-talkie.

"If I get my hands on Cox, I'm going to strangle him. There's no way he can approach that guy without endangering the hostages. Goddammit, we need control here. A cowboy cop is not what we need."

"Cox knows the perp," I said. "He knows the guy holding the hostages."

"What? What are you talking about?"

"Another long story."

"Jesus, Malone, you're just one big fat storybook, aren't you? Well, I don't have time to listen to them all right now. You stay put and keep your nose clean. This is police business. If the situation drags on, we'll light a campfire and let you tell some of your stories."

"Gracias," I said.

Sanchez grunted and moved off. I spotted another face I recognized—that of Officer Patrick Noon. He was standing a head above anyone near him, about thirty feet away from me. He was looking in my direction, but if he spotted me, he chose not to show it.

The van that had been inching its way through the crowd reached South Street. The rear doors flew open and a dozen or more helmeted policemen piled out. They were wearing external bulletproof vests and carrying automatic weapons. I spotted an identical van pulling up to the barricades from the south. A small army poured out of this one as well. Sirens sounded overhead, simultaneous with the **thwocka-thwocka-thwocka** of a low-flying helicopter. The elevated FDR Drive runs right past Pier 17, roughly level with the upper floors of the mall. I was sure that traffic had been stopped in both directions. I took a few steps out from under the highway and looked up. I spotted several slender rifle barrels resting on the guardrail. The sharpshooters were already in place. The firepower was building up.

Cox. I pictured him dashing across the hundred-yard open area to make his way to the pier building. This wasn't heroic, not any more than his shooting Roberto Diaz at point-blank range had been. I knew what it was. It was the same move as the one he'd pulled in the Municipal Building. A preemptive one. Cox had no intention of standing by while police negotiators attempted to set up a link to Angel. He couldn't risk it. Whatever Leonard Cox's entanglement was with Angel Ramos, it now appeared that he would do anything in his power to keep Angel from having the opportunity to spell it out.

Cox wasn't on any rescue mission. He was on the hunt.

Another burping siren sounded, this one from a black sedan making its way down South Street, the same direction I'd come from. A news van was hot on its trail. As the car eased to a stop, I ducked out from behind the tape and slipped unseen to the nearest fish stall and moved quickly behind it. I peeked back around the corner. Martin Leavitt was emerging from the sedan. I thought of James King's story about his cousin's crush on the younger Leavitt. The news van screeched to a halt, and Kelly Cole bolted from the passenger side and ran on tippy heels swiftly over to where Leavitt had paused to survey the scene. She was beckoning her cameraman to hurry along. Her hair bounced as if she were in a shampoo commercial. Even from this distance, I could see Leavitt lighting up as she approached. The man couldn't help himself; he was the ultimate flirt. I thought again about Margaret King, about seventeen-year-old Maggie King. Remy Sanchez was making his way over to the mayor. The news cameraman got his equipment up on his shoulder and flipped on his lamp. Cole reached for Leavitt's elbow to guide him closer, into the shot. He reached for hers as well. The two shared a little laugh. Even from where I was standing I could read the look on Sanchez's face. He obviously felt this was no time for a goddamn tea party.

The stalls of the fish market blocked me partially from view, allowing me to scoot unseen along the small seldom-used lip of the pier on the north side of the pavilion. I reached the pavilion and pushed quickly through the first set of double glass doors.

It was beginning to look a lot like Christmas. A forty-foot evergreen rose from the mall floor up to the other levels. It was decorated with large colored disks. They looked like psychedelic hubcaps. At the base of the tree was Santa's Workshop, now abandoned except for several mechanical reindeer whose heads swiveled left and right as if the animals were trying to figure out where everybody had gone. Thick silver strands of tinsel were draped everywhere, and most of the shopwindows had been frosted around the borders with spray-on snow. The sound system crooned "Silver Bells" to an empty house. I pulled out my .38.

Moving as swiftly as I could, I double-stepped it up the escalator to the second floor level and ducked into the nearest shop. It sold brightly colored wooden animals from South and Central America. A dozen Technicolor parrots were perched on colored loops hanging from the ceiling. I moved behind a blue gorilla the size of a small car and peered out the shopwindow.

There were two ways I could see for reaching the third level. One was to continue up the escalator I'd just been on. The other was to head down the low-ceilinged corridor of shops toward the rear of the pavilion. At the end of the corridor, a set of switchback stairs went up either side to the top level. My memory of the time Margo had dragged me here was that at the top of the escalator were several restaurants. The food court itself ran along an area corresponding to the corridor of shops on my level, then opened up to a large common area with tables and chairs and bolted-down lollipop tables for eating while standing. That was where the steps led to. It would have been nice to know if Ramos was holed up with his hostages on my end of the building or down at the far end. I glanced at the parrots. They weren't talking.

I didn't relish the idea of being delivered to Ramos via the escalator, so I decided to try the corridor. Between the shop and the far end of the corridor stood several market carts in the middle of the floor, the kind that sell bad jewelry and refrigerator magnets and various cheap gewgaws. I decided I'd make my way down the hallway cart by cart. They weren't much cover, but they were all I had.

I rubbed the gorilla's nose for good luck, then I took off out of the shop, keeping low, and made it to the first cart. "Silver Bells" had given way to "The Little Drummer Boy." **Pa-rum-pa-pum-pum.**

I dashed to the second cart and crouched behind it. A refrigerator magnet next to my head read: TIME EXISTS SO THAT EVERYTHING DOESN'T HAPPEN ALL AT ONCE. I liked that. I grabbed it and stuffed it in my pocket. I was halfway to the final cart when a shot sounded out and I felt a bullet zip by just inches from my face. I dove to the floor and slid the final few feet to the cart. A second shot rang out. This one took a chip off the cart, just above my head.

I made myself as small as I could and crawled beneath the cart, wedging myself between the wheels and the centering post. I flattened my cheek against the cold floor and eased my head forward, like a reluctant turtle.

Leonard Cox was crouched behind the railing at the top of the right-side stairway. His elbows were locked in front of him, and he was holding his service revolver in both hands. The gun bucked. The bullet hit something metal and ricocheted into the window of a toy store in front of me on the left. The exploding glass looked like water from a burst dam. I kissed the floor as bits of glass rained down all around me.

"Malone!" It was Cox. "Malone, it's the police! Hold your fire! Throw down your weapon!"

I knew immediately what he was doing. Cops carry transmitters on their shoulders, and my good friend Leonard Cox was setting it down for the record. In that instant, I knew Charlie's theory was correct. The so-called murder-suicide of Pearson and Cash. However the shootings went down, in the end it was Cox who'd set things up to look the way they had. Twisting and reshaping. Cox seemed to have a talent for it.

I had a lousy shot. I'd have to bring my shooting arm out from under the cart, and he'd have a free shot at me. Besides, I wanted to avoid firing my gun if at all possible. Cox would have a trickier time putting his self-defense story over on his superiors if there was no evidence that I'd fired at him.

"Malone!"

I didn't respond. I crawled slowly backward from under the cart and squatted on my haunches behind it. The toy store was the last shop in the corridor. Rising to a crouch, I grabbed hold of the cart's wooden handles, tilted it off its centering post and gave it a shove. It resisted at first, then moved. Keeping the cart between myself and Cox, I started rolling it forward, breaking into a slow run. As I neared the toy store, Cox fired again. I torqued the handles so that the cart began to tip. With a deep grunt, I shoved the cart with all my strength toward the shattered window and followed behind it, leaping at the last second through the window and rolling into a ball. Toys crashed down all around me in a clatter of plastic and metal. A toy drum set's cymbals gave a tinny crash. I rolled to a stop. There was a five-inch gash in the sleeve of my jacket. I sensed a warmth beneath it. I scooted immediately up against the wall, flat on the floor, and peered out over the pile of toys.

The tipped-over cart partially blocked my view—and kept me partially hidden—but I could see Cox clearly, up at the top of the stairs. He was still crouched behind the railing. I brought my .38 up to my nose, squinting along the barrel. I had a perfect shot.

Pa-rum-pa-pum-pum.

He pitched sideways. Simultaneously, I heard the shots. Cox started to rise to his knees, then spun around violently as a second volley of shots was fired. His gun dropped and his arm flailed for the railing, just missing it. His mouth dropped open and he toppled forward, belly flopping onto the top three steps. He didn't move. That was it. He looked as if he were glued to the spot.

I raced out of the toy store. From the floor above me, people were screaming. I heard another burst of automatic gunfire as I reached the stairs. I paused. Running up the stairs would be suicide. Blood was dripping down onto the railing next to me. I craned my neck and saw Leonard Cox's body. The entire building began to roar. It was the sound of helicopters. The sound was drowning out everything except the screaming. I couldn't remain where I was.

Move!

I spotted an elevator partway back down

the corridor and I ran to it and slammed the button. The helicopter roar gained volume and, with it, ferocity. The elevator door slid open and I got in. I hit 3. As the door slid closed I muttered a soft prayer.

39

ANGEL RAMOS WAS STANDING TWENTY FEET away when the elevator door opened. My gun was already up and aiming. My knuckles were white on the handle. Just as the elevator bumped to a halt, I'd noted the blood oozing from the gash in my coat sleeve. The warmth had given way to a hot searing pain. I realized what had happened. A large piece of the toy store's plate-glass window had sliced open my shooting arm when I dove through the window. A nasty thought tore through my brain as Ramos appeared before me: What if my trigger finger doesn't respond?

Ramos was cradling an Uzi rifle. He was in jeans and a white oversize Sean John sweatshirt. A black scarf covered his head. A black knapsack was on the floor between his feet.

He turned. Whether he actually saw me or not, I'll never know. Abruptly his body began to jerk as if he were having an epileptic seizure. The rifle clattered to the ground. Ramos's sweatshirt had a fit of its own, rippling in a breeze of gunfire. The splotches of red appeared even before the man had crumpled to the ground. It was over in seconds. His last movement—and he was probably already dead at this point—was his left leg. It kicked. His foot hit the Uzi, and the rifle skidded about ten feet along the floor.

The elevator door started to close, and I reached out with my gun hand and stopped it. A loud, metallic voice sounded. **"Lay down your weapon!"**

I did. I leaned down and skidded my accomplice across the floor. About ten feet. Just like Angel's. I stepped out of the elevator with my hands raised.

A police helicopter was floating in the air just off the end of the pavilion. The pilot was jockeying his stick to keep the craft in place. The sharpshooter was still aiming his rifle into the pavilion. The man holding the bullhorn was leaning out the side window of the bubble.

I turned to look in the other direction. Several dozen people—Angel's hostages— were moving forward as one. They all seemed to have forgotten how to walk normally.

40

THE PIER 17 PAVILION WAS FLOODED WITH police. The hostages were herded together and taken out as a group. Stretchers were brought in to remove the bodies of Cox, Angel Ramos and the food-court worker Ramos had shot, a young guy named Brian Vitrano. The top floor of the pavilion was cleared as quickly as possible so that the police bomb squad could come in and do their thing.

I was escorted out of the building and across the pier's open area by a pair of humorless policemen. One of them was Patrick Noon. "Evening, Noon," I'd said to him when he took hold of my good arm. He'd given me nothing back. Zero. Nada.

The setting sun on the far side of the island

hit the buildings along the Brooklyn waterfront and fired up a thousand windows with hot, dazzling gold.

I was taken to a waiting ambulance, where my coat was peeled off and my arm was triaged. While I was being worked on, I caught the rumor that one of the three people who'd been taken off to NYU Downtown Hospital was still alive. I knew without question that it wasn't Ramos. If there was a God who had a moment to spare for New York, I thought, it would be Brian Vitrano. He was our true hero du jour.

The EMS workers wrapped my arm in gauze and told me they would take me to the hospital to get some fresh blood.

Remy Sanchez was making his way over to me. He wasn't happy. "You could have gotten all those people in there killed. I could have your license pulled for a stunt like that. What the hell happened in there?"

"Cox tried to take me out."

"He tried to **kill** you?"

"I told you, Sanchez. He's a baddie." I corrected myself. "He **was** a baddie."

Sanchez shook his head. "**Is.** He's still alive."

My heart sank. And my head went light. I staggered, and an EMS guy grabbed hold of me. "He's lost blood," he said to Sanchez. "We're going to take him in."

"Wait," I said. I took a few calculated breaths, and the dizziness passed. I turned to Sanchez. "Cox was in it up to his teeth. He was in it with Ramos. They were a team, I'm convinced. **There's** your baddest apple, Captain. If I were you, I'd contact the doctors at the hospital and tell them to leave Cox in the hallway for a few hours. Those things do happen, you know."

Sanchez shook his head. "Something stank from the start," he said. "A bad cop'll cast a white shadow every time."

A bright light hit me. There was a rumbling in the crowd, and suddenly Kelly Cole was standing in front of me, holding a microphone and pressing a hand to her ear to keep an earplug from falling out. She flashed me a quick look of recognition, then barked urgently into the microphone. "Jim, I'm here with the man who was inside the pavilion when the shooting rang out. Could you tell us what it was like in there?" She thrust the microphone into my face.

"I don't remember a fucking thing," I said.

She snapped the microphone back and gave me a withering look. The sentiment was clear. **Fuck you, Malone.** The crowd parted behind her, and Mayor Leavitt strolled onto the scene. He acknowledged me with a nod, then tugged his tie tight as Cole wheeled around. She shoved the microphone forward and asked the mayor if he had any comment. Of course he did, but his words didn't register with me in any meaningful way. Leavitt stood in the harsh glare of the minicam and mouthed whatever it was he had to mouth. To me it was a silent movie starring Mr. Charisma. Mr. Bachelor Mayor.

I thought of Tommy Carroll's rant against the mayor just the night before. It seemed several lifetimes ago. If there really was to be a battle between the two men, Carroll was lost. He was beaten. The man chattering away to the city of New York and beyond was too young, too smart, too smooth, too appealing. There are some people to whom nothing bad ever sticks. They can walk through a mountain of muck and emerge clean and rosy. Survival and success just seem to be their birthright.

I heard Cole asking the mayor, "And where is Commissioner Carroll, Mr. Mayor? It looks like practically every cop in the city is here. Where's the commissioner?"

Leavitt addressed his answer directly to the camera. "Commissioner Carroll has been under a lot of strain lately. We all know it's been a rough time for the police department. I'm sad to report as well that Tommy's health hasn't been all that good. He's a proud man, and you'd never hear it from him. He always puts his job first."

"Then where is he?"

The mayor paused. As he did, my cell phone rang. I snatched it from my pocket and flipped it open. "Malone. Hold on."

I lowered the phone just as Martin Leavitt found the soulful expression he'd been looking for. He aimed it first at Kelly Cole, then at the camera. "I have no idea where the hell the commissioner is. He should certainly be here. Frankly, I'm a little concerned."

I raised the phone to my ear. "Malone. What?"

"Fritz?"

It was Margo.

"Yeah. What's up?"

For a moment I thought the shakiness was in the connection. Then I realized it was in Margo's voice. She was sobbing. "Oh God, Fritz. He's going to kill us. He's going to kill us both!"

I crushed the phone in my hand. **"What?"**

"He's going to kill us. Daddy and me. Oh God. Fritz. Whatever you do—"

The line went dead.

So did my heart.

Margo.

I took off running. I shoved the mayor out of my way, along with one of his security goons. The first several seconds, I was simply running blindly. **He's going to kill us both!** Then I focused. I sprinted through a gap between two police barricades and spotted Patrick Noon making his way over to a patrol car. I veered in his direction. Without thinking, I pulled my gun from my holster. Noon had no time to react.

"Get in!" I prodded the gun against his ribs. "Get in. There's a murder under way in Queens. Let's go!"

He paused.

"Get in!" He got the point. I ran around to the passenger side as he slid in behind the wheel. "Sirens," I barked, "The lights. Go, go, go!"

The officer frowned. He started up the car and put it in gear. "If this is bullshit, you're in deep."

"If you don't drive, **you're** in deep."

He drove. Because of the mess at the pier, we couldn't get onto the FDR until north of Chinatown. While Noon showed some good moves behind the wheel, I tried calling

Margo. No answer. Same thing with Charlie's number. I threw my phone onto the floor of the car. I'd sent her out there. How could I have been so perfectly **stupid**? I should have gone directly to Margo's after leaving her father's and fetched Donna Bia's phone myself. What was I thinking, involving her like that?

I looked out the window at the gray East River. Drown me. If anything happens to Margo or to Charlie, just drown me. Tie a rope around my leg and attach it to a car and send it off the Queensboro Bridge. **I'd sent her there.**

I turned to Noon. **"Drive!"**

Lights flashing and siren screaming at the top of its lungs, we raced over the bridge, and I directed Noon to Charlie's neighborhood. The officer looked over at me. "Plan?" He was cool, calm and collected. Good man. I took my cue.

"Plan. Okay." My right arm was throbbing. "Cut the sirens," I said. "Pull over. Here."

Noon brought the patrol car deftly to the curb in front of a florist. Charlie's street was two blocks away. I thought a moment, then I directed Noon to the intersection at the end of the block. The top of Charlie's house was visible from where we stopped. I took another twenty seconds to think.

"Okay. Here's how we do it."

I got out of the car and made my way down the alley that ran behind Charlie's house. I passed the house and went into the backyard of his next-door neighbors, Powell and Louise Harrison. Louise appeared at the back door. I put my finger to my lips, and she got the message.

The Harrisons are a retired couple. They have five grandchildren, a fact that Margo's mother likes to recycle to her daughter whenever I'm within earshot. Some years back, Powell and his son, Scott, built a slapdash tree house in the only tree in the Harrisons' backyard that could sustain one. Scott pounded a half-dozen two-by-fours into the tree trunk to serve as a ladder. There was a brief problem a few years ago with local teenagers finding their way up into the tree house late at night to indulge in any of several sports that teenagers generally indulge in. Charlie had solved the problem with several late-night vigils and a few revolver shots into the air.

I scurried up the tree, passed through the plywood tree house and shimmied out onto the thick branch that Charlie has been complaining to Powell about for twenty-three years. Charlie was convinced that with just the right kind of storm, the branch would break off and either land on his roof or go right through it. So far it hadn't. From the branch, I lowered myself soundlessly onto Charlie's roof. The pain in my injured arm was like fire. Blood had begun to ooze through the gauze.

I tried the windows first, suspecting they'd be locked. I was right. On to Plan B. I moved around to the far side of the house. I could see Noon's patrol car parked at the end of the block. I waved my arm three times in the air. Noon flashed his lights. A second later, his roof lights came on. I checked my watch, then made my way to the window to Margo's old room. I looked at my watch and counted down the final seconds. Four, three, two, one . . . I heard the not so distant squeal of tires.

I jabbed at the glass with my elbow just as Noon's siren and horn sounded full blast. He must have slipped the car into neutral, since the engine revved with a scream. By comparison, the tinkle of breaking glass was tiny. I hoped it was tiny enough. I'd know soon enough.

I unlocked the lock on Margo's window and let myself inside. I could hear voices from downstairs. I'd told Noon to wait in his car for two minutes before coming in, but that by all means he was to ignore that directive if he heard shooting. I took off my shoes and set them on the bed. I pulled my gun and made my way as catlike as I could through Margo's room and into the hallway. The voices from downstairs had stopped. I checked my watch. Thirty seconds, give or take. Our timing, I figured, would be approximate at best. I went down the short hallway to the top of the steps. I could see a corner of the living room, just enough to see the television set and Margo's mother's aquarium. The burbling of the filter was the only sound in the house.

Noon pounded on the door. By my calculations, he was early.

"Police! Open the door!"

I took a five count, then started down the steps.

Charlie was seated in his wheelchair on the far side of the room, facing the stairs. Next to him sat Margo. They were both looking up at me as I descended the top three stairs. There was a third person in the room as well.

Sitting next to Margo.

Holding a gun to her head.

My heart stopped. It's the devil you know.

Tommy Carroll got off his shot before I did. We both missed. I dropped and rolled down the steps. The front door flew open and Patrick Noon rushed into the house. Carroll swung his gun and fired another shot as Margo let out a scream. The tall officer dropped to the floor. Carroll swung his gun right back to Margo's head as I scrambled up onto all fours. He grabbed hold of her hair. I had time to do absolutely nothing. Zip.

"Drop the gun, Fritz," Carroll said. "It's a three count, then she's gone. I'm sorry. One—"

I skidded the gun along the floor. Noon had doubled over into fetal position and was groaning softly.

"Tommy," I said, "we've got to call an ambulance."

"Shut up."

"Tommy, he's a **cop.**"

"I said shut up."

I got up slowly from the floor. I saw now that the television set was on. Breaking-news coverage of the events at Pier 17. The volume was off. Carroll tilted his chin in the direction of the TV. He was perspiring profusely. For that matter, so was I.

"Charlie here was watching the tube when

I arrived. I saw your little act there with blondie. Nice language, Fritz."

I took a step forward and Carroll waved his gun at me. "Stop right there." He returned the gun to Margo's head. She hadn't said a word. Her hair had fallen into her face and she was giving me one of her darkest looks. It came to me as if it were at the far end of a long tunnel.

"Let her go," I said evenly. "Let them both go. For Christ's sake, get an ambulance out here. If you want to take me off somewhere and point your gun at me, let's do it. Leave them out of it. They have nothing to do with any of this."

"That's exactly what I came out here to find out," Carroll said. He refixed his grip on Margo's hair, pulling her head back.

My breath was short. "Let her go, Tommy. Or I swear—"

Carroll was having trouble with his own breath. "Or you swear **what**? Goddammit, I asked you to do one . . . simple thing. Just one. Locate Ramos. I should have known better. I know how you run everything by your old partner. I thought I'd come out here and see what kind of progress report old Charlie could give me. I can't say he was . . . being too cooperative." He tugged again on Margo's hair. "Then this one came dropping by. And look what she had with her."

I followed his eyes. I noticed that Donna Bia's cell phone was sitting on the coffee table, next to a stack of magazines. Over by the door, Patrick Noon attempted to rise up onto an elbow. He managed to make it halfway up, then collapsed again.

Charlie spoke up. "Your man's dying over there, Carroll. Why don't—"

"Shut up." Carroll inclined his head toward Noon.

"What does he know?"

"Jesus, Tommy, he doesn't know anything, either. Is this your latest method of damage control?"

Carroll considered me a moment. "What do **you** know?"

"Angel Ramos is dead," I said.

"I got that on the TV."

"Cox isn't."

He tried not to show his reaction, but he failed. "Bullshit. You're lying."

"I'm not. He got hit, but he's alive. So far, anyway."

"That's crap."

"It's not. It's fact. What's wrong? Do you have a problem with that? Cox is as corrupt a cop as they come, Tommy. What should you care if he lives?"

Carroll said nothing. He was trying to sort out whether I was bluffing. Margo started doing something strange with her eyes. She clenched them tightly, then opened them widely and looked off to her right. She did this several times. I saw what she was trying to say. When Noon had tried to rise, he'd rolled off of his service pistol. Carroll followed my eyes.

"One step in that direction and this one's gone." He pressed his pistol tighter against Margo's head, then he indicated Charlie. "Him too. I'm sorry, Fritz. That's how it has to go."

Charlie muttered, "Bastard."

Once more, I felt a shortness of breath. The edges of my vision were washing away as the scene in front of me seemed to be retreating. I was slipping into a tunnel-vision view of Margo and Tommy Carroll sitting a distant fifteen feet from me. Carroll was still speaking.

"What's up with Cox? Level with me. Is he really alive?"

I shuffled forward a step. "He's alive, Tommy. That's on the level. And something tells me if he pulls through, he won't be likely to keep his trap shut. Not if he thinks he can cut some sort of deal."

"He's . . . a bum." It seemed to take all of the big man's breath to get the sentence out.

"Maybe. But you know how prosecutors are. They'll make deals with bums so long as the bum can give up a bigger bum."

"Fuck you."

"Sorry. Was that a little too close to home?" I inched forward.

"I'll tell you who's the bum in all this. Goddamn Marty Leavitt. He's a sorry son of a bitch if ever there was one."

"You already gave me this speech last night."

"I didn't tell you **shit** last night. That son of a bitch is a rapist. You were on to that, weren't you, that nun thing? Damn smart-ass punk really fucking thought he'd gotten away with it. That stupid girl with her hundred stupid different stories . . . anyone with half a brain could tell she was protecting someone. There were at least four people questioned who told how she'd been mooning all over Leavitt. Big handsome ass hero, prosecuting her parents' killer." The police commissioner shook some of the sweat out of his eyes. He resembled an angry bear. "Who the hell prosecutes **him** when he goes off on this young girl and rapes her and beats her half to death? No one. He mauls this kid like a **beast,** then walks away. That's just not right, Fritz. You know that's not right."

I moved forward. "What did you know about any of that, Tommy? Your beat wasn't Brooklyn."

Carroll scoffed. "I know people. I knew Tony DiMarco. He was the lead investigator. He met with me one night. He called me in. He was in a fix. He suspected it was Martin Leavitt who'd attacked that girl. He laid it out for me. He had the case."

"Why didn't he just have Leavitt arrested?"

"Get real, Fritz. Leavitt was already Mr. Big out there. You pull someone like that in, even if you've got the goods, you're finished. You know what I'm saying. Leavitt had friends. A lot more friends than DiMarco. And Tony was six years from retirement. I gave him some pre-retirement advice. 'Drop it. Let Leavitt walk. The bastard will come up short someday. A shadow like that can't go away.' Give Tony credit—he argued with me about it. But I finally convinced him."

"Why'd you do that, Tommy? That's insane."

Margo had closed her eyes. Carroll brought up his free arm and wiped more sweat from his face. "Fucking right it was insane. You think I don't know that? Sometimes you've got to make the call. That's what I did. I gave that punk a pass. I let him walk." Carroll's eyes narrowed. He ran his tongue across his dry lips. "But the bastard finally came up short, Fritz. Prick thinks he can throw me to the wolves and I'm just going to sit on my ass and take it?"

I got it.

"Jesus, Tommy . . . you? **You** sent him those letters?"

He nodded tersely. "Leavitt saw the suicide note. When he heard about the nun who'd offed herself in Prospect Park, he went through the pipeline to get a copy of her suicide note. Stupidest thing he could have done. No one goes through the pipeline without me hearing about it. Your old man taught me that one. Make everybody out there your ear."

"What did Leavitt want with Margaret's suicide note?"

"If you ask me, he just wanted to see if she screwed him over at the end."

"She didn't. The note was just babble."

"Yeah. So was most of the crap in Nightmare's notes. Just enough of the same kind of babble for Leavitt to know he was screwed if he didn't do everything that was asked of him."

"The note I saw didn't mention anything about Margaret King."

"Of course not. Wise up, Fritz. What you saw was a copy. Leavitt typed that one up. He left out the real good stuff."

"Jesus, Tommy."

Carroll gave a hard smile. "**I** screwed that bastard over in the end. You think I'm letting a punk like that smear me? Hustle me out of office? I don't fucking think so. Marty Leavitt's not taking me down. That's just not going to happen. End of story. Sorry, Fritz."

"**You're** Nightmare," I said. "For Christ's sake, let's start talking evil, Tommy. What the hell kind of twisted crap are you trying to get away with?"

"Forget it. I'm not nothing anymore."

He released his grip on Margo and shoved her forward with so much force that she pitched onto the floor. Charlie jerked his chair around and I got exactly one step closer before Police Commissioner Tommy Carroll swiveled his gun, bit down on the end of the barrel and pulled the trigger. The roar was deafening. Charlie recoiled.

"Jesus Christ!"

Carroll slumped sideways. Margo continued along the carpet on her hands and knees. She reached me and rose up weightlessly from the floor as if she'd momentarily licked the pull of gravity. Her arms looped around my neck, and she buried her head under my chin.

"Fritz, Fritz, Fritz, Fritz . . ."

41

THE LITTLE GIRL IN THE BAGGAGE-CLAIM area looked so much like Shirley Temple that I did no fewer than three double takes. The mass of ringlets, the bright, intelligent eyes, the swollen-apple cheeks. She wore a short bell-shaped plaid dress and shiny black shoes, and I had no trouble imagining her hoofing it up the stairs to the arrivals hall with Bill "Bojangles" Robinson himself. Her mother was somewhat less glamorous. Around five foot four, she had her daughter's cheeks, though to less cute effect. No ringlets, and her face was etched with anticipation. The two were each wearing an oversize button with the face of a young bristle-headed man posing in front of an American flag. As the passengers began descending the stairs into the baggage area, the mother reached into her purse and handed her daughter a small American flag on a stick. Little Shirley Temple began jumping up and down; she could barely contain herself.

Me, I was able to contain myself. Airports generally put me to sleep. I positioned myself behind the phalanx of limo drivers who stood holding handwritten signs for the arriving passengers. BENNETT. FISK. WELCH. DALY. I spotted a discarded sign sticking out of a nearby trash bin and fetched it on a whim. I asked one of the drivers if I could borrow his Magic Marker, and I scribbled DORIS DAY on the back of the sign. A few minutes later, a real Shirley appeared. I spotted her as she was coming down the stairs. She was walking alongside a young serviceman on a pair of crutches. I recognized his face. The two were laughing about something. The little girl darted forward, waving her flag and shrieking. The serviceman gave my mother a quick nod and hopped on one foot quickly down the rest of the stairs, letting his crutches drop to the side as he leaned down to scoop his daughter up into his arms.

My mother turned and spotted me. Her face opened in a frozen laugh. "Ha! Doris Day! In your dreams."

I came forward and gave her a peck on the forehead. "Welcome home."

"You're cute, in your way, but where's Rock Hudson?"

"Rock's dead."

"Gay, too. How many times is one man going to break your mother's heart?" She raised a warning finger. "Don't answer that."

"You're looking good," I said, lifting her bag from her shoulder and slinging it over mine. "California must agree with you."

"It does. The people are as batty as they come, but they seem to be enjoying themselves. Half the girls are made of silicone, but they seem to be enjoying themselves, too. Tell you the truth, I couldn't live there." She flashed me a smile. "But I enjoyed myself." She gave me the once-over. "Say, you're looking nice and formal. This must be what it'd be like to have a lawyer for a son."

"They're burying Tommy this afternoon," I said.

She caught her breath. "Ah, Jesus. Tommy Carroll. Between your father and Tommy, that job's not holding such a good track record, is it? At least Tommy gets a full-fledged funeral. At least that."

"Let's get your suitcase."

We waited a few rounds at the carousel before her bag finally showed. The soldier with the crutches was standing nearby, his wife and his daughter hanging all over him. Shirley indicated him as I stepped forward to fetch her bag. "We were seated together. He told me I was pretty."

"Did you ask him, or did he just volunteer it?"

"What do you mean, did I **ask** him? Christ, you're a rotten son. He said I have nice eyes."

"You do. He's right. There's no green greener than the emerald green."

She made a soft clucking sound. "I could use a drink."

"Let's get into the city. I thought maybe you'd want to go to Tommy's funeral."

I wasn't just humoring her. About the eyes, I mean. They were still plenty sharp, plenty arresting. The old man used to wax like Yeats about Shirley Malone's eyes. And his blood wasn't even Irish.

"I see you let the place fall to hell without me."

"It's a tough old town," I said. "It bounces back."

She glanced quickly over at the soldier, then back at me. "Yeah, I know the feeling."

———

A MASSIVE POLICE SWEEP OF ANYONE WHO had ever even pronounced the name Angel Ramos had been launched within an hour of his death. Immunities, bargains and outright bribes were all employed. Sometime around three o'clock in the morning, Philip Byron had been located—alive—chained to an overturned washing machine in the basement of an abandoned row house about a mile from the Flea Club. He was dehydrated and suffering from almost no sleep in over seventy-two hours. He was taken immediately to the hospital for treatment. The infection that had set in on his mutilated hand was not as bad as it might have been. He made a brief nonspeaking appearance on television from his hospital bed, giving a wan thumbs-up with his good hand. The doctors expected a full recovery.

Patrick Noon pulled through as well. Tommy Carroll's bullet had shattered a rib and damaged a lung, but Noon was out of the hospital in a few days. Leonard Cox also survived his wounds. He was absent four feet of his small intestine, and he'd be in the market for a new kneecap, but the prognosis was that he would live to see both his trial and the many, many years of prison time that likely stretched beyond that.

I'd huddled for two days with Remy

Sanchez and lawyers from the district attorney's office and laid out for them all that I knew or presumed I knew concerning Margaret King, Leonard Cox, Roberto Diaz, Angel Ramos, Tommy Carroll and Mayor Martin Leavitt. I was, may I say, the center of attention.

When it became clear that Cox was going to survive his wounds, I suggested a tactic that was debated for several hours and finally agreed upon. I proposed that Cox not be informed of Tommy Carroll's suicide. He was kept away from radio and television and newspapers and from all personal visitors. His lawyers cried foul and declared that their client was also being kept away from his civil rights. Cox's doctors announced—per instruction—that the health of their patient required this near-complete isolation and that yes, they would duly testify to that effect in court if requested to do so.

Apparently, the health of their patient did allow him extensive visits from a particular Hispanic police captain. Remy Sanchez informed Cox that Tommy Carroll was not only alive but singing a most fascinating tune. Perhaps, Sanchez suggested, Cox would like to gargle some salt water and weigh in with a tune of his own.

"He thought he was singing a duet," Sanchez informed me over drinks at Mc-Hale's after a long session at Cox's hospital bedside. "But it was pure solo."

According to Sanchez, it was a strong performance. Cox set his sights on Police Commissioner Tommy Carroll. He was under the impression that by handing over Carroll, he was to receive substantial leniency in his own case. "Gosh, I don't know where he got that impression," Sanchez said. "He might claim it came from me, but I guess a guy in his position—all that medication and pain and everything—sometimes they just hear things."

Cox explained that it was Angel Ramos who had murdered Officer Thomas Cash out at the Brooklyn junkyard. Cash had arranged to meet with Ramos and had been wired to record their conversation in hopes of gathering information on his own partner, Jay Pearson, who was in thick with Angel. Or so said Cox. What Cash hadn't known was that word had leaked to Pearson about Cash becoming a stoolie, so Pearson had directed Ramos to take the officer out. Ramos did. Somehow he managed to wrest Cash's own service revolver from him and fired twice into the man's heart. Pearson then appeared on the scene.

Cox's guess was that Pearson was planning to kill Ramos, thus mopping up two potential problems at once. But Ramos caught the drift and shot Jay Pearson point-blank in the forehead. Angel fled. Cox and McNally answered the 911 call about shots being fired in the junkyard, and while Cox was attempting CPR on Cash, he discovered the wire. He removed the wire and the recorder while McNally was off radioing for assistance.

"Cox had the whole damn thing on tape," Sanchez told me. "I.A. was taking gas. They knew Cash was wearing the wire, and they knew it was missing when Cash's body got to the hospital. Because Ramos had used a service revolver on both men, Cox convinced McNally that they should rig the scene to look like a murder-suicide. No one really bought it. Cox swapped Pearson's and Cash's guns around, since Cash's gun was the one that had been fired. He put the gun in Pearson's hand and fired it into the ground, to get prints and residue. That was picked up on right away—the gun switch. The whole scene just didn't quite fit right. It was a hack job. They let the story go out there anyway. They decided two 'bad' cops taking their own justice was better than a double cop killer on the loose.

"Carroll knew Cox. Cox's old man had been with homicide out in Brooklyn, and Carroll had tracked the son's career, especially once it became clear that the son was going sour. Cox says that Carroll contacted him about a month ago. He said he wanted him to recruit a lowlife to take a shot at someone during the Thanksgiving parade. Just to shake things up, Cox says. Just to get the city on edge. He said he had fifty thousand dollars to play with.

"Cox knew immediately who his man was. He had the tape recording of Angel Ramos taking out not one but two New York City cops. Between the squeeze and the money, Ramos was an easy recruit. Cox told Carroll about Angel Ramos and added that Ramos had picked up some rudimentary bomb-making skills at Incarceration U. That's what got Carroll thinking on a larger scale. Ramos brought in Diaz to do the parade hit. The idea was that Cox and McNally would nab Diaz and whisk him away in the patrol car, presumably to let him escape later. That was crap, of course. It was just the way to let Diaz think he was safe. Diaz was an idiot. They were going to kill Diaz no matter what. According to Cox, though, it was Carroll who shot Diaz at the Municipal Building. Shooting McNally at the parade had not been part of the plan, and Carroll was furious. He personally took Diaz out for it. Then Ramos left the bomb at Barrymore's that night. It was supposed to be a small bomb, just a little flame-up, it wasn't necessarily supposed to kill anyone. Then Ramos did that nun act you told me about when he dropped off the next note. Sometime after he left the note at the convent in Riverdale, he went free agent. He nabbed Byron and decided to take over the game. From that point on, according to Cox, Carroll's orders were to find Ramos and kill him on the spot."

Sanchez added an extra matter that I had already figured out by then. According to Cox, his instructions as of the morning I went up to Riverdale and spoke with Sister Natividad had been to take me out as well. Carroll could see that I was beginning to deduce that Margaret King was somehow pivotal. He feared that I'd uncover why Leavitt was being blackmailed and, eventually, who was behind it. I suppose it's nice to know that the commissioner thought so highly of my skills.

It was Charlie who explained to me that when Carroll showed up at the house, the visit had been presented as a general query as to where I was in my investigation. As Carroll had said, he knew I'd be sharing whatever I was learning with Charlie. If it appeared that I had already shared too much, Carroll would decide how to proceed with Charlie. When Margo stumbled onto the scene with Donna Bia's cell phone, Carroll's dilemma doubled. According to Margo, it was when Carroll saw me on television from Pier 17—alive—that he ordered her at gunpoint to call me. No fool, Tommy. He knew I'd come flying.

SAY WHAT YOU WILL ABOUT WOMEN TAKING forever to get dressed to go out; Shirley Malone wasn't issued that chip. I dropped her off in front of her building, and by the time I'd located a parking spot two blocks away and made my way back to her place, she was waiting at the curb looking like the widow Jackie Kennedy herself. Well, as skinny, anyway. I made her go back inside and take off the veil. There are a lot of good things I can say about the woman, but you do have to keep an eye on her. It's just her temperament that she has a tendency to want to upstage.

My mother's apartment is located on Forty-eighth Street, a few doors in from Eleventh. We walked over to the Church of the Sacred Heart on Fifty-first near Tenth. There was already a large crowd milling about outside the church. As many were onlookers and press as were actually there for Tommy Carroll's funeral service. My mother had her arm looped through mine, and I felt it stiffen when she spotted Phyllis Scott emerging from a limo, followed by her son, Paul.

Shirley muttered, "Brunhilde and the pussycat." She stopped and produced a mirror and took a few pokes at her makeup. Phyllis and Paul made their way into the church without seeing us.

"I'm going to park you inside," I said. "I've got a little business to attend to."

"What sort of business?"

"Man stuff."

"Can I watch?"

I got her settled into a pew on the aisle about halfway down. Tommy's flag-draped casket was already positioned in the front of the church. The place was abuzz with low murmuring. My mother crossed herself and crawled onto the prayer bench. I noticed that there was a run going up the back of one of her stockings.

I continued to the front of the church and paused in front of Tommy's casket for as long as I could manage. Just how many police commissioner memorials is a person expected to attend in one lifetime? I moved over to the front pew and spent a few minutes with Betsy Carroll. She was holding up well enough.

"Bastard went out with his boots on," she said to me in a soft hoarse voice.

The press had been lavishing praise on the life and career of Tommy Carroll over the past several days. The impending ravages of his inoperable cancer were the explanation so far as to why the police commissioner had taken his own life. The smarter of the reporters sensed that there was a larger story to be told. I doubted they had any clue as to exactly how large. Soon enough they would.

"We'll get him into the ground," I said to Betsy. "I'm afraid it's going to be a short-lived peace."

She understood. Her husband's pathetically desperate hopes of going out with a clean legacy weren't going to be realized.

"He panicked," she said. "Big strong man like that. But in the end, he panicked."

I said nothing. She was right. Pride and fear. As far as I was concerned, making things right by Margaret King was simply how Tommy Carroll had attempted to justify his actions. Possibly in his own mind, he had believed in those motives. Maybe he had truly convinced himself. But ultimately, it was his determination not to allow Martin Leavitt to set the terms of his final public moment that had stuck in his craw. That was clear from the night I had seen him at home. That was what he couldn't stomach, and it was what had brought him to his poisonous decisions.

Betsy looked past me at her husband's casket. "What about that other thing?"

"I'm going to check on that right now," I said. "We're doing our best."

"I know Tommy doesn't deserve it, but I still hope—"

I cut her off. "We'll just have to see."

As I headed to the front of the church, I spotted my half sister. Elizabeth was crouched down in the aisle, talking with my mother.

Sanchez and I met outside the church. As planned. As I approached him, he gave a nod. "It's done. We're ready to roll."

As if on cue, there was a burping of police sirens and a black limousine was escorted to the open spot cordoned off by traffic cones directly in front of the church. The first to get out of the back was the mayor. He blinked a smile at the crowd, then turned to help Rebecca Gilpin make her way out of the car. Her maneuvering was made a little difficult on account of her crutches. The crutches were a deep maroon, matching the large clip half buried in her hair. The actress gave her high-wattage smile, then seemed to remember where she was and settled her features into pleasant repose.

Sanchez took a breath. "Here goes."

Before he had taken two steps, a figure came out of the crowd and planted herself in front of the couple. It was Tommy Carroll's assistant, Stacy. She said nothing. She simply stood there, her arms crossed loosely, and gave the mayor a withering look. Leavitt was clearly taken aback for several seconds, then found his footing.

"Um, Rebecca, I'd like you to meet Stacy . . ." He hesitated on the last name. "Kendall. Stacy worked very closely with Tommy. Stacy, this is—"

She cut him off. "I know who she is." Her normally monotonous voice wavered. "Does she know who I am?"

Leavitt's mouth opened, but for once there were no ready words.

Rebecca smiled sweetly. "Well, who **are** you, dear?"

Stacy's answer came in a hiss. **"I'm you."** She glared at Leavitt. "Except I guess I'm stupider."

Rebecca turned to Leavitt. "What?" Leavitt's face was nearly the color of the crutches. The sweet smile had drained from the actress's face.

Leavitt sputtered. "S-she's upset."

Rebecca gave him a withering look of her own. Stacy glanced over at Sanchez. Something in her eyes told me. She knew already. Friends in the right places. Sanchez came forward. As far as I could remember, this was the first time I'd ever seen an arrest come as a rescue.

"Mr. Mayor?" said Sanchez. "I need to see you for a moment."

Leavitt's response came out angrily. "What is it?"

"Sir? I think in private would be better." Sanchez tapped his fingers against his lapel.

Leavitt still hadn't caught on. "What is it, Captain?"

Sanchez kept a low, steady voice. "It's a warrant, sir. For your arrest. Multiple counts."

"My— I'm giving Commissioner Carroll's eulogy, Captain."

My cue. I stepped closer. "Actually, Mrs. Carroll says she would prefer it if you didn't," I said. "Sir."

The mayor grew bug-eyed. He was staring at Remy Sanchez's lapel. Maybe he could see the slight bulge of the warrant. "But . . . but it's been arranged."

"It's been unarranged," I said. "It's what the widow prefers. Tommy will receive a perfectly fine send-off, nothing to worry about." Lord help me, I couldn't keep the shit-eating grin off my face. "Sir."

42

A WEEK BEFORE CHRISTMAS, I TOOK Margo out for dinner. There was a Vietnamese place in Tribeca that she had been wanting to try. The menu confounded her with so many options that I finally called the waiter over and asked him to bring us six or seven of their most popular appetizers and a main course of fish.

"The biggest fish you've got. Preferably with the head still on."

Margo made a face. "Oooh."

She loved everything the waiter brought. She had so much fun with the octopus that I asked for a second helping. When the fish arrived, she remarked, "He looks like you."

"How do you know it's a he?"

She planted her chin in her palms and

smiled at me across the crowded table. "Because he looks like you."

We had ginger-and-green-tea ice cream
for dessert. Margo declared the whole meal
"heavenly."

"What we did to that country, and now
look. I actually feel a little guilty."

It was a cool evening, bordering on down-
right chilly. The temperature had dropped
noticeably while we'd been in the restaurant,
and we could see our breath. There'd been a
prediction of flurries. I asked Margo if she
was up for a little walk. She thought I was
taking her to the Hudson River Promenade,
but instead I turned east at Murray Street.
Her eyes widened with mock delight. "You're
taking me to the Dollhouse?"

"Sorry. No strip clubs tonight."

"Shoot." She tried to snap her fingers, but
they were too cold.

We skirted City Hall Park and made our
way down Fulton Street to the South Street
Seaport. Margo darkened as we crossed onto
the cobbled market area. "Scene of the crime.
How romantic."

The sound of singing was drifting our way.
In the middle of the cobbled area, a green
metal structure had been erected, reaching
some thirty or more feet high. The shape of

the structure—like the color—was intended to resemble a Christmas tree. There was a red-and-green chain running around the base of the structure, within which were several wrapped "Christmas presents" about the size of hay bales.

A sign hanging from the chain identified the structure as "The Chorus Tree." We didn't need the sign to tell us. Perched on small platforms running in increasingly shorter rows all the way up to the top of the tree were the carolers. They were singing a cappella, their frosty breath swirling up into the blackness. They were dressed in identical green coats and caps and were holding red flashlights made to look like candles. None of the carolers looked to be older than sixteen. A standing sign identified them as students of La Guardia High School for the Performing Arts. A person I assumed was their teacher stood facing them, conducting them through the range of holiday standards. As we watched, they segued from "Joy to the World" to "The Twelve Days of Christmas." Margo tugged on my sleeve.

" 'The Twelve Days of Christmas,' " she said in a low voice. "The path to madness."

I scanned the faces. There were thirteen girls and seven boys. I reached into my pocket and pulled out a folded newspaper clipping. It was from the **Post.** It was the lead story from the day after Margaret King's body had been found by the jogger in Prospect Park.

SISTER SUICIDE
Nun Ends Life in P'spect Park

The story included the photograph taken of Margaret King when she was in her early twenties. Dirty-blond hair. Slightly upturned nose. Large, dark eyes.

"There," I said, indicating a caroler about halfway up the tree. She was one in from the end. Margo looked back and forth between the newspaper photo and the caroler.

"That's her."

I nodded. "Grace Maynard."

"How did you find out?"

"How do you think? I'm not a shoe salesman, remember?"

"Right. Of course." She took the clipping from me and looked at it once more. "Margaret was already a mother when this picture was taken."

"Grace would have been around three at that point."

She handed the clipping back to me, and I put it back in my pocket. She looped her arm through mine and shivered. We rode out the rest of "The Twelve Days of Christmas," five golden rings and all. It turned out to be the final carol. At the conclusion, the small gathering of onlookers applauded. The conductor thanked us, and the carolers began coming down from the tree.

"She doesn't know a thing, does she?" Margo asked.

"About her mother?"

"Or about her father."

"If you were her parents, what would you do?"

Margo was silent a moment. Finally, she said, "I'm thinking I'm glad I don't have to figure that out."

Grace Maynard was goofing with the boy who had been standing next to her. They wielded their flashlights like sabers and were engaged in a mock swordfight. In his enthusiasm, the boy stumbled and nearly fell from his perch. A man in a huge fur hat standing next to me called out, "Come on, Lucius! Be more careful, will ya?"

Grace Maynard shined her little flashlight over at him. "It was my fault, Mr. Tuck! I'm sorry."

"Let's go," I said.

I looked back just once as Margo and I

headed for the street. Grace Maynard was chattering excitedly to a man and a woman. Her breath was popping from her mouth in bursts. Margo and I paused at the corner as a string of available taxis went by.

Margo looked up at me. "None of them good enough for you?"

"I thought maybe we'd walk some more. It's starting to snow."

I hadn't even noticed it until I'd said it. It was a very light snow. It could have almost been mistaken for ash.

"Where do you want to walk, big guy?" Margo asked. "Just around and around in circles?"

I thought about it. I couldn't say it sounded like a bad idea.

ACKNOWLEDGMENTS

Word on the street is that it's tedious to hear writers or actors or other such types giving gushing thanks to their agents. Well . . . too bad, this guy's earned it. My great thanks to Richard Pine of Inkwell Management—Mr. Cool—for his steadfast confidence in my work, his aplomb under fire, and his wise counsel and assistance while I was working on this book.

In addition, I want to thank Jonathan Karp for taking Richard's calls in the first place and for championing my book so powerfully at Random House. Likewise Gina Centrello (she of the astonishingly good taste) for all her enthusiastic support. And of course my shrewd and skillful editor, Mark Tavani, for bossing me around just the right amount in the name of getting it as right as right can be.

I've also received immeasurable support and guidance before, during, and after the writing of this book from Kadam Morten and the great loving crew at the Chakrasambara Buddhist Center in Chelsea. Everyone should be so fortunate.

ABOUT THE AUTHOR

Richard Hawke resides in New York City. This is his first novel. Visit his website at www.RHawke.com.